HIGH-TECH WAR

Floating in his balloon harness, Dalehouse held the crossbow up and sang, carefully attending to the notes he had been taught by the computers at Texas A&M. "I have brought you a gift."

The hydrogen-filled alien he called Charlie responded with a burst of song.

Danny moved on to the next sentence he had been taught. "You must come with me to find a *ha'aye'i*." That was hard to sing but Charlie seemed to understand; the song of thanks changed to a thin melody of concern.

Danny laughed. "Do not fear," he sang. "I will be a *ha'aye'i* to the *ha'aye'i*. We will destroy them with this gift, and the swarm will have no more need to fear."

It was a measure of the balloonist's trust in his friend from Earth that he was willing to embark on so fearful an adventure with him. The members of the flock *never* left it by choice. For more than an hour after they had dropped to a lower level and left the flock behind, Charlie's song was tenuous and sad. But then they dipped low under a bank of clouds and Charlie's song turned to active fear as from one of them dropped the predatory form of a killer.

"Watch," Danny cried, clumsily grasping the grip that had been designed for balloonist claws. At twenty meters he squeezed the trigger.

A dozen tiny metal spikes lashed out at the *ha'aye'i* spreading like the cone of fire of a shotgun shell. The creature screamed once in pain and surprise, and then had no more breath to scream with. It dr̶o̶p̶p̶ed past them, its horrid little face writhin̶g̶ ̶ ̶ ̶ ̶ ̶ ̶ ̶ing uselessly toward them. ̶ ̶ ̶ ̶ ̶

A ̶ ̶ ̶ ̶ ̶ ̶ ̶ ̶ ̶ ̶ ̶ ̶ ̶, and then a roaring paea̶ ̶ ̶ ̶ ̶ ̶ ̶ ̶ ̶ ̶ ̶ ̶ ̶ ̶ thing, 'Anny 'Alehouse̶ ̶ ̶ ̶ ̶ ̶ ̶ ̶ ̶ ̶ ̶us?"

"No̶ ̶ ̶ ̶ ̶ ̶ ̶ ̶ ̶ ̶ ̶for yourself!"

Baen Books By Frederik Pohl

Jem

Man Plus

Mars Plus (with Thomas T. Thomas)

The Starchild Trilogy (with Jack Williamson)

The Undersea Trilogy (with Jack Williamson)

Search the Sky (with C.M. Kornbluth)

The Years of the City (forthcoming)

FREDERIK POHL

JEM

BAEN

JEM

Copyright © 1978, 1979 by Frederik Pohl

A Baen Book

Baen Publishing Enterprises
P.O. Box 1403
Riverdale, NY 10471

ISBN: 0-671-87625-2

Cover art by David Mattingly

First Baen Printing, October 1994

Distributed by Simon & Schuster
1230 Avenue of the Americas
New York, NY 10020

Printed in the United States of America

·ONE·

WHEN DANNY DALEHOUSE first went to Sofia he did not know it for the first stage in a much longer journey, nor that he would meet some of his future companions. He had never heard of that larger destination, which bore the unattractive name of N-OA Bes-bes Geminorum 8426, or for that matter of the people. Their names were Nan Dimitrova and Captain Marge Menninger. The occasion was the Tenth General Assembly of the World Conference on Exobiology, and the time was not in any way bad for any of them. It was a springtime season, and for a moment there all the world seemed to be budding into sweet and friendly life.

There were three thousand people in the Great Hall of Culture and Science for the opening session, so many of them political that the five or six hundred scientists who were actively involved had trouble finding seats. Even the translators were doubled up in their booths. Handsome, hoary old Carl Sagan delivered the opening invocation, looking like a spry octogenarian instead of whatever incredible age he really was.

He was already wheeling forward to the rostrum as Dan Dale-house squeezed into a seat at the back of the hall. Dalehouse had never been in Bulgaria before. He had been drawn to the sunny parks, and he promised himself a look at the museum of centuries-old ikons under St. Stephan's Cathedral, a few blocks away. But he didn't want to miss Sagan, and the first plenary session was a tutorial on tactran reports. Some of the stuff he had never heard before. That was probably Sagan's work, he thought. Even as honorary joint chairman, Sagan passed the whole program through his nonsense filter. What was left was sure to be worth hearing. Sagan spoke briefly and cheerfully, and rolled away to a standing ovation.

Because the keynote speaker had been an American, the chairman of the tachyon-transmitter tutorial had to be from one of the other blocs. That was international etiquette. He was an Englishman from Fred Hoyle's Cambridge group. A few of the dignitaries from the Fuel Bloc stayed to hear him out of group solidarity, but most of the other political people left as inconspicuously as they could, and Dalehouse was able to move up to a better seat on the center aisle. He settled himself to tolerate the chairman's opening remarks, lulled by the scent of flowers coming through the open windows— Bulgaria made even less use of air conditioning than the United States.

Since Food and Fuel had already been heard from, protocol required that the next space go to People. So it was a Pakistani who read the first paper, entitled "Vital Signatures Reported from Bodies Orbiting Alpha Draconis, Procyon, 17-Kappa Indi, and Kung's Semistellar Object."

Dalehouse had been half drowsing, but as the title came through his earphones he sat up. "I never heard of some of those stars," he remarked to his neighbor. "Who is this guy?"

She pointed to her program and the name: Dr. Ahmed Dulla, Zulfikar Ali Bhutto University, Hyderabad. As Dale-house leaned over, he discovered that the flower scent was not coming from the windows but from her, and he took a closer look. Blond. A little plump, but with a solid, good-natured, pretty face. Hard to tell the age, but maybe about the same as his, which was mid-thirties. Since his divorce, Dalehouse had become more aware of the sexuality of women colleagues and chance-met females in general, but also more wary. He smiled thanks and sank back to listen.

The first part was not exciting. The reports on the probe to Alpha Draconis had already been published. He was not greatly interested in hearing again about the photometric measurements that established the presence of photosynthetic "plant" life in a reducing atmosphere. There were plenty of planets like that around that had been scanned and reported by the tachyon probes with their cargoes of instruments—the whole thing no bigger than a grapefruit, but miraculously capable of leaping interstellar distances in a week. The Pakistani seemed intent on repeating every word of every one of the reports, not failing to comment on the number of other reducing-atmosphere planets discovered and the apparent generally low level of evolved life on them. The Procyon probe had lost its lock, and the reports were at best ambiguous. Mercifully, Dulla did not dwell on the instrumentation. The data on 17-Kappa Indi sounded better—an oxygen atmosphere, at least, although the temperature range was bad and the signatures were sketchy—but the real prize was at the end.

Kung's Semistellar Object was not much larger than a planet itself. As stars went it was tiny, barely big enough to fuse nuclei and radiate heat, but it had a planet of its own that sounded like fun. Hot. Humid. Dense air, but about the right partial pressure of oxygen to be congenial to life—including the life of a human exploratory party, if anybody cared to spend the money to try it out. And the signatures were first-rate. Carbon dioxide. Traces of methane, but only traces. Good photometry. The only parameters missing were radio wavelengths; otherwise it sounded a lot like Miami Beach.

The Pakistani then went on to explain how Kung's Star had

been discovered by the big fixed radio dish at Nagchhu Dzong, in the Thanglha hills, and that the discovery had come about as a direct result of the wisdom and example of the late Chairman Mao. That was not in itself very interesting except to the other members of the People Bloc, who were nodding grave concurrence, but the planet seemed pretty strange. The translation had trouble keeping up with the Pakistani, and it wasn't Dalehouse's area of special interest anyhow, but he made out that only a part of one hemisphere was covered in the biotic study. Funny! Nor was he the only one fascinated. He looked up at the bank of translators, each in their individual glass cages, like nail clippers and pocket combs behind the windows of a vending machine. Each booth had its draped scarlet curtains tied back with a gold sash, very Slavic and incongruous, and behind them the translators looked like astronauts in their solid-state communications helmets. One of them was a young girl with a sweet, plain face, leaning forward to stare at the speaker with an expression of either incredulity or rapture. Her lips weren't moving; she seemed to be too entranced to function.

Dalehouse borrowed a pencil from the woman next to him and made a note in the margin of his program: *Invstgt Kung's Star, posbl survey grant.* He didn't name the planet. It didn't have a name yet, though he had heard some of the Peeps refer to it half reverently as Son of Kung. It would be called other things, and worse.

What can be said of someone like Danny Dalehouse? Grammar school, high school, college, graduate school; he got his Pretty Heavy Diploma at twenty-six, and jobs were scarce. He managed to teach freshman biology for a year, then a year on a grant in Tbilisi and more than a year of post-doctoral studies, so that he was past thirty before he caught on at Michigan State's new exobiology department. The marriage that had survived a year of living on cheese and white wine in Soviet Georgia began to dissolve in East Lansing. He was medium height, viewed charitably—about one seventy centimeters in his shoes—and slim. He wasn't particularly handsome, either. What he was was smart. He was smart enough so that in three years at Michigan State he had made himself one of the Food Bloc's top experts in reading the telemetry from a tachyon-transmitter probe and translating it into a good guess at how much life the signatures represented—even what kinds of life. Then he was smart enough to figure out that a telemetry interpreter who got to be nationally known for his skill was going to look too valuable where he was to be risked on a manned expedition to one of those fascinating, remote worlds. So he tapered off on the interpretation and resharpened his skills at mountain climbing, sailplaning, and long-distance running. You never knew what kind of athletic qualities you might need if you were lucky enough to be one of the fewscore people each year who got tossed to another star.

Being divorced was probably a plus quality. A man without much home life would be judged better able to concentrate on the job than someone mooning over wife and kids fifty light-years away. Dalehouse hadn't wanted Polly to leave. But when she did pack up and go, he was quick to see that the divorce wasn't all bad.

That night in the Aperitif Bar he ran into the blond woman again. He had gone to listen in on the headliners' news conference, but the crowd at that end of the bar was pretty thick, and most of them seemed to be actual reporters he didn't feel justified in shoving aside. Between their heads and cameras he caught glimpses of Sagan and Iosif Shklovskii sitting together in their life-support chairs at one end of the narrow room, having their picture taken, and passing smiling comments and an oxygen mask back and forth to each other. They rolled away toward the elevators, and most of the crowd followed them. Dalehouse opted for a drink and looked around the bar.

The blond was drinking Scotch with two small, dark, smiling men—no, he realized, she was drinking Scotch; they were drinking orange juice. The men got up and said good night while he was looking for a place to sit down, and he perceived the opportunity.

"Mind if I join you? I'm Danny Dalehouse, Michigan State."

"Marge Menninger," she said, and she didn't mind his joining her at all. She didn't mind letting him buy her another Scotch, and she didn't mind buying him one back, and she didn't mind going out for a stroll under the fat Bulgarian spring moon, and she didn't mind going to his room to open his bottle of Bulgarian wine; and, altogether, the day when Danny Dalehouse first heard of Kung's Star was a very successful and pleasurable one.

The next day, not quite so good.

It began well enough, in the early dawn. They woke in each other's arms and made love again without changing position. It was too early to get anything to eat, so they shared the last of the bottle of wine as they showered and dressed. Then they decided to go for a walk.

It had rained a little during the night. The streets were wet. But the air was warm, and in the lovely rose glow of sunrise, the Maria-Theresa-yellow buildings were warm peach and friendly.

"The next thing I want to do," said Dalehouse expansively, slipping an arm around Marge's waist, "is take a look at Kung's Star."

Marge looked at him with a different kind of interest. "You've got funding for that?"

"Well"—coming down—"no. No, I guess not. MSU launched four tactrans last year, but we've never had a grant for a manned probe."

She butted her head against his shoulder. "You're more of an operator than you look."

"What?"

"You don't come on real strong, Danny-boy, but you know what you're doing every minute, don't you? Like last night.

Those two Ay-rabs weren't getting anywhere trying to put the make on me. Then you just eased right in."

"I'm not sure I know what we're talking about."

"No?"

"No, not really." But she didn't seem about to clarify it, so he went back to what really interested him. "That planet sounds pretty great, Margie. Maybe even industry! Did you get that part? Traces of carbon monoxide and ozone."

She objected thoughtfully, "There were no radio signals."

"No. Doesn't prove anything. They wouldn't have heard any radio signals from Earth two hundred years ago, but there was a civilization there."

She pursed her lips but didn't answer. It occurred to him that something was troubling her, perhaps some female thing of the sort he had never considered himself very good at comprehending. He looked around for something to cheer her up and said, "Hey, look at those fellows."

They were strolling past the Dimitrov Mausoleum. In spite of the hour, in spite of the fact that there was no other human being in sight, the two honor guards stood absolutely immobile in their antic musical-comedy uniforms, not even the tips of the long curled feathers on their helmets quivering.

Margie glanced, but whatever was on her mind, sightseeing was not part of it. "It would be at least a two-year hitch," she said. "Would you really want to go?"

"I, uh, I think I'd miss you, Margie," he said, misinterpreting her point.

Impatiently, "Ah, no crap. If you had the funding, would you go there?"

"Try me."

"That Pak was so flaming pleased with himself. He's probably already got it all lined up with Heir-of-Mao for the Peeps to send a manned probe there."

"Well, that's fine with me, too. I don't want to go for political reasons. I don't care what country meets the first civilized aliens; I just want to be there."

"I care," she said. She slipped free of him to light a cigarette.

Dalehouse stopped and watched her cup her hands around the lighter to shield it from the gentle morning breeze. They had had a good deal to drink and not very much sleep. He could feel a certain interior frailty as a consequence, but Marge Menninger seemed unaffected. This was the first time he had gone to bed with a woman without the exchange of several chapters of autobiography. He didn't know her at all in his mind, only through his senses.

The other thing in Dalehouse's thoughts was that in the 10:00 A.M. session he had a paper to give—"Preliminary Studies toward a First Contact with Subtechnological Sentients" —and he wanted enough time to add some comments about the planet of Kung's Star.

He sneaked a glance at his watch: 7:30—plenty of time. The city was still quiet. Somewhere out of sight he could hear the first tram of the morning. Far down the street where they walked he could see two city gendarmes strolling hand in hand, their batons swinging from the outside hand of each. Nothing else seemed to be happening in Sofia. It made him think of his own home in East Lansing at that same promising time of day and year, when the university was running at half-speed for the summer sessions and on decent mornings he walked or biked to his office to enjoy the peace. And, of course, since the divorce, to get out of his empty house.

To be sure, he reminded himself, Sofia was not in the least like East Lansing: flat and urban, where his home was hilly and carpeted with solid quarter-acre split-levels. And Marge Menninger was not in the least like absent Polly, who had been dark, tiny, quick, and easily bored. What exactly was Marge Menninger like? Dalehouse had not quite made up his mind. She seemed to be different people. Yesterday in the Great Hall of Culture and Science she had been another academic colleague; last night, exactly what every all-American boy would like to find in his bed. But who was she this morning? They weren't strolling with their arms around each other's waists anymore. Marge was a meter away and a little ahead of him, moving briskly, smoking with intensity, and staring straight ahead.

She seemed to reach a decision, and glanced at him. "Michigan State University, Institute of Extrasolar Biology. Daniel Dalehouse, B.A., M.S., Ph.D. I guess I didn't tell you that I saw a preprint of your paper before I left Washington."

"You did?" He was startled.

"Interesting paper. Makes me think you're serious about wanting to go. Danny-boy, I might be able to help you."

"Help me how?"

"With money, dear man. That's all I've got to give. But I think I can give some to you. In case you didn't notice my name tag when you were taking my clothes off, that's what I do for a living. I'm with SERDCOM."

"Praise COM from whom all blessings flow," Danny said fervently; it was the annual grants from the Space Exploration, Research and Development Commission that kept Dalehouse's institute green. "How come I've never seen you when I go to Washington with my begging bowl?"

"I've only been there since February. I'm vice-secretary for new projects. Job didn't exist till the first of the year, and I wangled it. Before then I was teaching the stuff at my alma mater . . . among other subjects; we didn't have much of an extrasolar department. It's a small school, and it fell on hard times even while I was still an undergraduate. Well? What about it?"

"About what?"

"Were you creaming? Or do you want a grant for a manned trip to Kung's Star?"

"I do! Christ, yes, I do, I do."

She took his hand in one of hers, patted it with the other. "You may regard it as settled. Hello, what's this?"

"But—"

"I said settled." She was no longer looking at him; something had caught her attention. They had come to a large park, and off to their right was a mall leading up to a monument. Flanking the entrance to the mall were two heroic groups of bronze statuary.

Dalehouse followed her toward them, feeling dazed as well as hung over; it had not sunk in yet. "I suppose I ought to submit a proposal," he said tentatively.

"You bet. Send me a draft first before you put it through channels. ' She was examining the bronzes. "Will you look at this stuff!"

Dalehouse inspected them without interest. "It's a war memorial," he said. "Soldiers and peasants."

"Sure, but it isn't that old. That's a tommy gun that soldier is holding . . . and there's one on a motorbike. And look— some of the soldiers are women."

She bent down and inspected the Cyrillic lettering. "Damn. Don't know what it says. But it's the workers and peasants welcoming liberators, right? It has to be the last of the Big Ones—World War Two. Let's see, this is Bulgaria, so that must be the Red Army chasing the Germans out and all the Bulgarians bringing them flowers and hearty fraternal-solidarity handshakes and glasses of clear spring water. Wow! Jesus, Danny, both my grandfathers fought in this war, and one grandmother—two on one side, one on the other."

Dalehouse looked at her with amusement and fondness, if not full comprehension; it was strange to find anyone who took such an interest in actual foot-slogging fighting these days, when everyone knew that war was simply priced out of the market for any nation that wanted to survive. "What about your other grandmother? Some kind of slacker?"

She looked up at him for a moment. "She died in the bombings," she said. "Hey, this is fun."

The bronzes were certainly military enough for any war fan. Every figure was expressing courage, joy, and resolution in maximal socialist-realist style. They had been sculptured to fit in foursquare oblong blocks, with all the figures fitted into each other to conform; they looked a lot like a box of frozen sardines writhing around each other. Margie's interest in the sculpture was itself attracting interest, Dalehouse saw; the gendarmes had reached the end of their beat and were passing nearby on the return, watching benignly.

"What's so much fun about soldiers?" he asked.

"They're my trade, dear Dan. Didn't you know? Marjorie Maude Menninger, Captain, USA, late of West Point, or late of the practically late West Point, as I sometimes say. You should see me in uniform." She lighted another cigarette, and when she passed it to him for a drag he realized she had not been smoking tobacco.

She held the smoke, then exhaled it in a long plume. "Ah, those were the days," she said dreamily, gazing at the bronzes. "Look at that prunt holding the baby up in the air. Know what he's saying to the other soldier? 'Go ahead, Ivan. I'll hold the kid while you rape her mommy; then you hold the kid and it's my turn.'"

Dalehouse laughed. Encouraged, Margie went on. "And that young boy is saying, 'Hey, glorious Red Army soldier, you like my sister? Chocolate? Russki cigaretti?' And the WAC that's taking the flowers from the woman, she's saying, 'So, comrade! Stealing agricultural produce from the people's parks! Make no mistake about it, it's a long time in the camps for you!' Course, by the time the Soviets got here the Germans were finished anyhow, but—"

"Margie," he said.

"—still, it must have been pretty exciting—"

"Hey, Margie! Let's move on," he said uneasily. He had suddenly realized that the gendarmes were no longer smiling, and remembered, a little late, that all the municipal police had been given language lessons for the conference.

·TWO·

WHAT ONE COULD SAY about Ana Dimitrova was hardly necessary to spell out, because it was apparent on first meeting: she was a sweet, cheerful girl with a capacity for love. Sometimes she had the grinding tension headaches that were typical of the people whose corpora callosa had been cut through, and then she was disoriented, irritable, sometimes almost sick with pain. But she excused herself and bore them in private whenever she could.

She woke up early, as she had planned, and stole into the kitchen to make tea with her own hands. No powdered trash for Ahmed! When she brought it in to him he opened those heartbreaking long lashes and smiled at her, crinkling the dark brown eyes. "You are too good to me, Nan," he said in Urdu. She set the cup down beside him and bent to touch his cheek with hers. Ahmed did not believe in kissing, except under circumstances which, while she enjoyed them, were not included in her present plans.

"Let's get dressed quickly," she proposed. "I want to show you my good monster."

"Monster?"

"You'll see." She escaped his grasp and retreated to the shower, where she let the hot water beat on her temples for a long time. The solid-state helmet often brought on the headaches, and she did not want one today.

Later, while she was drying her long brown hair, Ahmed came in silently and ran his fingers along the narrow scar in her scalp. "Dear Nan," he said, "so much trouble to go to to learn Urdu. I learned it for nothing."

She leaned against him for a moment, then wrapped the towel around herself and scolded gently. "There is no time for this if we are going to see my monster in the dawn light. Also, it was not to learn languages that I had my brain split. It was only to be able to translate them better."

"We would not do such a thing in Pakistan," he said, but she knew he was only being dear.

Outside the bathroom door, listening to him squawk and grumble as the cold water hit him, Nan thought seriously about Ahmed. She was a practical person. She was quite willing to sacrifice a material good for a principle or a feeling, but she preferred to know clearly what the stakes were. For her love game with Ahmed, the stakes were pretty high. Bulgaria, like the Soviet Union, was among the most People-tolerant of the food-exporting nations, but the lines of international politics were still clear. They would be able to see each other only seldom and with difficulty unless one or the other of them renounced citizenship. She knew that one would not be Ahmed.

How deeply did she want to be involved with this dear Pakistani? Could she share a life in the crowded, slow cities of the People Bloc? She had seen them. They were charming enough. But a diet of mostly grain, a nearly total lack of personal machines, the inward-turning of the People Bloc minds—were they what she wanted? Congenial to visit, pleasant and quaint for a day or a month . . . but the rest of her life?

She dressed quickly without deciding the issue. One part of her mind was on what she was doing, the other on rehearsing her plans for that day's work at the conference; nothing was left for Ahmed. She made the bed while he was dressing, put away the washed dishes and glasses, and almost tugged him out the door.

The sky was bright pink, but the sun was just appearing; there was time if they hurried. She led him down the stairs—no waiting for the tiny cranked elevator—and out into the courtyard, then quickly away from the university to an intersection of two boulevards. She stopped and turned around.

"There, see?"

Ahmed squinted into the sunrise. "I see the cathedral," he grumbled.

"Yes, that's it. And the monster?"

"Monster? Is it in the cathedral?"

"It *is* the cathedral."

"St. Stephan's is a monster? . . . Oh! Yes, I think I see. Those windows up high, they are the eyes? And those windows lined up underneath. They are the teeth."

"It's smiling at us, do you see? And there are the ears, and the nose."

Ahmed was not looking at the cathedral any more, but at her. "You are such a strange girl. I wonder what sort of Pakistani you would make."

Nan caught her breath. "No! It's too much. Please don't talk like that." She took his arm. "Please, let's just walk."

"I have not had any breakfast, Ana."

"There's plenty of time." She guided him through the small park to the university, and down toward the larger one. She laughed. "Have you forgiven me for translating you so badly into Bulgarian?"

"I would not have known how bad it was if you had not told me."

"It was bad enough, Ahmed. I was looking at you when you were talking about this Kung's Star, and I forgot to translate."

He glanced at her cautiously. "Do you know," he said, "Heir-of-Mao is personally interested in this planet. It was he who chose the name for the quasi-stellar object. He was there at the observatory when it was discovered. I think—"

"What do you think, Ahmed?"

"I think exciting things will happen," he said obscurely. She laughed and lifted his hand to touch her cheek.

"Ana," he said, and stopped in the middle of the boulevard. "Listen to me. It is not impossible, you know. Even if I were to be away for a time, after that, for you and me, it would not be impossible."

"Please, dear Ahmed—"

"It is not impossible! I know," he said bitterly, oblivious of the fact that they were standing in the middle of the road, "that Pakistan is a poor country. We do not have food to export, like you and the Americans, and we do not have oil like the Middle Eastern states and the English. So we join with the countries that are left."

"I respect Pakistan very much."

"You were a child when you were there," he said severely. "But all the same it is not impossible to be happy, even in the People Bloc."

A trolleybus was coming, three cars long and almost silent on its rubber-tired wheels. Nan tugged him out of the way, glad for the chance to change the subject.

The difficulty with international conferences, she thought, was that you met political opponents, and sometimes they did not seem like opponents. She had not meant this involvement with someone from the other side. She certainly did not want its inconvenience and pain. She knew what the stakes were. As a translator with four fully mastered languages and half a dozen partials, she had been all over the world—largely within the Food Bloc, to be sure, but even so, that included Moscow and Kansas City and Rio and Ottawa. She had met defectors from the other sides. There had been a Welsh girl in Sydney; there were two or three Japanese on the faculty of the university, her own neighbors in Sofia. They always tried desperately to belong, but they were always different.

Both the morning and Ahmed were too beautiful for such unhappy thoughts. That part of her mind which daydreamed and worried went from worry to daydream; the other part of her mind, the perceiving and interpreting part, had been following some events across the boulevard and now commanded her attention.

"Look," she said, clutching at an excuse to divert Ahmed's attention, "what's going on over there?" It was on the Liberation Mall. The blond woman she had seen at one of the receptions was having an argument with two militiamen. One had her by the arm. The other was fingering his stun-stick and talking severely to a man, a youngish professorial type, also from the conference.

Ahmed said, uninterested, "Americans and Bulgarians. Let the Fats settle their problems between themselves."

"No, really!" Nan insisted. "I must see if I can help."

But in the long run all that Nan Dimitrova accomplished was to get herself arrested too.

It was the American woman's fault. Even an American should have known better than to make chauvinist-filth jokes about the Red Army within earshot of the police of the capital of the most Russophile of nations. If she hadn't known that much, at least she should have known better than to insist on her treaty right to have the American ambassador informed of the incident. Up to that point the militiamen were only looking for an opportunity to finish reprimanding the culprits and stroll away. Afterwards it was a matter with international repercussions.

The only good thing about it was that Ahmed didn't get involved. Nan sent him away. He left willingly enough, even amused. The rest of them, the two Americans and Nan herself, were taken to the People's Palace of Justice. Because it was a Sunday morning, they had to sit for hours on bare wood benches in an interrogation room until a magistrate could be found.

No one came near them. No one would have minded in the least, Nan was sure, if they had accepted the invitation of the open door and slipped silently away. But she did not want to do that by herself. The Americans were not willing to take the chance, the woman because she appeared to think some sort of principle was involved, the man evidently because the woman was involved. She eyed them with displeasure, especially the bleached blond, at least five kilos too well fed, even for the Food Bloc. You cannot choose your allies, she thought. The man seemed to be all right, if not too fastidious about whom he indulged his sexual pranks with. Still, as the time passed and the militiamen brought them croissants and strong tea, the confinement drew them together. They chatted cheerfully enough until the people's magistrate at last arrived, gruffly refused to hear any talk of treaties or ambassadors, instructed them in future to use the common sense God had given them and the good manners their mothers had no doubt taught them, and let them go.

By then they had completely missed the 10:00 A.M. session of the conference. Almost as bad, they had missed the special lunches arranged for the delegates. As it was a Sunday morning in spring, every restaurant in Sofia was booked full with private wedding parties, and none of them got any lunch at all.

That was the first time the three of them met.

The second was very much later, and very, very far away.

Danny Dalehouse found that a colleague had read his paper for him. So missing the morning session turned out not to have been an utter disaster, and in fact looked like producing a hell of a big plus. Margie was bright enough to realize she'd been dumb, and ego-strong enough to admit it. However serious Margie had been about the grant while strolling down the boulevard, full of wine, pot, and roses, now she was rueful enough to remember her promise.

All the way home from the conference in the clamjet, Dalehouse sat with his notebook on his knee, drawing up a proposal, until it was time to go to his bunk. By dawn they were over white-and-brown Labrador, the jet moving more slowly through the cold night air. Dalehouse ate his breakfast alone, except for a sleepy TWA stewardess to scramble his eggs and pour his coffee, and looked out at the clouds as the clamjet roller-coastered in and out of them, wondering what the planet of Kung's Star would be like.

· THREE ·

THE DAY AFTER Marge Menninger got back to her Washington office, she received Dalehouse's draft proposal. But she had already begun the process of getting it granted.

She had left the conference early to catch a ride on a NASA hydrojet, a rough and expensive ride but a fast one, back to her apartment in Houston. From there she had called the deputy undersecretary of state for cultural affairs. It was after office hours, but she got through with no trouble. Marge was on easy terms with the deputy undersecretary. She was his daughter. Once she had told him she'd had a pleasant trip she came right to the point:

"Poppa, I need a grant for a manned interstellar flight."

There was a short silence. Then he said, "Why?"

Marge scratched under her navel, thinking of all the reasons she could have given. For the advancement of human knowledge? For the potential economic benefit of the United States and the rest of the food-producing world? For the sake of her promise to Danny Dalehouse? All of these were reasons

19

which were important to someone or other, and some of them important to her; but to her father she gave only the one reason that would prevail: "Because if we don't do it the son-of-a-bitching Paks will."

"By themselves?" Even three thousand kilometers away, she heard the skepticism.

"The Chinese will put up the hard stuff. They're in it too."

"You know what it's going to cost." It wasn't a question; they both knew the answer. Even a tactran message capsule cost a couple million dollars to transport from one star system to another, and they weighed only a few kilos. What she had in mind was at least ten people with all their gear: she was asking for billions of dollars.

"A lot," she said, "but it's worth it."

Her father chuckled admiringly. "You've always been an expensive child, Margie. How are you going to get it past the joint committee?"

"I think I can. Let me worry about that, poppa."

"Um. Well, I'll help from this end. What do you want from me right now?"

Marge hesitated. It was an open phone connection, and so she chose her words carefully. "I asked that Pak for a copy of his full report. Of course, I'm a little handicapped until I get my hands on it."

"Of course," her father agreed. "Anything else?"

"There's not much I can do until I see the full report."

"I understand. Well. What else is new? How did you like our brave Bulgarian allies?"

She laughed. "I guess you know I got arrested."

"I only wonder it doesn't happen more often. You're a terrible person, love. You didn't get it from *my* side of the family."

"I'll tell mom you said that," she promised, and hung up; and so, by the time she was back in Washington, she had received by a private route a microfilmed copy of the Pakistani's entire report, already translated for her. She read it over diligently, making notes. Then she pushed them away and leaned back in her chair.

The son-of-a-bitching Pak had held back a *lot*. In his private report, three times as thick as the one he had read in Sofia, there was an inventory of major life forms. He hadn't mentioned that at all in Sofia. At least three species seemed to possess some sort of social organization: a kind of arthropod; a tunneling species, warm-blooded and soft-skinned; and an avian species—no, not avian, she corrected herself. They spent most of their time in the air, but without having developed wings. They were balloonists, not birds.

Three social species! At least one of them might well be intelligent enough to be civilized.

That brought her back to Danny Dalehouse, his paper on first contact with sentient life forms at the subtechnological level, and his draft proposal. She looked again at the bottom line of the proposal and grinned. Young Danny didn't have any hangups about asking for what he wanted. The bottom line was seventeen billion dollars.

Seventeen billion dollars, she reflected, was about the assessed valuation of Manhattan Island . . . the GNP of any of twenty-five or thirty of the world's nations . . . two months' worth of the United States fuel deficit in the balance of payments. It was a lot of money.

She put the papers and her notes in a bright red folder stamped MOST SECRET and locked them away. Then she began to get Danny Dalehouse what he wanted.

There was a lot to be said about Marge Menninger, and the most important thing was that she always knew what she wanted. She wanted a lot, and a lot of different things. Her motivations were clearly and hierarchically arranged in her mind. The third or fourth thing from the top was likely to be achieved. The second was a near certainty. But the one on top was ironbound.

A week later she had Dalehouse's final proposal and an appointment to testify before the House-Senate Joint Committee on Space Development. She used the week to good purpose, first to tell Dalehouse (on the phone, and spelled out by facsimile immediately afterwards) how to change his proposal to maximize its chances of approval, then to fill in the few gaps in her knowledge of what was required.

To throw a transmitter capsule or a shipload of human beings from one star to another, you first have to put them in orbit.

Tachyon transportation itself is a model of technological elegance. Once you have elevated your capsule to its proper charge state, it becomes obedient to tachyonic laws. It moves easily at faster-than-light speeds, covering interstellar distances to any point in the galaxy in a matter of days. It uses surprisingly little energy in the process. The paradox of the tachyon is that it requires more energy to go slow than to go fast.

Getting the capsule to the charge state is the hardest part. For that you need a rather bulky launch platform. The platform is expensive. More than that, it is heavy.

Getting the platform into orbit is not elegant at all. It is brute force. A hundred kilograms of fuel have to burn for every gram launched in the tachyon state. Fuel is fuel. You can burn oil, or you can burn something you make by using oil to make it—say, liquid hydrogen and liquid oxygen. Either way, in excess of half a million metric tons of oil had to burn to get ten people and minimum equipment on their way to Kung's Star.

Half a million metric tons!

It wasn't just the dollar value. It was four supertankers full of fuel, all of which had to come from one of the fuel-exporting nations, which were showing signs of throwing their weight around again. The QUIP-Three interbloc conferences (Quotas for Imports and Prices) were going badly for the food-exporting countries. If Marge didn't get the expedition well begun, with the necessary fuel tucked away in the big tank farms at Galveston or Bayonne, the increasing fuel prices would drive the costs well past even Danny Dalehouse's estimates.

When all the figures were safely transferred from paper to the inside of her head, Marge locked her desk in the Washington office. She headed for Hearing Room 201 in the old Rayburn Office Building with the knowledge that her work was cut out for her.

The obstacles might have deterred another person. Marge did not accept deterrence. Her disciplined mind dissected the immediate problem into its components, and she concentrated her attention on the attack for each. The problem with the joint committee separated easily into four parts: the chairman, the minority leader, the chief counsel for the committee, and Senator Lenz. She prepared her strategies for each.

The minority leader was her father's friend and could safely be left to him.

The chairman was ambitious to be president. He would be likely to make waves whenever he saw a chance for publicity. The way to deal with him was to keep a low profile and give him as little opportunity to take a campaign position as possible. After she was sworn in and read her prepared statement, he was the first to question her.

THE CHAIRMAN. Well, madam, I'm sure your motives are of the worthiest, but do you know how hard we're working here on the Hill to keep the deficit down?

CAPT. MENNINGER: I certainly do, Mr. Senator.

THE CHAIRMAN. And yet you expect us to give you God knows how many billion dollars for this project?

That was promising! He hadn't said "this hairbrained project" or "this preposterous extravagance."

CAPT. MENNINGER. I don't "expect" it, senator. I hope for it. I hope the committee will approve the proposal, because in my judgment it is an investment that will be returned manyfold for years and years to come.

THE CHAIRMAN. We can't spend the taxpayers' money on hopes.

CAPT. MENNINGER. I know that and appreciate it. It isn't hope I'm asking you to share. It's judgment. Not only mine, but the collective judgment of the best-informed experts in this area.

THE CHAIRMAN. Um. Well, there are many worthy claims based on very sound judgment. We can't grant all of them.

CAPT. MENNINGER. Of course, senator. I wouldn't be here if I wasn't confident of your fairness and competence.

THE CHAIRMAN. Well, do any of my distinguished colleagues have questions for this witness?

They did, but they were mostly perfunctory. The important people, like Senator Lenz and the minority leader, held back for another occasion; the minor members were principally concerned with getting their own positions on record.

The chief counsel was a trickier problem. He was smart. He was also wholly dedicated to making his bosses look good by keeping the joint committee out of trouble. Margie's hope was to make saying yes look less troublesome than saying no.

MR. GIANPAOLO. You spoke of returns on an investment. Do you mean actual cash or some abstract kind of knowledge or virtue?

CAPT. MENNINGER. Oh, both, Mr. Gianpaolo.

MR. GIANPAOLO. Really, Ms. Menninger? *Dollar* returns?

CAPT. MENNINGER. Based on prior experience and what is already known about this planet, yes. Definitely.

MR. GIANPAOLO. Can you give us an idea of what these dollar returns will be?

CAPT. MENNINGER. In broad terms, yes, Mr. Gianpaolo. The tactran reports indicate valuable raw materials and the presence of intelligent life—at least, a near certainty of the former and a strong possibility of the latter. Of course, these are only instrument reports.

MR. GIANPAOLO. Which, as I understand it, are subject to conflicting interpretations.

CAPT. MENNINGER. Exactly, Mr. Gianpaolo, and that is why it is necessary to send a manned expedition out. The whole reason for the expedition is to find out what we can't find out in any other way. If we knew what it would find, we wouldn't have to send it. But there is a different kind of return that I think is even more important. I think of it as "leadership."

MR. GIANPAOLO. Leadership?

CAPT. MENNINGER. The whole free world of food-exporting nations looks to us for that leadership, Mr. Gianpaolo. I don't believe any of us wants to fail them. This is an opportunity that comes only once in a lifetime. I am here because I cannot in all conscience take the responsibility for losing it. It is, in the final analysis, this committee's burden to carry.

Since nothing would be decided in open session, Marge was confident there would be time to make the members understand that that "burden" could best be unloaded by voting her the money.

If Marge Menninger had had her druthers, the testifying would have stopped there. But Gianpaolo was orchestrating the event. He was too wise to end on the note she preferred. He blunted her dramatic impact by dragging a long series of technical data out of her—"Yes, Mr. Gianpaolo, I understand that the planet's surface gravity is point seven six that of Earth, and its atmospheric pressure about thirty percent higher. But the oxygen level is about the same." He read her quotes about the "semi-greenhouse effect" and asked her what was meant by someone's remarks about "the inexhaustible reserve of outgassing from the cold side, as interior heat boils out volatiles." He got her, and himself, into a long complication about whether the designation of the star they were talking about was really Bes-bes Geminorum 8326 or Bes-bes Geminorum 8426 according to the New OAO General Catalogue—apparently both were given, because some typist made a mistake—until the chairman got restive. Then, satisfied that the audience was more than half asleep, he called for a ten-minute recess and returned to the attack.

MR. GIANPAOLO. Captain Menninger, I'm sure you know what it costs to launch a tachyon-transmitted space vessel. First—

CAPT. MENNINGER. Yes, sir, I believe I do.

MR. GIANPAOLO. First there is the immense expense of the launching vehicle itself. The costs for that alone, I believe, are in the neighborhood of six billion dollars.

CAPT. MENNINGER. Yes, sir. But as the vice-president announced in his message to the Tenth General Assembly of the World Conference on Exobiology, we already have such a launch vehicle. It can be used for a large number of missions.

MR. GIANPAOLO. But as the vice-president also announced, the time of that vehicle is fully booked. Prelaunch aiming time is as much as thirty days.

CAPT. MENNINGER. Yes, sir.

MR. GIANPAOLO. But your schedule calls for a launch to this— what is the name of it?

CAPT. MENNINGER. It has been referred to as "Son of Kung," sir, but that name is not official.

MR. GIANPAOLO. I hope not. You want a launch every ten days.

CAPT. MENNINGER. Yes, sir. Essential backup.

MR. GIANPAOLO. Which means canceling the mining survey mission to Procyon IV. I am sure you know that this planet has been identified as having a very dense core, with therefore a good potential for supplies of uranium and other fissiles for our power plants.

The British had sent that probe out. Meticulously they had announced that under existing international agreements they were making the telemetry public. That was all public knowledge. Gianpaolo was just getting on the record.

CAPT. MENNINGER. Yes, sir. Of course, that works out as a very marginal operation, considering the investment necessary to mine and refine uranium and to ship it to us back here. The Bes-bes Geminorum planet has much more potential—as I have already testified.

MR. GIANPAOLO. Yes, Captain Menninger, you have made us aware of your opinions.

And that was all hogwash. What the British had *not* announced, but what both Marge and Gianpaolo knew from previous briefing, was that British scintillation counters had found no ionizing radiation to speak of in Procyon IV's rather unpleasant atmosphere. Uranium there might be, but if so, it was thousands of meters deep. Marge was getting on the record too, although this particular record was private.

By the time she was through testifying, she was satisfied that things were moving in the right direction.

There remained the problem of Senator Lenz. He had far more muscle in the committee, and in the Senate generally, than anyone else—even the chairman. He had to be dealt with individually and privately, and Marge had plans for that.

She booked her return to Houston the long way around, by way of Denver. Her father drove her to Dulles Airport in his own car. Well, actually it wasn't his own. It belonged to a government agency. So did Godfrey Menninger, when you came right down to it. The car was both a perquisite of rank and an indispensable necessity in what he did for the agency; twice a day, other employees of the agency went over it with electronic sniffers and radio probes to make sure it had been neither bombed nor bugged.

God Menninger told his daughter, "You did pretty well at the hearing."

"Thanks, poppa. And thanks for that Pak's report."

"Had what you wanted in it?"

"Yep. Will you talk to the minority leader for me?"

"Already have, honey."

"And?"

"Oh, he's all right. If you get past Gus Lenz, I think you've got the committee taken care of. He didn't say much at the hearing."

"I didn't expect him to."

Her father waited, but as Marge did not go on he did not pursue the question. He said, "There's a follow-up on your Pakistani friend. He's at some kind of a meeting at K'ushui, along with some pretty high-powered people."

"K'ushui? What the hell is a K'ushui?"

"Well," said her father, "I kind of wish I could give you a

better answer than I know. It's a place in Sinkiang province. We haven't had, uh, very full reports yet. But it's not far from Lop Nor and not *too* far from the big radio dish, and Heir-of-Mao's been there five or six times in the past year."

"It sounds as though they're going to move."

"I would say so. I plugged in your estimates, and the best interpretation is that Heir-of-Mao's starting to do what you want us to do."

"Shit!"

"Not to worry," said her father. "I told that to the minority leader in strictest confidence. And I have no doubt he'll tell Gianpaolo. So it'll work for you, you know."

"I wanted to be first!"

"First doesn't always pick up the marbles, honey. How many people discovered America before the English put it in their pocket? Anyway, tell me what's so interesting about this planet."

Margie looked out at the high-rise apartments in the Virginia suburbs, ziggurats climbing away from the south exposure with the black-on-black textured squares of their solar heating panels.

"It was all in Ahmed Dulla's report, poppa."

"I didn't read it."

"Pity. Well, there's a little star with a lot of crummy little planets and one big one about the size of Earth. Gravity's a little lighter. Air's a little denser. It's a lot of real estate, poppa. And it reeks of life."

"We've found life before."

"Mosses and jellyfish! Crystal things that you can *call* alive if you want to. This is different. This is a biota as varied as our own, maybe. Maybe even a civilization. The planet's interesting in another way, too. It doesn't rotate, I mean relative to its primary—like the moon doesn't rotate relative to Earth. So the lit side of it has a sun in the sky all the time."

Her father listened comfortably, scratching his abdomen just below the navel, while his daughter went on about the planet. When she paused for breath, he said, "Wait a minute, honey." He leaned forward to turn on the radio; even in a routinely debugged car God Menninger didn't take chances. Over the twang of synthetic guitars he said, "There's something else you ought to know. The fuel countries are talking among themselves about a sixty percent price rise."

"Jesus, poppa! I'll never drink another shot of Scotch!"

"No, it's not the British this time. It's the Chinese, funnily enough."

"But they're people exporters!"

"They're anything-they-like exporters," her father corrected. "The only reason they're in the People Bloc is that they can swing more weight there. Heir-of-Mao plays his own game. This time he slipped the word to the Greasies that China was going to raise its own prices unilaterally, whatever the bloc votes to do. So that was all the hard-liners in Caracas and Edinburgh needed. The Saudis were for it, of course. They want to stretch out what oil they've got left. And the Indonesians and the rest of the little ones just have to go along with the big boys." He paused thoughtfully. "So your coming along with a chit for half a million tons of oil gets a little complicated right now."

"I see that, poppa. What are we going to do? I don't mean about my project, I mean the country."

"What we are not going to do," he said grimly, "is raise grain prices. We can't. Heir-of-Mao's joker is that the price rise is for export sales only. He considers any sales inside the People Bloc as domestic. So he's selling cheap to the Peeps, and that means they're getting what they need for irrigation and fertilizer at bargain-basement prices. If we raise the price we'll make it worth their while to stop importing in another three or four years. We could stand it in this country, maybe. But the Soviets, the Indochinese, the Bulgarians, the Brazilians, and the rest of the Latins—they couldn't handle it. Their economies would be wrecked. It would break up the bloc. No doubt that's what Heir-of-Mao has in mind."

He parked the car in the Dulles short-term lot. Before snapping off the radio he said, "It won't happen for a couple of months, I think. So you want to get your project on the way as fast as you can."

Marge slid out into the damp, hot evening air. The humped backs of boarding clamjets loomed over the parking lot hedge. They could hear the noise of two of them warming up and the gentler rush of another taking off.

Marge followed her father as he picked up her bag and started toward the terminal. "Poppa," she said, "can I tell the senator about, uh, that?"

"Christ, no! Not that he doesn't probably know it already. But *you* aren't supposed to know."

Surprisingly, she laughed. "Well, I was going to handle it a different way anyway. Hey, hold it, poppa. I'm not taking the Houston flight."

"You're not?"

"Uh-uh. I'm going home by a different route."

Menninger kissed his daughter good-bye at the check-in counter for the Denver clamjet. He watched her disappear into the gate tunnel with mingled admiration and rue. He had been thinking about asking just how she proposed to handle Senator Lenz, but he didn't have to. This was the flight Lenz would be on.

Because it was a night flight, the jet sat there for twenty minutes of preheating before it could take off. The passengers had to be aboard, and the stews scurried up and down with ear stoppers and sympathy. The best heat source there is is a jet turbine. The engines that would thrust the plane through the air in actual flight were now rotated inward, the shell-shaped baffles diverting the blast to pour countless thousands of BTUs into the clam-shaped lifting section.

Marge took advantage of the time to scrub her face, brush her hair, and change her makeup. She had seen the senator come aboard. She debated changing from her uniform into something more female and decided against it. Wasn't necessary. Wasn't advisable. It might look calculating, and Marge calculated carefully ways to avoid looking calculating.

The full-energy roar of the warm-up jets stopped, and everyone belted in for takeoff. That was a gentler sound. The clamjet bounced a few times and soared steeply up.

As soon as they were at cruising altitude Marge left her cubicle and ordered a drink in the forward first-class lounge. In a couple of minutes Senator Lenz was standing over her, smiling.

Adrian Lenz had two terms and two days seniority in the Senate; a friendly governor had appointed him to fill a forty-eight-hour vacancy just for the sake of the extra rank it would give him over other senators elected the same year. Even so, he was not much over forty. He looked younger than that. He had been divorced twice; the Colorado voters laughed about their swinging senator's bad luck but reelected him without much fuss. He could have been chairman of his own committee, but had chosen instead to serve on committees that were of more interest—and more visibility. One of these days "Gus" Lenz was going to be the President of the United States, and everyone knew it.

"Margie," he said, "I knew this was going to be a nice flight, but until now I didn't know why."

Margie patted the seat beside her. "You going to give me my seventeen billion?" she asked.

Lenz laughed. "You don't waste time, Margie."

"I don't have time to waste. The Peeps are going to go there if we don't. They're probably going to go anyhow. It's a race."

He frowned and nodded toward the stewardess; slight, dark, she wore her United Airlines uniform like a sari. When the drinks were served he said, "I listened to your testimony, Margie. It sounded good. I don't know if it sounded seventeen billion dollars' worth of good."

"There was some material in the supplementary statement

you might not have had a chance to read. Did you notice the part about the planet having its own sun?"

"I'm not sure."

"It's small but not very far away. The thing mostly radiates in the lower wavelengths. There's not too much visible light, but a hell of a lot of heat. And the planet doesn't turn in relation to it, so it's always hanging there."

"So?"

"So *energy*, senator. Solar power! Economical."

"I don't understand exactly what you're saying. You mean this substellar thing is hotter than our sun?"

"No, it's not nearly as hot. But it's a lot closer. The important thing is it doesn't move. What's the big problem with solar power here? The sun doesn't stay put. It wanders around all over the sky, and half the time it's not in the sky at all, because it's night here and so the sun's on the other side of the earth. I mean, look at our ship here. We had to preheat for nearly half an hour to get the gas light enough to lift, because it's after dark. On the side of the planet that faces its sun—the only side that interests me, Gus—it's never dark."

Lenz nodded and sipped his drink, waiting for more.

"It's never dark. It's never winter. The sun stays put, so you don't have to make your Fresnel lenses movable. And almost as important, the weather isn't a problem. You know what the score is on our own solar-power installations. Not counting clamjets in the daytime—because they're up over the clouds a lot of the time—we lose as much as twenty-five percent working time because the clouds cut out the sunlight."

Lenz looked puzzled. "This planet doesn't have any clouds?"

"Oh, sure. But they don't matter. The radiation is almost all heat, and it punches right through the clouds! Figure it out. Here we lose half the solar-generating time to night; another few percent to dawn and dusk, because the sun's so low it doesn't yield much power; as much as sixty percent additional for half the year because it's winter; and another twenty-five percent to cloud cover. Put them all together and we're lucky to get ten percent utilization. On this planet a cheaper installation can get damn near a hundred percent."

Lenz thought about that for a moment. "Sounds interesting," he said cautiously, and signaled for a refill.

Margie left him to sort things out in his own mind. Sooner or later it would occur to him to ask what good energy some hundred light-years away was going to do the voters in the state of Colorado on Earth. She had an answer for that, too, but she was content to wait until he asked for it.

But when he asked a question it caught her by surprise. "Margie? What've you got against the Paks?"

"Paks? Why—nothing, really."

"You seem to take this Ahmed's competition pretty seriously."

"Not on a personal level, Gus. I'm not *crazy* about Paks. But I've been on friendly terms with some. I had a Pak orderly when I was teaching at West Point. Nice kid. Kept my clothes ironed and never bothered me when I didn't want him around."

"That sounds like a nice appliance to own," Lenz observed.

"Yeah, yeah. I take your point." She stopped to think. "That's not where it's at, though. I'm not against Ahmed because he's a Pak. I'm against the Paks because they're the other side. I can't help it, senator. I root for my team."

"Which is who, Margie? Just the Food Bloc? Just the United States? Maybe just the female commissioned officers of the US Army?"

She giggled comfortably. "All of them, in that order," she agreed.

"Margie," he said seriously, "we're just shooting the bull here over a couple of drinks. I don't want to get too heavy."

"Why not, Gus? Order up a couple more drinks and let's get to it!"

He obeyed. While they were coming he said, "You're a nice

girl, Margie, but a little too bloody-minded. Pity you went to West Point."

"Wrong, Gus. The pity is that so few young Americans have the chance now."

He shook his head. "I voted to phase down the service academies and cut the military budget."

"I know you did. Worst vote you ever cast."

"No. There was no choice. *We can't afford war, Margie.* Can't you understand that? Even Pakistan could blow us off the map! Not to mention the Chinese and the Turks and the Poles and the rest of the People Bloc. Not to mention the British, the Saudis, the Venezuelans. We can't afford to fight anybody, and nobody can afford to fight us. And everybody knows it. They're not our enemies—"

"But they're competing with us, senator," said Captain Menninger, suddenly sitting up straighter and speaking with more precision. "Economically. Politically. Every other way. Remember Clausewitz: war is the logical extension of politics. I grant," she said quickly, "that we can't go that far. We don't want to blow up the planet. I know what you're saying. It's like that famous saying of—what was his name, the Russian cosmonaut? Years and years ago. Sevastianov, I think: 'When I was in space I saw how tiny the world was, and realized how important it was for all of us to learn to live together on it.' Well, sure, Gus. But learning to live together doesn't mean that some people can't live a little better than others. It's a fact of life! The Fuel people keep jumping their prices. And the People people keep demanding more money for their export workers, or else they'll keep them home, and what will we do for orderlies and airline stewardesses? And we compete back. Well, Gus, when I compete, I compete hard. I play to win! This Kung's Star planet is something I want to win. I think there's goodies on this planet. I want them for *us.* Us being defined as the Food Bloc, the United States, the state of Texas, the city of Houston, and all the other subdivisions you named or want to name, including blond ex-professors from

West Point, if you like, in descending order of size of community. Whichever community you want to talk about, if it's mine, I want it to be first, best, and most successful! I think that's what they call patriotism, senator. I really doubt that you want to knock it."

He looked at her thoughtfully over the new drinks, and raised his. "To you, Margie. You really are some kind of iron-pants."

She laughed. "All right," she said, softening. "I'll drink to that. Now, what about my bill?"

Lenz finished his drink and put it down. "For better or worse we're part of an economic community, and that's a fact of life for *you*, Captain Margie Menninger. You can't sell this to me as a United States venture. You might as a cooperative deal for the Food Bloc."

"Cripes, Gus! We'd still be paying for the whole thing!"

"Maybe ninety percent of it, yes."

"Then why not do it all and take it all?"

"Because," he said patiently, "I won't vote for that. So?"

Margie was silent for a moment, considering her priorities. She shrugged. "So all right," she said. "I don't mind if we include a few token gooks. Maybe two or three Canadians. A Brazilian. Maybe even a Bulgarian. In fact, there was a Bulgarian at the convention—"

She stopped herself. In mid-sentence it had occurred to her that in some sense she owed that Nan Whatever-it-was-ova a sort of a favor; but it had occurred to her simultaneously that the Bulgarian girl had been excessively close to the very Pak she was most worried about.

"No," she said, "on second thought I'm not sure I want a Bulgarian. They're too tiny a power to worry about, frankly. But maybe one or two people from the Soviets. If we send ten, and if at least six are genuine made-in-America US citizens, I can see bringing along a few from the rest of the bloc."

"Um." Lenz looked thoughtfully at her for a moment, moving slightly in his seat to the gentle pitching of the clamjet as it rose and fell through the night sky. "Well," he said, "we'll see." He smiled at her. "What shall we do with this night God has given us, Margie? It's too late to think hard and too early to go to sleep. Want to watch the stars for awhile?"

"Exactly what I want," she said, finishing the last of her drink and standing up. They made their way through the nearly empty lounge to the forward observation section and leaned against the padded rail. The clamjet was swooping gently over the rolling hills of West Virginia. Ahead of them Venus followed a crescent of a moon toward the horizon. After a while Lenz put his arm around her.

"Just checking," he said. "Old Iron-Pants."

Margie leaned against him contentedly enough. Lenz wasn't a big man. He wasn't particularly handsome either, but he was warm and muscular, and his arm around her felt good. There were worse ways of lobbying for votes than this, she reflected as she turned her face to his.

He came through. The full committee reported the bill out, and on a hot Georgia afternoon two or three months later, Margie was called away from her company to take a high-priority phone call. She had not bathed for three days; summer field maneuvers were conducted as close to real war conditions as possible. She was sweating, filthy with both camouflage paint and Georgia clay, and she knew she smelled pretty high. Also, her company was just about to take a hill that she had personally spotted and attacked, so when she got to the phone she was in no good mood. "Captain Menninger," she snarled, "and this goddamn better be important!"

Her father's voice laughed in her ear. "You tell me," he said cheerfully. "The President signed your bill ten minutes ago."

Marge sank back onto the first sergeant's immaculate chair, heedless of his looks. "Jesus, poppa," she said, "that's great!" She stared out at the walls of the command trailer without seeing them, calculating whether it was more important to get back to taking that hill with the rest of the weekend soldiers or to get on the phone and start Danny Dalehouse in motion.

"—what?" She had become aware that her father was still talking.

"I said there was some other news too, not quite so good. Your Pak friend."

"What about him, poppa?"

"That, uh, vacation he was going to take? He took it last week."

·FOUR·

THE PILOT was Vissarion Ilyich Kappelyushnikov. He was short and dark in the standard cosmonaut tradition, with a lot more Tatar in his family tree than his name would suggest. The expedition's eco-engineer was also a Soviet national, but Cossack-tall and fair-haired; his name was Pete Krivitin. The nominal commander of the expedition was an American, Alex Woodring. And they were all going at it at once. Alex was trying to arbitrate between the two Russians, helped by Harriet Santori, the translator. She wasn't really helping, but then the commander wasn't really succeeding at arbitrating. Kappelyushnikov wanted to land and get it over with. Krivitin wanted one more look at the probe reports before he would certify the landing site. Harriet wanted them all to act like adults, for heaven's sake. Woodring's difficulty was that until they landed, Kappelyushnikov was the captain of the ship and Alex's authority was only potential. And it had been going on for more than an hour.

Danny Dalehouse swallowed the desire to intervene again.

He loosened the straps of his deceleration couch and peered out the porthole. There was the planet, filling the window. From less than a hundred thousand kilometers, it no longer looked "away"; it was beginning to look "down." So let us the hell *get* there, he thought testily. These people didn't seem to realize they were screwing around with his personal expedition, which none of them would have been on if he hadn't persuaded that blond army female to authorize it.

A voice in his ear said, "Think we'll ever get there?"

Danny drew back. The woman beside him was Sparky Cerbo, as amiable a person as there was on the expedition; but after nineteen days of sharing less than twenty cubic meters of space, they were all getting edgy. The ongoing spat an arm's length away didn't make it any better.

"It doesn't look like much, does it?" Sparky went on, determinedly making the effort.

Dalehouse forced himself to respond. It wasn't her fault that he was sick of the sound, the sight, and the smell of her —and besides, she was right. Son of Kung didn't look like a proper planet at all. Danny knew what planets were supposed to look like. Some of them were red and bleak, like Mars. More often they were white or mottled white, like everything else from Venus through the gas giants. This one wasn't even trying to look right.

It wasn't so much the planet's fault as Kung's itself; as a star, it was simply incompetent. If Son of Kung had been in orbit around Earth's Sol, it would have looked pretty fine. It had much the same makeup as Earth. What it didn't have was decent sunlight. Kung glowered, not much brighter than Earth's moon during a total lunar eclipse. The only light that fell on Son of Kung was bloody red, and what it looked like from orbit was an open wound.

It would have helped some if it had had a real terminator, but Kung's light was so dim that there was no clear division between "daylight" and "night" sides—only a blurry transition from dark to darkest. Krivitin had assured them that once they landed and their eyes dark-adjusted, they would be able to see reasonably well. But from space that seemed doubtful. And for this, thought Danny, I gave up a perfectly good job at Michigan State.

The Russian language yelling peaked to climax and abruptly stopped. Krivitin, smiling as composedly as though the screaming match had been no more than a friendly chat about the weather, pulled himself around the lashed-down and nested machinery in the center of the main cubicle and peered in at them. "Sara, dear," he said in his perfect English, "you're wanted up front. You better come too, Daniel."

"We're going to land?" Sparky demanded.

"Most certainly not! Cappy has finally understood the necessity for another orbit."

"Hell," said Sparky, even her indomitable desire to please crumbling at last. Dalehouse shared her feelings: another orbit was close enough to another day, with nothing for him to do except try to stay out of the way.

"Yes, I agree," said Krivitin, "but Alex wants you to try to tap the Peeps' signals again."

Harriet complained, but Dalehouse stopped listening. He shucked off his straps and reached wearily for the cassettes of data he had stored away for deceleration.

He plugged in, put the speaker in his ear, and touched the switch. There was a slight tape hiss, an occasional scratch or click, and a distant, somber wail. Those were the sounds from the wolftrap lander. Its primary mission was to secure biological samples and test them in its built-in laboratories; but its microphones had picked up sounds that did not come from itself. He had listened to them fifty times already. After a time he shrugged, stopped the tape, and put in a different cassette.

This time the sounds were louder and clearer, with far more definition. The lander in this case had been a neutral-buoyancy floater with a small reserve of thrusting power and a locater for carbon dioxide. Like a female mosquito seeking a blood meal to fertilize its eggs, it was meant to drift until it found a trail of CO_2 and follow it until it found prey. Then it simply floated nearby as long as there were sounds for it to hear and transmit. But what sounds! Sometimes they resembled a chorus of bagpipes, sometimes a gang of teenage boys in a crepitation contest. Dalehouse had graphed the frequencies—from well below human hearing range to higher than a bat's squeak—and identified at least twenty phonemes. These were no birdcalls; this was language, he was certain.

Heat smote his exposed skin, and he turned back to the port; Kung had drifted into view, looking like a thin-skinned Halloween pumpkin with the embers of Hades inside its mottled surface. He squinted and pulled a neutral-density blind over the porthole; it was not dangerous to glance at it, but there was the chance of burning out your cornea if you stared too long.

In the warmth he felt sleepy. Why not? he thought, snapping off the tape. He leaned back, closed his eyes, and was just drifting off when he heard his name called. "Dalehouse! Krivitin! DiPaolo! Front and center, everybody."

He shook himself awake, wished for a cup of coffee, and pulled himself toward the workspace. Alex Woodring said, "You'd better all see this. The Peeps have filed another report, and Harriet's taped it for us."

Dalehouse wriggled closer for a better view of the video screen just as it blinked and lighted up. There was a plant on the screen, rust-red and fernlike, with raspberrylike fruits hanging from its fronds. "Roll the tape, Harriet," Woodring said impatiently. The images on the screen leaped and flickered, then stopped.

At first Dalehouse thought the picture was of another Klongan flower, possibly some desert succulent: red and yellow blobs oozing what he supposed was some sort of sap— Then it moved.

"Dear God," whispered somebody. Dalehouse felt something rise in his throat.

"What is it?"

"I think it used to be a white mouse," said Morrissey, the biologist.

"What *happened?*"

"That," said the biologist grimly, but with a trace of professional satisfaction, "is what I don't know yet. The Peeps are transmitting their voice reports in code."

"They're supposed to share information!" snapped Dalehouse.

"Well, maybe they will. I assume Heir-of-Mao will have his UNESCO delegation deliver a report. And when it's released in New York, Houston will no doubt send us a copy. But not very soon, I think. The picture was clear. When you come right down to it, that's all we need to know: Klong is not as hospitable as we would like. I—" He hesitated, then went on. "I don't think it's an infectious disease. It looks more like an allergic reaction. I can't really imagine an alien microorganism adapting that quickly to our body chemistry, anyway. I suspect we're as poisonous to them as they are to us, so for openers, we don't eat anything, we don't drink anything but our own sealed supplies and distilled water."

"You mean we're landing anyhow?" the Canadian electronicist said incredulously.

Captain Kappelyushnikov snarled, "*Da!*" He nodded vigorously, then muttered to the translator, who said smoothly:

"He says that that is why we came here. He says we will take all precautions. He says on the next orbit, we go."

Dalehouse played the strange songs from the mosquito probe a few times, but the equipment he needed to do any serious analysis had been stowed away and it made little sense to set it up again. Time to kill. Drowsily he peered out at the planet, and drifted off to sleep wondering what to call it. Kungson, Child of Kung, Son of Kung—"Klong, Son of Kung" was what one of the Americans had christened it—by any name, it was worrisome. When he woke he was given a tube of thick petroleum jelly to smear on himself—"Shuck your clothes and cover your whole body; maybe it will protect you from some kind of poison ivy or whatever that is until we get straightened out." Then he dressed again and waited. The electronicist had patched herself in to monitor any further ground transmissions and was pinpointing sources on a likris map of the sunward surface of Klong.

"There seem to be *two* stations broadcasting," Dalehouse commented.

"Yeah. Must be the base camp and, I suppose, somebody off on an expedition. There's the Peep base"—she touched a dot on the purplish sea, on one side of a hundred-kilometer bay—"and there's the other station." That was across the bay. "We know that's their base; we photographed it last time around. Nothing much. They aren't really set up yet, I'd say. That signal's pulse-coded, probably basic science data on its way to their orbiter for tachyon transmission back home."

"What's over on the other side of the bay?"

"Nothing much. There's a sort of nest of some of the arthropods there, but *they* don't have radio." She pulled the earpiece away from her temple and handed it to Dalehouse. "Listen to that signal."

Dalehouse put the phone in his ear. The sound was a staccato two-tone beep, plaintively repeated over and over.

"Sounds sad," he said.

The woman nodded. "I think it's a distress signal," she said, frowning. "Only they don't seem to be answering it."

·FIVE·

WHAT CAN BE SAID about a being like Sharn-igon that will make him come clear and real? Perhaps it can be approached in a roundabout way. Like this.

Suppose there is a kind and jolly man, the sort of person who takes children fishing, dances the polka, reads Elizabethan verse, and knows why Tebaldi was the greatest Mimi who ever lived.

Is this Sharn-igon?

No. This is only an analogy. Suppose we then go on to ask you if you have ever met this man. You hesitate, riffling through the chance encounters of a life. No, you say, a finger against your nose, I don't think so. I never met anybody like that.

And suppose we then say to you, But you did! It was a week ago Thursday. He was driving the A-37 bus you took from the station to the Federal Building, and you were late for your appointment with the tax examiner because this man would not change a five-dollar bill.

What do you say then? Perhaps you say, Christ, fellow! I

44

remember the incident well! But that was no amiable folk dancer. That was a bus driver!

That's how it would be with Sharn-igon. It's easy enough to imagine you meeting him (provided we don't worry about how you get there). Let's make the mind-experiment to see what would happen. Suppose you are standing outside of time and space somehow, like an H. G. Wells god looking down from a cloud. You poke your finger into the infinitesimal. You touch Sharn-igon's planet, and you uncover him. You look him over.

What do you see?

One might try to describe him to you by saying that Sharn-igon was politically conservative, deeply moral, and fundamentally honest. One might try to elicit your sympathy by saying that he (like who that you know?) was screaming inside with unhealed pain.

But would you see that?

Or would you glance and gasp and pull back your finger in loathing and say:

Christ, fellow! That's no person. It's an alien creature! It lives (lived? will live?) a thousand light-years away, on a planet that circles a star I have never even seen! And besides, it looks *creepy*. If I had to say what it looked like, giving it the best break I could, I would have to say that it looked like half of a partly squashed crab.

And, of course, you would be right. . . .

The way Sharn-igon looked to himself was something else again.

For one thing, he is not an instant invention for your eye to see. He is a person. He has relationships. He lives (will live?) in a society. He moves (moved?) around and through a dense web of laws and folkways. He wasn't like every other Krinpit (as his people called themselves), no matter how indistinguishable they might look to your eyes. He was Sharn-igon.

For example, although it was Ring-Greeting time, Sharn-igon hated Ring-Greeting. To him it was the loneliest and worst part of the cycle. He disliked the bustle, he resented the false and hypocritical sentiment. All the shops and brothels were busy as everyone tried to get gifts and to become pregnant, but it was an empty mockery in Sharn-igon's life, because he was alone.

If you had asked him, Sharn-igon would have told you that he had always hated Ring-Greeting, at least ever since his final molting. (When he was a young seed just beginning to wave on his male-mother's grate he loved it, naturally enough. All seeds did. Ring-Greeting was for kids.) That wasn't quite true. The cycle before, he and his he-wife, Cheee-pruitt, had had a very cheerful Greeting.

But Cheee-pruitt was gone. Sharn-igon signaled at his screen, almost stumbling over an Inedible Ghost that lay before it. There was no answer. He hesitated. Something—perhaps the ghost—seemed to be calling his name. But that was ridiculous. After a moment of indecision, he scuttled across the crowded run to the—call it a bar—to chew a couple of quick ones.

Look at Sharn-igon munching on strands of hallucinogenic fern among a crowd squeezed two or three deep around the Krinpit who was kneading and dispensing the stuff. He was a fine figure of a person. He was masculinely broad—easily two meters from rim to rim; and pleasingly slim—not more than forty centimeters to the tip of his carapace. In spite of his mood, unpaired males and females of all descriptions found him attractive. He was young, healthy, sexually potent, and successful in his chosen profession.

Well, that is not strictly true, because a paradox is involved.

Sharn-igon's profession was a form of social work. The more successful he was in terms of his own personal ego needs, the worse his society was. It was only when Krinpit were in trouble that they turned to persons like Sharn-igon. The Krinpit were socially interdependent to a degree not usually associated with a technological culture on Earth.

Maybe one could find that sort of close-knit clan among the Eskimos or Bushmen, where every member of the community had to be able to rely on every other or they would all die. For that reason Sharn-igon was happiest when he was least wanted. Ring-Greeting was bringing its usual crop of damaged egos born of loneliness amid the holiday cheer. He was busier than he had ever been, and so less happy.

Stand on your cloud and look down on Sharn-igon. To you he surely looks strange, and maybe quite repulsive, true. His crescent carapace is sprinkled with what look like chitinous sails. Some are a few centimeters high, some much smaller; and around them race, clicking and scraping, what look like lice. Actually, they aren't. They are not even parasites, except in the sense that a fetus is a parasite on its mother; they are the young. Sharn-igon is not the only Krinpit in the bar carrying young. Of the hundred individuals in the bar, eight or ten are in the brood-male phase. Sometimes one of the scurrying little creatures drops off or inadvertently gets carried off on the shell of another Krinpit as they rub together. They are instantly aware of what has happened and go wild in the attempt to get back. If they fail, they die.

Each end of Sharn-igon's shell is pleated chitin jointed with cartilage. That part is always in motion, expanding with accordion folds, tilting, spreading like a fan. He slides along the packed dirt floor or the bodies of Krinpit under him (in the conviviality of the bar no one minds being crawled on) on a dozen double-boned legs.

After he had had three quick ones and was feeling better, he left the bar and sidled down the turfy run, not hurrying, with no particular destination in mind. On each side of the run are what you might think of as rather shabby Japanese screens. They are not decorated in any way, but they are jointed and folded, and they come in all sizes. They set off the homes and commercial places, some of which, like the bar, are filled with scores of Krinpit, some almost empty. The screens too are studded with the tiny saillike projections, but otherwise they are unadorned. What you would notice at once is that they are not colored. The Krinpit do not understand color, and in the light of Kung's Star, blood-red and dusky, you would not see much color at first either, even if it were there.

That is how it would look to you, with your human eyes. How would it look to Krinpit eyes? Immaterial; it is a senseless question, because the Krinpit have no eyes. They have photo-sensitive receptors on their carapaces, but there is no lens, no retina, no mosaic of sensitive cells to analyze an image and translate it into information.

But if the scene was dark, it was also noisy.

Every one of the Krinpit was constantly booming its name —well, not its "name" in the sense that the name of Franklin Roosevelt's wife was Eleanor. The name was not an arbitrary convention. It was the sound each Krinpit made. It was sound that guided them, that palped the world around them and returned information to their quite agile and competent brains. The sonar pulses they sent forth to read the echoes were their "names." Each was different, and every one always being produced while its owner lived. Their main auditory apparatus was the drum-tight undersurface of the belly. It possessed a vent like a dolphin's that could produce a remark-able range of vowel sounds. The "knees" of the double-boned legs could punctuate them with tympanous "conso-nants." They walked in music wherever they went. They could not move silently. The exact sounds they produced were con-trollable; in fact, they had an elaborate and sophisticated lan-guage. The sounds which became their recognition signals were probably the easiest for them, but they could produce almost any other sound in the frequency range of their hear-ing. In this their voices were quite like humans'.

So wherever Sharn-igon went he was surrounded by that sound: *Sharn*, a rising protracted noise like a musical saw, overlaid with white hiss; *igon*, a staccato double drumbeat dropping down to the tonic again. It was not just Sharn-igon.

All the Krinpit were constantly making their basic name-sounds when they were not making others. It was not just the Krinpit. Their environment sang to them. Each of the enclosures was marked by wind-powered sound-making machines. Nearly all of them had ratchets or droning pipes or bull-roarers or circle-bowed strings clamoring out their own particular recognition signal.

So to a human eye Sharn-igon was a lopsided crab scuttling in a clattering mass of others, in hellish red gloom, with an inferno of raucous sound coming from every direction.

Sharn-igon perceived it quite differently. He was strolling aimlessly along a well-remembered street. The street had a name; it translates rather closely as "the Great White Way."

At the intersection of the Breeders' Wallow Sharn-igon fell into conversation with an acquaintance.

"Do you have knowledge of whereabouts of Cheee-pruitt?"

"Negative. Conjecture: statistically probable that he would be by lakeside of village."

"Why?"

"Some persons hurt or ill. Many onlookers. Several Anomalous Ghosts reported."

Sharn-igon acknowledged the statements and turned toward the lakefront. He recalled that there had seemed to be a ghost near Cheee-pruitt's residence some time before. And it was anomalous. Basically there were two kinds of ghosts. The Ghosts Above were common and easily "visible" (because they made so much noise) but returned no echo signal to speak of to a Krinpit's sonar. They were good eating when they could be caught. The Ghosts Below were almost invisible. They seldom made visible sounds and returned not much echo; they were mostly observed when their underground digging damaged a Krinpit structure or farm. They too were good eating and were systematically hunted for that purpose when the Krinpit were lucky enough to locate a nest of young.

But what were the anomalous ones, neither Ghosts Above nor Ghosts Below?

Sharn-igon scuttled through the Breeders' Wallow to the Place of Fish Vendors, and along the lakefront to the bright commotion at the Raft Mooring. There was something almost invisible bobbing in the gentle roll of the bay. Though the Krinpit used metal only very sparingly, Sharn-igon recognized the brightness of it; but the bright metal seemed to float over something so soft and immaterial that it returned no real reflection to his sounding. The bright part, though, not only reflected Sharn-igon's sounds almost blindingly, it generated sound of its own: a faint, high, steady whine, an irregular dry-sand rustle. Sharn-igon could not identify the sounds; but then, he had never seen a TV camera or a radio transponder.

He stopped one of the Krinpit moving irritably away from the group and asked what was happening.

"Some Krinpit attempted to eat the ghost. They are damaged."

"Did the ghost harm them?"

"Negative. After eating, they became damaged. One ghost is still there. Advise against eating."

Sharn-igon bounced sounds off the stranger more carefully.

"Have you too eaten of the ghost?"

"A very little, Sharn-igon. I too am damaged."

Sharn-igon touched mandibles and moved on, concerned about Cheee-pruitt. He didn't hear him anywhere in the crowd, but the din was blinding. At least two hundred Krinpit were scratching and sliding over each other's carapaces, milling around the bloody mass that had been one of the "ghosts." Sharn-igon halted and sounded the area irresolutely.

From behind him he thought he heard his own name, badly spoken but recognizable: *Sharn-igon.* When he turned, his highly directional sound sense identified the source. It was the ghost. The one that had seemed to speak his name. Sharn-igon approached it cautiously; he did not like its smell, didn't like its muffled, shadowy sound. But it was a curiosity. First his own name: Sharn-igon. And in between—what? Another name? It was certainly not a Krinpit name, but the ghost kept repeating it. It sounded like OCK med dool-LAH.

On the other shore of the Bay of the Cultural Revolution, fifty kilometers away, Feng Hua-tse rinsed the honey buckets in the purplish waters and carried them back toward the bubble cluster that was the People's Bloc headquarters. From the shore you couldn't see the landing craft itself at all. The extruded bubbles surrounded and hid it. Through the translucent walls of the nearest of them (they could have been made opaque, but the group decision had been that energy conservation was more important than privacy) he could see the vague shadows of the two women detailed as sick-bay orderlies. They had not been given the job because they were women. They had the job because they should have been in bed themselves. Barely able to stagger, they could more or less take care of themselves and the two bed cases. And there was no one to spare to do it for them.

Feng put the clean buckets inside the sick-bay bubble, resenting the waste of the precious nightsoil. But it was his own decision that the wastes from the casualties should be dumped in the bay rather than used to fertilize their tiny plot of garden. Until they were sure what had killed one member of the expedition and put four more on the sick list—nearly half their effectives wiped out at one stroke!—Feng would not risk contamination. It was a pity that their biologist was the sickest of the survivors; his wisdom was needed. But Feng had been a barefoot biologist himself in his youth, and he kept up the experiments with the animals, the tactran reports to Peking, and the four-times-daily examinations of the sick.

He paused in the radio room. The video screen that monitored the small party which had crossed the bay was still showing the same monotonous scene. Apparently the camera had been left on the raft, and apparently the raft had drifted in the slow, vagrant currents of the bay, so that the camera showed only an occasional thin slice of shoreline a quarter of a kilometer away. Once in awhile you could see one of the arthropods scuttling along, and now and again a glimpse of their low, flimsy buildings. But he had not yet seen either Ahmed Dulla or the Costa Rican who had gone with him.

Outside the bubble for the communications equipment the two West Indians were desultorily scooping dirt into woven baskets. Feng spoke sharply to them and achieved a momentary acceleration of pace. They were sick too, but it was not yet clear whether it was the same sickness as the others. They, he thought bitterly, should feel at home here. The heat and humidity were junglelike. What was worst was the lighting, always the same dusky red, never bright enough to see clearly, never dark. Feng had had a headache since they arrived, and it was his private opinion it was only from eyestrain. Feng, at least, had not eaten any of Son of Kung's food. In this he was luckier, or wiser, than the four in the sick bay and the one who had died, not to mention the dozen rats and guinea pigs they tested the stuff on. Feng swore. Why had he let that long-nosed hillman Dulla talk him into splitting their forces? To be sure, it had happened before the five became violently ill. Even so it had been a mistake. When he got back to Shensi, Feng admitted to himself, there would be a long day of self-criticism ahead.

If he got back.

We picked up two baskets of dirt in his shoulder yoke and carried them with him as he went to inspect the dam. That was his greatest hope. When it was completed, they would have electricity to spare—electricity to power the ultraviolet lamps, still stored in the landing craft's hold, that would turn the feeble, pale seedlings into sturdy crops. There was nothing wrong with this soil! No matter how many got sick, even if they died, it was not the soil's fault; Feng had rubbed it between finger and thumb, sniffed it, turned a spadeful over and gazed wonderingly at the crawling things that inhabited it. They were strange, but they meant the soil was fertile. What it did not have was proper sunlight. That they would have to make, as soon as the dam was built; and then, Feng swore, they would produce crops that any collective in Shensi province would envy.

It was raining as he started back, slow, fat, warm drops that ran down Feng's back under his cotton jacket. Another good thing: plenty of water. Not only was it good for the plants, but it kept the spores down, and Feng was highly suspicious of them as the source of the sickness. Even through the clouds he could feel the warmth of Kung Fu-tze. It was not visible, but it gave the clouds the angry, ruddy look of sky over a distant great city. It would stay that way until the air mass that carried the clouds moved away; then there would be that distant hot coal and the purple-black sky with its stars.

Feng took the forest path back to the headquarters, checking the traps. One held two multilegged creatures like landgoing lobsters, one dead, the other eating it. Feng dumped them both and did not reset the trap. There was no point in it. They were too shorthanded to bother with more animal specimens than they had already. Three of the traps were sprung but empty, and one was simply missing. Feng muttered to himself irritably. There was a lot they didn't know about the fauna of this fern forest. For one thing, what had stolen the trap? Most of the creatures they had seen were arthropods, buglike or crustaceanlike, none of them bigger than a man's hand. Bigger ones existed. The sentients in the settlement across the bay were proof of that—they were the size of a man. But the wild ones, if they existed, stayed out of sight. And there was something that lived in the tall, woody ferns. One could hear them, even catch a glimpse of them from time to time, but no one in the expedition had yet caught or even photographed one. It stood to reason that if there were small creatures there would be bigger ones to eat them, but where were they? And what would they look like? Wolf teeth, cat talons, crab claws . . .? Feng abandoned that line of thought; it was not reassuring. To be sure, the local fauna would no doubt find humans as indigestible as the humans had found the local fauna.

But they might not realize that in time.

It began to look as though humans would not find anything at all to eat on Klong. The biologist had been reduced to taking samples of microorganisms from each member of the party and culturing them on plates of agar. It was no longer possible to use laboratory animals. They had all died. And one by one he tried every promising-looking bit of plant or animal they brought him, dropping a broth of it onto the agar, and one by one each of them destroyed the darkening circle of growing bacteria. They were perfect antibiotics, except for one thing: they would have killed the patient more quickly than any disease.

Nevertheless. Ring the trees. Let them die. Ditch those soggy pastures. . . . But the trees did not appear to have a proper bark. In fact they weren't really trees. Slash and burn might not work here. But something would! One way or another, the fields of Child of Kung would prosper!

Feng became aware that his name was being called.

He turned away from the place where the last trap had been, trotting back toward the settlement. As he approached the beach and the fronds thinned, he saw one of the walking casualties waving in excitement.

Feng arrived out of breath. "What, what?" he grumbled.

"A radio message from the long-nose! It is a distress signal, Hua-tse."

"Tchah! What did he say?"

"He said nothing, Hua-tse. It is the automatic distress call. I tried to raise him, but there was no response."

"Of course," snarled Feng, gripping his hands together in anger. Another thing to admit to before the commune. Two members of the party endangered, perhaps lost, because he had foolishly permitted the division of their forces. Two irreplaceable persons—a hillman and a Hispanic, to be sure; nevertheless, persons. Their absence would be serious. And not just the persons. One of their three television cameras. The radio transponder. The precious plastic that had gone into making the skin of the boat. There was just so much of that. They had squandered a great deal on the bubbles to house the sick, the equipment, all their sparse possessions. That was foolishness, too; the fern forest was a limitless supply of woody stems for frames, fronds for ceilings and walls. In this drenched warmth they needed no more than that, but he had weakly permitted the blowing of bubble huts instead of using what nature provided.

Could they build another boat? It was by no means sure that there was plastic enough even for the hull and the sails; and when it was gone, where would they get more? Who could he send? Of their original eleven, one was dead, two were missing, and four were sick. Was it not even more foolish to further divide their forces, to attempt to repair the damage the first foolishness had cost? And what could they do if they did in fact build another boat and sail across the bay? That which had happened to the hillman and the Hispanic could just as well happen to whoever went after them. They had very little in the way of weapons, no more to spare than Dulla and the other man had taken with them in the first place, and little enough good that had done them—

"Are we going, Hua-tse?"

His attention was jarred back. "What?"

"Are we going to try to help our comrades?"

Feng gripped his hands tighter. "With what?" he demanded.

·SIX·

ON A PLANET that has no night the days are endless, Danny Dalehouse reflected, a meter down into the Klongan soil and at least that much more to go. His muscles told him he had been digging this latrine for at least eight hours. The discouragingly tiny spoil heap beside him contradicted them, and the ruddy glow that backlighted the clouds overhead offered no help. Latrine digging was not what he had signed on for. But it was something that had to be done, and he was clearly the most superfluous member of the party in line to do it—only why did it have to take so long?

They had been on the planet only three days (not that there were any days, but the old habits died hard), and already the pleasure was wearing thin. The parts that weren't actively unpleasant like digging latrines were a bore. The parts that weren't already boring were scary, like the madly violent thunderstorm that had blown away their first tent only hours after landing, or irritatingly uncomfortable, like the itchy

56

rashes they had all developed and the stomach troubles that had made the latrines so vital. And to make it worse, they seemed to have company. Kappelyushnikov had come swearing in Russian to report that a third tactran vessel had climbed down its charge state to orbit Klong. Greasies, no doubt. That meant everybody in the world was now represented on Klong. What price the solitary pioneer?

His spade struck air.

Danny lost his balance, spun, and came down in a fetal crouch into the pit, his face almost in the hole that had unexpectedly opened up. From it came a cool, musty smell. It made him think of unopened cellars and the cages of pet mice, and he heard quick, furtive movements.

Snakes? He rejected the thought as soon as he formed it. That was an earthly fear, not appropriate on Klong. But whatever it was could easily be even more deadly than a nest of rattlers. He leaped with prudent speed out of the trench and yelled, "Morrissey!"

The biologist was only a few meters away, sealing plant samples pickled in preservative into plastic baggies. "What's the matter?"

"I hit a hole, maybe a tunnel. You want to take a look?"

Morrissey looked down at the purplish seed pod in his forceps and back at Dalehouse's trench, torn. Then he said, "Sure, only I have to stow these away first. Don't dig any more till I finish."

That was a welcome order, and Dalehouse accepted it gratefully. He was getting used to taking orders. Even as a latrine digger he was subject to instant draft whenever some presently more valuable member of the expedition needed another pair of hands: Harriet to set up her radio, Morrissey to heat-seal his baggies, Sparky Cerbo to locate the canned tomatoes and the kitchen knives that had vanished during the thunderstorm—anyone. Twice already he had had to empty the landing vehicle's chemical toilet into a shallow pit and scrape the soil of Klong over it, because the rest of the crew couldn't wait for him to finish the job they were preventing him from finishing.

It was a drag. But he was on Son of Kung! He could smell the strange Klongan smells—cinnamon and mold and cut vegetation and something that was a little like mom's apple pie, but none of them really any of those things. He could see the Klongan landscape—he could see quite a lot of it, a shovelful at a time.

It was what he had expected in an expedition of specialists. Dalehouse was not a cook, not a farmer, not a doctor, not a radio surveyor. He had none of the hypertrophied skills that all the others possessed. He was the expedition's only generalist and would stay that way until they made contact with the local sentients and he could employ the communications skills he was advertised to have. Meanwhile he was stoop labor.

The Russian pilot, Kappelyushnikov, was yelling his name. "You, Danny, you come have drink. Put back sweat!"

"Why not?" Danny was pleased to notice that Cappy was holding aloft a glass containing a centimeter of water, grinning broadly. He had finally got the still to working. Dalehouse swallowed the few drops and wiped his lips appreciatively, then his slippery brow. Kappelyushnikov was right enough about that. In the dank, humid air they were both covered with sweat. The still was powered with a small oil-spray flame, which made it like burning hundred-dollar bills to operate. Later it would be moved to the lakeshore and driven by solar power, but right now they needed water they could drink.

"Very good, is it?" Kappelyushnikov demanded. "You don't feel faint, like is some poison? Okay. Then we go bring a drink to Gasha."

The translator had given herself command of the setting-up phase of the camp, and no one had resisted; she was spending hours over her radio trying to make sense of the communications, but she claimed the other half of her mind was able to keep track of everyone's duty assignments. She might have been right, Dalehouse thought. She was the least agreeable person on the expedition, and no one particularly wanted to disagree with her. She was also close to the least physically attractive, with stringy black hair and an expression of permanent disappointment. But she was grudgingly grateful for the water.

"Thank you for getting the still going. And the latrine, of course, Danny. Now if the two of you—"

"I'm not finished," Danny corrected. "Jim wants to check out a hole first. Is there anything new on the radio?"

Harriet smiled with closed lips. "We have a message from the Peeps."

"About that guy who's stuck?"

"Oh, no. Take a look." She handed over a facsimile film that said:

The People's Republics extend the hand of friendship to the second expedition to arrive on Child of Kung. Through peaceful cooperation we will achieve a glorious triumph for all mankind. We invite you to join us for the celebration of the fifteen hundredth anniversary of the writings of Confucius, after whom our star was named.

Dalehouse was perplexed. "Isn't that some kind of a winter holiday?"

"You are very well informed today, Dalehouse. It is in December. Our instructor called it the Confucian answer to Hanukkah, which is of course the Jewish answer to Christmas."

He frowned, trying to remember—already, it was becoming hard. "But this isn't even October yet."

"You are very swift indeed, Danny. So translate that, won't you?" requested the translator.

"I don't know. Are they saying something like, 'Don't bother us for a couple of months'?"

"Is more like to drop dead," the pilot put in.

"I don't think so. They aren't being unfriendly," Harriet said, recapturing the fax and squinting at it. "Notice that they referred to Kung Fu-tze by the latinized form of the name. That's a pretty courteous thing for them to do. Still—" She frowned. At best Harriet's eyes were always faintly popped, like a rabbit's, because of the heavy contacts she wore. Now her lips were pursed like a rabbit's too. "On the other hand, they were careful to point out we're the *second* expedition."

"Meaning they're the first. But what's the difference? They can't make territorial claims because they got here ahead of us; that's all spelled out in the UN accords. Nobody gets to claim any more than a circle fifty kilometers around a self-sustaining base."

"But they're pointing out that they could have."

Cappy was bored with the protocol. "Any love letters from the Oilies, Gasha?"

"Just a received-and-acknowledged. And now, about that latrine—"

"In a minute, Harriet. What about the Pak who's stranded?"

"He's still stranded. You want to hear the latest tapes?" She didn't wait for an answer; she knew what it would be. She plugged in a coil of tape and played it for them. It was the Peeps' automatic distress signal: every thirty seconds a coded SOS, followed by a five-second beep for homing. Between signals the microphone stayed open, transmitting whatever sounds were coming in.

"I've cut out most of the deadwood. Here's the man's voice."

Neither Dalehouse nor Kappelyushnikov included Urdu among their skills. "What is he say?" asked the pilot.

"Just asking for help. But he's not in good shape. Most of the time he doesn't talk at all, and we get this stuff."

What came out of the tape player was a little like an impossibly huge cricket's chirp and quite a lot like a Chinese New

Year festival in which Australian aborigines were playing their native instruments.

"What the hell is that?" Danny demanded.

"That," she said smugly, "is also language. I've been working on it, and I've sorted out a few key concepts. They are in some sort of trouble, I'm not sure what."

"Not as much as Pak is," grunted Kappelyushnikov. "Come, Danny, is time we go to work."

"Yes, that latrine is—"

"Not on latrine! Other things in life than shit, Gasha."

She paused, glowering at him. Kappelyushnikov was almost as dispensable as Danny Dalehouse. Maybe more so. After the expedition was well established, Dalehouse's skills would come into play, or so they all hoped, in making contact with sentient life. The pilot's main skill was piloting. A spacecraft by choice. If pressed, a clamjet, a racing vessel, or a canoe. None of those existed on Klong.

But what he had that was always useful was resourcefulness. "Gasha, dear," he coaxed, "is not possible. Your Morrissey still has his micetraps in the trench. And besides, now we have water, I have to make *wasserstoff.*"

"Hydrogen," Harriet corrected automatically. "Hydrogen? What in the world do you want with hydrogen?"

"So I will have a job, dear Gasha. To fly."

"You're going to fly with hydrogen?"

"You understand me, Gasha," the Russian beamed. He pointed. "Like them."

Danny glanced up, then ran for the tent and the one remaining decent pair of binoculars—two pairs of them, too, had turned up missing after the thunderstorm.

There they were, the windblown flock of balloonists, high and near the clouds. They were at least two kilometers away, too far to hear the sounds of their song, but in the glasses Dalehouse could see them clearly enough. In the purplish sky they stood out in their bright greens and yellows. It was true, Dalehouse verified. Some of them were self-luminous, like fireflies! Traceries of veins stood out over the great five-meter gasbag of the largest and nearest of them, flickering with racing sparks of bioluminescence.

"Damn," he snarled. "What are you saying, Cappy? Do you think you can fly up there?"

"With greatest of ease, Danny," the pilot said solemnly. "Is only a matter of making bubbles and putting *wasserstoff* in them. Then we fly."

"You've got a deal," said Dalehouse firmly. "Tell me what to do and I'll do it. I'll—wait a minute! What's that?"

The balloon swarm was scattering, and behind it, coming through the place it was vacating, was something else, something that beat with a rhythmic flash of light.

The sound reached him then. "It's a helicopter!" he cried in astonishment.

The chopper pilot was short, dark, and Irish. Not only Irish, but repatriated to the UK from eleven years in Houston, Texas. He and Morrissey hit it off immediately. "Remember Bismarck's?" "Ever been to La Carafe?" "Been there? I lived there!" When they were all gathered he said:

"Glad to meet you all. Name's Terry Boyne, and I bring you official greetings from our expedition, that's the Organization of Fuel-Exporting Nations, to yours, that's you. Nice place you've got here," he went on appreciatively, glancing around. "We're down toward the Heat Pole—ask my opinion, you folks picked a better spot. Where we are it's wind you wouldn't believe and scorching hot besides, if you please."

"So why'd you pick it?" asked Morrissey.

"Oh," said Boyne, "we do what our masters tell us. Isn't it about the same with you? And what they told me to do today was to come over and make a good-neighbor call."

Harriet, of course, stepped right in. "On behalf of the Food-Exporting States we accept your friendly greetings and in return—"

"Please to stow, Harriet?" rumbled Kappelyushnikov. "But we are not only other colony on Klong, Terry Boyne."

"What's 'Klong'?"

"It's what we call this place," Dalehouse explained.

"Um. 'Klong.' We've been told to call it 'Jem'—short for 'Geminorum', you see. Heaven knows what the Peeps call it."

"Have you been to see them?"

Boyne coughed. "Well, actually that's more or less what it's about, if you see what I mean. Have you people been monitoring their broadcasts?"

"Sure we have. Yours too."

"Right, then you've heard their distress signals. Poor sod, stuck with those beasts that our translator says call themselves 'Krinpit'. The Peeps don't respond. We offered to help out, and they as much as told us to fuck off."

Morrissey glanced at Harriet. Their translator was doing better than she. He said, "We've had much the same experience, Terry. They indicated we weren't welcome in their part of the world. Of course, they have no right to take that kind of a stand—"

"—but you don't want to start any bloc-to-bloc trouble," finished Boyne, nodding. "Well, for humanitarian reasons—" He choked, and took a great swig of the drink Morrissey had handed him, before going on. "Hell, let's be frank. For curiosity's sake, and just to see what's going on over there—but also for humanitarian reasons—we want to go and fish the guy out of there. The Peeps obviously can't. We suppose the reason they shut you and us out is that they don't want us to see how bad off they are. You folks can't—" He hesitated delicately. "Well, obviously it would be easier for us to go in with a chopper than for you to send an expedition overland. We're willing to do that. But not alone, if you see what I mean."

"I think I do," Harriet sniffed. "You want somebody to share the blame."

"We want to make it a clearly interbloc errand of mercy," Boyne corrected. "So I'm all set to go over there and snatch him out this minute. But I'd like one of you to go along."

Eight out of the ten members of the expedition were speaking at once then, with Kappelyushnikov's shouted "I go!" drowning out the rest.

Harriet glared around at her crew and then said petulantly, "Go then, if you want to, although we're so shorthanded here—"

Danny Dalehouse didn't wait for her to finish. "That's right, Harriet! And that's why it ought to be me. I can be spared, and besides—"

"No! I, *I* can be spared, Danny! And I am pilot—"

"Sorry, Cappy," said Danny confidently. "We already have a pilot—Mr. Boyne there—and besides, you have to make your *wasserstoff* so you can take me flying when I come back. And, two, making contact with alien sentients is my basic job, isn't it? And"—he didn't wait for an answer—"besides, I think I know the guy who's stuck there. Ahmed Dulla. We were both hassled by the cops in Bulgaria a couple of months ago."

Wook, wook, wook changed to *whickwhickwhickwhick* as the pilot increased the pitch of the rotors and the copter rocked off the ground and headed for a cloud. Danny clung to the seat, marveling at the profligacy with which the Fuel Bloc spent its treasure—four metric tons of helicopter alone, tachyon-transported from Earth orbit at what cost in resources he could not guess.

"You don't get airsick, do you?" shouted Boyne over the noise of the blades. Danny shook his head, and the pilot grinned and deflected the blade edges so that the chopper leaned toward and began to move after a bank of cumulus.

To Danny's disappointment, the flock of balloonists was out of sight, but there were still small and large creatures in the air, keeping their distance. Dalehouse couldn't see them very clearly and suspected they wanted it that way, staying at the limits of vision and disappearing into cloud as the copter came close. But below! That was laid out for him to enjoy as the chopper bounced along less than fifty meters over the tallest growth. Groves of trees like bamboo; clusters of thirty-meter ferns; tangles of things like mangroves, twenty or more trunks uniting to form a single cat's-cradle tangle of vegetation. He could see small things scuttling and leaping to hide as they twisted overhead, colors of all sorts. The unwinking red glower of the dwarf star toned down rock and water, but the brightest colors were not reflections. They were foxfire glow and lightning-bug tail, the lights of the plants themselves.

Of course Dalehouse had studied the maps of Klong, orbital photos supplemented by side-scatter radar. But this was different, seeing the landscape as they soared above it. Back along the shore was their own camp, on a narrow neck of land that locked off a bay from the wider ocean, or lake, a kilometer or two away. There was the lake (or ocean) itself, curving around like a bitten-into watermelon slice, and in the light from Kung almost the same color. Down the shore of it was the Peeps' encampment. Past that, off toward the part of Klong that lay just under the star, where the land was dryer and the temperatures even higher, was the Greasies' camp. Both of those were out of sight, of course. The copter swung out across the water. Boyne pointed, and Dalehouse nodded; he could see their destination just taking form through the gloomy haze, on the far shore.

Boyne had not been entirely frank, Dalehouse discovered. He had not mentioned that this was not his first flight to the Krinpit community. There had been at least two overflights before that, because there were photos of the layout. Boyne pulled a sheaf of them out of an elastic pocket in the door of the copter, sorted through them, and passed one over to Danny. "There, by the water's edge!" he bawled. His finger jabbed at a curled-up figure a few meters up the beach. Drawn up nearby was a plastic coracle, and there were sheds and more obscure structures all around. There were also some very unpleasant-looking creatures like square-ended crabs:

Krinpit. Some of them were suspiciously close to the huddled figure.

"Is he still alive?" Danny shouted.

"Don't know. He was a day or two ago. He's probably okay for water, but he must be getting damned hungry by now. And probably sick."

From the air the Krinpit village looked like a stockyard, most of the structures comprising only unroofed walls, like cattle pens. The creatures were all around, Danny saw, moving astonishingly quickly, at least when matched against his image of Earthside crustaceans. And they were clearly aware the chopper was approaching. Some raised up to point their blind faces toward it, and an ominous number seemed to be converging on the waterside.

"Creepy looking things, ain't they?" Boyne shouted.

"Listen," said Danny, "how are we going to get Dulla away from them? They don't just look creepy. They look mean."

"Yeah." Boyne rolled down his window and leaned out, circling the helicopter around. He shook his head, then pointed. "That your buddy?"

The figure had moved since the photograph had been taken, was no longer in the shelter of one of the sheds but a few meters away and lying outstretched, face down. Dulla didn't look particularly alive, but he wasn't clearly dead either.

Boyne frowned thoughtfully, then turned to Dalehouse. "Open that case between your feet there, will you, and hand me a couple of those things."

The "things" were metal cylinders with a wire loop at the end. Boyne took half a dozen, pulled the loops, and tossed them carefully toward the Krinpit. As they struck, yellow smoke came billowing out of them, forming a dense cloud. The Krinpit staggered out of the smoke as though disoriented.

"Just tear gas," Boyne grinned. "They hate it." He stared down. Nearly all the creatures that had been converging around the prostrate man were fleeing now . . . all but one.

That one was obviously in distress, but it did not leave the vicinity of the prone human being. It seemed to be in pain. It moved dartingly back and forth as though torn between conflicting imperatives: to flee; to stay; perhaps even to fight.

"What are we going to do about that son of a bitch?" Boyne wondered out loud, hovering over the scene. But then the creature moved painfully away, and Boyne made his decision. He dropped to the ground between the Krinpit and the unconscious Pakistani. "Grab 'im, Danny!" he yelled.

Danny flung open his door and jumped out. He scooped up the Pakistani with more difficulty than he had expected. Dulla did not weigh much over fifty kilos here, but he was boneless as rubber, completely out of it. Danny got him under the arms and more dragged than carried him into the helicopter while Boyne swore worriedly. The rotors spun, and they started to lift off, and there was a rushing, clattering scramble from the other side. Two hundred kilograms of adult Krinpit launched itself onto the side-pallet. Boyne gibbered in rage and jockeyed the controls. The chopper staggered and seemed about to turn on its side; but he got it straight and it began to pull up and away.

"What are you going to do, Boyne?" yelled Danny, trying to pull Dulla's legs inside so he could close the door. "You can't just leave that thing there!"

"Hell I can't!" Boyne stared worriedly at the stiff-jointed legs that were trying to scrape through the plastic to get at him, then turned the copter up and over the water. "I've always wanted a pet. Let's see if I can get this bugger home!"

By the time he got back to his own camp, full of wonder and worries, Dalehouse was physically exhausted. He made a quick report to the rest of the expedition and then fell into a dreamless sleep.

"Night" was an arbitrary concept on Klong. When he woke,

the sky was the same as it always was, clouds and the dull red cinder of Kung hanging far off center above.

It was back to work as usual. Kappelyushnikov, or somebody, had done some digging for him. He had less than an hour's work, mostly neatening up the edges. He welcomed it, because he had more than an hour's pondering to do.

After rescuing the Pakistani, Boyne had laid a beeline course for his own home base. He had not even asked if Dulla was alive; his attention was taken up to saturation by the hideous and very active creature only centimeters from his left ear and by the demands of piloting. Warned by radio, the Greasies had nets prepared. They had the Krinpit lashed and stowed before the beast knew what was happening. Then a quick meal while Dulla got some sort of emergency medical treatment, mostly cleaning him up and flowing a little glucose into his bloodstream. Then over the barren, hot ground to the Peeps' camp, where they left the sick man, accepted some haughty thanks from the Chinese in charge of the place, and took Dalehouse home.

All in all, he had been gone five or six hours. And every second filled with some new input to worry over in his mind.

He really begrudged them the Krinpit. There was no doubt the creature was intelligent. If the buildings hadn't proved that by themselves, its methodical attempt to gouge its way into the helicopter, and its patient acceptance of failure when the plastic proved too tough, bespoke thought. It had struggled only briefly when the Greasies threw the nets over it, then allowed itself to be hauled into a steel-barred cage. Only after the cage door had slammed behind it did it systematically cut through the netting to free its limbs. Dalehouse had spent all the moments he could spare just watching it and trying to make sense of its sounds. If only he had taken the brain-split at some point in his studies! He knew that Harriet or even that Bulgarian girl, Ana, could have reasoned out some sort of linguistic pattern, but it was only noise to him.

Then there was the wonder of the Greasy camp itself. Steel

bars! A helicopter! Bunks on legs, with metal springs! He could not begin to imagine what profligate burning of irreplaceable fuel had made it possible for them to hurl all that stuff at superlight speed to an orbit around Kung, and then to lower it safely to the surface of the planet. They even had air conditioning! True, they needed it; the surface temperature must have been well over forty so near to the Heat Pole. But no one forced them to settle where they would need the permanent drain of air conditioners to survive.

And by contrast, the Peeps. That was pathetic. Old What'sy had put the best face possible on it, but it was clear that the return of Dulla meant to him principally another casualty to try to take care of, with hardly anybody healthy enough to do the nursing—much less do anything else. He had proudly given the visitors to understand that another expedition was on the way, "nearly as big as our own." But how big was that?

Jim Morrissey interrupted his train of thought. The biologist had been out of the camp and had not heard the report; now he wanted it all over again, firsthand. Dalehouse obliged and then asked, "Did you catch anything in your micetraps?"

"Huh? Oh." Obviously that was long in Morrissey's past by now. "No. I ran a wire-tethered probe down the tunnel, but it kept hitting blind alleys. They're pretty smart, whoever they are. As soon as you broke into their tunnel they closed it off."

"So you don't have any animals to send back to Earth?"

"No animals? Never say it, never think it, Danny! I've got a whole menagerie. Crabrats and bugs, creepers and flyers. God knows what they all are. I think the crabrats are probably related to the Krinpit, but you can't really trace relationships until you do paleontology, and Christ, I haven't even made a beginning on the taxonomy yet. And plants—well, anyway, you might as well call them plants. They don't have stomata or mesophyll cells. Would you believe that?"

"Sure I would, Jim."

"Where the photosynthetic process happens I don't know," Jim went on, marveling, "but it's the same good old thing.

Starch production driven by sunlight, or what passes for sunlight—$6CO_2$ plus $6H_2O$ still yields $C_6H_{12}O_6$ and some spare oxygen, on Earth as it is in the heavens. Or the other way around."

"That's starch?" Dalehouse guessed.

"You bet. But don't eat any of it. And keep putting that jelly on your skin every time it rubs off. There're congeners in all that stuff that will do you in."

"Sure." Dalehouse's attention was wandering, and he hardly listened as Morrissey catalogued the vegetation he had so far identified on Klong: something like grasses that covered the plains; succulents like bamboo, with hollow stems that would make fine structural materials; forests of plants that looked like ferns but were fruiting and with woody stems. Some of them grew together from many trunks, like mangroves; others towered in solitary splendor, like redwoods. There were vines like grapes, spreading by transporting their hard-shelled seeds through the digestive tracts of animals. Some of them were luminous. Some were meat-eating, like the Venus flytrap. Some—

"That starch," Dalehouse interrupted, pursuing his train of thought. "Can't we eat it? I mean, sort of cook the poison out of it, like tapioca?"

"Danny, stick to what you know."

"No, really," Dalehouse persisted. "We're shipping a lot of mass in the form of food. Couldn't we?"

"No. Well, maybe. In a sense. It takes only a little bit of their proteins to kick off a reaction I can't handle, so don't experiment. Remember the Peeps' white mice."

"If they're plants, why aren't they green?"

"Well, they are, kind of. In this light they look purple because Kung's so red, but if you shine a flashlight on them they're a kind of greenish yellow. But, you know," he went on earnestly, "it's not the usual chlorophyll. Not even a porphyrin derivative. They do seem to use a magnesium ion—"

"I better get this finished up," said Danny, patting the biologist on the shoulder.

It was almost done. He lugged the chemical toilet from the lander and balanced it over the slit trench, and then reported to Harriet.

"All done. First-class American crapper ready for use."

She came over to inspect and then pursed her tiny lips. "Dalehouse, do you think we're animals? Can't you at least put a tent over it? And before it rains again, would you mind? Look at those clouds. Damn it, Danny, why do I have to tell everybody what to do around here?"

He got the tent up. But the storm, when it came, was a rouser. Lightning scored the entire sky, cloud to ground and air to air. Kung was completely obscured, not even a dull glow to mark where it hung in the sky, and the only light was the lightning itself. The first casualty was the power system. The second was Danny's outhouse tent, torn flying away by the eighty-kilometer gusts. By the time it was over they were drenched and miserable, and all of them were busy trying to put the camp together again. East Lansing had had no storms like Klong's, and Danny viewed with dismal foreboding the next few years on this treacherous planet. When he realized he had been more than twenty hours without sleep, he tumbled into bed and dreamed of a warm morning in Bulgaria with a pretty blond woman.

When he woke, Jim Morrissey was poking him. "Out. I get the bed next."

It wasn't really even a bed—just a sleeping bag on an air mattress—but at least it was warm and dry. Dalehouse reluctantly yielded it to the biologist. "So the camp survived?"

"More or less. Don't go near Harriet, though. One of her radios is missing, and she thinks we're all to blame." As he climbed into the bed and stretched his legs down to the warm interior, he said, "Cappy wants to show you something."

Danny didn't rush to see the pilot; odds were, he considered, that it was just some other stoop-labor job that needed doing. It could wait until he had something to eat—although, he reflected, chewing doggedly through a guaranteed full daily requirement of essential vitamins and minerals (it looked like a dog biscuit), eating wasn't a hell of a lot more fun than digging latrines.

But that wasn't what Kappelyushnikov had in mind. "Is no more manual labor for you and me for awhile, Danny," he grinned. "Have now been honored by appointment as chief meteorologist. Must make more *wasserstoff* to check winds, and you help."

"Harriet was real shook up by the storm," Dalehouse guessed.

"Gasha? Yes, that is what she wants, better weather forecasting. But what I want is exotic travel to faraway places! You will see."

Kappelyushnikov's still had been converted to solar power, a trough of brackish water from the lake running between aluminum reflecting V's, and the vapor trapped on a plastic sheet overhead. The drops slipped down into a tank, and part of the fresh water was being electrolyzed into hydrogen and oxygen. From the hydrogen collector, a seamless plastic balloon, a small compressor whirred at regular intervals to pump the gas into a heavy metal cylinder.

Kappelyushnikov checked the pressure gauge and nodded gravely. "Is plenty. Now you go borrow theodolite from head boss, Gasha. Do not take no for answer; and then I will show you something that will truly amaze you."

Fortunately for Dalehouse, Harriet was somewhere else when he went for the theodolite, a small sighting telescope that looked like a surveyor's transit. By the time he got back with it Kappelyushnikov had filled a plastic balloon with hydrogen and was expertly balancing its lift against the weight of a silver ruble. "My good-luck piece," he said dreamily. "Yes, fine. You have pencil?"

"What's a pencil? I have a ballpoint."

"Don't make fun of old-fashioned Soviet values," Kappelyushnikov said severely. "When I let go of balloon, you keep eye on watch. Every twenty seconds you tell me, I call off readings, you write down. You understand? Okay, let go."

The little balloon did not leap out of Dalehouse's fingers; it only drifted upward, bobbing gently as vagrant zephyrs caught it. In the still after the storm there was no strongly prevailing wind that Dalehouse could feel, but he could see the balloon move erratically. At each time-hack Kappelyushnikov read off right ascension and declination bearings. After the seventh reading he began to swear, and after the ninth he straightened up, scowling.

"Is no good! Lousy Kungson light! I cannot see. Next time we will tie on candle."

"Fine, but would you mind telling me what we're doing?"

"Measuring winds aloft, dear Danny! See how balloon curved around, started back way it came? Winds at different levels blow various individual different directions. Balloon follows. We follow balloon. Now we reduce readings, and soon I will truly astonish you with more than you wish to know about Klongan wind patterns."

Dalehouse squinted thoughtfully at where the balloon had disappeared into the maroon murk. "How are we going to do that?"

"Oh, Danny, Danny. How ignorant you Americans are! Simple trigonometry. I have right ascension sighting of balloon after twenty seconds, correct? So I have one angle of right triangle. Second angle must be ninety degrees—you understand that this is so? Otherwise would not be right triangle. So simple subtraction from one hundred eighty gives me angle remaining, and I have thus described triangle perfectly, except for dimension of sides. Okay. I now feed in dimension of first side, and simple transformation—"

"Whoa! You didn't measure anything. Where did you get the dimension of one side?"

"Altitude of balloon after twenty seconds, of course."

"But how do you know—"

"Ah," said Kappelyushnikov smugly, "that is why care is so important in weighing off balloon. With fixed lift, balloon rises at fixed rate. Lift is equal to one silver ruble, and so in each twenty seconds rises nine point seven three meters. We now perform same arithmetic for declination and we have fixed position of balloon in three-dimensional space. Here, walk while we talk." He took the jotted readings from Danny and scanned them, frowning. "Such terrible writing," he complained. "Nevertheless, I can read them perhaps well enough to feed into computer. Is very easy computation."

"Then why do you need a computer?"

"Oh, I could easily perform operations myself. But computer needs practice. Wait one, Danny."

While the Russian was mumbling to himself over the keyboard, Harriet poked her head in the tent. "What are you doing?" she demanded sharply.

"Important scientific research," said Kappelyushnikov airily, without looking up. To Danny's surprise, the translator did not react. She looked sullen, confused, and unhappy—not conspicuously different from her normal look. But her normal behavior was a good deal more abrasive than her demeanor now. She came quietly into the tent and sat down, thumbing dispiritedly through her translation notes.

"Have it!" cried the pilot happily, and pressed a command button. The liquid crystal over the computer flashed colored darts of light, then revealed a plot of wind arrows. "Colors of spectrum," Kappelyushnikov explained. "Red is lowest, up to fresh grass green for highest. You see? At fifty meters, wind heading one forty-five degrees, eight kilometers per hour. At one hundred meters, backing to ninety-five degrees and now fifteen kilometers. And so on. Triumph of Soviet technology."

Dalehouse nodded appreciatively. "That's very nice, but what do we want to know that for?"

"Meteorology," Kappelyushnikov grinned, winking and moving his head toward Harriet.

The woman looked up and burst out, "Cut that out, Vissarion. I'm in no mood for you to make fun of me. Tell Dalehouse your real reason."

The Russian looked surprised, and a little thoughtful, but he shrugged. "All right. Poor American Danny, you are helpless without your machines. But not I. I am pilot! I do not wish to be earthworm like one of those things we shit on in your latrine, Danny. I want something to fly. They will not give me fuel. They will not let me have structural materials for glider —would be easy, except for launching; plenty of winds here, you see. But Gasha says no, so what can I do? I look up and see balloonists floating around sky, and I say I also will be balloonist!" He pounded his fist on the top of the computer. "Have gas. Have navigation information for winds aloft. Have Soviet know-how. Have also little extra bonus of low gravity and high pressure of air. So now I will make little balloon, big enough for me, and I will pilot again."

A surge of enthusiasm infected Dalehouse. "Hey, that's great. Would it work?"

"Of course would work!"

"We could use it to take after those balloonists, get close to them. Harriet, do you hear that? It would give us a chance to try to talk to them."

"That's fine," she said, and Dalehouse looked at her more closely. Even for Harriet she looked sullen.

"What's the matter?" he asked.

She said, "I located the radio."

"The one that blew away in the storm?"

She laughed, like a cartoon figure laughing: *heh, heh, heh.* "It takes a real idiot to believe that one. How could it blow away? Goddamn thing weighs twenty kilos. It occurred to me it might be transmitting, so I listened, and it was. I tried RDFing, and I got a fix right away. Straight down," she said, staring at them. "The damn thing is right down underneath us in the ground."

A minute was still a minute. Danny made sure of that, because he had begun to doubt. His pulse was still forty-two in sixty seconds by the clock. He could hold his breath for three of the minutes and maybe a bit more. The small coinage of time had not altered in value. But one thousand four hundred and forty minutes did not seem to make a day anymore. Sometimes it felt as though a whole day had passed, and the clock said only six or seven hours. Sometimes it would occur to him to be tired, and the clock would show as much as thirty hours since he slept last. Fretfully Harriet tried to keep them all on some regular schedule, not because it seemed necessary, but because it was orderly. She failed. Within—what? a week?— they were sleeping when they wanted to and eating when they felt hungry and marking the passage of time, if at all, by events. The first near-visit by balloonists was after the big storm and before the Peeps received their reinforcement of personnel. The time Kappelyushnikov triangulated the missing radio for Harriet and discovered it was at least twenty meters underground was just after they sent their first reports and shipment of specimens back to Earth. And the time balloonists came to visit—

That was a whole other thing, the kind of event that changes everything fore and aft.

Dalehouse woke up with his mind in the sky. He did his chores. He helped Morrissey check his traps, prepared a meal of desecrated stew, fixed a valve in the shower stall by the lake. But what he was thinking of was Kappelyushnikov's balloons. Danny had talked him out of the big single hydrogen-filled bag: too big, too clumsy, too hard to manufacture, and above all too likely to kill its passenger if anything popped its skin. So they had painstakingly blown a hundred pibal-sized bags, and the Russian had knotted up a netting to contain them. The aggregate lift would be as much as you wanted. All it took was more balloons; you could multiply them to lift the entire camp if you liked. But if one or two popped, it did not mean a dead aeronaut. The passenger would descend reasonably slowly—to be more accurate, they were hopeful the passenger would descend slowly. He might damage himself, but at least he would not be spread flat across the Klongan landscape.

Kappelyushnikov would not allow Danny to do the final stages of filling and tying the balloons—"Is my neck, dear Danny, so is my job to make sure it stays okay."

"But you're taking so damn long. Let me help."

"*Nyet.* Is very clear," grinned the pilot, "that you think pretty soon you too will fly my balloons. Maybe so. But this time I am sole cargo. And besides, have still static lift tests to finish. Until then not even I fly."

Dalehouse moved impatiently away, disgruntled. He had been on Klong for—whatever length of time it was—a couple of weeks, at least. And the author of "Preliminary Studies toward a First Contact with Subtechnological Sentients" had yet to meet his first subtechnological sentient. Oh, he had seen them. There were burrowers under his feet, and he was sure he had caught a glimpse of something when Morrissey exploded a charge under a presumed tunnel. The Krinpit had been his fellow passenger for half an hour. And the balloonists were often in the sky, though seldom nearby. Three separate races to study and deal with! And the most productive thing he had done was dig a latrine.

He fidgeted his way into Harriet's tent, hoping to find that she had miraculously made some giant leap in translation of one of the languages—if they were languages. She wasn't there, but the tapes were. He played the best of them over and over until Kappelyushnikov came in, sweating and cheerful.

"Static test is good. Plenty lift. Now we let whole mishmash sit for a while, check for leaks. You are enjoying concert of airborne friends?"

"It isn't a concert, it's a language. I *think* it's a language. It's not random birdcalls. You can hear them singing in chords and harmonies. It's chromatic rather than——do you know anything about music theory?"

"Me? Please, Danny. I am pilot, not longhair fiddle player."

"Well, anyway, it's chromatic rather than diatonic, but the harmonies are there, not too far off what you might hear in, say, Scriabin."

"Fine composer," the Russian beamed. "But tell me. Why do you listen to tapes when you have real thing right outside?"

Startled, Danny raised his head. It was true. Some of the sounds he was hearing came from somewhere outside the tent.

"Also," Kappelyushnikov went on severely, "you are breaking Gasha's rice bowl. She is translator, not you, and she is very difficult lady. So come now and listen to your pink and green friends."

The balloonists had never been so close, or so numerous. The whole camp was staring up at them, hundreds of them, so many that they obscured each other and blotted out part of the sky. The red glower of Kung shone through them dimly as they passed before its disk, but many of them were glowing with their own firefly light, mostly, as Kappelyushnikov had said, pink and pale green. Their song was loud and clear. Harriet was there already, microphone extended to catch every note, listening critically with an expression of distaste. That meant nothing. It was just the way she always looked.

"Why so close?" Dalehouse marveled.

"I do not wish to break your rice bowl either, dear Danny. You are expert. But I think is possible they like what we put up for chopper pilot." And Kappelyushnikov waved to the strobe beacon on the tower.

"Um." Danny considered a moment. "Let's see. Do me a favor and get one of the portable floodlights. We'll see them better, and maybe it'll bring them even closer."

"Why not?" The Russian disappeared inside the supply tent and came back with the portable in one hand and the batteries in the other, cursing as he tried to avoid stumbling over the wires. He fumbled with it, and its dense white beam abruptly extended itself toward the horizon, then danced up toward the balloonists. It seemed to excite them. Their chirps, squeals, flatulences, and cello drones multiplied themselves in a shower of grace notes, and they seemed to follow the beam.

"How do they do that?" Harriet demanded fretfully. "They've got no wings or anything that I can see."

"Same as I, dear Gasha," boomed the Russian. "Up and down, to find a truly sympathetic current of air. Here, you hold light. I must watch experts and learn!"

The balloonists were coming closer. Evidently the light attracted them. Now that there was enough brightness to make the colors plain, the variety of their patterns was striking. There were cloudlike whorls, solid bands, cross-hatchings, dazzle designs that resembled World War I camouflage.

"Funny," said Dalehouse, staring longingly at the swarm. "Why would they have all those colors when they can't see them most of the time?"

"Is your opinion they can't," said Kappelyushnikov. "Light like beet juice is strange to us; we see only the red. But for them perhaps is— Ho, Morrissey! Good shot!"

Dalehouse jumped a quarter of a meter as the camp's one and only shotgun went off behind him. Overhead, one of the balloonists was spiraling toward the ground.

"I get," yelled Kappelyushnikov, and sprinted off to intersect its fall.

What the hell did you do?" blazed Dalehouse.

The biologist turned a startled and defensive face toward him. "I collected a specimen," he said.

Harriet laughed disagreeably. "Shame on you, Morrissey. You didn't get Dalehouse's permission to shoot one of his friends. That's the price you pay for being a specialist in sentients—you fall in love with your subjects."

"Don't be bitchy, Harriet. My job's hard enough. This'll

make it impossible. Shooting at them is the surest way to drive them away."

"Oh, sure, Dalehouse. Anybody can see they're stampeding in terror, right?" She waved a casual hand at the flock, still milling through the light and singing as they soared delightedly overhead.

Kappelyushnikov came back with a rubbery sac draped over his shoulder. "Almost had to fight off one of your Krinpit friends to get it," he growled. "Was big, ugly mother. Don't know what I would have done if he had truly contested ownership. But he scuttled away."

"There are no Krinpit around here," Harriet said sharply.

"Are now, Gasha. Never mind. See how pretty our new pet is."

The creature was not dead. It did not seem even wounded, or at least there was no blood. The shotgun pellets had blown a hole in the gasbag and nothing else. Its little face was working, looking like the countenance of an engorged tick, with great eyes staring at them. It was making the tiniest of sounds, almost like gasps.

"Disgusting," said Harriet, drawing back. "Why isn't it screaming?"

"If I knew the answers to questions like that," said Morrissey, dropping to one knee beside the creature to see it better, "I wouldn't have to collect specimens, would I? But at a guess, it would be if I hadn't shot the breath out of it. I think it uses the hydrogen for vocalizing. God knows what it breathes. Must be oxygen, of course, but—" He shook his head and glanced up. "Maybe I ought to collect a few more."

"No!"

"Christ, Dalehouse! You know, Harriet's right about you. Well—I know. At least let's see how phototropic they are. Hand me those shells." Kappelyushnikov passed over the plastic belt of ammunition, and Morrissey pawed through it until he found a signal flare.

"You'll set fire to them, Morrissey! That's hydrogen in those bags!"

"Oh, cripes." But the biologist aimed carefully to one side of the flock. More and more of them were entering into the beam, now steady, as Harriet had put it on the ground pointing up; the whole diffuse swarm was contracting into a knotted mass.

When the flare went off, the whole flock seemed to twitch like a single organism. They didn't swarm toward it. They stayed bunched in an ellipsoidal huddle along the axis of the beam of light; but their song changed to a frantic crescendo, and there seemed to be a systematic rearranging of positions within the flock. The smaller and less brightly colored individuals bobbed toward the lower portions of the school, and the larger and gaudier ones lifted toward the top. Dalehouse stared in fascination, so entranced that he did not realize his face was sticky and wet until Kappelyushnikov grunted in surprise.

"Hey! Is raining?"

But it wasn't rain. It was sweet and pungent on their lips, with an aftertaste that was animal and fetid; it fell like a gentle dew on their upturned faces and clung to their skins.

"Don't swallow any!" cried Morrissey in belated panic, but some of the people were already licking their lips. Not that it mattered, thought Dalehouse; the stuff was all over them. If it was poisonous, they were done for.

"You fools!" cried Harriet, stamping her foot. She had never been attractive, and now she looked like a witch, sallow face in a grimace, uneven teeth bared. "We've got to get this stuff off. Kappelyushnikov! You and Morrissey get buckets of water at once."

"*Da*, Gasha," said the pilot dreamily.

"*Now!*" she screamed.

"Oh, of course, now." He lumbered off a few steps, then paused and looked coquettishly back over his shoulder.

"Alyusha, dear. You help me get important water right away?"

The navigator simpered. She answered him in Russian, something that made Kappelyushnikov grin and Harriet swear. "Don't you clods know we're all in *danger?*" she cried, catching at Dalehouse's hand imploringly. "You, Danny, you've always been nicer to me than those other bastards. Help me get water."

He returned the pressure of her hand and whispered, "Hell, yes, honey, let's get some water."

"Danny!" But she wasn't angry anymore. She was smiling, allowing him to tug her toward the lakefront.

He ran his tongue over his lips again. Whatever the dew was, the more he tasted it the better he liked it: not sweet, not tart, not like fruit or meat, not like flowers. It was not like anything he had ever tasted before, but it was a taste he wanted more of. He saw Harriet touching her pointed tongue to her own thin lips and was suddenly seized with the need to taste that Klongan mist from her mouth. He felt the damp heat rising inside him and caught her roughly around the waist.

They kissed desperately, their hands busy ripping each other's clothes off.

It never occurred to them to think of hiding themselves. They cared nothing for what the others in the expedition might think of them, and the others cared no more for Harriet and Dalehouse. In couples and clusters the entire expedition was down on the ground in a mass fury of copulation, while overhead the swooping balloonists sang and soared through the searchlight and their gentle mist rained down on the human beings below.

·SEVEN·

ANA DIMITROVA sat in a window table of a Greek tea shop in Glasgow, writing industriously on her daily letter to Ahmed. She did not send them all. That would be ruinously extravagant! But every week, at the end of Sunday, she spread them out on a table and copied out the best parts, enough to fill four dots in a microfiche. It was never enough. She leaned forward into the northern sunshine, left elbow on the table next to the cooling cup of strong, sweet tea, head resting on the hand, oblivious to the noise of the lorries and the double-decker yellow-and-green buses on the Gallowgate road outside, and wrote:

—it seems so long since last I kissed your lovely eyelids and wished you good-bye. I miss you, dear Ahmed. This place is terrible! Terrible and strange. It smells of petroleum and internal-combustion engines, the smell of wicked waste. Well. They have only another five or ten years and then their North Sea oil will be gone, and then we will see.

The headaches have been very bad, I think because these languages are so uncouth. It is actual pain to speak in them. It will be all right, though, dear Ahmed. The headaches pass. The ache in my heart lasts much longer—

"More tea, miss?"

The harsh English words crashed into Nan's ear. She winced and raised her head. "Thank you, no."

"We'll be serving lunch in just a bit, miss. The souvlaki's very tasty today, cook says."

"No, no. Thank you. I must be getting back to my hotel." She had dawdled longer over the letter than was right, she thought remorsefully, and now she had to hurry, and the headache was back. It was not just that the woman was speaking English. It was the way she spoke it, the rough Scottish consonants that buzzed and rattled in the ear. Although in truth it did not much matter what language, or at least what non-Slavic language, she was hearing. The headaches were more frequent and more severe. It was probably because she had become a diplomatic translator. The international vocabulary of science was easy enough to translate, since so many of the words had the same roots in all languages. In diplomacy the risks were greater, the nuances subtler and more threatening. The choice of an adjective meant nothing in translating a report on X-ray polarimetry, but in a speech about locating a drilling claim on the Mid-Atlantic Ridge it might mean the difference between peace and war.

Nan paid her check and dodged cautiously across Gallowgate among the towering buses that so mischievously raced along the wrong side of the street. The diesel stink made her cough, and coughing made her headache worse.

And she was late. She was to be picked up for the airport at one, and it was past noon already. She walked virtuously past the shops (so bright and gay!) without looking in a single window. There were styles here that Sofia would not see for another year. But why bother? It would have been nice to buy new clothes to wear for Ahmed. With him so many billions of kilometers away, Nan wore what was easiest to put on and least likely to attract attention. Evenings she spent alone when she could, listening to music and studying grammar. Her best treat was to reread the sparse letters he had returned for her prodigious outflow—although they were not stimulating. From what he said, Son of Kung sounded a grim and awful place.

She cut through a corner of the Green to walk along the riverside toward her hotel, hoping to avoid the noise and the invisible, but not unsmellable, exhaust from all the vehicles. No use. Lorries rumbled along the embankment, and the sludgy surface of the Clyde itself was pocked with oil tankers and barges and creased with the wakes of hydrofoils. How did one *live* in a place like this? And it all could have been avoided. A little forethought. A little planning. Why did they have to put oil refineries in the middle of a city? Why stain their river with waste and filth when it could have been a cool oasis? Why be in such a rush to pump the oil from the bottom of the sea when it could have provided energy, even food, for another hundred generations? Why use oil at all, for that matter—especially in these packs and swarms of cars and lorries—when the city could have been built around public transportation, electrically powered, or powered with the hydrogen that Iceland, not so very far away, was so eager to sell.

But on Son of Kung . . .

On Son of Kung it could be all different. She wished she could be there. With Ahmed. Not just to be with Ahmed, she told herself stoutly, but to be part of a new world where things could be done properly. Where the mistakes of Earth could be avoided. Where one's children would have a future to look forward to.

Hers and Ahmed's children, of course. Nan smiled to herself. She was an honest person, and she admitted that Kungson seemed all the finer because Ahmed was there. If only she were not *here!* There were worrisome things between the lines of what he wrote. So many of his expedition had been sick. So many had died, just in the first days—and his only letters had been in those first days. Why, he himself could have— No. She would not countenance that thought. There was enough else to fret about. For example, the picture he had sent of himself. He had looked worrisomely thin, but what she had noticed most about the picture was the hand on his shoulder. The person who owned the hand was not visible, but Nan was almost sure it was a woman's hand. And that was even more worrisome.

"Miss Dimitrova! Hoy, there. Nan!"

All at once she perceived that her feet had carried her into the lobby of the hotel, and she was being greeted by a man she almost recognized. Dark, short, plump, a little past middle age, he had a diplomat's smile and wore clothes that, even across the immense old lobby, she was sure were real wool— if not cashmere.

He filled in the blank for her. "I'm Tam Gulsmit. Remember? We met at the FAO reception last month." He snapped his fingers for a forkboy. "Your bags are all ready—unless you care to freshen up? Have time for a drink?"

Now she recalled him well. He had been persistent in his attentions, even to the point of lying in wait for her as she came out of the powder room and drawing her into an offensively close conversation in the hall. She had explained to him that it was no use. It was not merely a question of being in love with someone else. That was not his concern; she did not have to tell him her reasons. It was a matter of socialist morality. V. I. Lenin had said it. Free love was all very well, but who would want to drink from a glass that every passerby had fouled with his lips? (And yet in Moscow, she remembered, the public drinking fountains had just such glasses chained to them, and each one surely smeared with a thousand lips.) Let the Fuel powers do what they liked—partner swapping, group orgies, whatever. She was not there to pass judgment, but a socialist girl from Sofia did not even smoke in the street, because she had been taught certain principles of behavior that did not leave her when she grew up.

"Sir Tam," she began—she remembered that he had one of those quaint British handles to his name—"it is a pleasure to see you again, but I must fly now to New York for the United Nations debate. I have no time—"

"All the time in the world, sweets, that's what I'm here for. Boy!"

Tardily the bellboy rolled up with his forklift, and that was scandalous, too: her one little zipper bag did not need a fuel-guzzling machine to carry it; she had toted it a kilometer at a time herself.

Sir Tam chuckled indulgently. "Aren't we quaint? This great, rambling old ruin—that's the Britishness of it, isn't it? We're great at backing a losing horse long past the point where anyone else would have chucked it in. Lucky for us we can afford it! Now, is there anything else you need to bring?"

"But truly, Sir Tam, a car is being sent to take me to the airport. It will be here any minute."

"Here already, sweetie. I'm it. Our Government have provided me with a Concorde Three, and I'd just rattle around in it by myself. When I heard that a friend of God Menninger's needed a lift I took the liberty of coming for you myself. You'll like it. There's plenty of room, and we'll make New York in ninety minutes."

Scandalous, scandalous! Of course the British could afford anything, ocean of oil under the North Sea, their octopus tendrils already grabbing at the Mid-Atlantic Ridge. But morally it was so wrong.

She had no chance to refuse. Sir Tam overcame all objections, and before she knew what was happening she was lifted gently by cherry picker into—dear God!—a supersonic hydrojet.

As soon as they belted up, in deep, foam armchairs with a suction-bottomed decanter and glasses already on a little table between them, the aircraft hurled itself into the air. The acceleration was frightening. The way the ground dropped away beneath them was not to be believed. Strangely, there was less noise than she had expected, far less than the warm-up roar of a clamjet.

"How quiet," she said, leaning away from Sir Tam's casually chummy arm.

He chuckled. "That's five thousand kilometers an hour for you. We leave the sound far behind. Do you like it?"

"Oh, yes," said Nan, trying to prevent him from pouring her a drink. She failed.

"Your voice sounds more like 'oh, no.' "

"Well, yes, perhaps that is so. It is terribly wasteful of oil, Sir Tam."

"We don't burn oil, sweetie! Pure hydrogen and oxygen—have to carry them both, this far up. Not an ounce of pollution."

"But of course one burns oil, or some other fuel, to make the hydrogen." She wondered if she could keep the conversation on propellant chemistry all the way across the Atlantic, decided not, and took a new tack. "It is frightening. One can see nothing from these tiny windows."

"What is there to see? You get turned on by clouds, love?"

"I have flown the oceans many times, Sir Tam. There is always something. Sometimes icebergs. The sea itself. In a clamjet there is the excitement of the landfall as one approaches Newfoundland or Rio or the Irish Coast. But at twenty-five thousand meters there is nothing."

"I couldn't agree with you more," said Sir Tam, unstrapping and moving closer. "If I had my way there'd be no windows in the thing at all."

Nan moistened her lips with the whiskey and said brightly, "But it is all so exciting. Could you perhaps show me around this aircraft?"

"Show you around?"

"Yes, please. It is so new to me."

"What's to see, love?" Then he shrugged. "Matter of fact,

yes, there are a few features I'd like to call to your attention."

She stood up gratefully, glad to get his hand off her knee. The headaches had lessened, perhaps because now they were breathing quite pure air instead of the Glaswegian smog, but she was annoyed. He had made it clear that they were the only passengers; that was not deceitful. But she had expected at least the chaperonage of the stewardesses, and they, all three of them, had retreated to their little cubbyholes in the aft of the aircraft. The little paneled lounge was far more intimate than she liked.

But worse was in store. What she had thought was a service cubicle turned out to be a tiny, complete bedroom suite. With —could one believe it?—a *waterbed*. Easily a metric ton of profligately wasted mass! For nothing, surely, but profligately immoral purposes!

"Now there," said Sir Tam over her shoulder, "is a feature worth studying. Go ahead, Nan. Let your impulses carry you. Try it out."

"Certainly not!" She moved away from his touching hand and added formally, "Sir Tam, I must tell you that I am an engaged person. It is not correct for me to allow myself to be in a situation of this kind."

"How quaint."

"Sir Tam!" She was almost shrieking now, and furiously angry, not only with him but with herself. If she had used a tiny bit of intelligence she would have known this was coming and could have avoided it. A delicate hint that this was the wrong time. A suggestion of—what? Of a social disease, if necessary. Anything. But she was trapped, the waterbed before her, this gland case behind, already with his lips against her ear, whispering buzzingly so that her headache exploded again. Desperately she caught at a straw.

"We—we were speaking of Godfrey Menninger?"

"What?"

"Godfrey Menninger. The father of my good friend, Captain Marge Menninger. You spoke of him in the hotel."

He was silent for a moment, neither releasing her nor trying to pull her closer. "Do you know God Menninger well?"

"Only through his daughter. I was able to keep her from going to jail once."

His arm was definitely less tight. After a moment he patted her gently and stepped away. "Let's have a drink," he said, ringing for the stewardesses. The satyr's smile had been replaced by the diplomat's.

The conversation was back on its tracks again, for which Ana was intensely grateful. She even managed to return to the little cubicle with the armchairs and to persuade the stewardess to bring her a nice cup of strong *chai* instead of the whiskey Gulsmit suggested. He seemed greatly interested in the story of Margie Menninger's little episode, in every detail. Had they been fingerprinted? Was the people's magistrate a court of record, whatever that was? Had Ana spoken to anyone in the militia about the incident later on, and if so what had they said?

Such trivial things seemed to interest him, but Nan was content to go on dredging up memories for him all the way across the Atlantic, as long as it meant his keeping his hands to himself. When she was wrung dry he leaned back, nursing the new drink the stewardess had poured for him and squinting out at the blue-black and cloudless sky.

"Very interesting," he said at last. "That poor little girl. Of course, I've known her since she was tiny." It had not occurred to Ana that Margie Menninger had ever been tiny. She let it pass, and Sir Tam added, "And dear old God. Have you known him long?"

"Not in a personal sense," she said, careful not to add lying to the fault of being untruthful. "Of course he is of great importance in cultural matters. I too am deeply concerned about culture."

"Culture," repeated Sir Tam meditatively. He seemed about to produce a real smile but managed to retain the diplomatic one instead. "You are a dear, Nan," he said, and shook his wristwatch to make the red numerals blink on. "Ah, almost there," he said regretfully. "But of course you must allow me to escort you to your hotel."

The morning session of the UN was exhausting. There was no time for a real lunch because she had to post-edit the computer translations of what she had already translated once that morning before they could be printed. And the afternoon session was one long catfight.

The debate was on fishing rights for Antarctic krill. Because it was food, tempers ran high. And because sea lore is almost as old an area of human interest as eating, the translation was demanding. There were no places where she could coast, no technical words that were new-coined and common to almost all languages. Every language had developed its own words for ships, seamanship, and above all, eating, at the dawn of language itself. Only three of Nan's languages were in use—Bulgarian, English, and Russian. The Pakistanis were not involved in the debate, and there were plenty of others proficient in the Romance languages. So there were long periods when she could listen without having to speak. But there was no rest even in those periods; she needed to remember every word she could. The UN delegates had the awful habit of quoting each other at length—sometimes with approval, sometimes with a sneer, always with the risk of some tiny hairsplit that she had to get just right. Her headaches were immense.

That was, of course, the price you paid for having the two hemispheres of your brain surgically sliced apart. Not to mention the stitching back of parts of them that kept you from stumbling into things or falling down, or the DNA injections that left your neck swollen and your eyes bulging for weeks at a time and sometimes caused seizures indistinguishable from epilepsy. That had been a surprise. They hadn't told her about those things when she signed up to become a split-brain translator—not really. You never did know what pain was going to be until you had it.

What made the whole day an order of magnitude worse was that she was starved for sleep. Sir Tam had followed her to her very door and then planted a foot inside it. His hands had been all over her in the limousine all the way in from the airport. The only way she could think to get rid of him was to pretend such exhaustion that she could not stay awake another second, even though it was just after lunch, New York time. And then she found she had talked herself into it.

So she did go to sleep. And woke up before midnight with the chance for any more sleep gone. And what was there to do with the eleven hours before the morning session would begin?

A letter to Ahmed, of course. A few hours with English irregular verbs. Another hour or so listening to the tapes she had just made to check her accent. But then she was tired and fretful. What she needed most was a walk from her apartment past the university into the fresh morning air of the park, but that was ten thousand kilometers away in Sofia. In New York you did not go walking in the fresh morning air. And so she had turned up for duty in the translator's booth feeling as though a hard day's work was already behind her, and her head throbbing and pounding in two different rhythms, one in each temple. . . .

Her mind had wandered. She forced it back. It was Sir Tam asking for the floor now, and she had to put his words into Bulgarian.

His face was purple-red, and he was shouting. With one half of her brain Nan wondered at that while the other half was automatically processing his words. So much passion about such little fish! Not even fish. They were some sort of crustacean, weren't they? To Nan, "krill" was something that old-fashioned peasant grannies stirred into their stews to give them body. It came as a grayish-white powdery substance that you bought in jars labeled "fish protein concentrate." You knew that it was good for you, but you didn't like to think about what organs and oddities were ground up to make it. In food-rich Bulgaria, nobody grew excited about the stuff.

But Sir Tam was excited. The Fuel Bloc needed it desperately, he shouted. Had to have it! Was entitled to it, by all the laws of civilized humanity! The Fuel Bloc already possessed the fleets of long-range factory ships that could seine the cold Antarctic Ocean. He quoted *Pacem in Maris* and the British-Portuguese Treaty of A.D. 1242. The tiny bodies of the creatures that made up the krill, he declaimed, were absolutely essential to British agriculture, being the very best kind of fertilizer for their crops.

At which the Uruguayan delegate interrupted, snarling, "Agriculture! You are using this essential protein to feed to animals."

"Of course," Sir Tam replied stoutly. "We are not blessed with the advantages given your country, Señor Corrubias. We do not have immense plains on which our cattle can graze. In order to feed them properly, we must have imports—"

Someone in the American delegation laughed out loud, not a pleasant laugh, and the Uruguayan drummed on his desk derisively. "So it is cattle you feed, Sir Gulsmit? But we have it on the evidence of your own Ministry of Health that you give the krill to your cats and budgies! Do you then make minced kitten patties, perhaps? Or fresh chops of parrakeet?"

Sir Tam looked long-sufferingly at the president pro tem. "Sir, I must ask the courtesy of the floor."

The president was a spare Ghanaian who had not once glanced toward any speaker. He did not do so now. His eyes stayed on the letters he was signing one by one as his secretary put them before him. He said, "I would request of the delegate from Uruguay that he reserve his remarks until the delegate from the United Kingdom has concluded."

Sir Tam beamed graciously. "Thank you. In any case, I am almost finished. Of course, some part of our imports of krill does find its way into pet food, some part into protein additives for the justly famous British beef, some part into fertilizer to help us grow the vital foods that nature has otherwise denied us. Is that a matter for this body? I think not. What is of concern is the behavior of member states in their conduct of world affairs. We infringe no international treaty in continuing the long British tradition of the sea, in harvesting what is freely available to all in international waters, and of course in making suitable use of those pelagic areas which, by existing treaties freely arrived at by the member states, have long been reserved to us. But even this is not relevant to the motion before us today! That motion, I remind you, relates only to the proposal for a United Nations peacekeeping team to supervise the Antarctic fisheries. 'Peacekeeping,' my dear fellow delegates. A team to keep the peace. And therefore our position is clear. No such team is needed. The peace has been kept. There have been no incidents. There certainly will be none of our making. The United Nations has better things to do than to seek solutions for problems that do not exist."

And he sat down, managing to do so with a bow to the president pro tem, a sardonic grin for the Uruguayan, and yes, even a wink for Ana, up in the translator's booth! She shook her head in distress at this frivolous-minded person. But perhaps he was serious after all, for he was already writing something on a scrap of paper and beckoning a page, even as the Ghanaian finished signing his letters, slapped his portfolio shut, glanced at the clock, and managed not to catch the Uruguayan delegate's eye as he said, "I am informed that the address of the next delegate may occupy a substantial period of time. Since it is now four, I suggest we recess this debate until ten o'clock tomorrow morning."

A buzz rose up from the floor. Nan leaned back for a long moment, massaging her temples before she stood up and allowed herself to contemplate the next half hour: a quick meal, a bath, and then a lovely long sleep—

No. It was not to be. As she opened the door to the booth the page dashed up, out of breath, and handed her the note from Sir Tam. It said:

Absolutely essential you attend the party in the DVL, and that I have the pleasure of escorting you.

So there was no rest, no rest. She might have refused the invitation. But Sir Tam had taken the precaution of telling the head of the Bulgarian mission to the United Nations about it, and she was no sooner in her room than he was on the phone insisting she go.

She bathed quickly and dressed in what she guessed might be appropriate, then trotted back across the street from her hotel to the great quaint oblong building, so unlike its newer and fortresslike neighbors. Her head was pounding all the way. Diffidently she whispered her name to the guard at the Distinguished Visitors Lounge. He consulted a list, smiled frostily, and let her in.

What a tumult! How much smoke, and what odors of food and drinks! And there was Sir Tam, to be sure, tiny bouquet of flowers in one hand, the other hand on the shoulder of a plump, dark, grinning man whom Nan did not at once recognize but who was the very Uruguayan with whom Sir Tam had been exchanging insults an hour before.

"Nan! Ho, Nan! Over here!" He was beckoning her to him. She could not think of a reason for refusing, and knew before it happened that Gulsmit would be *touching* her again. And it happened just that way. The flowers turned out to be a bouquet of Parma violets, outrageously out of season and, of course, for her. Gulsmit insisted on pinning the corsage on her demure bodice himself, taking much more time over it than was necessary while the others in his little conversational group jovially pretended not to notice.

It angered Nan that the Scot should put himself on such terms of evident intimacy, especially in this hyperactive atmosphere, where people who had been trading threats with each other all day were now laughing and mingling and drinking together. Not only that. Every person in this little group was from a rival bloc. What would the head of her delegation say?

Sir Tam and the Saudi were Fuel. The Uruguayans were People. So were the two jolly Chinese women in their spike-heeled shoes and neo-Mao jackets of silk brocade and metal thread.

"You'll never guess, Nan," grinned Sir Tam after introducing her, "what our friends have up their sleeves for tomorrow. Tell her, Liao-tsen."

The older of the Chinese women laid her hand on Ana's arm, smiling. Clearly she had been drinking a great deal. Her consonants were fuzzy, but she said, comprehensibly enough, "The People's Republic of Bengal will put forward an emergency resolution. It is a very pretty resolution, Miss Dimitrova. All about 'the alleged multinational expedition of the Food-Exporting Powers' and their 'acts of violence against the natives of Son of Kung.' "

"Violence? What is this about violence?" demanded Nan, startled and suddenly fearful. If there was fighting on Kungson . . . if Ahmed found himself in the middle of a war . . .

"That's the funny part, dear girl," chuckled Sir Tam. "It seems your friend God's little junket has begun shooting down harmless balloonists. But not to worry. I don't think it's going to pass. It's not a party matter, is it, Señor Corrubias?"

The Uruguayan shrugged. "There has been no official consultation among the People's Republics, that is true."

"And unofficial?" Gulsmit probed.

Corrubias glanced at the elder Chinese woman, who nodded permission, and said, "I can tell you my personal opinion, and that is that the acts of violence we have heard described are not of much importance. Can one really get upset about rubber jack-o'-lanterns floating around in the sky?"

"There is also the matter of the underground race," said the Chinese woman. She took another sip of her drink, looking merrily mysterious over the top of it at Sir Tam, before going on comfortably, "But that too . . . well, a few burrows broken into, that's all. After all, how can we be sure that the creatures who inhabit them are indeed intelligent? We would not object to a Nebraska farmer, for example, opening a mole run as he plowed his corn paddies."

"One might also," said Ana boldly, surprising herself at the harshness of her voice, "speak of the crustacean race that has suffered some casualties." But Sir Tam stopped her by a gentle pressure on the shoulder. She did not protest. She had suddenly begun to fear that it was Ahmed's group that had caused those casualties, about which she knew so worryingly little.

"I would really enjoy watching you two fight it out," said Sir Tam, laughing to take the menace out of his words. But Nan wondered if he didn't really mean it. She also wondered why he was so carefully and publicly possessive of her, arm around her shoulder, hovering over her drink and refilling it from every passing tray. Surely all these foreign people would suppose they had been in bed together! She blushed at the thought. It would have been bad enough to be guilty of an immoral dalliance, like any common tart, and to have it known. But she was not even guilty! The name without the game—how awful! Why would Sir Tam go out of his way to create such an impression? Could it be that the lax morality of the Fuel people was such that he valued the appearance of sexual adventure as much as the relationship itself? Was he trying to show that he was still sexually potent? And what sort of people was she living among here?

"Please excuse me for a moment," she said, glancing about as though looking for a woman's w.c. But as soon as she was well away from Sir Tam, she circled around the white-paneled room to the buffet tables. At least she would bring up her blood sugar. Perhaps that would relieve the headaches and the exhaustion, and then she would think of a way to relieve the pressure from Sir Tam.

The table would have been lavish even in Sofia! But was it not the Tibetans who were giving this party? And why did they feel obliged to spread so wasteful a display of food? Caviar that certainly did not come from the Himalayas; delicate fruit ices that surely were unknown in their sparse, high valleys; pâtés in the original wooden boxes from France. And look what they had done! The centerpieces were carved replicas of the races of Kungson! A balloonist, half a meter thick, in butter! A crustacean carved from what looked like strawberry sherbet! A long, almost ratlike creature—was it a burrower?—made from foie gras! And there, standing next to her, was a distinguished-looking gray-haired man who was directing a pale-haired younger man to fill a plate from the display. A spoonful of the burrower, a few slices of some sort of meat, a croissant, a scoop from the balloonist to butter the roll. He caught her eye and smiled pleasantly without speaking.

It was all incredibly ostentatious. It quite took Ana's appetite away. She looked away from the food and saw Sir Tam across the room, eyes on her. Strangely, he nodded encouragement and pointed—to whom? To the graying, tall man next to her?

She looked more carefully. Had they ever met? No. But he had a face she seemed to know, from a photograph, she thought—but a photograph that had meant something to her.

She turned to speak to him, and the pale-haired man was suddenly between them, polite but at a state of readiness. For what? Did they think she was an assassin?

Then she remembered where she had seen the face. "You're Mr. Godfrey Menninger," she said.

His expression was inquiring. "Yes?"

"We've never met, but I've seen your picture in a newspaper. With your daughter. I'm Ana Dimitrova, and I met your daughter a few months ago in Sofia."

"Of course you did! The angel of rescue. It's all right, Teddy," he said to the younger man, who stepped back and began collecting silverware for Menninger's plate. "How nice to meet you at last, Ana. Margie's here somewhere. Not near the food, poor thing. She has her mother's metabolism. She can't even look at a layout like this without putting on a kilo. Let's go find her so you can say hello."

Captain Menninger was sipping her Perrier water and allowing a fifty-year-old Japanese attaché to think he was making headway against her defenses when she heard her father's voice behind her.

"Margie, dear, a surprise for you. You remember Ana Dimitrova?"

"No." Marge studied the woman carefully, not competitively but in the manner of someone trying to learn a terrain from a map. Then the card file in her head clicked over. "Yes," she corrected herself. "The Bulgarian woman. How nice to see you again."

It was not anything of the kind, and she intended the Bulgarian bint to understand that. On the other hand, Margie had no particular wish to make an enemy of her, either. There might be a time when her connection with that Pak she was screwing—Dulla? Yes. Ahmed Dulla, member of the first Peeps' expedition to Klong—could be a useful line to pursue. So she turned to the Japanese and said:

"Tetsu, I'd like you to meet Nan Dimitrova. She was such a help to me in Bulgaria. You know how foolish I am about making jokes—I just can't help this mouth of mine. It says things that get me into the most terrible trouble. And so, of course, I said something ridiculously awful. Political, you know. It could have had really sticky consequences. And along came Nan, total stranger, just a good person, and got me out of it. How is that nice young man you were with, Nan?"

"Ahmed is on Kungson," said Nan. She was unwilling to give offense, but she was not obliged to like this plump blond's nasty little put-down games.

"Is he! Why, that's a coincidence. You remember Dr. Dalehouse, of course? He's there too. Perhaps they'll meet." She saw that her father's aide had just signaled something to him and added, "Poppa, you're looking worried. Am I saying something awful again?"

Godfrey Menninger smiled. "What I'm worried about is that if I'm going to give you a lift to Boston, it's time we were on our way. You do remember you have a date at MIT tonight?"

"Oh, dear. I'd forgotten." Wholly untrue. Margie had not forgotten the time of her date, which was the following morning, and she had no doubt that her father had not either.

"Also," he went on, "you'll be sneezing and scratching if we stay here much longer. Or had you also forgotten that you are allergic to flowers?"

Margie had never in her life been allergic to anything, but she said, "You do take such good care of me, poppa. Nan, I'm sorry this was so short, but it's really nice seeing you again. And Tetsu, don't be a stranger next time you're in Houston. Stop by and say hello." The Japanese hissed and bowed. Of course, Margie reflected, she could be out of town if he ever did happen to show up in Houston. Not that it mattered. She had already accomplished her objective. Past a certain age, even going to bed with a man did not give you quite as firm a grip on his emotions as communicating the impression that you certainly would like to if you ever got the chance.

In her father's car, with the bodyguard-aide sitting in front, she said, "Now what was that all about, poppa?"

"Maybe your little Bulgarian friend isn't quite as much of a country girl as she seems. Teddy swept her as a matter of routine. There was a microphone in her corsage."

"Her? Bugged? That's a crock!"

"That's a fact," he corrected. "Maybe her delegation put it on her, who knows? That place was full of sharks. It could have been any one of them. And speaking of sharks—"

"You want to know what I picked up," she said, nodding, and told him what the Japanese had said about the Bengali resolution.

He leaned back in the seat. "Just the usual UN Mischief

Night, I'd say. You turn over my garbage can, I throw a dead cat on your roof. Are they going to press it?"

"He didn't say, poppa. He didn't seem to take it very seriously."

Her father rubbed the spot below his navel thoughtfully. "Of course, with the Peeps you never know. Heir-of-Mao has an investment in Klong. The Bengalis wouldn't be starting anything they didn't clear with the Forbidden City."

Margie's hair prickled erect at the back of her neck. "Are you saying I should worry? I don't want my mission withdrawn!"

"Oh, no. No chance of that, honey. Relax, will you? You're too much like your old lady. She never did learn to swing with the action. When the PLO kidnapped you I thought she'd have a nervous breakdown."

"She was scared shitless, poppa. And you never turned a hair." Not even, she thought, when your own four-year-old daughter was bawling into the jetliner's radio.

"But I knew you were going to be all right, honey. I really did."

"Well, I'm not bringing that up again, ol' buddy." Margie folded her hands in her lap and stared out the window. Between the UN complex and the airport there was no building, no street, that Margie had not seen a dozen times before. She was not really seeing them now. But they helped spur and clarify her thoughts, the long tandem buses hobbling down the slow lanes, the apartment dwellers walking their dogs, the school kids, stores, police on their tricycles, sidewalk vendors with their handmade jewelry and pocket computers. Thomas Jefferson, as he returned to Monticello, might have looked out of his stagecoach in just the same detached but proprietary way at the slaves weeding his crops.

She said slowly, "Listen, poppa. I want to get our mission reinforced. Now."

"What's the hurry?"

"I don't know, but there's a hurry. I want it done before the

Peeps and the Greasies cut us off at the roots or get enough
of their own people up there to own Kungson. I want us there
first and biggest, because I want it all."

"Shit, honey. Didn't they teach you about priorities at the
Point? There's the krill business and the Mid-Atlantic Ridge
and the Greasies threatening to raise their prices again—do
you have any idea how tough all this is? I've only got one
stack, and there's only room for one thing at the top of it."

"No, poppa, I don't want to be told how hard it is. Don't
you understand this is a whole planet?"

"Of course I do, but—"

"No. No buts. I guess you don't really understand what it
means to have a whole planet to play with. For us, poppa, all
for *us*. To start from scratch with, to develop in a systematic
manner. Find all the fossil fuels, develop them in a rational
way. Locate the cities where they don't destroy arable land.
Plant crops where they won't damage the soil. Develop industry where it's most convenient. Plan the population. Let it
grow as it is needed, but not to where you have a surplus:
good, strong, self-reliant people. American people, poppa.
Maybe the place stinks now, but give it a hundred years and
you'd rather be there than here, I promise. *And I want it.*"

Godfrey Menninger sighed, looking in love and some awe
at the oldest and most troublesome of his children. "You're
worse than your mother ever was," he said ruefully. "Well, I
hear what you say. The Poles owe us one. I'll see what I can
do."

TechTowTwo sprawled over the bank of the Charles River,
more than twice the cubage of all the old brick buildings put
together. There were no classrooms in Technology Tower
Two. There was no administration, either. It was all for research, from the computer storage in the subbasements to the
solar-radiation experiments that decorated the roof with sau-
cers and bow ties.

The Massachusetts Institute of Technology had a long tradition of involvement with space exploration, going back even before there was any—or any that did not take place on a printed page. As early as the 1950s there had been a design class whose entire curriculum revolved around the creation of products for export to the inhabitants of the third planet of the star Arcturus. The fact that there was no known planet of Arcturus, let alone inhabitants of it, did not disturb either teacher or students. Techpersons were used to unhinging their imaginations on demand. In the Cambridge community that centered around MIT, Harvard, the Garden Street observatories, and all the wonderlands of Route 128 there had been designers of interstellar spacecraft before the first Sputnik went into orbit, anatomists of extraterrestrials when there was no proof of life anywhere off the surface of Earth, and specialists in interplanetary communications before anyone was on the other end of the line. Margie Menninger had taken six months of graduate studies there, dashing from Tech to Harvard. She had been careful to keep her contacts bright.

The woman Margie wanted to see was a former president of the MISFITS and thus would have been a power in the Tech world even if she had not also held the title of assistant dean of the college. She had arranged a breakfast meeting at Margie's request and had turned out five department heads on order.

The dean introduced them around the table and said, "Make it good now, Margie. Department heads aren't crazy about getting up so early in the morning."

Margie sampled her scrambled eggs. "For this kind of food, I don't blame them," she said, putting down her fork. "Let me get right to it. I have about ten minutes' worth of holos of the autochthons of Son of Kung, alias Klong. No sound. Just visible." She leaned back to the sideboard and snapped a switch, and the first of the holographic pictures condensed out of a pinkish glow. "You've probably seen most of this stuff anyway," she said. "That's a Krinpit. They are one of the three intelligent, or anyway possibly intelligent, races on

Klong, and the only one of the lot that is urban. In a moment you'll see some of their buildings. They're open at the top. Evidently the Krinpit don't worry much about weather. Why they have buildings at all is anyone's guess, but they do. They would seem much the easiest of the three races to conduct trade with, but unfortunately the Peeps have a head start with them. No doubt we'll catch up."

The head of the design staff was a lean young black woman who had limited her breakfast to orange juice and black coffee and was already through with it. "Catch up at what, Captain Menninger?" she asked.

Margie took her measure and refused combat. "For openers, Dr. Ravenel, I'd like to see your people create some trade goods. For all three races. They're all going to be our customers one of these days."

The economist took his eyes off the holo of a Krinpit coracle to challenge Margie. " 'Customers' implies two-way trade. What do you think these, ah, Klongans are going to have to sell us that's worth the trouble of shipping it all those light-years?"

Margie grinned. "I thought you'd never ask." She pulled an attaché case off the floor and opened it on the table in front of her, pushing the plate of eggs out of the way. "So far," she said, "we don't exactly have any *manufactured* objects. But take a look at this." She passed around several ten-centimeter squares of a filmy, resilient substance. "That's the stuff the balloonists' hydrogen sacs are made out of. It's really pretty special stuff—I mean, it holds gaseous H_2 with less than one percent leakage in a twenty-four-hour period. We could supply quite a lot of that if there was a specialty market for it."

"Don't you have to kill a balloonist to get it?"

"Good question." Margie nodded to the economist with a lying smile. "Actually, no. That is, there are other, nonsentient races with the same body structure, although this one is, I believe, from one of the sentients. How about a market? If I remember correctly, the Germans had to use the second stomach of the ox when they were building the *Hindenburg*."

"I see," said the economist gravely. "All we need to do is contact a few Zeppelin manufacturers." There was a general titter.

"I'm sure," said Margie steadily, "that you will have some better idea than that. Oh, and I ought to mention one thing. I brought my checkbook. There's a National Science Foundation grant for research and development that's waiting for someone to apply for it." And for that gift too, I thank you, poppa, she thought.

The economist had not become the head of a major department of the faculty without learning when to retreat. "I didn't mean to brush you off, Captain Menninger. This is actually a pretty exciting challenge. What else have you got for us?"

"Well, we have a number of samples that haven't been studied very carefully. Frankly, they aren't really supposed to be here. Camp Detrick doesn't know they're gone yet."

The group stirred. The dean said quickly, "Margie, I think we all get the same picture when you mention Camp Detrick. Is there anything connected with biological warfare in this?"

"Certainly not! No, believe me, that doesn't come into it at all. I sometimes go out of channels, I admit, but what do you guess they'd do to me if I broke security on something like that?"

"Then why Camp Detrick?"

"Because these are alien organisms," Margie explained. "Except for the sample of balloonist tissue, you'll notice that every item I've got here is in a double-wrapped, heat-sealed container. The outside has been acid-washed and UV-sterilized. No, wait—" she added, grinning. Everybody at the table had begun looking at their fingertips, and there was a perceptible movement away from the samples of tissue on the table. "Those balloonist samples are okay. The rest, maybe not so okay. They've been pretty carefully gone over. There don't seem to be any pathogens or allergens. But naturally you'll want to use care in handling them."

"Thanks a lot, captain," said the designer stiffly. "How can you be so sure about the tissue?"

"I ate some three days ago," she said. She had their full attention now and swept on. "I should point out that the grant naturally includes whatever you need to insure safe handling. Now, this group contains plant samples. They're photosynthetic, and their principal response is in the infrared range. Interesting for you agronomists? Right. And these over here are supposed to be art objects. They come from the Krinpit, the ones that look like squashed cockroaches. The things are supposed to 'sing.' That is, if you're a Krinpit and you rub them on your shell, they make some interesting sounds. If you don't have a chitinous shell, you can use a credit card."

The woman from design picked up one of them gingerly, peering at it through the transparent plastic. "You said you wanted us to develop some kind of trading goods?"

"I sure do." The last thing Margie pulled out of her dispatch case was a red-covered mimeographed document. The words MOST SECRET were dazzle-printed on the jacket. "As you can see, this is classified, but that's just military hang-ups. It will be turned over to the UN in about ten days anyway, or most of it will. It's the most comprehensive report we've been able to prepare on the three principal races of Klong."

All six of the faculty members at the table reached for it at once, but the design woman was fastest. "Um," she said, flipping through it. "I've got a graduate student who would eat this up. Can I show it to him?"

"Better than that. Let's leave this copy and the samples with our friends, and let's you and I go talk to him."

Fifteen minutes later Margie had succeeded in getting rid of the department head, and she and a slim, excitable young man named Walter Pinson were head to head. "Think you can handle it?" asked Margie.

"Yes! I mean, well, it's a big job—"

Margie put her hand on his arm. "I'm sure you can. I'd

really appreciate it if you'd tell me how you plan to go about it, though."

Pinson thought for a moment. "Well, the first thing is to figure out what their needs are," he offered.

"That's fascinating! It must be pretty difficult. I would hardly know where to start. Offhand, I'd say their biggest need, all of them, is just staying alive. As you'll see, everything on the planet spends a lot of its time trying to eat everything else, including the other intelligent races."

"Cannibalism?"

"Well, I don't think you can call it that. They're different species. And there are a lot of other species that are trying to eat the intelligent ones."

"Predators," said Pinson, nodding. "Well, there's a starting point right there. Let's see. For the predators like the balloon-ists, for instance, anything that would set them on fire would help protect the sentients. Of course," he added, frowning, "we'd have to make sure that these were used only to defend the sentients against lower forms of life."

"Of course!" said Margie, shocked. "We wouldn't want to give them weapons to start a war with!" She glanced at her watch. "I've got an idea, Walter. I didn't have much of a breakfast, and it's getting on toward lunch. Why don't you and I get something to eat? There's a place I used to know when I was a graduate student. In a pretty frowsty old motel, but the food was good—if you have the time, I mean?"

"Oh, I have the time," said Pinson, looking at her apprecia-tively.

"It's up past Harvard Square, but we ought to be able to get a cab. And please let me—I have an expense account, and it's all your tax money anyway." As they walked toward the eleva-tor, a mob of undergraduates flocked toward a lecture hall. Looking toward them, Margie asked, "Do you by any chance know a student named Lloyd Wensley? I think he's a fresh-man."

"No, I don't think so. Friend of yours?"

"Not really—or anyway, not since he was a little kid. I used to know his family. Now, about these, ah, implements for self-protection—"

Several quite pleasant hours later, Margie got into a cab outside the old motel. If the food had not been really as good as she remembered it, the rooms still came up to standard. As they approached Harvard Square she had an impulse. "Go down Mass Ave," she ordered the driver. "I want to make a little detour." After a few blocks she directed him into a side street, and looked about.

She recognized the neighborhood. There was the super-market. There was Giordan's Spa, and there, over the barber-shop, only now it was over a hardware store, was the three-room corner apartment where she had lived with Lloyd and Lloyd Junior through the ten months that measured both her graduate year and her marriage. It was the closest Marge had ever come to motherhood, fill-in to a six-year-old for the real mother who had died when he was three. It was the closest she had ever come to wifehood, too, and closer than she would ever come again. Old Lloyd! Thirty years old when she was nineteen, and so fucking *courtly* in the Officers' Club that you'd never guess what he was like in bed. Not even if you'd tried him out a time or two, as Margie had been careful to do. Just looking up at the window of their bedroom made Marge's neck ache with the memory of being head-jammed into a corner of the bed, half choked with pillows, so Lloyd could pump himself dry as quickly as convenient. As often as convenient. When he thought convenient. You didn't ask a cuspidor for permission to spit in it, or a wife for sex. The cuspidor couldn't struggle, not if you had it jammed into position just right, and it wouldn't cry out. Neither would the wife, espe-cially with the six-year-old stepson only marginally asleep just outside the door.

She ordered the driver on.

It would have been nice to see Lloyd Junior, all grown up.

But better not. Better the way it was. She hadn't seen either of the Lloyds since the annulment, and no use pressing your luck. It had been a pretty frightening, dehumanizing experience for a young girl; how lucky she was, thought Margie, that it hadn't scarred her forever!

When she got back to her hotel there was a taped message from her father: "To hear is to obey. Catch a news broadcast."

She turned on the bedside TV while she packed, hunting for an all-news station. She was rewarded with five minutes about the latest Boston political corruption scandals, and then an in-depth interview with the Red Sox's new designated hitter. But at last there was a recap of the top international story of the day.

"In a surprise move at the United Nations this morning, the top Polish delegate, Wladislas Prczensky, announced that his government has accepted the challenge presented by the Bengali resolution. The Food powers have agreed to send out an investigatory commission with broad powers to investigate the alleged cases of brutal treatment of native races on the planet whimsically called 'Klong' or 'Son of Kung.' There will be no representatives of major powers such as the United States or the Soviet Union on the commission, which will be made up of UN peacekeeping officers from Poland itself, Brazil, Canada, Argentina, and Bulgaria."

·EIGHT·

DANNY DALEHOUSE reached out to grab the theodolite as it tipped in the soft ground. Morrissey grinned and apologized. "Must've lost my balance."

"Or else you're stoned again," said Dalehouse. He was angry—not just at Morrissey. In the candor of his heart he knew that most of his anger was at the fact that Kappelyushnikov was flying and he was not. "Anyway," he went on, "you've knocked this run in the head. Next time why don't you just go sleep it off?"

They had all been freaked out by the stuff the balloonists had sprayed on them, and from time to time, for days afterward, all of them had recurring phases of lust and euphoria. Not only were Morrissey's more intense, but Dalehouse was pretty sure the biochemist was still exposing himself. He had discovered that something in the semen or sperm of the male balloonists was highly hallucinogenic—better than that, was the long-sought-after true aphrodisiac fabled in song and story. It wasn't Morrissey's fault that his researches put him

110

clear out of it from time to time. But he shouldn't have insisted on helping with the theodolite readings.

Far overhead Kappelyushnikov's cluster of bright yellow balloons gyrated as the pilot experimented with controlling his altitude to take advantage of the winds at various levels. When he was finished tracking them they would have basic information that could allow them to cruise the skies. Then Dalehouse's turn would come. But he was tired of waiting.

"Cappy," he said into the radio, "we've lost the readings. Might as well come on down."

Harriet was walking toward them as Kappelyushnikov's answer came through. It was in Russian; Harriet heard, and flinched irritably. That was in character. She had been a perfect bitch about the whole thing, Dalehouse thought. When they returned to normal after that first incredible trip, she had flamed at him, "Animal! Don't you know you could have got me pregnant?" It had never occurred to him to ask. Nor had it occurred to her, at the time. It was no use reminding her that she had been as eager as he. She had retreated into her hard defiant-spinster shell. And ever since, she had been ten times as upright as before and fifty times as nasty to anyone who made sexual remarks in her presence or even, as with Kappelyushnikov just now, used some perfectly justifiable bad language.

"I've got some new tapes for you," Harriet sniffed.

"Any progress?"

"Certainly there's progress, Dalehouse. There's a definite grammar. I'll brief the whole camp on it after the next meal." She glanced up at Cappy, having a last fling with his balloon as half a dozen of the Klongan gasbags soared around him, and retreated.

A definite grammar.

Well, there was no use trying to hurry Harriet. "Preliminary Studies toward a First Contact with Subtechnological Sentients" seemed very far away! Dalehouse counted up the score. It was not impressive. They had made no contact at all with the crablike things called Krinpit or with the burrowers. The gasbags had been hanging around quite a lot since the day they had showered the expedition with their milt. But they did not come close enough for the kind of contact Danny Dalehouse wanted. They bounced and swung hundreds of meters in the air most of the time, descending lower only when most of the camp was away or asleep. No doubt they had been trained to avoid ground-limited creatures through eons of predation. But it made it hard for Danny.

At least, with the gasbags in sight, rifle microphones had been able to capture quite a lot of their strident, singing dialogue—if dialogue was what it was. Harriet said she detected structure. Harriet said it was not birdsongs or cries of alarm. Harriet said she would teach him to speak to them. But what Harriet said was not always to be believed, Danny Dalehouse thought. The other thing he thought was that they needed a different translator. The split-brain operation facilitated language learning, but it had several drawbacks. It sometimes produced bad physical effects, including long-lasting pain. Once in awhile it produced personality changes. And it didn't always work. A person who had no gift for languages to begin with came out of surgery still lacking the gift. In Harriet's case, Danny would have guessed all three were true.

They had transmitted all the tapes to Earth anyway. Sooner or later the big semantic computers at Johns Hopkins and Texas A&M would be checking in, and Harriet's skills, or lack of them, would stop mattering so much.

What Danny needed, or at least what Danny wanted, so badly he could taste it, was to be up there in the sky with one of the gasbags, one on one, learning a language in the good old-fashioned way. Anything else was a compromise. They'd tried everything within their resources. Free-floating instrumented balloons with sensors programmed to respond to the signatures of life; wolftraps for the Krinpit; buried microphones for the burrowers; the rifle mikes and the zoom-lens cameras for the gasbags. They had kilometers of tape, with pictures and sounds of all manner of jumping, crawling, wriggling things, and in all the endless hours hardly as much as ten minutes' worth that was any use to Danny Dalehouse.

Still, something had been accomplished. Enough for him to have composed a couple of reports to go back to Earth. Enough even for his jealous colleagues at MSU and the Double-A-L to pore over eagerly, even if not enough to satisfy Danny. It was still learning, even if much of it was negative.

The first thing to perish was the pretty fable of three independent intelligent races living in some sort of beneficent cooperation and harmony. There was no cooperation. At least, they had seen no signs of that, and many to the contrary. The burrowers seemed never to interact with the others at all. The gasbags and the Krinpit did, but not in any cooperative or harmonious way. The balloonists never touched ground, as far as Danny had seen, or at least not on purpose. There were at least a dozen species that enjoyed eating balloonists when they could catch them—sleek brown creatures that looked a little like stub-winged bats, froglike leapers, arthropods smaller than the Krinpit—not least of them, the Krinpit themselves. If a gasbag ever drifted low enough for one of them to reach it, it was dead. So the entire lives of the balloonists, from spawn to fodder, were spent in the air, and their ultimate burial was always in the digestive tract of some ground-bound race—so tawdry a fate for so pretty a species!

Kappelyushnikov was coming in low and fast, tossed by the low-level winds. He pulled the rip cord on his balloon at five meters and dropped like a stone, wriggling out of the harness to fall free. He tumbled over and over as he landed, then got up, rubbing himself, and ran to catch the deflated balloon cluster as it scudded before the breeze.

Danny winced, contemplating his own first flight. The last

little bit of ballooning was going to be the hardest. He turned to help Cappy pick up the fabric, and a rifleshot next to his head made him duck and swear.

He spun around, furious. "What the hell are you up to, Morrissey?"

The biologist put the rifle at shoulder-arms and saluted the tumbling form of one of the hovering gasbags. "Just harvesting another specimen, Danny," he said cheerfully. He had judged height and wind drift with precision, and the collapsed bag was dropping almost at their feet. "Ah, shit," he said in disgust. "Another female."

"Really?" said Danny, staring at what looked like an immense erection. "Are you sure?"

"Fooled me too," Morrissey grinned. "No, the ones with the schlongs aren't the males. They aren't schlongs. I mean, they aren't penises. These folks don't make love like you and I, Danny. The females sort of squirt their eggs out to float around in the air, and then the boys come out and whack off onto them."

"When did you find all that out?" Dalehouse was annoyed; the rule of the expedition was that each of them shared discoveries as soon as made.

"When you were bugged at me for being stoned out of my mind," Morrissey said. "I think it has to do with the way they generate their hydrogen. Solar flares seem to be involved. So when they saw our lights they thought it was a flare—and that's when they spawned. Only we happened to be underneath, and so we got sprayed with, uh, with—"

"I know what we got sprayed with," Dalehouse said.

"Yeah! You know, Danny, when I took up this career they made dissecting specimens sound pretty tacky—but every time I go near one of the males' sex glands I get high. I'm beginning to like this line of work."

"Do you have to kill them all off to do it, though? You'll chase the flock away. Then how am I going to make contact?"

Morrissey grinned. He didn't answer. He just pointed aloft.

Dalehouse, in justice, had to concede the unspoken point. Whatever emotions the gasbags had, fear did not seem to be among them. Morrissey had shot down nearly a dozen of them, but ever since the first contact the swarm had almost always stayed within sight. Perhaps it was the lights that attracted them. In the permanent Klongan twilight, there was no such thing as "day." The camp had opted to create one, marked by turning on the whole bank of floodlights at an arbitrary "dawn" and turning them off again twelve clock hours later. One light always stayed on—to keep off predators, they told themselves, but in truth it was to keep out the primordially threatening dark.

Morrissey picked up the balloonist. It was still alive, its wrinkled features moving soundlessly. Once down, they never uttered a sound—because, Morrissey said, the hydrogen that gave them voice was lost when their bags were punctured. But they kept on *trying*. The first one they had shot down had lived for more than forty hours. It had crept all around the camp, dragging its gray and wrinkled bag, and it had seemed in pain all of that time. Dalehouse had been glad when it died at last, was glad now when Morrissey plunged the new one into a killer bag for return to Earth.

Kappelyushnikov limped up to them, rubbing his buttocks. "Is always a martyr, first pioneer of flight," he grumbled. "So, Danny Dalehouse. You want go up now?"

An electric shock hit Danny. "You mean *now*?"

"Sure, why not? Wind isn't bad. I go with, soon as two balloons fill."

It took longer than Dalehouse would have thought possible for the little pump to fill two batches of balloons big enough for human passengers—especially since the pump was a hastily rigged nonsparking compressor that leaked as much gas as it squeezed into the bags. Dalehouse tried to eat, tried to nap, tried to interest himself in other projects, and kept coming back to gaze at the tethered clusters of bags, quietly swelling with hydrogen, constrained by the cord netting that surrounded them.

The weather had taken a turn for the worse. Clouds covered the sky from horizon to horizon, but Kappelyushnikov was stubbornly optimistic. "Clouds will blow away. Is positive skies will be clear." When the first pinkening of sky began to show, he said decisively, "Is okay now. Strap in, Danny."

Mistrustfully, Dalehouse buckled himself into the harness. He was a taller but lighter man than the Russian, and Kappelyushnikov grumbled to himself as he valved off surplus hydrogen. "Otherwise," he explained, "you go back to state of Michigan, East Lansing, *shwoosh!* But next time, not so much wasting gas."

The harness had a quick-release latch at the shoulders, and Dalehouse touched it experimentally.

"No, no!" screamed Kappelyushnikov. "You want to pull when you are up two hundred meters, fine, pull! Is your neck. But don't waste gas for nothing." He guided Danny's hands to the two crucial cords. "Is not clamjet, you understand? Is free balloon. Clamjet uses lift to save fuel. Here is no fuel, only lift. Here you go where wind goes. You don't like direction, you find different wind. Spill water ballast, you go up. Spill *wasserstoff*, you go down."

Dalehouse wriggled in the harness. It was not going to be very much like sailplaning over the eastern shore of Lake Michigan, where there was always a west wind to bounce off the bluffs and keep a glider aloft for hours. But if the Russian could do it, he could do it. I hope, he added to himself, and said, "All right, I think I have the hang of it."

"So let's go," cried the Russian, grinning as he slipped into his own harness. He bent and picked up a fair-sized rock, gesturing to Danny to do the same. The other members of the expedition were standing back, but one of them handed Danny a rock, and at Kappelyushnikov's orders they untethered the balloons.

Kappelyushnikov danced over toward Danny like a diver stilting across a sea bottom. He came as close as he could under the bulk of their balloons, peering into his face. "You are all right?" Danny nodded. "So drop the rock and we go!" Kappelyushnikov cried. And he cast his own rock away and began to float diagonally upward.

Dalehouse took a deep breath and followed his example, watching the Russian move upward.

Nothing seemed to happen. Danny did not feel any acceleration, only that his feet seemed to have gone abruptly numb and there was no sensation of pressure on their bottoms. Because his eyes were on Kappelyushnikov he neglected to look down until he was fifty meters in the air.

They were drifting south, along the coastline. Far above them and inland, over the purple hills that marked the edge of the fern forest, the extended swarm of balloonists was grazing on whatever tiny organisms they could find floating in the sky. Below and behind was the dwindling campsite. Danny was already higher than the nose of their return rocket, the tallest object in camp. Off to his left was the sea itself, and a couple of islands in the muddy waters, covered with many-trunked trees.

He wrenched his attention away from sight-seeing; Kappelyushnikov was shouting at him. "What?" Dalehouse bellowed. The gap had widened; Cappy was now forty meters above him and moving inland, evidently in a different air layer.

"*Drop . . . little . . . water!*" shouted the Russian.

Dalehouse nodded and reached tentatively for the valve cord. He pulled at it with a light touch.

Nothing happened.

He pulled again, harder. Half a liter of ballast sprayed out of the tank, drenching him. Danny had not realized that the passenger was directly under the ballast tank, and gasping, he vowed to change that element of design before he went up again.

But he was flying!

Not easily. Not with grace. Not even with the clumsy control that Kappelyushnikov had taught himself. He spent the first hour chasing Cappy across the sky. It was like one of the fun-house games where you and your girl are on different rotating circles of a ride, when neither of you can take a step except to change from one spinning disk to another. Though Kappelyushnikov did all he could to make capture easy, he never caught the Russian—not that first time.

But—flying! It was exactly the dream he had always had, the dream everyone has had. The total conquest of the air. No jets. No wings. No engines. Just gently swimming through the atmospheric ocean, with no more effort than floating in a saltwater bay.

He reveled in it, and as time went on—not in the first flight or the tenth, but the supply of hydrogen was limitless, if slow in coming, and he made as many flights as he could—he began to acquire some skill.

And the problem of reaching the gasbags turned out to be no problem at all.

He didn't have to seek them out. They were far more skilled at flying than he, and they came to him, bobbing around like great jack-o'-lanterns with hideous ticklike faces, peering inquisitively into his own face, and singing, singing. Oh! how they sang.

For the next week, or what passed on Klong for a week, Dalehouse spent every minute he could in the air. The life of the camp went on almost without him. Even Kappelyushnikov was more earthbound than he. There was nothing to hold Dalehouse there, and he found himself almost a stranger when he landed, slept, relieved bladder and bowels, ate, filled his balloons, and soared again. Harriet snapped at him for demanding more than she could handle in translation. The camp commander complained bitterly at the waste of power in generating hydrogen. Jim Morrissey pleaded for time and help in collecting and studying the other species. Even Cappy was surly about the wear and tear on his balloons. Danny didn't care. In the skies of Klong he was alive. He progressed from feckless interloper to skilled aeronaut; from stranger to, almost, one of the great drifting swarm. He began to be able to exchange at least rudimentary ideas with some of the gas-bags, especially the biggest of them—two meters across, with a pattern that looked almost like a tartan. Danny named him "Bonnie Prince Charlie," lacking any clue as to what the gas-bag called itself. *Him*self. Danny began to think of him as almost a friend. If it had not been for his physical needs, and one other thing, Dalehouse would hardly have bothered re-turning to the camp at all.

The one other thing was Harriet.

He could not do without her help in translation. It wasn't enough. He was convinced a lot of it was wrong. But it was all he had in the endeavor to communicate with these beauti-ful and monstrous creatures of the air. He raged to the rest of the encampment and insisted on his complaints being relayed to Earth; he insulted her almost to the point of tears —from eyes that he would have sworn had never felt them before. It was not enough to suit him . . . but voyage by voyage, hour by hour, some sort of communication began to build up.

You never knew what part of your learning was going to be useful. Those long sessions of Chomsky and transactional grammar, the critiques of Lorenz and Dart, the semesters on territoriality and mating rites—none of them seemed very helpful in the skies of Klong. But he blessed every hour of sailplaning and every evening with his local barbershop quar-tet. The language of the gasbags was music. Not even Manda-rin made such demands on pitch and tonality as did their songs. Even before he knew any words, he found himself chiming in on their chorus, and they responded to it with, if not exactly welcome, at least curiosity. The big plaid one even learned to sing Danny Dalehouse's name—as well as he could with a sound-producing mechanism that was deficient in such basic phonemes as the fricative.

Danny learned that some of their songs were not unlike terrestrial birdcalls; there was one for food, and several for danger. There seemed to be three separate warning sounds, one for danger from the ground, and two for dangers, but evidently different kinds of dangers, from the air. One of the terms sounded almost Hawaiian, with its liquids and glottal stops; that seemed to belong to a kind of feral gasbag, a shark of the air that appeared to be their most dangerous natural enemy.

The other—Dalehouse could not be sure, and Harriet was not much help, but it appeared to relate to danger from *above* the air; and not just danger, but that kind of special macho risk-taking danger that involved mortal peril, even death, but was infinitely attractive for reasons he could not perceive. He puzzled over that for hours, making Harriet's life a living hell. On that point, no solution. But the tapes went back to Earth, and the computer matches began to come back, and Harriet was able to construct sentences for him to say. He sang, "I am friend," and, heart-stoppingly, the great crosshatched gasbag he called Charlie responded with a whole song.

"You are, you are, you are friend!" And the whole chorus joined in.

The fickle Klongan weather cooperated for eight calendar days, and then the winds began to rise and the clouds rolled in.

When the winds blew, even the gasbag swarm had trouble keeping station with each other, and Danny Dalehouse was blown all over the sky. He tried to keep the camp in range; and because he did, so did the whole swarm. But in the effort they were widely separated. When he decided to give up at last, he called good-bye and heard in response the song that seemed to mean "sky danger." Dalehouse repeated it; it seemed appropriate enough, considering the weather. But then he became conscious of a deep fluttering sound behind the whine of the winds—the sound of a helicopter.

Dalehouse abandoned the flock, climbed high enough to find a return wind, then jockeyed himself expertly down through the cross-breezes toward the camp. There it was, dropping through the frayed bottom of a cloud: the Greasy copter, with a Union Jack on its tail strut. So profligate of energy! Not only did they ship that vast mass through tachyon transit at incredible cost, but they had also shipped enough fuel to allow the pilot to take joyrides. And what was it carrying slung between its skids? Some other kind of machine! Typical Greasy oil-hoggery!

Danny swore disgustedly at the wastefulness of the Greasies. With a fraction of the kilocalories they poured out in simple inefficiency and carelessness he could have had a decent computer, Kappelyushnikov could long since have had his glider, Morrissey could have had an outboard motor for his boat and thus a nearly complete selection of marine samples by now. There was something wrong in a world that let a handful of nations burn off energy so recklessly simply because they happened to be sitting on its sources. Sure, when it was gone, they would be as threadbare as the Peruvians or the Paks, but there was no comfort in that. Their downfall would be the world's downfall. . . .

Or at least *that* world's downfall. Maybe something could be worked out for *this* one. Planning. Thought. Preparation. Control of growth so that scarce resources would not be pissed away irrevocably on foolishness. A fair division of Klong's treasures so that no nation and no individual could profit by starving others. An attempt to insure equity to all—

Dalehouse's train of thought snapped as he realized that he had been daydreaming. The winds had carried him farther than he intended, almost out over the sea. He vented hydrogen frantically and came down almost in the water, falling fast. He picked himself up and watched the ripped cases of the balloons floating out of reach in the water. Cappy would be furious.

At least he wouldn't have to carry them on what looked like a long walk back up the shore to the camp, he thought. It was some consolation, but it didn't last long. Before he was halfway back it began to rain.

And it rained. *And* it rained. It was no such ferocious, windslamming storm as had hit them soon after the landing, but it lasted most tediously and maddeningly long, far past the point where it was an incident, or an annoyance, to the point, and past the point, where it seemed they were all sentenced to fat, oily drops turning the ground into mud and the camp into a steam bath for all the miserable rest of their lives. There was no chance of ballooning. There were no native balloonists in sight to follow anyway. Kappelyushnikov grumpily seamed and filled new balloons in the hope of better times to come. Harriet Santori tongue-lashed everyone who came near her. Morrissey packed samples in his tent and pored over mysterious pictures and charts, coming out only to stare furiously at the rain and shake his head. Danny composed long tactran messages to SERDCOM and the Double-A-L, demanding gifts for his gasbag friends. Krivitin and Sparky Cerbo concocted some kind of witches' brew from the native berries and got terribly drunk together, and then even more terribly sick as their bodies strove to defend themselves against the alien Klongan protein traces in the popskull. They very nearly died. They surely would have, exploded Alex Woodring, shaking with anger, if they had done any such moron's trick earlier; the first total vulnerability had dwindled to reactions that no longer brought death—only protracted misery. Danny inherited the job of tending them and, at Harriet's angry insistence, of packaging samples of their various untidy emissions for Jim Morrissey to analyze.

Morrissey was crouched over his pictures and diagrams when Danny came in, and when his duty was explained to him, he flatly refused it. "Cripes, Danny, I've got no equipment for that kind of thing. Throw those samples in the crapper. I don't want them."

"Harriet says we must know how serious the poisoning is."

"We already know that, man. They got real sick. But they didn't die."

"Harriet says you can at least analyze them."

"For what? I wouldn't know what to look for."

"Harriet says—"

"Oh, screw Harriet. 'Scuse me, Danny; I didn't mean to remind you of your, uh, indiscretions. Anyway, I've got something better for us to do now that the rain's stopping."

"It hasn't stopped, Jim."

"It's slowing down. When it does stop, Boyne's going to be coming around to collect the backhoe I borrowed from him. I want to use it first."

"For what?"

"For digging up some of our light-fingered friends." He pointed straight down at the floor of the tent. "The ones that swiped Harriet's radio."

"We already tried that."

"Yes, we did. We found out that the important thing is speed. They'll close up the tunnels faster than you'd believe, so we've got to get in, get moving, and get to where they are before they have a chance to react. We'll never have a clear field to pick them up otherwise—unless," he added offhandedly, "we flooded the tunnels with cyanide first. Then we could take our time."

"Is that all you think of—killing?" Dalehouse flared.

"No, no. I wasn't suggesting it. I was *excluding* it. I know you don't like killing off our alien brothers."

Dalehouse took a deep breath. He had seen enough of the balloonists to stop thinking of them as preparations and learn to consider them, almost, as people. The burrowers were still total unknowns to him, and probably rather distasteful—he thought of termites and maggots and all sorts of vile crawling things when he thought of them—but he wasn't ready for genocide.

"So what were you suggesting?" he asked.

"I borrowed a backhoe from Boyne. I want to use it before

he takes it back. The thing is, I think I know where to dig."

He gathered up a clump of the papers on the upended footlocker he was using for a desk and handed them over. The sheets on top seemed to be a map, which meant nothing to Dalehouse, but underneath was a sheaf of photographs. He recognized them; they were aerial views of the area surrounding the camp. Some he had taken himself, others were undoubtedly Kappelyushnikov's.

"There's something wrong with them," he said. "The colors look funny. Why is this part blue?"

"It's false-color photography, Danny. That batch is in the infrared; the bluer the picture, the warmer the ground. Here, see these sort of pale streaks? They're two or three degrees warmer than what's on either side of them."

Dalehouse turned the pictures about in his hands and then asked, "Why?"

"Well, see if you figure it out the same way I did. Look at the one under it, in orthodox color. You took that one. Turn it so it's oriented the same way as the false-color print—there. Do you see those clumps of orangey bushes? They seem to extend in almost straight lines. And those bright red ones? They are extensions of the same lines. The bushes are all the same plant; the difference is that the bright red ones are dead. Well, doesn't it look to you like the pale lines in the false-color pictures match up with the lines of bushes in the ortho? And I've poked a probe down along some of those lines, and guess what I found."

"Burrows?" Dalehouse hazarded.

"You're so damn smart," grumbled Morrissey. "All right, show me some real smarts. *Why* are those plants and markings related to the burrows?"

Dalehouse put down the pictures patiently. "That I don't know. But I bet you're going to tell me."

"Well, no. Not for sure. But I can make a smart guess. I'd say digging out tunnels causes some sort of chemical change in the surface. Maybe it leeches out the nutrients selectively? And those plants happen to be the kind that survive best in that kind of soil? Or maybe the castings from the burrowers fertilize them, again selectively. Those are analogues from Earth: you can detect mole runs that way, and earthworms aerate the soil and make things grow better. This may be some wholly different process, but my bet is that that's the general idea."

He sat back on his folding campstool and regarded Danny anxiously.

Dalehouse thought for a second, listening to the dwindling plop of raindrops on the tent roof. "You tell me more than I want to know, Jim, but I think I get your drift. You want me to help you dig them up. How are we going to do that fast enough? Especially in the kind of mud there is out there?"

"That's why I borrowed Boyne's backhoe. It's been in position ever since the rain began. I think the burrowers sense ground vibrations; I wanted them to get used to its being there before we started."

"Did you tell him what you wanted it for? I got the impression they were digging burrows themselves."

"So did I, and that's why I didn't tell him. I said we needed new latrines, and by gosh, we do—sometime or other. Anyway, it's right over the best-looking patch of bushes right now, ready to go. Are you with me?"

Danny thought wistfully of his airborne friends, so much more inviting than these rats or worms. But they were out of reach for the time being . . .

"Sure," he said.

Morrissey grinned, relieved. "Well, that was the easy part. Now we come up against the tough bit: convincing Harriet to go along."

Harriet was every bit as tough as advertised. "You don't seriously *mean,*" she began, "that you want to drag everybody out in a *downpour* just for the sake of digging a few *holes*?"

"Come on, Harriet," said Morrissey, trying not to explode. "The rain's almost stopped."

"And if it has, there are a *thousand* more important things to do!"

"Will be fun, Gasha," Kappelyushnikov chipped in. "Digging for foxholes like landed oil-rich English country gentlemen! Excellent sport."

"And it isn't just a few holes," Morrissey added. "Look at the seismology traces. There are big things down there, chambers twenty meters long and more. Not just tunnels. Maybe cities."

Harriet said cuttingly, "Morrissey, if you wonder why none of us have any confidence in you, that's just the reason. You'll say any stupid thing that comes into your head. Cities! There are some indications of shafts and chambers somewhat bigger than the tunnels directly under the surface, yes. But I would not call them—"

"All right, all right. They're not cities. Maybe they aren't even villages, but they're something. At the least, they are something like breeding chambers where they keep their young. Or store their food. Or, Christ, I don't know, maybe it's where they have ballet performances or play bingo— what's the difference? Just because they're bigger, it follows that they're probably more important. It will be less likely, or at least harder, for them to seal them off."

He looked toward Alex Woodring, who coughed and said, "I think that's reasonable, Harriet. Don't you?"

She pursed her lips thoughtfully. "Reasonable? No, I certainly wouldn't call it *reasonable*. Of course, you're our leader, at least nominally, and if you think it wise for us to depart from the—"

"I do think it's a good idea, Harriet," Woodring said boldly.

"If you'll let me finish, please? I was saying, if you think we should depart from the agreement we all made that group decisions should be arrived at *unanimously*, not by a vote or some one person throwing his weight around, then I suppose I have nothing further to say."

"Gasha, dear," said Kappelyushnikov soothingly, "shut up, please? Tell us plan, Jim."

"You bet! First thing we do is open up as big a hole as we can with the backhoe. All of us are out there with shovels, and we jump in. What we want is specimens. We grab what we see. We should take them pretty much by surprise, and besides," he said, with some self-satisfaction, "two of us can carry these." He held up his camera. "They've got good bright strobes. I got that idea from Boyne when we were drinking together; I think that's what they do at the Greasies'. They go in with these things, partly to get pictures and mostly to dazzle them. While they're temporarily blinded we can grab them easily."

Dalehouse put in, "Temporarily, Jim?"

"Well," Morrissey said reluctantly, "no, I'm not real sure about that part. Their eyes are probably pretty delicate—but hell, Danny, we don't even know if they have any eyes in the first place!"

"Then how do they get dazzled?"

"All right. But still, that's the way I want to do it. And we'll take walkie-talkies. If anything, uh, goes wrong—" He hesitated and then started over. "If you should get disoriented or anything, you just dig *up*. You should be able to do that with your bare hands. If not, you just turn your walkie-talkie on. We might be unable to get voice communication from under the surface, but we know from the radio that was stolen that we can at least get carrier sound, so we'll RDF you and dig you out. That's if anything goes wrong."

Kappelyushnikov leaned forward and placed his hand on the biologist's mouth. "Dear Jim," he said, "please don't encourage us anymore, otherwise we all quit. Let's do this; no more talk."

Predictably, Harriet would have nothing to do with the venture, and she insisted that at least two of the men stay behind—"In case we have to dig you heroes out." But Sparky

Cerbo volunteered to go in, and Alicia Dair claimed she could run the backhoe better than anyone else in the camp. So they had half a dozen in coveralls, head lamps, goggles, and gloves, ready to jump in when Morrissey signaled the digging to start.

He had been right about the mud; there wasn't any, except right around the main paths of the camp, where they had trodden the Klongan ground cover to death. But the soil was saturated, and the backhoe threw as much moisture as it did dirt. In less than a minute it had broken through.

Morrissey swallowed, crossed himself, and jumped into the hole. Alex Woodring followed, then Danny, then Kappelyushnikov, di Paolo, and Sparky Cerbo.

The plan was to break up into pairs, each couple to follow one tunnel. The trouble with the plan was that it was predicated on there being more than two directions to take. There weren't. The pit they dropped into was not much more than a meter broad. It smelled damp and—and *bad*, Danny thought, like a stale cage of pet mice; and it was no more than a tunnel. Di Paolo jumped down onto Danny's ankle, and Sparky Cerbo, following, got him square in the middle of the back. They were all tangled together, cursing and grumbling, and if there was a burrower within a kilometer that didn't know they were coming, that burrower, Danny thought, would have to be dead.

"Quit screwing around!" yelled Morrissey over his shoulder. "Dalehouse! Sparky! You two follow me."

Dalehouse got himself turned around in time to see Morrissey's hips and knees, outlined against the glow from his head lamp, moving away. The cross-section of the tunnel was more oval than round, shallower than it was broad; they couldn't quite move on hands and knees, but they could scramble well enough on thighs and elbows.

"See anything?" he called ahead.

"No. Shut up. Listen." Morrissey's voice was muffled, but Dalehouse could hear it well enough. Past it and through it he thought he heard something else. What? It was faint and hard to identify—squirrellike squeals and rustlings, perhaps, and larger, deeper sounds from farther away. His own breath, the rubbing of his gear, the sounds the others made all conspired to drown it out. But there was *something*.

A bright flare made him blink. It hurt his eyes. It came from Morrissey's strobe, up ahead. All Dalehouse got of it was what trickled back, impeded by the rough dirt walls almost without reflectance. In the other direction it must have been startling. Now he was sure he heard the squirrel squeals, and they sounded anguished. As well they should, Danny realized, with a moment's empathy for the burrowers. What could light have meant to them, ever, but some predator breaking in, and death and destruction following?

He bumped into Morrissey's feet and stopped. Over his shoulder, Morrissey snarled, "The fuckers! They've blocked it."

"The tunnel?"

"Christ, yes, the tunnel! It's packed tight, too. How the hell could they do that so fast?"

Dalehouse had a moment's atavistic fear. Blocked! And in the other direction? He rolled onto his side, extinguished his light, and peered back between his feet down the tunnel. Past Sparky's crouching form he could see—he was sure he could see—the reassuring dim red glow from the Klongan sky. Even so, he could feel the muscles at the back of his neck tensed and painful with the ancient human terror of being buried alive, and he suddenly remembered that the direction they had taken was the one that went under the backhoe. What if its weight crushed the roof through and pinned them? "Ah, Jim," he called. "What do you think? Should we get back to the barn?"

Pause. Then, angrily, "Might as well. We're not doing any good here. Maybe the guys had better luck the other way."

But Cappy and the others were already outside, helping them out as they emerged. They had got only eight or nine meters into their tunnel before it was blocked; Dalehouse's group had gone more than twice as far. It came out the same in the end, though, Dalehouse reflected. Incredible that their reactions could be so fast! No doubt they had been trained into them over endless Klongan millenia. Whatever the reason, it was not going to be easy to collect a specimen, much less try to make contact. Danny thought of his airborne friends longingly; how much nicer to fly to make contact than to wiggle through the mud like a snake!

Kappelyushnikov was brushing him off, and then, more lingeringly, doing the same for Sparky Cerbo. "Dearest girl," he said, "you are disgracefully filthy! Let us all go swim in lake, take our minds off troubles."

Good-naturedly the girl moved away from his hand. "Maybe we should see what Harriet wants first," she suggested. And, sure enough, Harriet was standing at the entrance to the headquarters tent, a hundred meters away, evidently waiting for them to come to her.

As they straggled in, she looked them up and down with distaste. "A total failure, I see," she said, nodding. "Of course, that was to be expected."

"Harriet," Jim Morrissey began dangerously.

She raised her hand. "It doesn't matter. Perhaps you'll be interested in what has happened while you were gone."

"Harriet, we were only gone twenty or thirty minutes!" Morrissey exploded.

"Nevertheless. First there was a tactran signal. We're being reinforced, and so are the Peeps. Second—" She stepped aside to let them pass through into the tent. The others who had stayed behind were clustered inside, looking, Dalehouse thought, curiously self-satisfied. "I believe you wanted a specimen of those underground creatures? We found one trying to steal some of our supplies. Of course, it would have been easier if so many of you hadn't been wasting your time on foolishness, so you could have helped when we needed you—"

Kappelyushnikov bellowed, "Gasha! Get to point, right now. You caught specimen for us?"

"Of course," she said. "We put him in one of Morrissey's cages. I was quite severely scratched doing it, but that's about what you can expect when—"

They didn't let her finish; they were all inside and staring.

The stale mouse-cage smell was a thousand times stronger, almost choking Danny Dalehouse, but there it was. It was nearly two meters long, tiny eyes set close together above its snout, squeezed tight in anguish. It was squealing softly— Danny would almost have said brokenheartedly—to itself. It was gnawing at the metal bars of the cage and simultaneously scrabbling at the plastic flooring with duckfoot-shaped claws. It was covered with a sort of dun-colored down or short fur; it seemed to have at least six pairs of limbs, all stubby, all clawed, and all incredibly strong.

Whatever its teeth were made of, they were *hard;* one of the bars of the cage was almost gnawed through. And its squeals of pain never stopped.

·NINE·

THE SWARM WAS half fledglings now, tiny balloonets that had just cast off their parachuting threads of silk and now struggled bravely to keep up with the great two-meter adult spheres. In the constant chorus of the swarm, the fledglings' voices were as tiny as their gasbags. Their shrill peepings used the least possible amount of hydrogen, to preserve their precarious lift balance against the few drops in their ballast bladders.

Charlie patrolled majestically through the swarm, driving the bulk of his body reprovingly against a cluster of infant balloonets who were singing against the swarm melody, rotating his eye patches to scan the skies for *ha'aye'i*, listening to the countersongs of praise and complaint from the other adults of the swarm, and always, always, leading them as they sang. There was much praise, and much complaint. The praise he took for granted. To the complaint he attended with more care, ready either to remedy or rebuke. Three females sang despairingly of little ones who dropped

132

their flying tails too soon, or who could not hold their hydrogen and so drifted helplessly down to the voracious world below. Another pealed a dirge of anger and sorrow, blaming the deformed fledglings on the Persons of the Middle Sun.

This was just; and Charlie led the swarm in a concurrence of sympathy and advice. "Never"—(*Never, never, never,* sang the chorus)—"never again must we breed near the New Suns."

The females chorused agreement, but some of the males sang in counterpoint, "But how can we know which is real Heaven-Danger and which is not? And where may we breed at all? The Persons of the Three Suns are under all our air!"

Charlie's answering song was serene. "I will ask my friend of the Middle Sun. He will know." (*He will know, he will know,* chorused the swarm.)

But a male sang a dire question. "And when the swarming rapture is on us, will we remember?"

"Yes," sang Charlie. "We will remember because we must." (*We must, we must.*)

That should have settled it. And yet, the song of the swarm was not at peace. Undertones buzzed and discorded against the dominant themes. Even Charlie's own song faltered now and then, and repeated itself when it should have burst into triumphant new themes. Currents were stirring under the surface of his mind. They never reached consciousness; if they had, no power could have kept him from expressing them in song. But they were there. Worries. Doubts. Puzzles. Who were these Persons of the Three Suns? Where had they come from? They seemed the same, as like as any swarms of balloonists. Yet Charlie's friend 'Anny 'Alehouse had explained that they were not the same.

First there had been the Persons of the Small Sun. They had seemed no more than another species of devouring Earth-Danger creatures in the beginning, although they had created a tiny sun almost at once. But their camp was almost at the

limit of Charlie's range, and the swarm had not troubled
themselves about those Persons.

Then there was the group of Charlie's friend; and almost
at once, the third group, the Persons of the Big Sun. They
were worrisome! Their sun was always shining brightly,
brighter than the Heaven-Danger at its brightest. Since it was
almost the deepest of Charlie's instincts to swarm in the direction of a bright light, it was actual pain to turn and swim away
from the Big Sun. They had almost been trapped when the
Persons first arrived—when all three of the parties of Persons
of the Suns arrived—because each of them came roaring
down through the air on a pillar of Sun-Flame. But none had
been close enough to cause them to swarm. By the time the
flock had maneuvered near, the flames were gone and the
lights were darkened. Then the Persons of the Big Sun had
sent one of themselves up into the air in the great queer thing
that fluttered and rattled; it was harder than the *ha'aye'i* Sky-
Danger, and even more deadly. Something about it drew balloonists into its swinging claws, and more than a dozen of
Charlie's swarm had been ripped open and gone fluttering
down to ground, helpless, despairing, and silent. Now they
avoided it in fear and sorrow. Two out of three of the groups
of New Persons, and both to be avoided! The one because
they killed, the other because they did not fly at all, were no
more than any other Ground-Danger, would not have been
thought to be Persons at all—

Except for 'Anny 'Alehouse.

Charlie sang of his friend, who redeemed his whole race.
Anny 'Alehouse and his sometimes companion, 'Appy—they
were Persons! They flew as Persons flew, by the majesty and
the grace of the air itself. It was a sad thing that even their
Middle Sun had flared like a true Heaven-Danger and caused
the flock to breed poorly. But it did not occur to Charlie to
blame Morrissey's flare on Dalehouse or Kappelyushnikov; it
did not occur to him to think of blame at all. When Kung
flared, the balloonists bred. They could not help it. They did

not try. They had never developed defenses against a false flare, one lacking in the actinic radiation that helped them make their hydrogen and triggered their fertility. They had never needed any—until now. And they had no way to learn a defense.

The swarm was drifting toward a swelling cumulus cloud; Charlie swelled his singing sac and boomed out, "Hive up, my brothers!" (*Hive up, hive up,* came the answering chorus.) "Hive up, sisters and mates! Hive up, young and old! Watch for *ha'aye'i* in the wet shadows! Huddle the little ones close!"

Every member of the swarm was singing full-throatedly now as the swarm compacted, swimming into the ruddy-pink, cottony edges of the cloud. They could see each other only as ghosts, except for the oldest and biggest males, whose luminous markings gave them more visibility. But they could hear the songs, and Charlie and the other senior males patrolled the periphery of the swarm. If *ha'aye'i* were there, the males could not defend the swarm—could not even defend themselves to any purpose. But they could sing warning, and then the swarm would scatter in all directions, so that only the slowest and weakest would be caught.

Cumulus clouds formed at the top of updrafts of warm air, and the *ha'aye'i* often sought them out to supplement their comparatively weak lift. There was always a price; what the *ha'aye'i* gained in speed and control, not to mention claws and jaws, they paid for in smaller lifting bags, so that for them it was always an effort to stay in the air. The *ha'aye'i* were sharks of the air. They never slept, never stopped moving—and were always hungry.

But this time the swarm was lucky. There were no killer balloons in the cloud, and they emerged intact. Charlie trumpeted out a song of thanksgiving as the flock entered clear air again. All joined.

The swarm was drifting toward the Heat Pole. Charlie rotated his eye patches to catch clues of the movement of the air. He always knew in what direction the winds blew on each level; he was taught by the movement of cloudlets, by the fluttering of dropped fledgling silk, most of all by a lifetime of experience, so that he did not have to think of how to capture a favorable wind; he *knew*, as surely as any New Yorker hurrying down Fifth Avenue knows the number of the next cross street. He did not want to stray too far from his friend of the Middle Sun, whom he had not seen for some time. He trumpeted for the swarm to rise a hundred meters. The other males took up his song, and from all the gasbags, great and small, drops of water ballast fell. There would be no trouble replacing it for the adults, who were naturally and automatically catching and swallowing the tiny misting of dew during their passage through the clouds. The smaller ones made hard work of it. But they valiantly released swallowed gas into their bags, and the females watchfully butted the littlest ones higher. The swarm stayed together at the new level as its drift changed back in the direction of the camp of the Middle Sun.

No *ha'aye'i* in sight. Plenty of water on their skins to lick off and swallow, part to hold as ballast, part to dissociate into the oxygen they metabolized and the hydrogen that gave them lift. Charlie was well content. It was good to be a balloonist! He returned to the song of thanksgiving.

They were nearing the edges of their territory, and another swarm bobbed high above them a few kilometers away. Charlie observed them without concern. There was no rivalry between swarms. Sometimes two of them would float side by side for long periods, or even coalesce. Sometimes when two swarms were joined, individuals from one would adhere to another. No one thought anything of that. From that moment they were full members of their new swarm and joined in its songs. But it was more common that each should stay in its own unmarked but known volume of air. They grazed the pollen fields of their own home air without coveting those of their neighbors. Though after half a dozen breedings there might be no single individual still alive of the original swarm, the swarm itself would still drift placidly over the same ten thousand square kilometers of ground. One place was almost like another. Over any one of those square kilometers the sustaining air was always around them. The pollen clouds blew through them all.

Still, some parts of their range were more attractive than others. The mesa where the Persons of the Big Sun had built their shining shells and lit their blazing lamps had been one of their favorites, pollen drifting down off the hills in a pleasant stream, and few *ha'aye'i*. Charlie sang sorrowfully of his regret as he thought of it, now that they must avoid it for all time to come. The bay of the ocean-lake where 'Anny 'Alehouse lived was, on the contrary, usually to be avoided. The water evaporating from the sea meant columns of rising cloud, and killer balloons no doubt in half the columns. If any member of the swarm had chosen to question Charlie's decision to return there, it would have been quite reasonable to do so, in practical terms. But in terms of the lives of the balloonists themselves it was quite impossible. Their group decisions were never questioned. If a senior adult sang, "Do thus," it was done. Charlie was the most senior of adults, and so his song usually prevailed. Not always. Now and then another adult would sing a contrary proposal ten minutes later, but if Charlie returned to his own ten minutes after that, there was no complaint. Each of the other adults loyally picked up his song, and the swarm complied.

There was also the consideration that Charlie had brought to the swarm his friend of the Middle Sun, with his astonishing and fascinating new sounds. This was a Person! Puzzling, yes. But not like those earthbound grubbers of the Small Sun or the strange creatures of the Big Sun who flew only with the help of killing machines. As the swarm drew near the camp of the Middle Sun, all of the adults rotated their bodies so that their tiny faces, like the features of engorged ticks, looked downward, anxious to spy 'Anny or 'Appy. Even the balloonets were caught up in the happy fever of the search; and when the first of the swarm spotted Danny rising to meet them, the song of the flock became triumphant.

How strange 'Anny 'Alehouse looked this time! His lifting sac had always been disagreeably knobby and lacking in any decent coloration, but now it was swollen immensely and knobbier than ever. Charlie might not have recognized him if there had been more than one other like him in all the world to confuse him with. But it was 'Anny all the same. The swarm swallowed hydrogen and dropped to meet him, singing the song of welcome Charlie had invented for his friend.

Dalehouse was almost as overjoyed to see the swarm again as the swarm was to see Dalehouse. It had been a long time! After the storm there had been the time for cleaning up; and before they were through the second ship had dropped out of the tachyon charge state to bring them new people and a whole host of new equipment. That was fine enough, but to make them welcome and to integrate the new things into the old had taken time—more than time. Some of what they had brought had been gifts for the balloonists, and to deliver the gifts meant more load had to be lifted, which meant a bigger cluster of balloons, which meant making and filling new ones and redesigning the ballasting system to compensate. Danny was far from sure it had been worth it.

But there had also been half a kilo of microfiches from the Double-A-L, and those had been worth a lot. Professor D. Dalehouse was now a name to conjure with among xenobiologists. They had quoted his reports in every paper. And the papers themselves had given much to think of. Among the conferees at Michigan State a battle had raged. In the evolution of the balloonists, where was Darwin? When a female scattered her filamentary eggs into the air of Klong like the burst of a milkweed pod and all the males spewed sperm at once, where was the selection of the fittest? What kind of premium on strength, agility, intelligence, or sexual attraction would make each generation somehow infinitesimally more "fit" than the one before in an ontogeny where all the males spurted all their genes into a cloud of mixed female genetic material, with the wind for a mixer and random chance deciding who fathered which on whom? The balloonists kept no Leporello lists. Well any one of them might have fathered a *mille-tre;* but if so he never knew it.

Charlie could have settled the debate if asked. All the balloonists were sexually mature as soon as they were able to drop their spider-silk parachute threads and float free. But all balloonists were not equal in size.

The older, the bigger. The bigger, the more sperm or eggs they flung into the collective pool. Human beings, by contrast, cease to play a part in evolution before half their lives are over. Wisdom does not come at twenty-five. By the time there is a significant difference between a Da Vinci and a dolt the days of breeding are over. Selection plays no further part. Nor does it in resistance to the degenerative diseases of the old, which is why in two million years the human race has not selected against cancer, arthritis, or arteriosclerosis. Raunchy young cells have been disciplined by the stresses of fifty thousand generations. But past the breeding age the cell runs out of programming. It doesn't know what to do next. It begins to fall apart.

With the balloonists it was different. The Charlie-sized giants among them sprayed half a liter of mist-of-sperm into each receptive cloud of eggs, while the tiny first-swarm male balloonets squeezed out hardly a drop. The Charlies had proved their fitness to survive by the most conclusive of tests: they had survived.

Dalehouse was eager to try to settle questions like that as he called to Charlie and swung in to meet him, even more eager to try the new language elements the big computers on Earth had generated for him. What was occupying most of his attention, though, was his gift from Earth. Like the swarm's greeting song, it was an example of the thing his society did best. It was a weapon.

It was not entirely a free gift, Dalehouse reflected, but then there is nothing without a price. Charlie's song cost him some of his reserve of lifting gas, as the songs that were their life always cost the swarm. If they sang, they vented gas. If they vented gas, they lost lift. If they lost lift, sooner or later they drifted helplessly down to the eager mouths on the surface and were eaten. Or, almost as bad, had to live on there, helpless and voiceless, until they were able to accumulate and dissociate enough water molecules to recharge their stocks—quickly if Kung was kind enough to flare for them, painfully slowly otherwise. It was a price they paid gladly. To live was to sing; to be quiet was to be dead anyway. But in the end, for most of them, it was the price of their lives.

The price of the gift Danny Dalehouse brought was the lives of the five balloonists who had been sent back to Earth in the return capsule.

The designers at Camp Detrick had made good use of the samples. The two who were dead on arrival were dissected at once. Those were the lucky ones. The other three were studied *in vivo*. The biggest and strongest of them lasted two weeks.

The Camp Detrick experimenters also had a price to pay, because eight of them came down with the Klongan hives, and one had the severe misfortune to have his skull fill up with antigenic fluid, so that he would never again for the rest of his life stress an experimental subject. Or, indeed, hold a fork by himself. But probably the balloonists who had been his subjects would not have thought that price unfair.

Danny Dalehouse unslung the lightweight carbine from one shoulder and practiced aiming it. Its stock was metal shell, and sintered metal at that; it weighed hardly a kilogram, but half that weight was in high-velocity bullets. It was poor design. He felt sure the recoil would kick him halfway across the sky if he fired it, and anyway, what was the use of high-velocity bullets? What target was there in the Klongan air that needed that sort of impact to destroy it? But the word from Earth brought by the reinforcement party that had been labeled a UN peacekeeping committee was that it must be carried. So he carried it.

He put it back and, somewhat uncomfortably, took Charlie's gift off the other shoulder. Now, that was more like it. Somebody somewhere had understood what Charlie's people could do and what they needed in order to protect themselves against predators. It weighed even less than the carbine, and it contained no propellants at all. Its tiny winch could be operated by the claws of a Charlie to tighten a long-lasting elastic cord. Its trigger was sized to fit a balloonist, and what it fired was a cluster of minute needles or, alternatively, a capsule of some sort of fluid. Needles were for airborne predators. The fluid, or so Danny was told, was against creatures like the crabrats, if a balloonist was forced down and needed defense; and it would only incapacitate them without killing.

It would tax all of Dalehouse's linguistics to convey any part of that to Charlie, but the way to get it done was to begin. He held the crossbow up and sang, carefully attending to the notes he had been taught by the computers at Texas A&M. "I have brought you a gift."

Charlie responded with a burst of song. Dalehouse could understand no more than a few phrases, but clearly it was a message of gratitude and polite inquiry; and anyway, the little tape recorder at his belt was getting it all down for later study.

Danny moved on to the next sentence he had been taught. "You must come with me to find a *ha'aye'i.*" That was hard to sing; English does not come with glottal stops, and practicing it for an hour had left Dalehouse's throat sore. But Charlie seemed to understand, because the song of thanks changed to a thin melody of concern. Danny laughed. "Do not fear," he sang. "I will be a *ha'aye'i* to the *ha'aye'i.* We will destroy them with this gift, and the swarm will no more need to fear."

Song of confusion, with the words *the swarm* repeated over

and over, not only by Charlie but by all his flock.

The hardest part of all was yet to come. "You must leave the swarm," sang Dalehouse. "They will be safe. We will return. But now just you and I must fly to seek a *ha'aye'i.*"

It took time; but the message ultimately seemed to get across. It was a measure of the balloonist's trust in his friend from Earth that he was willing to embark on so fearful an adventure with him. The members of the flock *never* left it by choice. For more than an hour after they had dropped to a lower level and left the flock behind, Charlie's song was querulous and sad. And no *ha'aye'i* appeared. They left the Food Bloc camp far behind, drifting down the shore of the sea-lake and then across a neck of it to the vicinity of the Peeps' tattered colony. For some time Dalehouse had been wondering if the Texas computers had really given him the right words to sing. But then Charlie's song turned to active fear. They dipped low under a bank of clouds, warm-weather cumuli that looked like female balloonists turned upside down, and from one of them dropped the predatory form of a killer.

Danny was uneasily tempted to slay this first one with his own carbine. It was frightening to see the *ha'aye'i* stoop toward them. But he wanted to demonstrate his gift to Charlie.

"Watch!" he cried, clumsily grasping the grip that had been designed for balloonist claws. He circled the swelling form of the airshark in the cross-haired sight, designed for balloonist eye patches, feeling the low vibrations of Charlie's muttered song of terror. At twenty meters he squeezed the trigger.

A dozen tiny metal spikes lashed out at the *ha'aye'i,* spreading like the cone of fire of a shotgun shell. One was enough. The shark's bag ripped open with a puff of moisture. The creature screamed once in pain and surprise, and then had no more breath to scream with. It dropped past them, its horrid little face writhing, its claws clutching uselessly toward them, meters away.

A bright trill of surprise from Charlie, and then a roaring

paean of triumph. "This is a great good thing, 'Anny 'Ale-house! Will you slay all the *ha'aye'i* for us?"

"No, not I, Charlie. You will do it for yourself!" And hanging in the air, Danny showed him the clever little crank that worked the elastic cord, the simple breech that the cluster of needles dropped into. For a creature who had never used tools before, Charlie was quick to grasp the operation. Dalehouse had him fire a practice round at a cloud and then watched patiently while the balloonist painfully wound the winch for himself and loaded again.

They were no longer quite alone. Unbidden, the swarm had drifted after them and was floating half a kilometer away, all their eye patches rotated toward them, their distant song sweet and plaintive, like a puppy's lonely begging to be let in. And down below, the Peeps' camp was near; Dalehouse could see one or two upturned faces curiously staring at them. Let them look, he thought virtuously; let them see how the Food-Exporting Powers were helping the native races of Klong, if they had so little to do with their time. There were only a handful of them left of the original expedition, and their much-boasted reinforcements showed no signs of arriving.

Reinforcements. Reminded, Dalehouse began the rest of his message for Charlie. "This gift," he sang, "is yours. But we would ask a gift of you, too."

"What gift?" sang Charlie politely.

"I do not know words," sang Danny, "but soon I will show you. My swarm-mates ask you to carry some small things to other places. Some you will drop to the ground. Some you will bring back." Teaching Charlie how to point the cameras and sound-recording instruments was going to take forever, Dalehouse thought glumly; and how were they ever going to tell him where to drop the clusters of wolftrap sensors and seismic mikes? What seemed so simple on Earth was something else entirely on Klong—

"Beware, beware!" sang the distant, frantic voices of the swarm.

Tardily Danny looked around. The *ha'aye'i*'s rush caught them unaware. It came from behind and below, where Dalehouse had not thought to look. And Charlie, fondling his new toy and trying to understand what Dalehouse wanted of him, had been careless.

If it had not been for the distant shrieking of the swarm, the creature might have had them both. But Charlie spun faster than Dalehouse, and before Danny could unlimber his carbine the balloonist had shown how well he had learned his lesson by killing the killer. Either of them could have reached out and caught the long, wicked claws of the *ha'aye'i* as it fell past them; it was that close.

"Well done!" yelled Dalehouse, and Charlie pealed in rapture:

"Well, well done! How great a gift!" They rose to rejoin the swarm—

Lances of golden fire reached up faintly toward the flock from the Peeps' camp below.

"My God!" shouted Danny. "The fools are setting off fireworks!"

The rockets exploded into showers of sparks, and all through the swarm balloonists were bursting into bright hydrogen flame.

·TEN·

WHEN DULLA WAS AWAKE, which was not much of the time, he was only blurrily conscious of what was going on. At first there had been a recurrent *whick, whick* that he could not identify, and some person who seemed vaguely familiar manhandling him into whatever it was that was making the sounds. Then pain—a lot of pain. Then long periods when people were talking to him or around him. But he felt no impulse to answer. In his brief conscious times he discovered by and by that he was no longer in pain. The treatment the Greasies had given him had been unpleasant, but it seemed to have done the trick. He was alive. He was rehydrated. The swellings had gone down. He was no longer blind. He was only very weak.

When he woke up and realized that he was not only awake but actually seemed able to keep his eyes open for awhile, Feng Hua-tse was standing by his cot. The Chinaman was looking very stretched out, Dulla thought with some contempt; he looked even worse than Dulla himself felt.

"You are feeling better?" Feng asked sadly.

Dulla thought it over. "Yes. I think so. What has happened?"

"I am glad you are feeling better. The long-noses brought you here from the place of your beetle friends. They said you would live, but I didn't think so. It has been a long time. Do you want to eat?"

"Yes—no," Dulla corrected himself. "I do, but not at this moment. I want the w.c. first."

"Shall I help you?"

"No. I can do it myself."

"I am glad of that, too," said Feng, who had been functioning as bedpan orderly for all the days of Ahmed Dulla's recovery and longer before that than he cared to remember. The Pakistani raised himself painfully from the inflatable cot and moved slowly toward the slit-trench latrine.

He gazed disapprovingly around the camp. One of the noises he had been hearing identified itself for him: a slapping, rasping sound that turned out to be the waterwheel. So at least there should be power. But where were the promised floodlights, the growing crops, the comforts? Where were all the people?

Feng had followed him and stood gazing mournfully as Dulla relieved himself. "Why do you stand there?" snapped Dulla, tying up his pajama cord and making hard work of it. "What has happened? Why has so little been done?"

The leader spread his hands. "What can I say? There were ten of us. Two died with you in this venture you found so necessary. One other died here. Two were so ill they had to be returned to Earth—by courtesy of the Greasies. We had no one well enough to fly the return capsule. The Italian is asleep, and the two women are gathering fuel."

"Gathering fuel! Are we become peasants again, Feng?"

The leader sighed. "I have done my best," he said. It was a sentence he had been saying over and over to himself for a long time. "Help is coming. Heir-of-Mao himself has ordered it. Two great ships, material and persons, soon—"

"Soon! And until then, what? Do we do nothing?"

"Go back to bed," said Feng wearily. "You exhaust me, Dulla. Eat if you will. There is food. The Fats gave it to us; otherwise there would be none."

"And now we are beggars," sneered Dulla. He swayed and caught hold of Feng's shoulder. "For this I studied and came all these light-years! For this I almost died! How foolish we will all look when we return in disgrace to Earth!"

Feng shook his head heavily. He disengaged the Pakistani's hand from his shoulder and stepped downwind—the man was odorously unwashed. He did not need to hear any of this. He knew it for himself. He had accepted the charity of the Fats for the food without which they all would have starved; of the Greasies for the rescue of Dulla and for the return to Earth of the sick members of the expedition—who would no doubt even now be telling their debriefers how badly Feng Hua-tse had managed the expedition with which he had been entrusted. There would be large-character posters going up in K'ushui about that even now. They would be very critical of him. When they got back to Earth—if they got back—the best hope he had was to become a barefoot biochemist along the Yellow River again.

Of course, if somehow they mercifully spared him until the two great ships arrived—

Ah, then! He had pored over the tactran messages and pictures yearningly. The second ship would bring not ten, not fifteen, but a majestic thirty-four new persons. An agronomist! Someone to take up Feng's own pitiful beginnings, the mushrooms he had sown, the wheat seedlings he had coaxed to sprout—the fittest of them would survive, and the fittest of their descendants would flourish. There were two more translators, both split-brained, one of them a skilled littoral pisciculturist as well. The Great Water might yet yield food they could eat. A doctor—no, Feng corrected himself, a fully schooled surgeon with a world reputation in the treatment of traumatic injuries. True, he was nearly two meters tall and black as a boy-child's hair, by his photograph. But still. Three of the new additions had had limnology crash courses, and one of them, who had once been an officer in the Red Guards, had also had three years of experience as a scout in the Gobi, and later in the Himalayas.

And the worldly goods the other ship would carry! Photovoltaic generators, capable of pouring out 230-volt a.c. in really significant quantities. Plastic to spare. Pioneering tools —axes and machetes, and a few rifles for the collection of specimens as well as for "game." Folbots. Magnesium-frame bicycles. A doubly redundant computer with no fewer than six remote-access terminals. Radio equipment. Laser equipment. Food. More food; food enough for all of them for many months . . .

It seemed a dream!

But what was not a dream was that very surely, Feng knew, among those thirty-four persons would be one who would come over to him and quietly say, "Feng Hua-tse? I am directed by Heir-of-Mao to receive your report on why your custodianship of this project has not lived up to expectations." And then would come the sweating time. There would be no excuses accepted. He would not be interested in the mushrooms that were refusing to grow or the specimens that Feng himself had painfully kept alive. He would only be interested in why three had died and two had been sent home and ten had accomplished so very little.

All this was in Feng Hua-tse's mind, but all he said was, "Go back to sleep, Dulla. I am out of patience with you."

Dulla did not go back to sleep. Anger had given him strength. What he did was wake up the Italian.

"Oh, you are alive again?" Spadetti yawned and rubbed the blue-black stubble on his chin. "We thought you were going to die," he said cheerfully. "I almost bet a day's ration on it. I would have been very angry to lose."

"I have been talking to Feng, that bungler!"

"It is not all Uazzi's fault, Dulla. We were the first. We made the mistakes that must be made so others can learn."

"I did not want to be teacher to the Fats and the Greasies! I did not want them here at all. This can be our planet, to shape as we will!"

"Yes," admitted Spadetti, "I had some such thought myself. But, *chi sa*, what can you do? Each step seemed right at the time. Even yours, to make friends with the natives—"

"Those beasts! One cannot make friends with them."

"Oh, not true, Dulla. Our rivals have succeeded. The Fats have balloonists carrying their cameras all over the planet, or so they promise on the tactran. The Greasies are teaching their moles and earthworms how to burrow under our camp and listen to what we say. Perhaps they are listening now."

"Nonsense! How stupid you are!"

"Stupid, perhaps, but no, it is not entirely nonsense," smiled the Italian, unoffended. "Perhaps I have made it a little bit of a joke, but I am not sure that I am joking. And what have we accomplished? I will be more exact, Dulla. What did you yourself accomplish, except to get two people killed, when you visited our *frutti-del-mare* friends? We failed. It is as simple as that." He yawned and scratched. "Now, Dulla, *per favore*, let me wake up by myself a little? I am not so happy with this reality around me that I want to leave my dreams so rudely."

"Drink your wine and dream then," said Dulla coldly.

"Oh, Dulla! But that is not a bad idea. If one only had a true wine instead of this filth."

"Pig," said Dulla, but softly enough that Spadetti did not have to admit he had heard it. He returned to his cot and sat heavily on the edge of it, ignoring Spadetti's soft-voiced imprecations as he tasted the jungle juice he had made for himself. Perhaps it would kill him. Why not? The smell of it kept Dulla from wanting to eat, though he knew he should; he judged he had lost ten kilos at least since landing on Son of Kung, and he could not spare very many more. He sat breathing heavily, sucking through a straw at a flask of flat, tepid water from the still. By and by he noticed that there was a plastic pouch under his bed. He upended it and covered the cot with a drift of tiny white fiche prints.

"I see you have found your love letters," called the Italian from across the tent. "Unfortunately, I cannot read your language. But she is quite a pretty girl."

Dulla ignored him. He gathered them up and carried them to the radio shack, where the only working viewer was. Spadetti had been right; they were almost all from the Bulgarian girl, and they all said much the same thing. She missed him. She thought of him. She consoled her lonely sorrow with the memory of their days together in Sofia.

But in the photographs there was Ana in Paris, Ana in London, Ana in Cairo, Ana in New York. She seemed to be having an interesting time without him.

Rich countries! At bottom, were they not all the same, whether the wealth was in fuel or in food? Wealth was wealth! A greater distance separated him from the fat Bulgarians than from—from even the Krinpit, he thought, and then realized almost at once that he was being unjust. Nan was not like that. But then, she had had the advantage of spending much of her childhood in Hyderabad.

Away from the smell of the Italian's imitation wine, Dulla realized he was hungry. He found some cracked corn and ate it while he went through Ana's letters quickly, and then, more slowly, the synoptics from Earth. Much had happened while he was out of it. The Fats had been reinforced from Earth— it was called a UN peacekeeping team, but that deceived only the most naive. The Greasies had established a satellite astronomical observatory and were monitoring changes in the radiation of Kung. There were problems with the satellite, and the results were unclear. Even so, Dulla studied the reports with fascination and envy. That should have been his own project! It was what he had trained for, all those graduate years. What a waste this expedition was! He glanced distastefully at the gaping rents in the tent, at the instruments that were scattered out to rust because there was no one to use them. So much to be done. So much that he could not think where to begin and so could do nothing.

There was a racket outside which made Dulla glance up, frowning—Feng and the Italian quarreling about something, and behind them the distant squawking of a herd of balloonists. If Heir-of-Mao had been a little more openhanded, and if Feng had been a bit less of a fool . . . then they might have had a helicopter, like the Greasies, or the wit to make balloons, like the Fats, and he too might have had the chance to fly with the flocks. That chance was lost. Even the Krinpit, whom he himself, Ahmed Dulla, had resolved to make contact with, were as strange to him as ever. It was not fair! He had taken the risk. He remembered well how he had felt as he lay helpless among the curious, jostling masses of crablike creatures. If they hadn't tried to eat the other two first, he knew he would have wound up as a meal. And for nothing. The one Krinpit they had a chance to communicate with, to keep for a specimen, Feng had allowed to be stolen by the Greasies.

There were sudden new sounds from outside, hissing white sounds that made Dulla get up and peer out of the tent. He saw flames reaching toward the sky and Feng struggling with the Italian while one of the Jamaican women swore angrily at them both.

"What is happening here?" Dulla demanded.

The Italian pushed Feng away and turned toward Dulla, his expression repentant. "Uazzi wished to greet our friends," he said, peering aloft. The rockets had climbed up into the maroon murk and exploded, and there were smaller explosions all around them. Balloonists had caught fire from the shower of sparks. "I helped him aim, but perhaps—perhaps my aim was not good," he said.

"Foolish one!" cried Dulla, almost dancing with rage, "Do you see what you have done?"

"I have burned up a few gasbags. Why not?" grumbled Spadetti.

"Not just gasbags! Rub the wine out of your eyes and look again. There! Is that a gasbag? Do you not see it is a human being hanging there, wondering why we have tried to kill him, anxious to return to his base with the Fats or the Greasies and report that the People's Republics have declared war? Another blunder! And one we may not survive."

"Peace, Dulla," panted Feng. "It does not matter if the Fats and the Greasies are angry at us now. Help is on the way."

"You are as big a fool as he! Shooting off fireworks like some farm brigade celebrating the overfulfillment of its cabbage quota!"

"I wish," said Feng, "that you had not been rescued, Dulla. There was less struggle here when you were with the Krinpit."

"And I wish," said Dulla, "that the Krinpit who tried to kill me was our leader here instead of you. He was less ugly, and less of a fool."

That Krinpit was many kilometers away, and at that moment almost as angry as Dulla. He had been driven to the brink of insanity with the infuriating attempts of the Poison Ghosts of the Fuel camp to converse with him, with hunger, and above all with the continual blinding uproar of the camp.

In the noisy, bright world of the Krinpit there was never a time of silence. But the level of sound was always manageable: sixty or seventy decibels most of the time, except for the occasional thunderclap of a storm. It almost never reached over seventy-five.

To Sharn-igon, the Fuel camp was torture. Sometimes it was quiet and dim, sometimes blindingly loud. The Krinpit had no internal-combustion engines to punish their auditory nerves. The Greasies had dozens of them. Sharn-igon had no conception of how they worked or what they were for, but he could recognize each of them when it was operating: high clatter of the drilling machine, rubbery roar of the helicopter, rattle and whine of the power saws, steady chug of the water pump. He had arrived at the camp almost blind, for the nearness of the helicopter's turbojet had affected his hearing just as staring at the uncaged sun would damage a human's eyes; the afterimage lasted for days and was still maddeningly distorting to his perceptions. He had been penned behind steel bars as soon as he arrived. However hard he gnawed and sawed, the bars of the cage would not give. As soon as he made a little scratch in one it was replaced. The Poison Ghosts troubled him endlessly, echoing his name and his sounds in a weirdly frightening way. Sharn-igon knew nothing of tape recording, and to hear his own sounds played back to him was as shattering an experience as it would be for a human to see his own form suddenly appear before him. He had realized that the Poison Ghosts wanted to communicate with him and had understood a tiny portion of what they were trying to say. But he seldom replied. He had nothing to say to them.

And he was nearly starving. He survived, barely, on the little he would eat of what they put before him—mostly vegetation, of which he disdained the majority as a human being would spurn thistle and grass. His hunger was maddeningly stimulated because he could smell the tasty nearness of Ghosts Below penned near him, and even a Ghost Above now and then. But the Poison Ghosts never brought him any of these to eat. And always there was the blinding roar of noise, or the equally unpleasant silences when the camp slept and only the faint echo from tents and soft bodies kept him company. Human beings, scantily fed on bread and water in an isolation cell, with bright lights denying them sleep, go mad. Sharn-igon was not far from it.

But he clung to sanity, because he had a goal. The Poison Ghosts had killed Cheee-pruitt.

He had not learned to tell one from another in time to know which was the culprit, but that was a problem easily solved. They were all guilty. Even in his madness it was clear to him that it was proper for him to kill a great many of them to redress their guilt, but what had not become clear to him was how. The chitin of claw and shell-sword were rubbed flat and sore against the bars, and still the bars held.

When all the sounds were out he chatted with the Ghost Above, straining longingly against the bars. "Desire to eat you," he said. If it had not been for the bars, the Ghost Above would have been easy prey. It had lost most of its gas and was crawling about the floor of a cage like his own. Its song was no more than a pathetic whisper.

"You cannot reach me," it pointed out, "unless you molt. And then I would eat you." Each spoke in its own language, but over thousands of generations all the races of Klong knew a little of the language of the others. With the Ghosts Above you could not help being exposed to their constant singing, and even the Ghosts Below could be heard chattering and whistling in their tunnels. "I have eaten several of you hard-shells," the Ghost Above wheezed faintly. "I particularly like the backlings and the first molt."

The creature was boasting, but Sharn-igon could believe the story easily enough. The balloonists fed mostly on air-borne detritus, but to make their young healthy they needed more potent protein sources now and then. When the breeding time was on, the females would drop like locusts to scour the ground clean of everything they could find. Adult Krinpit in shell were too dangerous, but in molt they were fair game. Best of all was a clutch of Ghosts Below caught on their thieving raids to the surface—for Krinpit as well as balloonist. The thought made Sharn-igon's salivary glands flow.

"Hard-shell," whispered the Ghost Above, "I am dying, I think. You can eat me then if you like."

In all honesty, Sharn-igon was forced to admit, "You may be eating me before that." But then he perceived that something was strange. The Ghost Above was no longer in its cage. It was dragging slowly across the floor. "How escape?" he demanded.

"Perhaps because I am so close to death," sang the Ghost Above faintly. "The Killing Ones made a hole in my sac to let the life out of me and then closed it with a thing that stuck and clung and stung. But it has come loose, and almost all my life has spilled away, and so I was able to slide between the bars."

"Wish I could slide through bars!"

"Why do you not open the cage? You have hard things. The Killing Ones push a hard thing into a place in the cage when they want to, and it opens."

"What hard thing are you speaking of? I have worn my shell to pulp."

"No," sighed the balloonist. "Not like your shell. Wait, there is one by the door. I will show you."

Sharn-igon's conception of keys and locks was quite unlike a human's, but the Krinpit too had ways of securing one thing to another temporarily. He chattered and scratched in feverish impatience while the dying gasbag slowly dragged itself toward him, with something bright and hard in its shadowy mouth.

"Could push hard thing into place in my cage?" he wheedled.

The Ghost Above sang softly to itself for a moment. Then it pointed out, "You will eat me."

"Yes. Will. But you very close to dying anyway," Sharn-igon pointed out, and added shrewdly, "Sing very badly now."

The balloonist hissed sadly without forming words. It was true.

"If push thing in place in my cage so that I can go free," bargained Sharn-igon, "will kill some of the Poison Ghosts for you." He added honestly, "Intend to do that in any case, since they killed my he-wife."

"How many?" whispered the balloonist doubtfully.

"As many as I can," said Sharn-igon. "At least one. No, two. Two for you, and as many as I can for me."

"Three for me. The three who come to this place and cause me pain."

"All right, yes, three," cried Sharn-igon. "Anything you like! But do quickly, before Poison Ghosts come back!"

Hours later, at almost the last of his strength, Sharn-igon staggered into a Krinpit village. It was not his own. He had seen the sounds of it on the horizon for a long time, but he was so weak and filled with pain that it had taken him longer to crawl the distance than the tiniest backling. "Sharn-igon, Sharn-igon, Sharn-igon," he called as he approached the alien Krinpit. "Am not of your place. Sharn-igon, Sharn-igon!"

A gravid female scuttled past him. She moved slowly because she was near her time, but she ignored his presence.

That did not surprise Sharn-igon. It was what he had expected. Indeed, each lurching step into the alien village was harder for him than the one before, and he was a professional empathizer. "Sharn-igon," he called bravely. "I would speak to one among you, although I am not of this place."

There was no answer, of course. It would not be easy to make contact. Each village was culturally as well as geographically isolated from every other. They did not fight. But they did not interact. If a party of Krinpit from one village chanced upon an individual or a party from another, they depersonalized each other. One Krinpit might push another from a different village out of the way. Two alien Krinpit might each take an end of a many-tree trunk that was barring their mutual way. Both would lift. Neither would address the other.

Genetically the villages were not isolated. The seedlings dropped from their he-father's backs when they were ripe to do so, wherever they might be. If they chanced to be near an alien village when they did—and if they were lucky enough to make their way to it without becoming food for a Ghost Below or any other marauder—they were accepted there as readily as any autochthon. But adults never did such a thing.

On the other hand, an adult had never found himself in Sharn-igon's position—until now.

"Sharn-igon, Sharn-igon," he called over and over, and at last a he-mother crept toward him. It did not speak directly to him, but it did not retreat, either. As it moved, it softly made the sound of its name: Tsharr-p'fleng.

"Have had good Ring-Greeting, alien brother?" Sharn-igon asked politely.

No answer, except that the sound of the stranger's name grew a trifle louder and more assured.

"Am not of this place," Sharn-igon acknowledged. "Most unpleasant for me to be here. Am aware is unpleasant also for you. However, must speak with you."

Agitatedly the other Krinpit scratched and thumped its name for a moment and then managed to speak. "Why you here, Sharn-igon?"

He collapsed on the knees of his forelegs. "Must have food," he said. The balloonist had been so very thin and frail that he made only half a meal, and of course Sharn-igon had been careful not to eat any part of the Poison Ghosts. He was not sure he had succeeded in killing all three, but two at least were certain, and the other would be a long time recovering. That settled the score for the balloonist.

But not for Cheee-pruitt.

If Sharn-igon had not been a professional empathist he could not have broken through the barriers between villages. As it was, it took much time and all of his persuasion; but at the end of it Tsharr-p'fleng helped him to a dwelling pen and ministered to his needs.

Sharn-igon devoured the crabrat they brought him while Tsharr-p'fleng engaged in agitated conversation with others of the village just outside the wall. Then they came in and ranged themselves around Sharn-igon, listening to him eat. He ignored their polite scratches of curiosity and concern until every morsel was gone. Then he pushed away the splintered carapace and spoke.

"Poison Ghosts killed my he-wife and did not eat him."

A flickering sound of disgust.

"They captured me and held me in a place without doors. They removed my backlings and took them away. I do not think they were eaten, but I have not heard them since."

Brighter sounds—disgust mixed with sympathy and anger.

"Moreover, they have also captured Ghosts Above and Ghosts Below and many of the lesser living things, and have eaten none of them. I therefore killed three of the Poison Ghosts. Intend to kill more. Are you back-mates with the Poison Ghosts?"

The he-mother rustled and spoke with contempt. "Not those! Their back-mates are the Ghosts Below."

Another said, "But Poison Ghosts have ways of killing. They have spoken to us in our language and told us to beware of them, lest they kill us."

"Beware of what? What did they tell you to do?"

"Only to refrain from harming any of them, for then they will kill all in our village."

Sharn-igon said, "The Poison Ghosts do not speak truth. Listen! They say they come from another world, like stars in sky. What are these stars?"

"They say they are like heat from sky," muttered the other.

"Have felt heat from sky. Have felt no heat from these other stars. I hear nothing from them. No matter how loud I shout, hear no echo from any of them."

"We have said these things ourselves," said Tsharr-p'fleng slowly. "But we are afraid of the Poison Ghosts. They will kill us, without eating."

"They will; it is true," said Sharn-igon. He paused. Then he went on. "Unless we kill them first. Unless all of our villages together fall upon them and kill them, without eating."

·ELEVEN·

MARGE MENNINGER'S HAIR was no longer blond. The name on her passport was not Margie Menninger. According to her travel orders, she was now a major, en route to a new duty station; and although the orders authorized a delay en route, it was unlikely that the general who signed them had contemplated that it would be spent in Paris.

In the little room of her hotel she fidgeted over the so-called croissant and what passed for orange juice, and phoned down to the concierge to see if the message she was expecting had arrived.

"I regret it, Meez Bernardi, but there is nothing," sighed the concierge. Marge took another bite of the croissant and gave it up. France was nominally part of the Food Bloc—by the skin of its teeth, and by the relabeling of Algerian wine for export—but you couldn't prove it by what they gave you for breakfast.

She was tired of this room, with its leftover smells of *khef* and sexual athletics from its previous occupants. She wanted to move around and couldn't. And while she was fretting away time in this room, the Peep ships were going through pre-launch, the training of backup crews for the next Food Bloc mission was limping along without her, and God only knew what disasters were taking place in Washington and at the UN.

She abandoned the breakfast and dressed quickly. When she came downstairs, of course there was a message at the concierge's desk, on a flimsy blue slip of paper:

Miss Hester Bernardi will be picked up at 1500 hours for her appointment.

It had obviously been there all along. Margie did not bother to reprimand the concierge; she would take care of that at tipping time. She pushed her way out into the Rue Caumartin, deciding what to do next. Six hours to kill! And for the life of her she could not think of any productive use to make of them.

It was a warm, drizzly day. The stink of gasoline drenched the air over the Place de l'Opéra. Food Bloc or not, France was cozy with the Ay-rabs, as well as with the Peeps. That was another reason you could not trust the frogs, Margie thought darkly. One of her grandfathers had marched into this city in Wehrmacht gray, and the other, in the opposite direction a few years later, in American olive drab, and both of them had passed on to her their feelings about the French. They were inconstant allies and unreliable subjects, and the few who ever seemed to have any sense of national purpose usually wound up having their heads shaved or chopped by the many who did not. In Margie's view, the French were not a bit better than the English, the Spanish, the Italians, the Portuguese, the Asians, the Africans, the Latins—and about ninety percent of the Americans too, when you came right down to it.

But the immediate problem was not what was wrong with humanity, but what she could do with this day. There was only one answer. She could do the thing most American women came to Paris to do. She could shop.

She not only could shop, she must; it was the best way of avoiding attention. She not only must, she wanted to.

It was one of Margie's most closely guarded secrets that periodically she went on shopping binges, out of one store and into another, pricing fabric, trying on dresses, matching shoes with gowns. In her little Houston apartment there were two closets, plus half of what was meant to be a guest room, filled with her purchases. They were thrown jumbled onto shelves, pushed under a bed in their original store bags: sweaters she would never wear, material half-sewn into drapes that would never be hung. Her living room was spartan, and her bedroom was always immaculate, because you never knew who might drop in. But the secret rooms were part of the hidden personality of Margie Menninger. None of what she bought was very expensive. It was not because she was economical. She had unaccounted funds at her disposal, and the prices never mattered. But her taste was for quantity rather than quality. Periodically she would wage war against the overflow, and then for awhile Goodwill and the Salvation Army would fatten off her discards. But a week later the hoard would have grown again.

Margie did not bother with the tourist traps along the Champs Élysées or with the tucked-away boutiques. Her tastes were for stores like Printemps, Uniprix, and the Galeries Lafayette. The only fly in the ointment was that she could not buy anything. She could not carry it where she was going and did not want to attract attention by leaving it, so she tried on, and she priced, and for six hours she made the lives of a score of Parisian shopgirls a living hell. That didn't bother Margie Menninger at all. By the time the taxicab picked her up at her hotel, punctually on the tick of three o'clock, her good nature was restored. She leaned back against the hard plastic seat of the cab, ready for what was to come next.

The driver stopped at the Place Vendôme long enough for

another passenger to jump in. Behind tourist shades was the face of her father, which was no surprise to Margie.

"Bonjour, honey," he said. "I brought you your toy."

She took the camera he offered her and hefted it critically. It was heavier than it looked; she would have to be careful not to let anyone else pick it up.

"Don't try to take pictures with it," he said, "because it won't. Just hang it around your neck on the strap. Then, when you get where you're going"—he pushed the shutter lever, and the casing opened to reveal a dull metal object inside— "this is what you give your contact. Along with a hundred thousand petrodollars. They're in the carrying case."

"Thank you, poppa."

He twisted in the seat to look at her. "You're not going to tell your mother that I let you do this, are you?"

"Christ, no. She'd have a shit hemorrhage."

"And don't get caught," he added as an afterthought. "Your contact was one of Tam Gulsmit's best people, and he is going to be really ticked off when he finds out we turned him. How are things going at Camp Detrick?"

"Good shape, poppa. You get me the transport, I'll send some good people."

He nodded. "We've had a little lucky break," he offered. "The Peeps fired on one of our guys. No harm done, but it makes a nice incident."

"Didn't he fire back, for Christ's sake?"

"Not him! It was your old jailhouse buddy, the one from Bulgaria. As near as I can tell, he doesn't believe in the use of force. Anyway, he did exactly what I would have told him to do. He got the hell out of there and reported back to the UN peacekeeping force, and he had tapes and pictures to prove what he said." He peered out the window. They had crossed the Seine. Now they were creeping through heavy traffic in a working-class neighborhood. "This is where I get out. See you in Washington, love. And take care of yourself."

Early the next morning Margie was in Trieste. She was not Hester Bernardi anymore, but she wasn't Marge Menninger either. She was a sleepy Swiss-Italian housewife in a sweaty pantsuit, driving to the Yugoslav border in a rented Fiat electrocar with a crowd of other Sunday-morning shoppers looking for cheap vegetables and bargains in Yugoslavian kitchenware. Unlike them, she drove straight through to Zagreb, parked the car and took a bus to the capital.

When she reached Belgrade, the object her father had given her was at the bottom of a plastic shopping bag with an old sweater and a shabby pocketbook on top of it. And she had had very little sleep.

Margie could not have grown up in the household of Godfrey Menninger without learning the easy dialogue of espionage. In all the world, she was the only person with whom her father had always been open. First because she was too little to understand, and so he could speak freely in her presence. Then because she had to understand. When the PLO kidnapped her she had been terrified past the point a four-year-old can survive, and her father's patient explanations had been the only thing that let her make sense of the terror. And finally, because he trusted her to understand, always, that the grotesque and lethal things he did had a purpose. He never questioned that she shared that purpose. So she had grown up in an atmosphere of drops and liquidations and couriers and double agents, at the center of a web that stretched all around the world.

But now she was not at the center of the web; she was out where the risks were immense and the penalties drastic. She walked quickly down the busy streets, avoiding eye contact. The closet-sized shops had their doors open, and confusing smells came out of them: a knifelike aroma of roasting meat from a dressmaker's (when had she eaten last?), the sting of unwashed armpits from what seemed to be a costume-jewelry boutique. She crossed, dodging a tram, and saw the office she was looking for. The sign said Electrotek Münschen, and it was over a sweatshop where fat, huge men in T-shirts worked at belt-driven sewing machines.

She checked her watch. There was more than an hour before her first possible contact. The man she needed to meet was a short, slim Italian who would be wearing a football blazer with the name of the Skopje team. Of course, no one like that was in sight yet—even if he turned up for the first rendezvous, which her father had warned was unlikely.

Down the block there was a cluster of roofed sheds surrounding a gabled two-story building that looked like any American suburban town's leftover railroad station. A farmers' market? It seemed to be something like that. Margie pushed her way through crowds of women in babushkas and women in minifrocks, men in blue smocks carrying crates of pink new potatoes on their shoulders, and men with a child on each hand, studying counters of chocolates and jellies. It was a satisfyingly busy mob. She was not conspicuous there.

She was, however, hungry.

Strawberries seemed to be in season. Margie bought half a kilo and a bottle of Pepsi and found a seat on a stone balustrade next to an open suitcase full of screwdrivers and cast-aluminum socket wrenches. What Margie wanted most was a hamburger, but no one seemed to be selling anything like that. But others were eating strawberries, and Margie was confident she looked like any one of them, or at least, if not like them, like some housewife who might have stopped en route to any ordinary destination to refresh herself.

At two punctually she was back in front of Electrotek München, studying a Belgrade bus guide as instructed. No short, slim Italian appeared. Twice she caught snatches of words that seemed to be in English, but when she looked up from her bus guide and glanced casually in that direction, she could not tell which of the passersby had spoken. She pitched the bus guide into a corner sewer and walked angrily away. The second appointment was not until ten o'clock at one of the big old luxury hotels, and what in God's name was she going to do until then?

She had to keep moving. It was very hard to stroll for more than seven hours, however many Camparis and soda you are willing to stop and drink. God bless, she passed something that called itself, in Cyrillic letters, an Expres-Restoran, and when she realized that it was a cafeteria, one problem at least was solved. She pointed at something that looked like roast chicken and probably was, and with the mashed potatoes and bread that went with it, at least she was full. Full of time. She emptied herself of as much of it as she could: a stroll through the botanical gardens, a long window-shopping stroll down the Boulevard Marshal Tito. And then it began to rain. She retreated into a *bioskop* and watched a Czech comedy with Serbo-Croatian subtitles until nine. The only problem was staying awake; but when she got to the hotel there was a real problem. Ghelizzi did not show up there either.

By now she was almost dizzy with fatigue, her clothes were sweaty and rain-stained, and she was sure she was beginning to smell. Poppa had not really thought these arrangements through, she thought with some bitterness. It should have occurred to him that the waiters at the hotel bar would not fail to notice a sweaty, dirty foreign woman among all their marble and their string trios. If she had been a man, it might not have mattered. A man could have been checking out the hotel whores—the skinny, dark-at-the-roots blond playing solitaire by the fireplace, the plump one with the bright red hair who had left the aperitif lounge twice in one hour, with different men, and was back again, ready for the next. Margie refused another Campari and sent the waiter for a Turkish coffee. The next appointment was not until the following afternoon, and where would she sleep?

The whores had rooms. If she had been one of them . . .

The idea did not disturb Margie in any moral way, but it took only a second for her to discard it as impractical. Even if she had a room, the waiters would surely throw her out to protect the existing monopoly the first time she looked toward one of the solitary males. They were already looking at her with interest and beginning to take the cloths off some of the tables in the farther end of the room.

Margie picked up her coffee and moved to the table of the streaked blond. She spoke to her in English, confident that in a tourist hotel the girls would be fluent in the necessary words in any major language.

"How much for all night?" she asked.

The blond looked scandalized. "For yourself? How disgusting! I could not possibly do such a thing with a woman."

"Fifty dinars."

"One hundred."

"All right, one hundred. But I have very special tastes, and you must do exactly as I ask."

The blond looked skeptical, then shrugged and signaled the waiter. "First you must buy me a real Scotch whiskey while you explain what these tastes are. Then we will see."

In the morning Margie woke up refreshed. She used the whore's tiny shower to get clean, dressed quickly and paid the woman off with a smile.

"May I ask a question?" the whore offered, counting the money.

"I can't stop you from asking."

"This thing you had me do, simply rubbing your neck each time you woke until you fell asleep again? Is that truly satisfying to you?"

"You wouldn't believe how satisfying," smiled Margie. She strolled grandly out of the hotel, nodding politely to the local police in their baggy gray uniforms open at the neck, hands on the guns in the cardboard holsters. A few blocks down the boulevard took her to the London Cafe, and there, nursing a beer at one of the indoor tables, was the slim, short Italian wearing a Skopje football cap.

She sat down and ordered a coffee, then visited the

women's w.c. When she came back the Italian was gone. The bag she had left on her chair did not appear to be disturbed, but her exploring fingers told her the camera was gone, and in its place was a guide folder about the hovercraft cruise to the Iron Gorge.

She made her way back across the border the same way she had come. By the time she was in Trieste again and able to resume the identity of the Swiss-Italian housewife, she was fully restored. On the clamjet to Paris she locked herself in the toilet and studied the contents of the travel folder.

How Ghelizzi had come to be a person of trust in Sir Tam's army of spies was beyond her; he had not impressed her as being the sort of man one would repose faith in. But he had delivered the goods this time. The little device was on its way, and the complete file of secret tactran messages between Earth and the Fuel Bloc camp on Klong was in her hands in microfiche. Her father would be very proud.

·TWELVE·

What Ana Dimitrova had seen of the United States was what she had seen of most of the world: airports, hotel rooms, meeting halls, city streets. So at first she looked around with lively interest as the electrobus whined along an eight-lane superhighway toward the place she had been ordered to report to. So much open space, not even farmed! And contrarily, so many places lined up one after another as they passed through communities—places to eat, places to sleep, places to drink, places to buy gas. What prodigious devourers these Americans must be to keep them all flourishing!

More than half of her companions in the bus were Americans, and they were busy devouring, too, several smoking in flagrant disregard of the signs, a couple chewing gum, three in the back seat passing around a bottle in a brown paper bag. The army sergeant who had offered her part of a chocolate bar was now offering the Canadian agronomist woman some round hard candies with holes in them. Nan was making an effort to like the others because she surely would be seeing

a lot of them in training. It wasn't easy. One by one, each of
the American men had made friendly overtures to her which
turned in seconds into sexual ones. Even the Vietnamese
colonel, so tiny and delicate that she had sat down next to him
at first, thinking he was a woman, had begun to make personal
remarks in his beautiful high-pitched English. She had
changed seats six times so far and now resolutely sat staring
out the window even though she was no longer seeing anything. Such compulsive consumers—she could not help feeling that they seemed obliged to consume her as well.

She touched the tiny microfiche from Ahmed at the bottom
of her blouse pocket. She had no reader for it, but she needed
none. As always it was formal, not very rewarding, and extremely short:

> My dear Ana,
>
> I appreciate the letters you have been sending and think
> of you often.
>
> With great affection,
> Dulla

He could have spent a few P$ more, she thought resent-
fully, and then, as always, brought herself up sharply. Ahmed
was from a poor country. Even fiched and faxed, the cost per
square centimeter of a letter from Kungson to Earth was very
high. (But in her own letters she had poured money out like
water. (But she could not judge him; she had not had the life
experience of measuring every penny. (But it was not just the
economy of space and money—how much more he could
have said if he had chosen, in even fewer words!—it was the
economy of emotion that she begrudged.))) Three deep in
parentheses, she took her mind off Dulla and resolved to think
about more profitable subjects, and then realized the bus had
stopped.

Three uniformed Americans had entered by the driver's
seat. One of them gestured for silence and said to the bus at

large, "You people are welcome, and let's see some ID."

Craning her neck, Nan could see a barricade with two other soldiers standing by it. They were not at attention, but they were watching the bus quite carefully, and she observed that what had looked like a well-clipped hedge stretching away on both sides of the barrier had barbed wire inside it. How curious. They were treating this place as though it were some sort of military installation rather than a center for preparing scientists and support personnel for a peaceful expedition to Kungson. Big-power customs were so strange to her. When the MPs came to her, she handed her passport over and smiled at the tall black one who was studying it. He returned her look impassively.

"Name?"

Of course, it was right there, next to his thumb. "Ana Elena Dimitrova."

"Place of birth?"

"My place of birth? It is Marek, Bulgaria. That is a city south of Sofia, not far from the Yugoslavian border."

"Put your thumb here, please." She pressed against the little pad he extended to her and then on a square white card, which he tucked into her passport. "Your papers will be returned to you later," he said, and then unbent. "You like to dance? There's a nice group at the club tonight. Ask for me if you don't see me. Name's Leroy."

"Thank you, Leroy."

"See you later, honey." He winked and moved along. Ana found a tissue and wiped the ink off her thumb wonderingly. These Americans were even worse than Sir Tam—not just the Americans, she corrected herself, thinking of the Vietnamese colonel and his agile, tiny hands. Would it be like this always? Would it not be even worse when she was part of the small colony on Kungson and they were all living in each other's pockets anyway?

But at least then Ahmed would be somewhere near! In the wrong encampment, yes. But she would find a way to see him.

Let her just get on the same planet with him again, and they would be together! It made the whole ordeal seem worthwhile.

By the next day, not even that made it seem altogether attractive. She could not have attended Leroy's dance that night if she had wanted to. There was no time. Issue of new clothing: "You will wear these here fatigues at all times, except when instructed by your instructors." Assignment to quarters: "You will maintain cleanliness at all times. At all times all personal possessions are to be kept in your footlockers." Preliminary briefing: "You will fall out at oh six hundred hours for breakfast. From oh seven hundred to eleven hundred you will participate in your individual refresher courses of instruction in the application of your specialized skills on Klong. From twelve hundred to sixteen-thirty you will complete your survival course to teach you your survival skills for surviving in the environment of Klong. From eighteen hundred to lights out at twenty-two hundred you will conduct your personal affairs except when required to participate in additional refresher courses or survival instruction. Weekends? Who's the guy who wants to know about weekends? Oh, you. Well, there aren't any weekends here." By the time all that was finished it was nearly midnight, and then Ana dragged her suitcase to the tiny, bare room that had been assigned to her, coldly furnished like the showcase cell in a county jail, only to find out that her roommate was the Vietnamese colonel. Even here rank had its privilege. But Ana was having none of it, and so it was back to the billeting office and a good deal of argument, and by the time she was able to get to sleep in a new room with a female roommate it was nearly two.

Breakfast was discouragingly huge—eggs and sausage and cereal, and breads with jams and marmalades, and peanut butter in opened liter cans on every table—and for dessert they spent an hour receiving inoculations. None of them were painful, but from the grins and jokes of the medics Ana knew that they would be later on. And then she lined up with the other two dozen of her detachment in a wet, cold wind, and they were marched off to their various refresher courses in the application of their specialized skills. Ana's tiny group included the Canadian woman and two men unknown to her, and they wound through the camp streets, past a baseball field and a bowling alley, between barracks and anonymous buildings with armed guards patrolling before them, out into an open field half a kilometer square. In the center of it was a sort of tethered balloon shaped like a sausage, fifty meters long, with guards around the perimeter and three of them grouped before the entrance. There was a fence surrounding the whole thing, and more guards at the gate in the fence; and before any of them were permitted inside, they had to go through the same tedious business of checking IDs one more time.

Off to one side there was a tall chimney coupled to the main tent by a flexible plastic tube. The chimney roared. Though there was no smoke, the shimmering at the top showed that some very hot gases were boiling high into the air out of it. It did not seem to serve any function that Ana could guess. But then, neither did the weapons that all the permanent personnel carried. Who were they meant to be used against? What possible enemy threatened a training base for a scientific expedition which, after all, was in a sense the property of the entire world?

When she finally got through the gates and the guards, she found herself in a long, open shed covered with the opaque white plastic of the bubble. The atmosphere was damp and heavy, filled with strange smells, and the lighting was sultry red. At first she could see very little, but she was aware that people were moving about between rows of what seemed to be smaller, transparent bubbles. The lighting came from a bank of gas-glow tubes, all red, and there was not very much of it.

The guide who had brought her to this place was speaking to her. "Are you all right?"

"Yes, I think so. Why not?"

"Sometimes people can't stand the smell."

She sniffed gingerly: pepper and spice and jungle rot. "No, it is fine."

The Canadian woman said, "Everything sounds funny."

"There's positive pressure in the outer shell. Your ears probably popped a little. That's so that if there's any air leakage it will all be inward, not out, and of course the air from this chamber gets incinerated at fifteen hundred degrees as it is pumped out—maybe you saw the chimney."

"One has heard stories of dangerous diseases," Nan ventured.

"No. There aren't any. Oh, sure," the guide went on gloomily, "you can get killed around here. But that's allergies, not disease, and you've all had your shots for them. Dimitrova, you're for linguistics. You come with me; the rest of you stay right here till I get back."

He led her through the hothouselike room, past the rows of plastic bubbles. As her eyes became dark-adapted she could see that each of them contained some sort of specimen —mostly plants, and some of them were immense. One towered ten meters, nearly to the top of the shell. It looked like a giant cluster of ferns, and Ana marveled at the money that had been spent to transport that immense mass over the light-years. Apart from the outside roaring of the incinerator, the sounds of pumps, and the noises the people in the shell made, there were sounds she could not identify—a sort of faint, wailing, high-pitched song, and groaning, clattering noises. They came from where she was heading for. The guide said, "Welcome to our zoo."

And then she saw the balloonist.

She recognized it at once; there could not be another creature as strange as that anywhere in the universe! But it looked . . . damaged. It was tethered inside a cage. Its great bubble was throbbing but almost limp, sagging against the ground. She stared, fascinated, and saw that a flexible plastic coupling had been taped neatly to a hole in the gasbag, and the plastic line went to a cylinder of gas. A woman with a tape recorder was crouched by the cylinder, adjusting the gas valve as she listened to the balloonist's plaintive song.

No wonder the voice sounded so faint! He was operating at a fraction of normal pressure, far too little to let him fly, only enough to let him gasp a sobbing sort of song. The woman looked up and said, "You're Dimitrova? I'm Julia Arden, and this"—pointing at the balloonist—" is Shirley. She's singing about her childhood right now."

Ana shook hands courteously, staring at the sad, wrinkled little creature. Those sounds did not seem like language! She could not imagine understanding them, much less translating them, no matter how many times they halved her brain! She said doubtfully, "I will do my best, Mis Arden, but do you think you can really teach me to talk to that?"

"Me? Maybe not. I'll help, and so will the computers, but the one who's going to teach you is Shirley herself. She loves to sing to us. Poor thing. She doesn't have much else to do with her time, does she?"

Nan looked at the creature for a moment and then burst out, "No, but what a shame, really! Can you not see she is in pain?"

The other woman shrugged. "What do you want me to do about it?" Her tone was less hostile than defensive. "I don't suppose Shirley volunteered for this duty, but then, neither did I. Your job is learning her language, Dimitrova, and let's get on with it."

"But to see a creature in pain—"

Julia Arden laughed and then shook her head. "Sweetie, you only got here last night. Wait a day or two. Then you can talk to me about pain."

From 0700 to 1100 Ana Dimitrova stretched the muscles of her mind until she thought she would die of it, and from 1200 to 1630 she balanced the diet by doing the same to her body.

Julia Arden had been right. Within forty-eight hours Ana was an expert on pain. She woke up each morning with a hazy overcast of brightness that she knew was the foretaste of migraine. She went to bed each night with so many aches, throbs, and bruises that it took all the will she had to refrain from swallowing the pills they had given her. She could not afford pills. She needed her mind alert, even while she slept, because sleeping was only another kind of study for Ana, with the taped calls of the balloonists murmuring under her pillow all night long.

The headaches, all right—they were something she was used to. Worse than that, the shots were producing their effect. Her skin was covered with little blisters and bumps, some that itched, some that were tender, some downright painful every moment of time. Not just pain. She wheezed and coughed. Her eyes ran uninterruptedly, and so did her nose. She was not alone; everyone in her group was having the same reaction to the allergy shots. If this was the prophylaxis, what could the illness itself be like? And then she saw the holos of the unfortunate Peeps who had died of their reactions before the countermeasures had been developed, and they defined for her the difference between prophylaxis and reality. It was not comforting to her. It was terrifying! How had Ahmed fared in all this? He had said nothing in his letters, but perhaps he was only being brave.

And every afternoon—feel well, feel ill, no matter—there she was out on the exercise field. Push-ups and five-hundred-meter runs, obstacle courses and rope climbing. Her hands were raw, then blistered, then calloused. Even through the coveralls her knees were scraped bloody. Everywhere on arms and legs where there was not a pimple or a blister, there was a bruise.

To be sure, she scolded herself, for all of this there was a clear purpose! Kungson was no picnic dell; it was a place of strange and perhaps lethal dangers. These measures, however brutal, were only to help her meet those dangers and conquer them. If she had not volunteered for the job, she had also not refused it when offered.

And finally, the most potent argument of all. It was the way to Ahmed. So she did her best all the time and was secretly proud of the fact that some of the others were doing less well than she. The tiny Vietnamese colonel, Nguyen Dao Tree, fell in a heap from the knotted ropes one afternoon and was taken to hospital. (He was back the next day, limping but game.) One woman, an older one, perhaps almost forty, fell flat on her face halfway up a rocky hill; she was taken away too, and she did not return.

One made quick friendships in such a place. She learned to call the colonel "Guy" and to respect his quick mind and sense of humor. She learned, too, to avoid being alone with him or with the sergeant, Sweggert—or indeed with any of the men, all of whom seemed to possess special reserves of strength when in the presence of an attractive female. Or an unattractive one. Her roommate, Corporal Elena Kristianides, was certainly not pretty, but more than once Nan staggered back to find the door locked and sounds of faint moans and giggles inside. When at last admitted, she always said forgivingly, "Please, it is all right, Kris. Do not speak of it." But it was not all right. She needed her sleep! Why didn't they need it too?

As days became weeks the fatigue lessened, the bruises healed, the reactions to the antiallergens diminished. The headaches stayed the same, but Nan was used to them, and she learned to take part in the friendly chatter in the mess hall. Always there were such stories! They were going to Kungson on a one-way trip and were expected to breed there and raise a new race of humans. They were not going to Kungson at all, but to a new planet, not yet announced or even named. They were not going into space at all. They were going to be parachuted onto the Scottish coast to commandeer the oil refineries. They were going to Antarctica, which was going to become a new Food Bloc colony, since a process had been discovered for melting the ice cap. At first Ana was frightened by such stories, then amused, then bored. She began making up stories of her own and found them as quickly passed along as any other. But some of the stories seemed true. Even some terrible ones: an unexplained accident in space that had destroyed the Peeps' resupply ships and even their tachyon-transit satellite itself. She let herself be late for dinner that night to listen to the evening news; sure enough, it was official. How terrifying! What would it mean to Ahmed? But then the news went on to say that the expeditions of the Fuel and Food blocs had offered help to the expedition of the People's Republics, and with her heart full, Ana hurried to the dining room, demanded attention, and proposed that they all sign a letter of sympathy and good wishes to their colleagues of the People's Bloc. The faces all turned to her, then whispered among themselves, half-embarrassed, but in the long run they let her write the letter, and they all signed. The next afternoon her training supervisor even excused her early to carry the document to the office of the camp commandant. He listened to her blankly, read the document three times, and then promised to send it through channels. At dinner that night she reported glowingly what had happened, but her news was drowned in other news. There were three new stories. First, that they were to receive a large shipment of new trainees the next day. Second, that a date had been set for their flight to Kungson, less than three weeks in the future. And third, contradictorily, that the whole project was about to be canceled.

Such stories! Nan stood up angrily, rapping her fork against her thick chinaware cup. "How can you all believe this nonsense?" she demanded. "How can all of these be true at once?" But not many of the others were paying attention, and she felt a tug at her elbow.

It was the colonel, who had, as he often did, squeezed in between Ana and her roommate at the table in order to try his fortunes one more time. "Sweet, beautiful Ana," he said, "don't make a fool of yourself. I know something of these stories, and they are all true."

That one of them was true was proved the next morning. Sixty-five more persons arrived at the base, and Ana knew one of them! It was the blond woman who was Godfrey Menninger's daughter.

Of course, everything was turned topsy-turvy. All of the billeting accommodations were changed to make room for the new arrivals—no, not for that reason alone, Ana realized, because most of the new ones, and quite a few of the old ones, were housed in another barracks half a kilometer away. Nan lost her WAC corporal roommate and feared at once that she would get Colonel Guy back again. But that did not happen. He went to the other barracks, and Nan was moved in with the Canadian woman, whose specialty seemed to be growing food crops in unusual circumstances. Marge Menninger caught sight of Nan in the crowd and waved to her. But they had no chance to speak—not that Ana had any particular reason to want to speak to the American, anyway—and in all the confusion, she was nearly an hour late for her morning session with the female balloonist.

The creature was no longer a specimen to Ana. She was a friend. Into the cognitive half of Ana's brain the songs of the balloonists had poured. In the first day she had learned to understand a few simple phrases, in a week to communicate abstract thoughts; now she was almost fluent. Ana had never thought of herself as having any kind of a singing voice, but the balloonist was not critical. They sang to each other for hours on end, and more and more Shirley's songs were sad and despairing, and sometimes even disconnected. She was, she told Ana, the last survivor of the dozen or more of her species who had been wrenched from Kungson and hurled to this inhospitable place. She did not expect to live much longer. She sang to Ana of the sweetness of warm pollen in a damp cloud, of the hot, stinging sadness of egg-spraying, of the communal joy of the flock in chorus. She told Ana that she would never sing in the flock again. She was thrice right. She would not have dared sing with her voice so pitifully harsh and weak because the gas pump gave her only faltering tones. She had no chance of being returned to Kungson. And she knew death was near.

Two days later she was dead. Ana arrived at the zoo to find her cage empty and Julia Arden supervising the sterilization of its parts.

"Don't take on," she advised gruffly. "You've learned all you need to know."

"It is not for the learning that I weep. It is because I have lost someone dear."

"Christ. Get out of here, Dimitrova. How did they let a jerk like you into this project in the first place? Crying over a dead fartbag and sending love letters to the Peeps—you're really out of it!"

Ana marched back to the barracks, threw herself down on her cot, and allowed herself to weep as she had not done in months—for Shirley, for Ahmed, for the world, and for herself. "Out of it" described her feelings exactly. How had everything become so hideous and complex?

That afternoon in the exercise field was an ordeal. The physical strain was no longer a real problem, but for some days now the "exercises" had taken a new turn. All of them, her own original detachment as well as the new arrivals, had been working less to strengthen their muscles and reflexes than to learn to handle unfamiliar equipment—unfamiliar to Ana, at least. She observed that all of the new people, and some of the old, had obviously had experience with it already. Such equipment! Heavy hoses like water cannon, backpack tanks and nozzles like flamethrowers, lasers, even grenade launchers. For what grotesque purpose was all this intended? Tight-lipped, Ana did as she was told. Repeatedly she found herself in difficulties and had to be bailed out by one of the others. The colonel saved her from incinerating herself with a flamethrower, and Sergeant Sweggert had to rescue her when the recoil of her water cannon knocked her off her feet.

"Please do not concern yourself," she gasped furiously, pulling herself erect and reaching once more for the hose. "I am quite all right."

"Hell you are," he said amiably. "Lean into it more, honey, you hear? It doesn't take muscle, just a little brains."

"I do not agree."

He shook his head. "Why do you get so uptight, Annie?"

"I do not like being trained in the use of weapons!"

"What weapons?" He grinned at her. "Don't you know this stuff is only to use against vermin? Colonel Menninger spelled it all out for us. We don't want to kill any sentients; that's against the law, and besides, we'll all get our asses in a crack. But all the intelligent ones got little cousins, crabrats and airsharks and things that dig around in the dirt and come out and chew your ass off. *Those* are what we're going to use this stuff for."

"In any event," said Ana, "I do not require assistance from you, sergeant—even if I believed you, or your Colonel Menninger, which I do not."

Sweggert looked past her and pursed his lips. "Hello, there, colonel," he said. "We was just talking about you."

"So I noticed," said Margie Menninger's voice. Ana turned slowly, and there she was. Looking, Ana observed without regret, quite poorly. The shots were having their way with her; her face was broken out in cerise blotches, her eyes were red and running, and her hair showed dark roots. "Get on with it, sergeant," she said. "Dimitrova, see me in my room after chow."

She turned away and raised her voice. "All right, all of you," she cried. "Get your asses down! Let's see how you crawl!"

Rebelliously Ana dropped to the ground and practiced the way of worming herself across an open field that she had learned the day before. These were infantry tactics! What nonsense for a scientific expedition! She conserved her anger carefully, and it lasted her the rest of the afternoon, through dinner, and right up to the moment she knocked on Menninger's door in that other barracks halfway across the base.

"Come in." Lt. Col. Menninger was sitting at a desk in a white, fluffy dressing gown, rimless granny glasses on her nose, a half-eaten dinner tray pushed to one side. She looked up from some papers and said, "Take a seat, Ana. Do you smoke? Would you like a drink?"

The angry fires inside Ana banked themselves. But they were still ready to blaze out. "No, thank you," she said, in general, to all.

Margie stood up and poured herself a scant shot of whiskey. She would have preferred marijuana, but she did not care to share a joint with this Bulgarian. She sipped a centimeter off the top of the drink and said, "Personal question. What have you got against Sweggert?"

"I have nothing against Sergeant Sweggert. I simply do not care to make love with him."

"What are you, Dimitrova, some maximum women's libber? You don't have to ball him on the parade ground. Just let him give you a hand when he wants to."

"Colonel Menninger," Ana said precisely, "are you ordering me to encourage his sexual overtures so that I can complete the obstacle course more readily?"

"I am not ordering you to do diddly-shit, Dimitrova. What is it with you? Sweggert comes on to everything with a hole in it. It's his nature. He comes on to me, too. I could put the son of a bitch in Leavenworth for the places his hands have been on the drill field. But I won't, because he's a good sol — Because he's essentially a good person. He'll help you if you let him. You can always tell him to fuck off later on."

"This I consider immoral, Colonel Menninger."

Margie finished her drink and poured half of another. "You're not too happy here, are you, Ana?"

"That is correct, Mis Menninger. I did not ask for this assignment."

"I did."

"Yes, no doubt, perhaps you did, but I—"

"No, that's not what I mean. I asked for it for myself, but I also asked for it for you. I picked you out by name, Ana, and it took hell's own conniving to make the Bulgarians turn you loose. They think you're pretty great at translating." She tossed down the rest of the drink and took off her glasses. "Look, Ana, I need you. This project is important to me. It should be important to you, too, if you have a spark of patriotism in your body."

"Patriotism?"

"Loyalty, then," said Margie impatiently. "Loyalty to our bloc. I know we come from different countries, but we stand for the same thing."

Ana found herself more puzzled than angered by this strange American. She tried to sort her feelings out and express them exactly. "Bulgaria is my home," she began. "I love my home. The Food Bloc—that is a much more abstract thing, Mis Menninger. I understand that in a world of two hundred nations there must be alliances and that one owes one's allies some sort of allegiance, or at least courtesy. But I cannot say I feel loyalty. Not to the Food Bloc."

"To the whole human race then, honey," said Margie. "Don't you see it? You just said it for yourself—a world of two hundred nations. But Klong can be a world of *one* nation! No fighting. No spies. No cloak-and-dagger shit. Who colonized America?"

"What?" It took Ana a moment to realize she was supposed to answer the question. "Why—the English? Before them, the Dutch."

"And before them maybe the Italians and Spaniards, with Columbus, and maybe, for Christ's sake, anybody you like— the Vikings, the Polynesians, the Chinese. Who knows? But the people who live in America now are the *Americans*. And that's who's going to live on Klong in another generation or two. The Klongans. Or whatever they call themselves. A single race of human beings. Never mind where they come from here! They'll be all the same, all part of the same wonderful . . . well, dream. I don't mind calling it a dream. But you and I can make it come true, Ana. We can learn how to live on Klong. We can build a world without national barriers and without the kind of senseless competition and rapacity that have ruined this one. Do you know what it means to have a whole new world to start over on?"

Ana was silent. "I—I have had some thoughts of that sort myself," she admitted.

"Of course you have. *And I want to make it happen.* I want to lay the foundations for a world society that understands planning and conservation and cooperation. Do you know how much we're putting into this? *Four ships.* Nearly ninety people. Thirty-five tons of equipment. The invasion of Europe cost less than this one launch, and believe me, everybody involved is screaming. It costs too much. It upsets the Peeps. The Greasies will raise their prices. We need the resources to solve the problems of the cities. Half the Congress would like to call it off tomorrow—"

"One has heard rumors," Ana said cautiously, "that the launch may be canceled."

Margie hesitated, and a shadow crossed her face. "No," she corrected. "That will not happen, because it is too important. But that is why I asked for you, Ana. If we can send ninety people, they must be the best ninety people there are. And you are the best translator I could find." She reached out and touched Ana's sleeve. "Do you understand?"

Ana drew away as soon as she could without giving offense, her thoughts uncertain. "Y-yes," she said unwillingly, and then, "but, on the other hand, no. What you say is most persuasive, Mis Menninger, but what has it to do with the use of flamethrowers and other weapons? Are we to build this fine monolithic world by destroying everyone else?"

"Of course not, Ana!" cried Margie, with as much shock and revulsion in her voice as she knew how to put there. "I give you my word!"

There was a silence. "I see," said Ana at last. "You give me your word."

"What else would you have me do?"

Ana said thoughtfully, "One has so little contact with the rest of the world here. I would like very much an opportunity to discuss this with others. Perhaps with my own delegation at the United Nations?"

"Why not?" exclaimed Margie. She looked thoughtful for a moment and then nodded. "I'll tell you what. As soon as training's over we're all going to get three days off. I'm going to New York myself. Come with me. We'll eat some decent food, go to a few parties. And you can talk it over with anyone you like. Agreed?"

Ana hesitated. At last, unwillingly, she said, "All right, Mis Menninger. That sounds attractive." It did not, for many reasons, but as a just person Ana had to concede that it sounded at least fair.

"Fine, honey. Now, if you don't mind, I'm overdue for a long, hot bath."

Margie locked the door behind the Bulgarian woman and ran herself a tub with some satisfaction. What the stupid prunt didn't know was that she was leaving Camp Detrick direct for the launch pad. The next chance she would have to talk anything over with anybody would be on Klong, and there let her say whatever she liked.

But Ana Dimitrova was only one problem, and maybe the easiest to solve. "One has heard rumors that the launch may be canceled" indeed! If Dimitrova had heard them, then everybody had heard them, and maybe the rumors were close to being true.

Margie allowed herself five minutes of luxurious soaking in the tub. When she got out she draped a towel around her body, not from modesty but from distaste; the shots had raised angry red welts all over her skin, and even with the ointment and the pills they itched. She did not want to be seen like that. Certainly not by the senator. It was bad advertising for the merchandise.

As she was dialing Adrian Lenz's private number she looked at herself in the mirror, frowned, and switched to voice only. "Hello, honey," she said as soon as he was on the line. "I'm sorry there's no picture, but this place doesn't have all mod. cons., and anyway"—she giggled—"I don't have any clothes on."

"Hello, Margie." Senator Lenz's voice was neutral. It was the sort of tone one uses to a brother-in-law or an airport security guard; it said, I acknowledge there is a relationship between us, but don't push it. "I assume you're calling me about your proposed new launch."

"Just 'proposed,' Adrian? You voted for it three weeks ago."

"I know my own voting record, Margie."

"Of course you do, Adrian. Listen, I didn't call you up to quarrel with you."

"No, you didn't," said the senator. "You called me up to try to keep me in line. I was pretty sure you'd call. I'm even pretty sure of what you're going to say. You're going to tell me that we've got a hell of a big investment in Klong now and if we don't nourish it the whole thing might go down the tube."

"Something like that, senator," Marge Menninger said reluctantly.

"I was sure of it. You know, we've heard those arguments before. Every time the DoD wants something outrageous they start by asking some piss-ant amount as a 'study grant.' Then a little more because the study showed some really promising idea. Then some more because, gosh, senator, we've gone this far, let's not waste it. And then, the next thing you know, we've got some stupid new missile or antiballistic defense system or nuclear bomber. Not because any sensible person wants it, but because there was no place to stop. Well, Margie, maybe this is the place to stop Klong. Three days from now there's a committee meeting. I don't know which way I'm going to vote, because I don't have all the information yet. But I'm not making any promises."

Margie kept the disappointment out of her voice, but she was less successful with the anger. "This project means a hell of a lot to me, Adrian."

"Don't you think I know it? Listen, Margie, this is an open line, but I thought you might be interested in something. I've got tomorrow's early edition of the *Herald* here, and there's a story from Peiping. 'Authoritative sources' say that repair crews at their tactran satellite have definite evidence that the explosion which destroyed the satellite and two transport ships was of suspicious origin."

"I watch the news, Adrian. I saw that. And there was another story, too, that said that dissident elements within the People's Republics were thought to be responsible."

The senator was silent. Margie would have given a lot to have seen the expression on his face just then, even at the cost of revealing the sorry condition of her own, and her hand reached out to restore the vision circuit to the call. But then the senator said, "I guess that's all we should say under the circumstances, Margie. I agree with you about one thing. You've gotten us into this pretty deep." And he broke the connection.

Margie sat thoughtfully blow-drying her hair for the next ten minutes, while her mind raced. Then she picked up the phone and dialed the orderly room. "Colonel Menninger here," she said. "Notify the training officer that I will not be present for tomorrow's formations, and have transportation ready for me at oh eight hundred. I need to go to New York."

"Yes, ma'am," said the OD. He was not surprised. All members of the project were restricted to the base, and the orders said there were no exceptions. But he knew who had written the orders.

Margie sat impatiently in the audience section of the Security Council chamber, waiting to be called. The delegation from Peru was explaining its recent vote at considerable length while the other nine members of the council waited in varying degrees of fury to explain each other's. The question seemed to have something to do with the territorial limits for fishing fleets. Normally Margie would have paid close attention, but her mind was a good many light-years away, on Klong. When the young black woman came to fetch her for her appointment she forgot about Peru before she had left the auditorium.

The woman conducted her to an inconspicuous room marked Authorized Personnel Only and held the door open for her without going, or looking, inside.

"Hello, poppa," said Margie as soon as the door was closed, turning her cheek to be kissed.

Her father did not kiss her. "You look like hell," he said, his voice flat and without affection. "What the fuck have you been teaching these 'colonists' of yours?"

Margie was caught off guard; it was not any of the questions she had expected from him, and certainly not what she had come to discuss. But she responded at once. "I've been teaching them survival tactics. Exactly what I said I was going to teach them."

"Take a look at these," he said, spreading a sheaf of holoflat pictures before her. "Art exhibits from Heir-of-Mao's private collection. Cost me quite a lot to get them."

Margie held one up, wiggling it slightly to get the effect of three-dimensional motion. "Makes me look fat," she said critically.

"These came out of the pouch of a courier in Ottawa. You recognize them, I guess. There's one of your boys throwing a grenade. And a nice shot of a flamethrower drill. And another one of a girl, I won't say who, stabbing what looks a hell of a lot like a Krinpit with what looks a hell of a lot like a sword."

"Oh, hell, poppa, that's no sword. It's just a flat, sharp knife. I got the idea from watching the stew chef opening up oysters at the Grand Central Clam Bar. And that Krinpit's only a dummy."

"Hell's shitfire, Margie! That's combat technique!"

"It's survival, dear," she corrected. "What do you think? The biggest and ugliest dangers our boys and girls are going to face are the Krinpit and the burrowers and the balloonists and, oh, yes, not to forget the Greasies and the Peeps. I'm not advocating killing, poppa, I'm just teaching them how to handle themselves if killing is going on." Her face clouded. "All the same, I wish I knew who took those pictures."

"You will," he said grimly. "But it doesn't matter; those are just copies. The Peeps have the originals, and Tam Gulsmit's probably got a set of his own by now, and the Peeps and the Greasies on Klong are going to hear about it by next week at the latest, and interexpedition friendship is over. Did you listen to the debate in the council?"

"What? Oh, sure—a little."

"You should have listened a lot. Peru has just extended its ocean borders to a thousand kilometers."

Margie squinted, perplexed. "What does that have to do with maybe some fighting on Klong?"

"Peru wouldn't do that without a lot of backing from somebody. They're nominally Food, sure, because of the anchovy catch. But they don't have a pot to piss in when the fish go deep, so they try to keep friendly with the other blocs."

"Which one?"

Her father pushed the corners of his eyes up. He did not do it because there was any risk of this supersensitive room being bugged; it was only a reflex not to speak the name of Heir-of-Mao unnecessarily.

Margie was silent for a moment while the card sorter in her

brain ordered her hierarchy of priorities. She came back to Number One. "Poppa," she said, "Peru can stick their anchovies in their ear, and I'm not going to lose sleep about which one of my people is a spy, and if we get a little scandal about combat training we'll survive it. None of it's going to matter in two or three weeks, because we'll be there, and that's what I came to see you about. Adrian Lenz is crawfishing. I need help, poppa. Don't let him cancel us out."

Her father leaned back in his chair. Margie was not used to seeing Godfrey Menninger looking old and tired, but that was how he looked now.

"Sweetie," he said heavily, "do you have any idea how much trouble we're in?"

"Of course, I do, poppa, but—"

"No, listen. I don't think you do. There's a tanker aground on Catalina Island today, with six hundred thousand tons of oil that isn't going to get to Long Beach. Wouldn't matter, normally. Southern California keeps plenty of reserves. But their reserves got diverted to your project, so they're low now. Unless they get that tanker afloat in forty-eight hours, Los Angeles is going to spend the weekend in a brownout. What do you think is going to be the public reaction to that?"

"Well, sure, a certain amount of shit is going to—"

He raised his hand. "And you saw the story in this morning's papers. The Peeps know their tactran satellite was deliberately destroyed."

"No, it wasn't! That was an accident. The bomb was just supposed to knock out the supply ship!"

"An accident in the commission of a crime becomes part of the crime, Margie."

"But they can't prove— I mean, there's no way in the world that they can pin it on me unless—"

She looked at her father. He shook his head. "The Italian isn't going to tell them anything. He's already been taken out."

So poor Guido was not going to live to spend his hundred

thousand petrodollars. "He gave good value," she said. "Look what you got out of his microfiches. You have proof that the Greasies set up their base where they did because they had seismic scans to show oil under it. That's against treaty right there."

"Don't be a child, Margie. What does 'proof' have to do with it? Sir Tam and the Slopies can't prove you handed Ghelizzi the bomb, but they don't have to prove, they only have to know. And they do. Peru proves it. Not to mention a few other little news items you may not have heard about yet, like the American embassy in Buenos Aires being fire-bombed this morning. That's a little message from Sir Tam or Heir-of-Mao, I would judge. What do you suppose the next message is going to be?"

Margie realized she had been scratching her blisters and made herself take her hand away. "Oh, shit," she said glumly, and thought hard while her father waited.

But really, she reflected, the basic rules were unchanged. The equation of power was utterly clear. No nation could afford to fight any other nation in the whole world anymore. Food, Fuel, and People each owned enough muscle to smash both the others flat, and all of them knew it. Worse than that. Even the tiniest nation had a minute sliver of muscle of its own, gift of the breeder reactors and the waste reclaimers. Not enough to matter in a global sense, no. But Peru could enforce its decisions if driven to. Ecuador could kill Washington or Miami, Denmark could destroy Glasgow, Indonesia could obliterate Melbourne. Fire-bombings and riots—well, what did they matter? There was a permanent simmer of border incidents and small-scale violence. Each year, a few thousand injured, a few scores or hundreds dead. But the lid never blew off, because everybody knew what would happen.

"Poppa," she said, "you know nobody can do anything *really* serious. The balance of power prohibits it."

"Wrong! The balance of power breaks down as soon as somebody makes a mistake. The Peeps made one when they fired rockets at our gasbags on Klong. *I* made one when I let you carry that bomb to Belgrade. It's time to pull the fuses, honey."

For the first time in her adult life, Margie Menninger felt real fear. "Poppa! Are you saying you're not going to help me with Lenz?"

"I'm saying more than that, Margie. I agree with him. I'm seeing the President tomorrow, and I'm going to tell him to scrap the launch."

"Poppa!"

He hesitated. "Honey, maybe later. After things quiet down—"

"Later's no good! You think the Peeps aren't going to reinforce as soon as they can get another satellite up there? And the Greasies? And—"

"It's settled, Margie."

She looked at him, appalled. This was the God Menninger that his whole agency knew and she had rarely seen. It wasn't her father she was looking at. It was a human being as implacable and determined as she herself had ever been, and with the accustomed support of a great deal of power to back his decisions up.

She said, "I can't change your mind." It wasn't a question, and he didn't give it an answer.

"Well," she said, "there's no reason for me to hang around here then, is there? Good-bye, poppa. Take care of yourself. I'll see you another time."

She did not look at him again as she got up, collected her brown leather officer's bag and her uniform cap, and let herself out.

If her father was as determined as she, the other side of the coin was that she was no less determined than he. She stopped in the visitors' lounge and entered a public phone booth to dial a local number.

The woman on the other end was a strikingly handsome human being, not a sex symbol but a work of art. "Why,

Marjorie," she said. "I thought you were off doing spy stuff for your father or something—Marjorie! What's the matter with your face?"

Marge felt her blotched chin. "Oh, that. That's just a reaction to some shots. Can I come over to see you?"

"Of course, lover. Right now?"

"Right this second, mom." Margie hung up the phone and hurried toward the elevators. But before she entered them she stopped in a ladies' room to check her makeup.

Marge Menninger's mother lived, among other places, in the residential tower section of one of New York City's tallest and most expensive skyscrapers. It was an old-fashioned place, built when energy was cheap, so that it made economic sense at that time to economize on insulation and rely on huge inputs of BTUs all winter long and continuous air conditioning all summer. It was one of the few that had not been at least partly rebuilt when oil reached P$300 a barrel, and it would have been ruinously expensive for most tenants—even most well-to-do tenants. The condominium apartments were no more expensive to buy than any others in a good neighborhood. But if you had to ask what the maintenance costs would be, you couldn't afford them. Alicia Howe and her present husband didn't have to ask.

The butler welcomed Margie. "How nice to see you, Miss Menninger! Will you be using your room this time?"

"Afraid not, Harvey. I just want to talk to mom."

"Yes, Miss Margie. She's expecting you."

As Alicia Howe rose to be kissed, she made a quick, all-seeing inventory of her daughter. Those awful splotches on her complexion! The clothes were passable enough, as army uniforms went, and thank heaven the child had been born with her father's smiling good looks. "You could lose a couple of kilos, lover," she said.

"I will, I promise. Mom, I want you to do me a favor."

"Of course, hon."

"Poppa's being a little difficult about something, and I need to go public. I want to hold a news conference."

Alicia Howe's husband owned a lot of television: three major-city outlets and large interests in a dozen satellite networks. "I'm sure one of Harold's people can help you out," she said slowly. "Should I ask what the problem is?"

"Mom, you shouldn't even know there's a problem."

Her mother sighed. She had learned to live with God Menninger's off-the-record life while they were married, but since the divorce she had hoped to be free of it. She never talked to her ex-husband. It wasn't that she disliked him—in her heart, she still thought him the most interesting, and by a long way the sexiest, of her men. But she could not cope with the knowledge that any little slip of the tongue from him to her, and from her to anyone, might bring catastrophic consequences to the world.

"Honey, I do have to tell Harold something."

"Oh, sure, mom. But not as a problem. What I want to talk about is Kl—Jem. The planet Jem. I'm going there, mom."

"Yes, of course, you told me that. In a year or two, maybe, when things settle down—"

"I want to settle them down, mom. I want the United States to send enough muscle up there to make it fit to live in. Fit for you to visit someday, if you want to. And I want to do it now. I'm supposed to leave in eighteen days."

"Margie! Really, Margie!"

"Don't take on, will you? It's what I want."

Alicia Howe had not been able to prevail against that argument in more than a dozen years. She had no hope of prevailing against it now. The thought of her daughter flinging herself through space to some terrible place where people died disgustingly was frightening. But Margie had demonstrated a capacity for taking care of herself.

"Well," she said, "I guess I can't send you to your room.

All right. You haven't told me what you want me to do."

"Ask Harold to get me onto one of his newsmaker programs. He'll know how to do it better than I can tell him. They're backing away from my planet, mom, cutting the funding, complaining about the problems. I want the public to know how important it is, and I want to be the one to tell them." She added strategically, "Poppa was right behind me on this at first, but now he's changed his mind. He wants to call the whole thing off."

"You mean you want to put the squeeze on your own father?"

"Exactly right."

Alicia Howe smiled. That part was sure to appeal to her current husband. She spread her hands resignedly and moved toward the phone. "I'll tell Harold what you want," she said.

Ana Dimitrova sat with her eyes closed in a broad, low room, elbows on a ring-shaped table, head in her hands, earphones on her head. Her lips were moving. Her head twitched from side to side as she tried to match the rhythms of the taped balloonist song that was coming over the headset. It was very difficult, in large part because it was not a balloonist's voice making the sounds. It was a Krinpit's. The tape had been made several weeks before, when Detrick's last surviving Krinpit had had no one left to talk to but Shirley, the one surviving balloonist.

But her name had not been Shirley. Her name, rather beautiful, had been *Mo'ahi'i Ba'alu'i*, which meant something like Sweetly Golden Cloud-Bearer. Krinpit rasps and tympani did not easily form the balloonist sounds. But Shirley had understood him—no, Ana corrected herself, Mo'ahi'i Ba'alu'i had understood him. Ana was determined to do the same, and so she played and replayed sections of the tape:

Ma'iya'a hi'i (these creatures unlike us) *hu'u ha'iye'i* (are vicious animals).

And Cloud-Bearer's response:

Ni'u'a mali'i na'a hu'iha. (They have killed my song).

Ana pushed the headphones off her ears and allowed herself to rub her eyes. The headaches were very bad tonight. And this awful room! Twenty headsets and tape-control panels before twenty identical hard-backed chairs, all around the ring. So bleak! So unsympathetic!

Unsympathetic? Ana clucked her lips at herself. That was one of the English language's booby-trap words: sympathetic, *simpatico.* They sounded so much alike. But they did not mean the same thing, and it was embarrassing to a translator of Ana's skills to fall into the blunder of confusing them. It proved she was too tired to work anymore this night, and so she switched off the tape decisively, hung the earphones on their hook, and stood up to go. She intended to wish a courteous good night to those few other eager project personnel who had shared her desire to put in overtime at the tape ring. But there weren't any. They had all left while she was concentrating.

It was nearly eleven o'clock! In six hours she would have to be getting out of bed!

Hurrying down the empty company street toward her room, Ana paused halfway, changed course, and entered the dayroom. Really, these headaches were too bad! But there was a dispensing machine in the dayroom, and sometimes one of the American soft drinks containing caffeine would constrict the blood vessels and reduce the thumping, thumping throb long enough for her to get to sleep.

But as she dropped a dollar into the machine and waited for the cup to fill, it seemed to her that coming here had been a mistake, after all. Such an ear-drubbing of noise! A dozen couples were dancing frenziedly to a stereo at one end of the room. At the other a young Oriental man had a guitar, and a group was singing with him, quite at cross-purposes to the music on the stereo. Quite uncaring. And even more noise came from the television alcove: a babble of excited voices, laughter. What could they be watching? She drifted closer to peer at the screen. Someone was lifting a pillowcase out of a sonic washer and exclaiming rapturously over its pristine shine. Were these people excited over a commercial?

"Oh, Nan," cried her roommate, elbowing toward her. "You missed it. She was *wonderful.*"

"What? What did I miss? Who was wonderful?"

"Lieutenant Colonel Menninger. It was really super. You know," confided the woman, "I never really liked her. But tonight she was just beautiful. She was on the six o'clock news. It was just a little person-to-person interview, like a follow-up to a story about Jem. I don't know why they picked her, but I'm glad they did! She said such wonderful things! She said Jem gave hope to all the unhappy people of the world. She said it was a planet where all the old hatreds could be forgotten. A place where—what did she say?—yes, a place where each child could elect a morality and an idea, and have the space and the freedom to live his life by it!"

Ana coughed Coca-Cola in a fine spray into her cupped hand. "Colonel Menninger said that?" she gasped.

"Yes, yes, Nan, and she said it beautifully. We were all touched. Even people like Stud Sweggert and Nguyen the Tryin' were *really* moved. I mean, they even kept their hands to themselves. And the newscaster said something about sending troops to Jem, and Colonel Menninger said, 'I'm a soldier myself. Every country has soldiers like me, and every one of us prays we'll never have anything to do. But on Jem we can do something useful! Something for peace, not for destruction. Please let us do it.'—What?"

Nan had been marveling to herself in Bulgarian. "No, no, please go on," she said.

"Well. And just now they repeated parts of it on the late report, and they said the public response has been incredible. Telegrams, phone calls. To the White House and the UN and the networks—I don't know where all."

Ana forgot her headache. "Perhaps I have been doing Colonel Menninger an injustice. Truly, I am amazed."

"Well, I am too! But she made me feel really good about what we're doing, and everyone's talking about it!"

And they were. Not only in the barracks dayroom. Senator Lenz's phones were ringing, and it was constituents urging him to make sure the heroes on Jem got support. Newsrooms around the country were watching the electronic tally of calls from the public: Jem, Jem! Spot pollsters were reporting great and growing public concern. God Menninger's phone rang only once, but the person on the other end was the President of the United States. When he hung up, Menninger's face was tense and stern, but then it relaxed and he broke into a smile. "Honey," he said to empty space, "damn your black heart, you do your old man proud."

·THIRTEEN·

FOR TWENTY KILOMETERS Charlie and his flock tried to follow the little biplane as it chugged and bounced through the sky of Jem. No use. The balloonists soared high, swooped low, found winds that carried them toward the heat pole, but never fast enough to keep up. Charlie sang a mournful farewell song into his radio as they turned away, and the sound penetrated even the noisy rattle of the little engine inside the plane. "Too much noise," shouted Kappelyushnikov cheerfully into Danny Dalehouse's ear. "Turn off, please?"

"Let me say good-bye first." Dalehouse sang into the tiny radio, then switched it off. Far behind and half a kilometer overhead, the flock bobbed acknowledgment. Dalehouse craned his neck to see forward, but the camp of the Greasies was of course nowhere yet in sight. They were flying almost directly toward the Heat Pole—"southeast" by the convention of considering the poles of rotation as north and south, however irrelevant that was to compasses and sextants—and it was uphill almost all the way. How foolish of the Greasies to locate their camp in the least hospitable part of the planet! But who could figure why the Greasies did things?

Kappelyushnikov leaned over and slapped him on the shoulder. "You wish to puke?" he called encouragingly, pointing over the side of the cockpit. Dalehouse shook his head. "Is all right, you know," Cappy went on. "Is little rough, yes. We are fighting winds, not making love to them like in balloon. But you have truly outstanding aircraft technician in charge!"

"I'm not complaining." And in fact, he had no reason to complain. The biplane was a technological marvel on Klong —on Jem, as they were supposed to call it now, he reminded himself. At least they were flying! The Greasy camp was hard to reach any other way. There were no cars on Jem, because no roads. Only a tracked vehicle could go very far, and even the Greasies did not have them to spare. Because, in their pigheaded way, the Greasies had camped ten kilometers from the nearest usable water, boats were out. You could fly there for this semi-summit meeting that was supposed to make everyone on Jem friends again. Or you could walk. And Dalehouse spared a thought of compassion for the poor, proud, pedestrian Peeps, who were no doubt doing just that somewhere below.

So just to be flying was a triumph, although he wished Cappy had not brought up the subject of airsickness. It was not so much the motion that was bothering him as the food they had been eating. With twenty-two more mouths to feed, the old catch-as-catch-can meal style was down the drain. Unfortunately, the new people had brought their appetites, but they had forgotten to pack a chef to satisfy them. The food was unbearable. No one dared complain. The person who bitched would be the next cook.

Still, the community was growing. The third resupply ship had brought a great deal! This sputtering little two-winged airplane, folded and stacked and foolish-looking, but demonstrably workable, because it was working. The little plutonium-powered machines and instruments that had given Morrissey sensors to study the Creepies in their tunnels under the ground and Dalehouse himself radios to pass on to Charlie. A new Argus orbiter to photograph clouds and help them predict the weather. Or at least to guess at it a little more accurately.

It had even helped them in their attempts to make contact with sentients. Sort of. Charlie was delighted with his crossbow and his radio. Jim Morrissey had taken another tack. He had used the new power auger to make three widely spaced holes along a Creepy burrow. The end holes held soft charges of explosives, the center one a hose connected to the exhaust of the auger's little gasoline putt-putt. When Morrissey blew the charges he sealed both ends of that section of the tunnel, and the carbon monoxide caught four burrowers before they could dig away. By then they were no good for Dalehouse's purposes, of course, but they were a joy to Morrissey.

Even further marvels were on their way. The third resupply had brought eight metric tons of equipment, but according to the tactran messages the next would bring nearly fifty, plus maybe a hundred additional personnel. It would be a city! The summons to the meeting at the Fuel camp had not only been a welcome tour of Jem, it had been a reprieve from the tedium of erecting tents to receive the reinforcements.

What the tactran had failed to say was just what the reinforcements would be used for. They certainly needed any number of specialists they didn't have. A *real* cook. A dentist. Some better-looking women. A better translator . . . reminded, Dalehouse leaned back to see how Harriet was faring behind him.

The translator was most uncomfortably curled up in a space no more than a meter square, and studded, at that, with bolts and levers that must have been tattooing Harriet's hips and ribs indelibly. If she had been anyone else Dalehouse would have thought of some friendly, commiserating remark. For Harriet he could find none. Her eyes were closed. Her expression registered resignation to the palpable injustice of being the smallest of the three of them, and thus the one to be squeezed into the tiny rear compartment.

"Getting close," Kappelyushnikov bawled in his ear.

Dalehouse leaned forward, rubbing at the glass as though the Jemman murk were on the inside rather than all around. There was nothing but maroon cloud—

Then the stark white rim of the Heat Pole glittered through a break. And something else. The clouds themselves were clearly bright. As the biplane tunneled out of the last of the cloud bank they were leaving, Dalehouse saw the cause before him.

"Jesu Crist!" cried Kappelyushnikov. "Have they no shame?"

The light was the Oily camp. It stood out on the horizon like a bonfire, penetrating Jem's dour maroon murk with beacons, lighted windows—my God, Dalehouse marveled, even streetlamps! It was no longer an expeditionary camp. It looked like a small town.

The vertical beacon dipped and swept across the biplane to acknowledge their approach, then courteously away so that they were not dazzled. Kappelyushnikov muttered inaudibly into his radio mouthpiece, listened for a moment, and then began to circle.

"What's the matter?" Dalehouse demanded.

"Is nothing the matter, only we are no longer in hurry," said the pilot. "Peeps will be unavoidably one hour detained, so let us study this miracle before landing on it."

A miracle it very nearly was. There were only about forty people in the Greasy camp, but they seemed to have almost that many buildings. *Buildings,* not tents or plastic huts. What had they made them out of? And what buildings! Some were barracks, some seemed individual bungalows. One looked more like a tenth-size copy of the Eiffel Tower than like a structure one could live or work in. Another was a good twenty-five meters in length. And—what was that curious, shallow, round petaled cone on the far side of the camp? It seemed to be constructed of bent strips of shiny metal arrayed around a central black cylinder. Could it be a solar generator? If so, it was almost megawatt size! And—that stubby tower with the horizontally rotating fan. Wasn't that the exhaust from an *air conditioner*?

Harriet had roused herself and was leaning forward over Dalehouse's shoulder to see. Her breath buzzed annoyingly in his ear as she said sternly, "That is a . . . *lascivious* waste!"

"Oh, yes, dear Gasha!" cried the pilot. "How wonderful would be if we, too, could afford one!"

Over the rattles and groans that came from his Krinpit escort, Ahmed Dulla heard a sputtering distant sound. "Put me down. Wait. Try to be quiet," he called peevishly in the mixture of Urdu and their own language that made communication possible between them. Or sometimes did. He lowered himself from the litter in which they had been carrying him and climbed onto a knee of a many-tree, pushing aside the pinkly glowing fronds to stare around the sky. A tiny two-winged aircraft was chuttering along just below cloud level. "So. Another triumph of technology arrives," he said.

The Krinpit, Jorrn-fteet, reared back to study him more carefully, its stubby claws waving. "Your meaning is not loud," it rattled.

"No matter. Let us move on." Dulla was in no mood for a nice chat with these grossly hypertrophied bugs, however useful they were to him. "Go carry the litter and my bag; I will walk," he ordered. "It is too steep here for riding." They were climbing from the shallow valley of the river now, up through the last of the forested slopes onto the dry highlands. The vegetation began to change from many-trees and ferns to things like succulents, stubby barrels with glowing, bright red, luminous buttons. Dulla looked at them all with distaste. Study the plants, find new products; it is in this way that my fathers became independent of the machines of the outside world. So Feng Hua-tse had advised before he left; but Dulla was an astrophysicist, not an herbal healer, and he had no intention of following the fool's instructions.

There was no overhang between him and the sky now, and he could see the little biplane circling, far off toward the bright white line of the Heat Pole. So. The Greasies had their helicopter, the Fats now had a plane, and what did the representative of the People's Republics have to take him to this meeting? A litter carried by animals that looked like squashed crustaceans. Dulla fumed. If Feng had listened to him, they would have insisted that the three-party meeting be held at their own camp. So they would have been spared this humiliation of arriving on a plastic frame carried by creatures out of some children's nonsense fable—if not the humiliation of exposing to the Fats and the Oilies the meanness of their encampment. What a disaster! And all Feng's fault, or Heir-of-Mao's. The expedition should have been properly supplied and reinforced in the first place, but leave it to the Chinamen to hoard coppers to the ruination of the project.

Without warning the Krinpit stopped, and Dulla, lost in his thoughts, almost tripped over them. "What, what?" he complained. "Why are you standing here?"

"A very loud thing moves quickly," rattled Jorrn-fteet.

"I do not hear anything." But now that he was awakened from his reverie he did see something, a swell of dust behind the hills. As he watched, a machine topped the rise, coming toward him. It was still a kilometer away, but it looked like a half-track.

"Another triumph of conspicuous waste," sneered Dulla. "How dare they come for me, as though I could not make the journey by myself?" The Krinpit rattled inquiringly, and he added, "Never mind. Put down the litter; I will carry my knapsack myself now. Hide yourselves. I do not want the Greasies to see you."

But the words conveyed no meaning to the Krinpit. A Krinpit could never hide from another Krinpit as long as they were close enough to hear each other. Dulla struggled to explain. "Go back to the place behind the hill. The Greasies will not hear you there. I will return in the space it took us to come up from the river." He was not sure they understood that, either. The Krinpit had a clear sense of time, but the vocabulary of terms to mark its units did not map well from one language based on a diurnal cycle to another which had evolved on a planet without easy temporal reference points. But they lurched away obediently, and Dulla walked steadily toward the approaching half-track.

The driver was a Kuwaiti, apparently a translator, because he greeted Dulla in flawless Urdu. "Would you like a lift?" he called. "Jump in!"

"You are very courteous," smiled Dulla. "Indeed, it is a little warm for strolling today." But it was not courtesy at all, he fumed internally, it was only more of their damnable arrogance! Ahmed Dulla was quite sure that he was the only person on Jem whose native language was Urdu, and here the Greasies had made sure they had someone who could speak to him! As though he himself were not already proficient in four other languages!

The time would come, he promised himself, when he would humble the ostentatious swine. So he rode up over the gullied hills toward the Greasy camp, chatting amiably with the Kuwaiti, remarking politely on the fine appearance of their camp, his face smiling and his heart swelling with rage.

The official host for the meeting was named Chesley Pontrefact, London-born but not of native roots that went many generations back. His skin was purplish brown and his hair white wool. Coded tactran messages had given Dulla a good deal of background on every member of the Greasy expeditions, as well as the Fats, and he knew that Pontrefact was an air vice-marshal and nominal commander of the Greasy expedition. But he also knew that real power belonged to one of the civilians from Saudi Arabia.

Pontrefact bustled about the long conference table (wood! shipped all the way from Earth!) offering drinks and smokes. "Brandy do you, Dr. Dalehouse?" he inquired solicitously. "And perhaps a Coca-Cola for you, sir? I'm afraid we don't have orange juice, but at least there's ice."

"Nothing, please," said Dulla, seething. Ice! "I suggest we begin our meeting, if that is convenient."

"Certainly, Dr. Dulla." Pontrefact sat down heavily at the head of the table and glanced inquiringly around. "Mind if I take the chair, just for form's sake?"

Dulla watched to see if any of the Fats were going to object and spoke a split second before they did. "Not at all, Marshal Pontrefact," he said warmly. "We are your guests." But one should show courtesy to guests, and what was this seating arrangement but a deliberate insult? Pontrefact at the head, two of his associates at the foot—the Kuwaiti translator and a woman who could be no one but the Saudi civilian who was the Greasies' decision maker. On one side of the table were all three of the Fats—Dalehouse, their Russian pilot, and their own translator; and on the other—only himself. How much more deliberately could they point out that he was alone and insignificant? He added diffidently, "Since we are all conversant, I believe, with English, perhaps we can dispense with the translators. It is an old saying of my people that the success of a conference is inversely proportional to the square of the number of participants."

Quickly, "I shall stay," said the Fats translator. Pontrefact raised his white-caterpillar eyebrows but said nothing; Dulla shrugged politely and gazed toward the chair, waiting for the proceedings to begin.

The Saudi whispered to the interpreter at some length. Across the table, Dalehouse hesitated, then got up to extend his hand to Dulla. "Good to see you looking fit, Ahmed," he said.

Dulla touched his hand minimally. "Thank you." He added grudgingly, "And thank you for assisting in returning me to my own camp. I have not had a chance to express my gratitude since."

"Glad to help. Anyway, it's good to see someone from your expedition—we don't see many of you, you know."

Dulla glared. Then, stiffly, "I have come a long way for this meeting. Can we not begin?"

"Oh, hell," said Pontrefact from the head of the table. "Look, mates, the whole reason for this meeting is to try to work together better. We know what a balls-up our masters have made at home. Shall we see if we can do a bit better here?"

Dulla said happily, "Please limit your observations to your own people." It was as he had suspected; the Greasies were going to insult everyone but themselves. Let this West Indian whose grandfather was a ticket collector on the London Underground make a fool of himself if he chose. Not of the People's Republics.

"But I'm in dead earnest, Dr. Dulla. We invited you here because it's clear we are all working at cross-purposes. Your own camp is in serious trouble, and we all know it. The Food people and our own lot are a bit better off, yes. But you don't have a proper doctor, do you, Dr. Dalehouse? Not to mention a few other things. And we can't be expected—that is, we don't have limitless resources either. Under the UN resolution we are all supposed to cooperate and divide the responsibilities. Particularly the science. We undertook the geology, and you can't say we haven't played fair about that. We've done a great deal."

"Indeed so," put in Kappelyushnikov blandly. "Is pure coincidence that most is in personal vicinity and relates primarily to fissionables and to salt domes."

"That is, to petroleum," Dulla agreed. "Yes, I think we are all aware of that, Marshal Pontrefact." How thoughtful of the Fats and the Greasies to begin quarreling among themselves so soon!

"Be that as it may," the chairman went on doggedly,

"there's a hell of a lot to be done here, and we can't do it all. Astronomy, for instance. We did orbit a satellite observatory, but—as I am sure you know—it ran into malfunctions. Let me show you something." He got up and moved to a likris screen on the wall. When he had fiddled with it for a moment the crystals sprang into varicolored light, showing some sort of graph. "You've seen our solar generator. This shows the solar input for our power plant. As you see, there are spikes in the curve. This may not seem important to you, but our generator is a precision instrument. It isn't going to do its job properly if the solar constant isn't, well, constant."

Dulla stared in black envy at the graph. That was what he was here for, after all—because he was a specialist in stellar studies! He hardly noticed when Dalehouse put in, "If Kung is acting up, it may mean more to us than a few wiggles in your power supply."

Pontrefact nodded. "Of course it may. We notified this to Herstmonceux-Greenwich with a copy of the tape. They're quite upset about it. Kung may be a variable star."

"Hardly," sneered Dulla. "It is known that a few flares are possible."

"But it is not known how many, or how big; and that's exactly what we need to know. What, if I may say, we confidently expected to know from the astronomical researches that were meant to be conducted by your expedition, Dr. Dulla."

Dulla exploded. "But this is too much! How can one practice astrophysics when one is hungry? And whose fault is that?"

"Certainly not ours, old chap," Pontrefact said indignantly.

"But someone blew up our ships, *old chap.* Someone killed thirty-four citizens of the People's Republics, old chap!"

"But that was—" Pontrefact stopped the sentence in mid-syllable. He made a visible effort to control his temper. "Be that as it may," he got out again, "the plain fact is the work's got to be done, and someone's got to do it. You have the instruments and we don't, at least not until proper telescopes arrive from Earth. We have the manpower, and you evidently don't."

"I beg your pardon. Allow me to inform you of my academic standing. I am director of the Planetology Institute at Zulfikar Ali Bhutto University and have graduate degrees in astrophysics from—"

"But no one's disputing your degrees, dear man, only your fitness to function. Let us send our own astronomer over. Better still, let Boyne airlift your equipment here, where there's better seeing—"

"Certainly not! Not either!"

"I really don't think that's quite fair, do you? We've certainly cooperated in providing food, for instance—"

"Such food! For your people, not for ours: all flour, hardly any rice."

Dalehouse said placatingly, "We'll turn up some rice for you if that's what you like."

"How gracious of you!" Dulla sneered.

"Now, wait a minute, Dulla. We've done our best for you —and we have a couple of complaints of our own, if you want to know. Like shooting at me!"

Dulla grimaced. "That was only Hua-tse's foolishness with fireworks. The People's Republics have already expressed their regrets."

"To whom? The dead balloonists?"

"Yes," sneered Dulla with exaggerated humility, "of course, it is so; we do apologize to your close friends, the comic gasbags. And to yours too, sir, the vermin who dig in the earth and whom you find so useful!"

"If you mean the Creeps," said Pontrefact, his control of his temper wearing thin, "at least we don't use them as litter bearers."

"No! You use them to help you exploit the mineral riches! Is it not true that there has been radiation disease among them?"

"No, it isn't! At least, not here. We did use a few to dig samples for us in other areas, and yes, they did encounter some radiation, but I must say that I resent the imputation that we are exploiting the natives."

"Oh, I am sure you would not do that, Marshal Pontrefact, especially as your own ancestors must have experienced so much of that from the other side, as it were."

"Now, look here, Dulla!"

But Pontrefact was interrupted by the Saudi woman, who said: "I think we should recess for lunch. We have much to discuss, and shouting at each other will not help. Let's resolve to try to do better in the afternoon."

But the afternoon session, if quieter, did not seem very productive to Danny Dalehouse. "At least we got a decent meal out of it," he said to Kappelyushnikov outside the longhouse where they had met.

"Is as ashes in my mouth," growled the Russian. "Oh, how many nice things they have here. Not just food."

That was not to be argued. Across from the meetinghouse a new building was going up. A tracked dumpster deposited a scoop of earth into a hopper; the man running it shoved a lever forward, there was a high-pitched whine, and moments later, the sides fell away and the operator lifted out a finished panel of hard brick. The trick was in adding something to the compacted earth as a stabilizer.

"And have you seen what's up on the hill?" asked Harriet with jealousy in her tone. On the slopes above the colony there were terraced rows of green seedlings. *Green!* The Greasies were using banks of incandescent plant lights to grow Terrestrial food!

"Feel like time when I was seventeen years," said Kappelyushnikov. "Kid sailplane pilot, winner of All-Region Height and Endurance Contest, fresh from Nizhniy Tagil, walking down Kalinin-Prospekt first time in life, and oh, my God, how overwhelming was Moscow! Trams, skyscrapers,

bookstores, restaurants." He pointed to the plasma column of
the solar generator, with its rosette of reflectors around it. "Is
daunting, dear friends. No wonder Greasies call us here to
issue orders of day. They have muscle to enforce!" He
shrugged, then grinned as they rounded the last barracks and
saw the little landing field. "Hoy! Boyne!" he shouted.
"Come say good-bye to country cousins!"

The Irish pilot hesitated, then came toward them. "Hello,"
he said noncommittally. "I've just been putting our friend
Dulla on a jeep on his way home."

"He didn't seem in a very good mood," Dalehouse observed.

The pilot grinned. "His feelings were hurt, I'd say. He
didn't want us to see that he was using Krinpit transportation
to get here. You didn't know that? They came up the river by
boat, and then the Krips carried him up eight or ten kilometers until we picked him up."

Harriet said spitefully, "He might have been in a better
mood if you hadn't gone out of your way to insult him, Dalehouse."

"Me? How?"

"He thought you were making a joke about the fact that so
few of the Peeps have survived. His face went all tight."

Dalehouse protested. "I didn't mean anything like that.
He's such a thorny son of a bitch."

"Forget," advised Kappelyushnikov. "He is such close
friend of cockroaches, let them worry about his feelings."

"Well, I don't understand that either, Cappy. The Krinpit
almost killed him."

"Then how is possible they become native bearers for fine
Pakistani sahib as he daringly marches through jungle?"

"I can explain that," Boyne said gloomily, "although I can't
say I like it. That first Krinpit you and I carried here, Dalehouse, the one that calls itself Sharn-igon? It's mad at all
human beings. Apparently its girlfriend, or actually I think it
was a boyfriend, died from the first contact with the Peeps,

and it just wants to get even. Only its idea of getting even seems to be to make as much trouble for as many human beings as it can. It's raised a hell of a fuss with the Krips near here; we can't make any contact with them at all. I guess it thinks the Peeps are pretty well screwed, so it's willing to help them screw the rest of us. Looks damn bad for the future, if you ask me."

He was walking along with them toward the airstrip, but his manner seemed reserved; he made no eye contact with any of them, and what he said was more of a monologue than a conversation.

Kappelyushnikov said placatingly, "Hey, Boyne, you pissed about something?"

"Me? Why should I be?" But Boyne still did not look at him.

Kappelyushnikov glanced at the others, then back to the pilot. "Hey, Boyne," he wheedled. "We two are members of great interstellar brotherhood of pilotry, should not be pissed at each other."

"Look, it's not you personally," said Boyne angrily. "I got my ass eaten out for lending you chaps the backhoe, not to mention talking a little more openly than I was supposed to about what we were doing here."

"But we're all in this together," Dalehouse put in. "It's like Pontrefact said at the meeting. We're supposed to share information."

"Oh, Ponty's got the right idea, but that's supposed to go both ways. You didn't see fit to mention some of your own little deeds, did you? Like arming the balloonists against the Krinpit?"

"We didn't! I mean, that's my own department, Boyne. We've given them a few simple weapons to protect themselves against the *ha'aye'i*, that's all."

"Well, they've been using them against everything they can catch. Not to mention that business with the Peeps' supply ship."

"That was an accident!" Dalehouse said.

"Sure it was. Same as it's an accident that your plane—" He hesitated, then closed his mouth.

"Come on, Boyne, what are you trying to say?" Dalehouse demanded.

"Nothing. Forget it." Boyne glanced back toward the camp, then said rapidly, "Look, this peace conference was a bust, right? Nothing got settled. And the way things are going— well, I've got a bad feeling. The local Krips are gassing our Creepies in their burrows every once in awhile—that's Peeps' doing, I suppose. The Peep ship gets blown up; you say it's an accident, but the gen says CIA. You're giving the Loonies weapons. And your plane—well, shit, man," he said, glaring at Kappelyushnikov. "I've got eyes. So right now I don't feel like having a heart-to-heart, all right? Maybe some other time. So, so long, and have a nice flight home." He nodded briskly and turned back to the Greasy base.

Kappelyushnikov broodingly watched him go. "I too have bad feeling," he said. "About dear friend and fellow pilot Boyne, too. Questions I would like to ask, but this is not good time."

"I'd like to know more about what they're using the Creepies for," Dalehouse agreed. "And frankly, that bit about our being responsible for the Peeps' accident is beginning to get under my skin. Do you think there's any possibility it could be true?"

Cappy regarded him thoughtfully. "You are very nice person, Danny," he said sadly. "Perhaps you do not wonder enough. Like, do you wonder why Greasies have landing strip when gillicopter lands anywhere?"

"That hadn't occurred to me," Dalehouse admitted.

"Occured to me," said the Russian. "Just like occurred to Boyne to wonder why strange little hatch dear Gasha rode on is in our plane. You and Gasha look at it, you say, 'Oh, what a nuisance. Cannot understand purpose.' But when pilot looks at it, Boyne or me, we say at once, 'Oh, how strange that aircraft designed for peaceful exploration has built-in bomb bay.' "

Thirty meters below the airstrip, Mother dr'Shee woke with the smell of cyanide in her splayed nose, too faint to be dangerous, too strong to ignore. The Shelled Devils were at it again.

She yipped peremptorily for the brood-member on duty. It turned out to be t'Weechr, the runt of the litter and the one the others saddled with the least attractive jobs—including, she realized justly, attending to the wants of the Mother when she first woke up. There were only seven in this present brood of hers, and all of them male, and none of them the size or the strength or the wit of their father. It was a loose and unsettling time, and it spoiled her temper.

"Food," she ordered harshly. "And drink. And someone to groom me while I am waiting."

T'Weechr said humbly, "There is no one but me, Brood Mother. I will be quick with the food and groom you while you eat."

"And why is there no one?"

"The New Devils are teaching, Brood Mother. All are commanded to be present."

"Tssheee." If dr'Shee had been a human, the sound would have been a grunt, written "Humph" for convenience's sake. But she was not actually displeased, merely fretful; and when t'Weechr returned it was not only with tubers and a shell of water, but there were even some fresh leaves and fruits from Above.

"Taken or given?" she demanded, sniffing them suspiciously.

"These were gifts of the New Devils, Brood Mother," the youth apologized.

"Tssheee." They were, however, tasty, and she was hungry. She defecated neatly into the shell when she was finished, and t'Weechr folded it closed.

"Is there any other service, Brood Mother?" he asked, licking a final strand of her fur into neatness.

"No. Be gone." He touched noses and wriggled away to deliver the package to the rotting rooms. The next brood would mix it with the planting mud and plaster it into the ceilings of the farm tunnels when they prepared the next crops. By then it would be well aged, and of great value in growing the tubers.

Runt or not, t'Weechr was a good child. She would miss him when the litter matured and scattered. And that time was not far off. At every awakening now, her dugs had been smaller and harder. The breeding males knew it, and every time she left her nest they wriggled close to touch her, nose to anus, testing to see how near she was to courtship. Only yesterday the male with the scarred leg had said, half-jesting, "What would you like next time, dr'Shee? Krinpit shell? A live Flying Devil? The head of a New Devil?"

"Your own head," she had said, half-irritated, half-flirtatious. He had snorted laughter through the spreading folds of his nose and crept away, but he would be back. It was not an unpleasing thought. Dr'Shee's brood-sister had mated with that one, two litters ago. A fine brood, three females! And the sister had said he was indefatigable at rut. Well. A proper courtship was a proper courtship, but she could not help hoping that he might turn out to be the male with the finest gift to lay before her.

Faint and distant vibrations in the earth set her whiskers to quivering. That was the New Devils, too. Time was when such tremors had meant only a particularly violent thunderstorm Above, or perhaps the crash of a falling many-tree. Now the New Devils scraped and shoved hillocks and boulders around at will, and the earth was no longer easy to her senses. As she moved around her chamber, sniffing and touching to make sure everything was in its place, it was touch and smell and taste that principally guided her. Sometimes her males had plastered bits of fungus and vegetation into the walls along with the secretions that made their tunnels hard and water-proof, and from the plant decay there was some faint glow. Dr'Shee appreciated the light but did not need it. For her people, eyes were almost a handicap, especially on their infrequent dashes to the Surface, when only the densest of clouds and worst of storms dimmed Kung's radiance enough for them to bear.

"Greeting, dr'Shee."

She sniffed in startlement and then recognized the female at the entrance to her chamber. "How are you, qr'Tshew? Come in, come in."

The other female entered, and dr'Shee said at once, "I will send for food."

"I have eaten," said qr'Tshew politely. "What lovely courtship gifts." She fondled dr'Shee's collection. Six breedings, six fine gifts: a hard thing stolen from the New Devils that no one understood; the leg of a crabrat—that had been her first gift, and the least worthy, but in some ways the most satisfying of her courtship gifts; even the claws of a balloonist. Every one had been stolen from the Surface itself, at great risk, and delivered to her at a cost. Few males survived more than two or three mad, half-blind dashes to the Surface to steal courtship gifts. The enemies were everywhere.

Manners satisfied, qr'Tshew came to the point. "The father of my last brood has died of a bad breathing," she said. "Also three young of other mothers."

"What a pity," said dr'Shee. She was not referring to the male, of course; once a male had achieved breeding he was done, for that female. But to have young die of the cyanide gas!

"I fear for our way of life," said qr'Tshew primly. "Since the New Devils came, our litters have not been the same."

"I have had the same thought," dr'Shee admitted. "I have spoken of it to my sisters."

"And I to mine. I and my sisters have thought something we wish to share. Our young are being taught things by the

New Devils. Dr'Shee, shouldn't we mothers learn what the litters are learning?"

"But they are learning ways of bringing death! You and I are mothers, qr'Tshew!" Dr'Shee was shocked.

"The Krinpit bring death to us, do they not? The broods in the upper galleries have blocked off the tunnels where the bad air came from, but is it not certain that the Shelled Devils will break through again and more bad air will come?"

"I cannot bring death, except of course for food."

"Then let us eat them, shells and all," said qr'Tshew grimly. "Touch closely, dr'Shee. There is a story—" She hesitated. "I do not know how true it is. It came from a Krinpit and might as well have come from a Flying Devil." That was an old saying to indicate dubiousness, but in this case, dr'Shee realized, it was actually true. "This Shelled Devil taunted one of my sister's brood by saying that New Devils had destroyed an entire city of our race. He said the New Devils thought of us as vermin and would not rest until we were all gone. That is why they have given the Krinpit the bad air."

"But the New Devils are teaching our litters how to destroy Krinpit."

"The next part of the story is puzzling, but I think it is so. The Shelled Devil says that there are three kinds of New Devils. One kind destroyed the city. Another kind gave them the bad air with which they harm us here. And the kind that teaches our litters is a third kind. They have destroyed Flying Devils and Krinpit, as well as persons of the two other kinds of their own race. But they do not destroy us."

Dr'Shee thrashed her long, supple body in agitation. "But that is not true!" she cried. "They have taken several litters from their classes to some other place, and only a few have returned. And they have been weak and slow, and speak of their brood-mates dying!"

"My sisters and I have heard this also," agreed qr'Tshew.

"Tssheee!" The petaled folds of dr'Shee's nose were rippling furiously. "It feels," she said at length, "as though the teaching of bringing death is not a bad thing. If we bring death to the Krinpit, then they will not be able to bring more bad air to us. If we help our New Devils to bring death to the others, then they will not be able to aid the Krinpit or the Flying Devils against us."

"I have had this same thought, dr'Shee."

"I have a further thought, qr'Tshew. Once we have brought death to these others, perhaps we can then bring death to our own New Devils."

"And then our litters will be ours again, dr'Shee!"

"And our burrows will be safe and dark. Yes! Do not go away, qr'Tshew. I will summon t'Weechr and he will begin to teach us these lessons!"

·FOURTEEN·

EVEN IN JEM'S favorable conditions—air denser, gravity less than Earth—there was a peremptory equation of lift. Danny Dalehouse could carry whatever he liked simply by adding balloons to his cluster. Charlie had no such power. He could carry what he could carry, and there was an end to it. To carry any of Dalehouse's gifts meant sacrificing ballast and therefore mobility. To carry them all was impossible. When Dalehouse scolded him for giving the crossbow to a flock-mate—at a time when the *ha'aye'i* seemed everywhere!—Charlie sang placatingly, "But I must keep the speaker-to-air! I cannot have both, cannot have both."

"And if you are killed by a *ha'aye'i*, what good will the radio do you?" But Charlie didn't even seem to understand the question. He and the flock were singing a sort of rhapsody about the speaker-to-air and how it enriched their chorus; and Dalehouse abandoned the effort.

Charlie's possession of the radio wasn't all good. It meant that Dalehouse could really keep in contact with the flock from the ground as long as they stayed in line of sight or somewhere near it, and that fact had not escaped Major Santangelo, the new camp commandant. It was getting less easy to escape into the air. At the same time, it was getting less attractive to stay in the camp. Santangelo had established command at once. He had proved it by sending Harriet and Alex Woodring off to try to make contact with a distant tribe of burrowers, hopefully uncontaminated by contact with the Greasies. And the camp was being run along increasingly strict military lines.

Dalehouse broke through the flock's song. "I must return. Four more flocks of our people are joining us, and I wish to be there when they arrive."

"We will come with you, we will come with you—"

"No, you won't," he contradicted. "Too many *ha'aye'i* near the camp." That was the truth, and that, too, was a consequence of the "gifts" he had given them. Since the Oilies had found out that Santangelo's "scientific instruments" were being used by the balloonists to keep tabs on what was going on in their camp they had taken to shooting down every balloonist that came within a kilometer of them. So balloonists were growing locally scarce, and the predators hungry.

"Fly by the Wet Valleys," he commanded. "Learn if our people are well there."

"No need," sang Charlie. "See the wings of your friend 'Appy coming from there even now!" And back behind the shoreline, there it was, Cappy's little biplane coming back from visiting the outpost, circling in for a landing.

"Then good-bye," sang Dalehouse, and expertly vented hydrogen until he came down to the level of the onshore winds that carried him back to the camp.

He was getting really good at ballooning, and he was smiling as he drifted down over the commandant's pet project, the little mud fort on the shore, and dropped to earth on the first bluff. He gathered up the deflated balloons, slung their loose-netted bulk over his shoulder, and walked happily enough up to the hydrogen shed.

That was the end of happiness. Half the camp was gathered around Kappelyushnikov and Santangelo, farther up the hill. Jim Morrissey and half a dozen others were coming toward him, their faces grim. Dalehouse caught Morrissey's arm as he passed. "What's the matter?" he demanded.

Morrissey paused. "Trouble, Danny. Something's happened to the outcamp. Harriet, Woodring, Dugachenko— they're missing. Cappy says the camp's been ripped apart, and they're gone."

"Harriet?"

"All of them, damn it! And there's blood and Krinpit tracks all over the place. Let go, we've got to get down to Castle Santangelo—in case they invade by sea, I guess. Anyway, you'd better get up there and see what your orders are."

Orders! How like an army officer to overreact and start issuing orders in all directions! Dalehouse let them go past and walked belligerently up to the group around Santangelo and the pilot. Someone was saying, "—I didn't know there were any Krinpit in the Wet Valleys."

"If you were in Beverly Hills you wouldn't know there were any rattlesnakes in California, either, but if you wandered around Hollywood Hills they'd bite your ass off. That's enough for arguing," the major said. "Those of you with assigned defense posts, get to them. We've got four ships coming in in the next twenty hours. It'd be a good time for anybody to catch us off guard, and we're not going to be caught. Move it!"

Dalehouse, who had been given no assigned defense post, was not anxious to get one. He moved away briskly with the others as the group broke up, circling around the outskirts to approach the communications shack.

Inside, the comm team on duty was watching a continually shifting display of moving symbols against a green grid of coordinate lines: the four resupply ships, already in orbit around Jem, making their final course corrections before dropping down to the surface. Dalehouse had expected Kappelyushnikov to show up there, and he did, moments after Dalehouse himself.

"Ah, Danny," he said dismally, "you have good taste for finding nice place to fuck off. Wait one while I see if asshole traffic controller has accidentally got ships in right orbit." He peered into the screen, grumbled at the crew on duty, then shrugged and returned to Dalehouse. "Is on course," he reported. "Now question is, is course right? We find out. Poor Gasha!"

"Are you sure she's dead?"

"Have not seen corpus delicti, no. But Danny, there was very much blood, two liters at least."

"But you didn't see the bodies."

"No, Danny, did not. Saw blood. Saw tents chopped up to fine Venetian lace, clothes all over, food, radio smashed, little scratchy bug-tracks everywhere I looked. No bodies. So I yelled some, listened, poked into bushes. Then came home. So poor Gasha, not to mention poor Alexei and poor Gregor."

Danny shook his head wonderingly. "The Krinpit are damn noisy beasts. I don't see how they could catch the camp by surprise, and if they weren't surprised they should've been able to take care of themselves. Santangelo made them carry guns."

Kappelyushnikov shrugged. "You want to, I fly you there and you study scene of crime for yourself. Right now, excuse. First ship is about to come out of orbit, and I must keep controller up to personal high standard of accuracy."

Half the personnel in the first ship were a combat team—a fact which would have come as a distinctly unpleasant shock to Dalehouse at one time but now seemed less so. While they were still in orbit, the Vietnamese colonel commanding them had been briefed by radio, and the squad formed up outside the ship as they debarked, and immediately drew weapons and trotted to reinforce the perimeter guards. The second ship was also mostly military, but among the faces was one Dalehouse recognized. It took him a moment to make the connection, but then it was clear: the Bulgarian girl who had interceded for him and Marge Menninger in Sofia. He called to her and waved; she looked startled, then smiled—rather attractively, he thought—and called a greeting.

That was as far as it went just then, for by that time the new colonel had conferred with Major Santangelo, and the whole camp was mobilized. The Vietnamese—his name was Tree—commandeered Kappelyushnikov and the airplane, and they were gone for more than two hours, orbiting the camp in widening circles, first at high altitude, then nearly brushing the tops of the trees. All the tents had to come down. By the time the third rocket landed the tents were up again, now lined up six to a row, four rows paralleling each other, in what had become a company street. At each corner of the encampment pits were dug, and out of the third ship came machine guns and flamethrowers to go into them, while the few rankless nonspecialists who had not been tapped for unloading, tent detail, or pit digging had been set to pounding steel stakes into the ground ten meters outside the limits of the camp. Among the third ship's cargo were two huge reels of barbed wire, and by the time the last ship began its drop they had been strung along the stakes.

For once the Jemman skies were almost clear as the fourth ship came into sight high over the far horizon of the ocean-lake. First there was a broad, bright, meteoritic splash of light as the ablative entry shields soaked up the worst of the excess energy and spilled it away in incandescent shards. Then the ship itself was in naked-eye range, falling free for a moment. A quick blue-white jet flare made a course correction. Then the trigger parachute came free, pulling the three main chutes after it. The ship seemed to hang almost motionless in the ruddy air; but slowly, slowly it grew larger until it was almost overhead, two hundred meters up. Then the chutes were jettisoned and the ship lowered itself, on its blinding, ear-destroying rockets, to the beach.

Dalehouse had seen, he counted, five of those landings now, not including the one he himself had been in. They were all almost miraculous to watch. And they were all different. The ships themselves were different. Of the new four, only one was the tall, silver shape of his own ship. The other three were squat double cones, ten meters from rounded top to rounded bottom as they crouched on their landing struts, nearly twenty meters across at their widest.

The first person out of the ship was Marge Menninger.

It was not a surprise. The surprising part was that she hadn't come earlier. Dalehouse realized he had been half-expecting her on every ship that landed. She looked tired, disheveled, and harried, and obviously she had been sleeping in her olive-drab fatigues for all of the transit-time week. But she also looked pretty good to Dalehouse. The female members of the Food Bloc party had not been chosen for their sexuality. Apart from a rare occasional grapple with someone he didn't really like very much—sometimes impelled by tickling one of the balloonists into parting with a few sprays of joy-juice, sometimes by nothing more than boredom—Dalehouse's sex life had been sparse, joyless, and dull. Margie reminded him of better times.

Margie had also come up in the world since Sofia; the insignia on her collar tabs were no longer captain's bars but full colonel's eagles, and as she moved aside to let the rest of the troops debark, Colonel Tree and Major Santangelo were already beginning to report to her. She listened attentively while her eyes were taking inventory of the camp, the defense perimeter, and the progress of the debarkation. Then she began speaking in short, quick sentences. Dalehouse was not close enough to hear the words, but there was no doubt that the sentences were orders. Tree argued about something.

Good-humoredly, Margie slipped her arm around his shoulder while she answered, then patted his bottom as he moved off, scowling, to do as he was told. She and Santangelo moved up toward the command center, still talking; and Dalehouse began to revise his notions of what to expect from seeing Margie Menninger again.

But as they approached where he was standing, she caught sight of him and threw out her arms. "Hey, Dan! Beautiful to see you!" She kissed him enthusiastically. "You're looking real fine, you know? Or as close to fine as you can in this light."

"You, too," he said. "And congratulations."

"On what, being here? Oh, you mean the eagles. Well, they had to give me that to handle Guy Tree. Dimitrova ought to be around somewhere. Have you seen her? Now if we could only get the Pak to come for a visit, we could all have a nice time talking over good old days in the Bulgarian slammer."

"Colonel Menninger—"

"All right, major, I'm coming. Stay loose, Dan. We've got catching up to do."

He stared after her. In the old Rotsy days in college, before he had dropped out as it became clear that nobody would ever need to fight wars anymore, colonels had seemed quite different. It wasn't just that she was female. And pretty, and young. Colonels had seemed to have more on their minds than Margie Menninger did—especially colonels coming into a situation where the panic button had been so recently pressed.

A husky man in a sergeant's uniform was speaking to him. "You Dr. Dalehouse? There's mail for you at the library."

"Oh, sure. Thanks." Dalehouse took note of the fact that the sergeant's expression was both surprised and a little amused, but he understood both reactions. "Nice kid, the colonel," he said benevolently. He didn't wait for an answer.

Most of the "mail" was from Michigan State and the Double-A-L, but one of the letters was a surprise. It was from Polly! So long ago, so far away, Dalehouse had almost forgotten he had ever had a wife. He could think of no reason why she would be writing him. Nearly everyone in the first two parties had also received mail, and the lines at the viewers were discouraging. Dalehouse put the collection of fiches in his pocket and headed for Kappelyushnikov's private store of goodies in the hydrogen shed. The pilot had long since scrounged the things he deemed essential to the good life on Jem, and among them was his own microfiche viewer. With considerable curiosity, Dalehouse slid his ex-wife's letter into position.

Dear Daniel:

I don't know if you knew that Grandfather Medway died last summer. When his will was probated it turned out he left the Grand Haven house to us. I guess he just never got around to changing the will after our divorce.

It isn't worth a whole lot, but of course it's worth something—the lawyer says its assessed value is $43,500. I'm a little embarrassed about this. I have this strong feeling that says you're going to say you'll waive your share. Well, if that's really what you want I'd appreciate it if you'd sign a release for me and have it notarized—is there anybody there who's a notary? Otherwise, will you tell me what you'd like to do?

We are all well, Daniel, in spite of everything. Detroit had another blackout last week, and the rioting and looting were pretty bad, and the new emergency surtaxes are going to be hard to handle. Not to mention the heatless days and the moratorium on daytime TV and the scary news about international politics. Most people seem to think it's because of what's going on up where you are— but that's not your fault, is it? I remember you with a lot of affection, Daniel, and hope you do me.

Pauline

Sitting on the edge of Kappelyushnikov's personal cot, Dalehouse put the viewer down thoughtfully. The Grand Haven house. It was really only a bungalow, at least fifty years old and only sketchily modernized. But he and Polly had spent their honeymoon in it, in a snowy January with the wind whipping up over the bluff from Lake Michigan all day and all night. Of course she could have the house. Somebody in the camp could probably notarize a quitclaim, at least legally enough to satisfy some up-country surrogate court.

He stretched out on the cot, thinking about his ex-wife and her letter. News from Earth had not seemed either very interesting or very relevant, and Dalehouse had spent a lot more time thinking about the balloonists and the complications of life on Jem than about the brief paragraphs on the camp wall newspaper. But Polly made it sound serious. Riots, looting, blackouts, heatless days! He decided he would have to talk to some of the new people as soon as they quit bustling around and getting settled. That Bulgarian girl, for instance. She could fill him in on what was really happening back home, and, besides, she was a pretty nice person. He lay drowsily trying to decide whether it was better to do that now or to keep on enjoying the private space to think his own thoughts.

The decision was taken out of his hands. "Hello, Dr. Dalehouse," came Ana Dimitrova's voice. "Mr. Kappelyushnikov said you'd be here. But I must confess I was not sure he was in earnest."

Dalehouse opened his eyes and sat up as Cappy and the girl stooped through the entrance to the shed. The pilot's expression made it clear that, whatever he had told the girl, he had hoped there would be no one there, but he rallied and said, "Ah, Anyushka, you must learn to trust me. Here is old friend to see you, Danny."

Dalehouse accepted the formal handshake she offered. She had a nice smile, he observed. In fact, if she had not chosen to wear her hair pulled severely back and avoid the use of makeup, she could have been quite attractive.

"I was hoping to get a chance to talk to you, Miss Dimitrova."

"Heavens, Ana, please. Old cellmates must not be formal with each other."

"But on other hand," said the pilot, "must not impose on dear Danny, who is no doubt hungry and must get to mess hall at once or risk missing excellent dog-meat-and-slime meal."

"Nice try, Cappy," Dalehouse acknowledged. "No, I'm not hungry. How are things on Earth, Ana? I've just been hearing some bad stories."

Her expression clouded. "If the stories you have heard have been of violence and disaster, then, yes, that is how things are. Just before we left the television news spoke of martial law in the city of Los Angeles, and also in several cities of Europe. And there was some sinking of an Australian naval vessel off the coast of Peru."

"Dear God."

"Oh, there is much more than that, Dr. Dalehouse—Dan. But we have brought all the recent newspapers, as well as tapes of television programs—it is really quite an extensive library, I understand. I believe there are more than twenty thousand books in microfiche, at Colonel Menninger's express orders."

"Twenty thousand books?" Dalehouse shook his head. "You know, I never thought of her as a reader."

Ana smiled and sat cross-legged on the floor before him. "Please, let us be comfortable. I too am sometimes astonished at Colonel Menninger." She hesitated, then said, "She is not, however, always to be relied on. I had expected some time to consult with my government before coming here, on her promise. But it did not happen. None of us were allowed to leave the camp until we were flown to the launching point. Perhaps it was because she did not want to risk exposing us to the unstable conditions we might have found."

"As bad as that?"

"Worse," growled Kappelyushnikov. "You see, Danny? We should be grateful to be here on safe tropical-paradise planet like Jem, where only once in awhile isolated party gets wiped out by giant cockroaches."

"That's another thing," said Danny. "Marge Menninger doesn't seem particularly worried, after the flap yesterday."

"No reason to worry, dear Danny. I and little Vietnamese colonel have scoured every centimeter from ten klicks in all directions, using magnetometer, IR scanners, and good piloting eyes. Is no metal thing bigger than breadbasket anywhere around, I promise, and not more than three, maybe six, creatures larger than crabrat. So sleep safely tonight, Danny. In own bed," he added pointedly, and did not need to add "soon."

Nan was quicker than he. "That is good advice, Cappy," she said, standing up. "I think I will take it for myself."

"I will escort you," rumbled Kappelyushnikov. "No, do not disturb self, Danny. I see you are quite tired."

Ana sighed. "Gospodin Kappelyushnikov," she scolded, "apart from the fact that I am tired and quite disoriented from all these new experiences, you and I have barely met. I do hope that we will be friends. Please don't make that difficult by behaving like some Cossack with a peasant maid."

Cappy looked abashed, then angry. Then he grinned. "Anyushka, you are fine Slavic girl. Yes, we will be friends at once. Later on, perhaps more—but," he added hastily, "only in proper Soviet style, no premature touching, all right? Now let us all three stroll through pleasant Jemman murk to your tent."

Ana laughed and slapped him on the shoulder. "Russian bear! Come, then." She led the way outside and stood for a moment, glancing around at the quieting camp. The floodlights that marked official "day" were out, but Kung was clear and ruddy in the sky overhead. "I do not know if I can get used to a world where it is never night," she complained.

"Is severe handicap for certain purposes, yes," Kappelyushnikov agreed. They climbed the bluff and walked along it toward the female tent area. At the very edge, surrounded by a border of rounded stones in lieu of a lawn, was a tent larger than the others. It already had a flat rock before it stenciled *Col. M. Menninger, Commanding.*

"Margie's doing herself well," Dalehouse commented.

"Is privilege of rank," said Kappelyushnikov, but he was staring down the beach at the four new ships, one tall and slim, three squat, resting on their landing struts.

"That's strange, isn't it?" Dalehouse said. "Those three are quite unlike the others."

Cappy glanced at him. "You are truly observant, Danny." But his tone was strange.

"All right, Cappy. What's the secret?"

"Secret? Simple pilot is not told secrets. But I have eyes, and I can make conjectures."

"Come on, Cappy. You're going to tell us your conjecture sooner or later. Why not do it now?"

"Two conjectures," he corrected. "First, observe shape of three new spacecraft. Imagine sliced in half, forming two little cones each. Then imagine all six cones set on base around perimeter of camp, and the glass removed from those long, narrow ports that are so unnecessary for navigation of space. What have we then?"

"Upside-down cones with unglazed long, narrow ports," Dalehouse guessed.

"Yes, exactly. Only when installed on defense perimeter we have other name for them. We call them 'machine-gun emplacements.'" He sighed. "I think is triumph of two-faced engineering design, not accident, that this is so."

"But one can scarcely believe that," objected Ana. "This is, after all, a peaceable exploration party, not an invading army!"

"Yes, also exactly. Is only coincidence that so many members of peaceable exploration party are also soldiers."

Both Dalehouse and the girl were silent, studying the landed spaceships. "I would like not to believe you," said Ana at last. "But perhaps—"

"Wait a minute!" Dalehouse interrupted. "Those three ships—they don't have any return stage! That's why they're so short!"

Kappelyushnikov nodded. "And that is second conjecture," he added heavily. "Only is not really conjecture. Library of twenty thousand books is not light reading for weekend. Spacecraft that come apart to make forts are not for round trip. Vessels without return-capsule capability are not accident. Total of sum is clear. For many of us, is not intended we ever go back to dear old planet Earth."

Getting into the Jemman sky again the next day was a victory for Dalehouse, and he did not know how many more of those victories he would have. The day had begun unpromisingly. As soon as the "morning" lights were on he had found a mini-memo on the bench inside his tent door to let him know that, as from 0800 hours that standard day, he was to consider himself under military discipline with the assimilated rank of captain. On the way to breakfast he had passed an orderly carrying two covered trays into Margie's tent. An orderly! Not even the late Harriet Santori had gone that far. And on the way back past the tent, the Vietnamese colonel had been coming out.

Who Marge Menninger kept in her bed was no concern of his, and all this other military Mickey Mouse was irrelevant to his purpose on Jem. All the same, Dalehouse was not enjoying his flight as much as usual that day.

For one thing, Charlie and his flock were nowhere around —partly because Major Santangelo had insisted they overfly some of the other parts of Jem to bring back intelligence. Mostly because Dalehouse himself was reluctant to have them there, with so many *ha'aye'i* waiting in the clouds to prey on them. At least he had insisted they stay a full two kilometers away from the Greasy camp; maybe that was enough for safety. Meanwhile, Dalehouse had his lightweight carbine with him, and he was hoping to take out at least a couple of

the *ha'aye'i* before Charlie drifted back. There was already
one balloonist in the camp as a sort of combination convales-
cent and pet, waiting for his *ha'aye'i*-ripped gasbag to mend
enough for flight. Dalehouse didn't want Charlie to join him.

Trying to look appetizing, he drifted under the base of a
low cumulus humilis. It was exactly the sort of place the airsharks chose for hiding. But if there was one in the cloud it
wasn't hungry just then.

He vented gas and dropped away from the cloud as the
updraft began to suck him toward it; if there were *ha'aye'i*, he
wanted to meet them in clear air, not where they could be
upon him before he could shoot. A return flow carried him
back toward the camp, and he looked down from half a kilometer on a busy scene. About twenty people were still unloading the new ships. Others were clearing brush and forest to
widen the perimeter around the camp, and up past the camp
toward the hills, in a natural meadow of thorn-bearing ground
vines, a tiny tractor was plowing furrows. That was new! The
tractor must have come out of one of the ships, and the
furrows looked exactly as though someone was planning to
farm.

That was reasonable enough, and even good news—certainly they could use fresh vegetables, and if the Greasies
could grow them so could the Fats. But something about it
troubled Dalehouse. He couldn't put his finger on it; something about using soldiers to farm? Forced labor on land?

He dismissed the thought; he was getting too low.

He vented some ballast, and the water sluiced down on the
newly plowed land like a toy-scale rain shower. The thing that
was tickling his memory was beginning to be annoying. For
some reason, it reminded him of his undergraduate anthro-
pology professor, a gentle and undemanding man a lot like
Alex Woodring—

Like Alex Woodring, who was dead. Along with Gasha and
the Bulgarian corporal he had never really come to know.

He was having none but depressing thoughts. His reserves

of hydrogen and ballast were getting a little low, and evidently the *ha'aye'i* had learned to distinguish between a balloonist and a human being swinging from a netted cluster of bags. They were not to be tricked this day. Reluctantly he swung back over the beach, vented gas, and dropped to the pebbly sand.

By the time he had picked up and stowed the deflated balloons Margie Menninger was approaching, along with the woman sergeant who was her orderly. "Nice flying, Danny," she said. "Looks like fun. Will you take me up with you sometime?"

He stood regarding her for a moment. She really looked very pretty, even in the maroon Kung-light that darkened her lips and hid the gold of her hair. Her fatigues were new and sharply pressed, and her short hairdo flopped becomingly as she moved. "Any time you say, Marge. Or is it 'colonel'?"

She laughed. "All you brand-new officers are the same, very rank conscious. We're off duty right now, Danny, so it's Marge. You'll learn."

"I'm not sure I want to learn how to be a soldier."

"Oh, you'll catch on," she promised. "Tinka, take the point. Let's go for a walk, shall we?"

The sergeant moved out ahead of them, trotting to the barbed-wire enclosure. The troops in the pit at the corner lifted a section of the wire aside so the three of them could pass through; the sergeant in charge gave Margie a soft salute, and she nodded pleasantly back.

"If a person went swimming in this water," she said, "would she find herself being eaten up by something?"

"Not so far. We do it all the time."

"Looks pretty tempting. Care to join me?"

Dalehouse shook his head, not in negation but in wonder. "Margie, you're something. I thought colonels had to keep busy, especially when they think their troops need armed guards and barbed-wire fences day and night."

"Dear Danny," she said good-naturedly, "I haven't been a

colonel very long, but I taught the theory of it to a couple thousand plebes at the Point. I think I have a pretty good grasp of the basic principles. A colonel doesn't have to do much; she just has to see that everybody else gets everything done. I already put in four hours of pretty solid work this morning."

"Yes, I saw Colonel Tree coming out of your tent."

She looked at him thoughtfully. She didn't comment but went on, "As to your other point, the perimeter watch is SOP from now on, but there are patrols in the woods and aerial reconnaissance every hour, and besides, Tinka's a qualified expert with all hand weapons. I think you'll be all right."

"I wasn't worried about my personal safety."

"No, you weren't. You were worried about the troops under my command, and on their behalf I thank you for your concern." She grinned and patted his arm. "Hold on a minute." She fished a cigarette case out of her pocket, ducked behind him to get out of the wind, and expertly lit up. She inhaled deeply and held it, passing him the joint. When she exhaled, she called to the sergeant, "Tinka!"

"Yes'm."

"Next batch of dope you clean for us, save the seeds. Let's see if we can grow the little buggers here."

"Yes'm."

Danny took a long hit, beginning to relax. Being with Margie Menninger was never dull, at least. As he slowly exhaled he looked her over in some admiration. She had adjusted at once to the heat, the disconcertingly low gravity, the thick air that had troubled them all for weeks. She was some kind of woman.

By the time they had finished passing the joint back and forth they were out of sight of the perimeter guard where the beach widened under a high, bare bluff. Margie stopped, looking around. "Seems as good as any," she commented. "Tinka, take your position."

"Yes'm." The sergeant scrambled agilely up the side of the

bluff to the top, and Margie shucked her fatigues. She wore nothing underneath. "If you're coming, come. If not, stay and help Tinka keep watch." And she splashed into the water.

Dope, company, or whatever, Dalehouse was feeling better than he had all day. He laughed out loud, then skinned out of his own clothes and joined her.

Ten minutes later they were both back on the beach, lying not very comfortably on their clothes, waiting to dry.

"Ouch," said Margie. "If I ever get any extra people for punishment detail, I think I'll see if they can get the rocks out of this sand."

"You get used to it."

"Only if I have to, Danny. I'm going to make this a nice camp if I can—good duty. For instance, you know what we're going to have tonight?"

He rolled his head to look at her. "What?"

"The first official Jemman Food-Exporting Bloc encampment dance."

"A *dance*?"

She grinned. "See what I mean? Those turkeys who were running this place never thought of that. But there's nothing to it: spread out some flats on the dirt, put a few tapes in the machine, and there you are. Saturday night special. Best thing in the world for morale."

"You are probably about the US Army's best colonel for having fun," Dalehouse said.

"For all the rest of being a colonel, too, Danny. Don't you forget it."

"Well, I won't, Margie. I believe it. Only it's kind of hard to remember under the, ah, present circumstances."

"Well, I'll put my clothes back on if it'll help you concentrate. This isn't just fun and games. I wanted to talk to you."

"About what?"

"Whatever you want to tell me. How you think things are going. What isn't being done that ought to be. What you've learned being here that I haven't found out yet."

He propped himself up on an elbow to look at her. She returned his gaze serenely, scratching her bare abdomen just above the pubic hair. "Well," he said, "I guess you've seen all the reports about making contact with the sentients."

"Memorized them, Danny. I even saw some of the sentients at Detrick, but they weren't in very good condition. Especially the Creepy."

"The burrower? We haven't had very good luck with them."

"Piss-poor, I'd say."

"Well—yes, that's fair. But we did get about ten specimens, two of them alive. And Morrissey has a whole report on them not transmitted yet. He says they're farmers—from underneath, which is kind of an interesting idea. They plant some kind of tubers in the roofs of their tunnels. He was planning to talk to that expert you were supposed to bring—I don't know her name."

"Sondra Leckler? She didn't come, Danny. I had her scratched."

"Why?"

"Political. She's Canadian." She looked at him thoughtfully. "Does that fact mean anything to you?"

"Not a thing."

"No, I didn't think so. Canada voted for Peru's thousand-mile limit in the UN. That's cozying with the Peeps, right there. And everybody knows Canada's got the hots for the Greasies because of their goddam Athabasca tar sands. They're politically unreliable right now, Danny. There were four Canadians scheduled for this shipment, and I scratched all their asses right off."

"That sounds pretty paranoid," he commented.

"No, realistic. I've got no time to teach you the facts of life, Danny. What else? I don't mean about the burrowers."

He regarded her thoughtfully. She lay on her back, hands behind her head, comfortable in her nudity as she squinted toward the glowing red Kung. For a slightly plump girl her waist curved beautifully into her hips, and her breasts were rounded even while she lay flat on her back. But under that blond hair was a brain Dalehouse did not fully understand.

He dropped back and said, "Well, there's the balloonists. I know the most about them. Our regular flock is off toward the Heat Pole, but there's another one out over the water. They're basically territorial, but—"

"You were at the Greasy camp awhile ago, weren't you?"

"Yeah. When we were still on visiting terms. Is that what you want me to tell you about?"

"Among other things."

"All right. They've got a hell of a lot of stuff we don't, Margie." He described the machine that molded building blocks, the plasma generator, the farm, the air conditioning, the *ice*.

"Sounds pretty nice," she commented. "We'll have all that stuff too, Danny, I promise you. Did you see a plane and four gliders?"

"No. There was an airstrip—Cappy commented on it; it didn't make sense, with just a helicopter. But they didn't have a plane then."

"They do now. I thought they'd sneaked a reinforcement in that you didn't catch. Did you know about the base on Farside?"

"*Farside?* You mean the dark half of Jem? What the hell would anyone want there?"

"That's what I need to find out. But they've got it. Why do you think I stayed four extra orbits before I came down? I made damn sure I photomapped and radar-surveyed everything I could; I know every satellite around Jem, I know every spot on the surface that's using energy, and I don't like all of what I know. The Farside base was a real shock. Did you see any children in the Greasy camp?"

"Children? Hell, no! Why would—"

"Well, I think they're moving whole families in, Danny,

which seems to indicate they've got more than an exploring expedition in mind."

"How could you tell whether they had children from space?"

"No way, Danny. I didn't say the orbital reconnaissance was the *only* way I knew what was going on with the Greasies. One other thing. No, two. Have they got a baseball field?"

"Baseball?" He was sitting up now, staring at her. "What the hell would they do with a baseball field? Cricket, maybe, and no doubt football, but—"

"That's a break," she said, without explaining. "Last question. Did you happen to run into a fellow named Tamil?"

"I don't think so." Dalehouse thought hard. "Wait a minute. Short fellow with a shaved head? Chess player?"

"I don't know. He's an Indonesian."

"Well, I'm not sure, but I think there was a petrochemist with a name like that. I didn't talk to him. I don't think he spoke English."

"Pity." Margie ruminated for a moment, then sat up, shading her eyes. "Are those your balloonists out there?"

As Dalehouse turned to look, Margie was standing, taking a few steps toward the shore, and what he looked at was not the sky but her. The artist Hogarth had said that the most beautiful line in nature was the curve of a woman's back, and Margie, silhouetted against the ruddy sky, was a fine figure of a woman. Half-amused, Dalehouse realized by the stirrings in his groin that he was beginning to display interest. But only beginning. The stimulus was that beautiful and remembered butt; the suppressant was the things she said. He would be some little while figuring out just how it was he did feel about Margie Menninger.

Then he got his eyes past her and forgot the stirrings. "There are *ha'aye'i* out there!" he said furiously.

"What'ys?"

"They're predators. That's not our regular flock; they just

drifted in, because of the lights, most likely. And those clouds are full of *ha'aye'i*!" The flock was close enough to be heard now, singing loudly, only a few hundred meters away. And far beyond and above them three slimmer shapes were swooping toward them.

"That's a what-you-call-it there? Jesus! Look at that mother," she cried, as the first of the airsharks expertly ripped at the bag of a huge female, slipped past, turned end-for-end, and reversed itself. It came back ten meters lower to catch the deflated balloonist as it fell, braying its death song. "That's a fucking *Immelmann* that thing just did! Nobody's done that since World War One!"

"This isn't a performance, damn it! They're dying!" Two more of the predators had struck, and two more balloonists were caught farther down the shore. But at least it was not Charlie's flock. None of those victims were friends. "See that stuff coming out of the female?" he asked. "Those are her eggs. They're long spider-silk kind of things. They'll float around forever, but they won't be fertilized because none of the males have—"

"Fuck her eggs, little buddy. I'm rooting for the shark! What a killing machine! Shit, Danny, I can see why things are going badly here. You people picked the wrong allies. We ought to team up with the sharks!"

Dalehouse was scandalized. "They're animals! They're not even intelligent!"

"Show me a professor," she said, "and I'll show you a fart-brain. How intelligent do you have to be to fight?"

"Christ. The balloonists are our friends. We've got them doing surveillance for us. The *ha'aye'i* would never do that. Now you want us to line up with their natural enemies?"

"Well, I can see there might be problems." She stared wistfully at the *ha'aye'i*, which had ripped away the inedible bag and was now feasting on the soft parts of its still-living prey. "Too bad," she said philosophically. She stepped back toward Danny, still watching the spectacle, and took his hand.

"You're really sure about this? There's no way to persuade our gooks to get along with the sharks?"

"No way at all! Even if you could somehow reach the *ha'aye'i* to explain what you wanted. The *ha'aye'i* don't even sing. That's the whole meaning of life to balloonists. They could never deal with creatures that didn't sing."

"Oh?" Margie looked at him thoughtfully. Then she released his hand and sat down again, leaning back on her arms and looking up at him. "Tell me, Danny, would you like to make me sing?"

He stared at her. Why, she was sexually excited by watching the slaughter!

He glanced at the top of the bluff, where the back of the head of the orderly was motionless in sight. "Maybe we'd better be getting back," he said.

"What's the matter, sweetie? Don't like having an audience? Tinka won't bother us."

"I don't care about her."

"Then what?" she asked cheerfully. "Hey, I bet I can guess. You're hassled about the colonel."

"Tree? He's got nothing to do with me."

"Aw, come off it, sweets." She patted the ground beside her. After a moment, he sat down, not very close. "You think I've been getting it on with old Nguyen the Tryin'."

"No. I don't think it, I know it."

"And suppose I have?"

"Your business," he said promptly. "I'm not saying it isn't. Maybe I've got some sexist-pig notions, but—"

"But no maybe. You fucking well do, Danny-boy." She was smiling without softness now.

He shrugged. "Let's go back, colonel."

"Let's stay here. And," she said, "I've got the rank on you, and when a colonel says 'let's' to a captain, what it means is *do it.*"

There was no more stirring in Dalehouse's groin; he was both angry and amused at his own anger. He said, "Let's get this straight. Are you ordering me to fuck you?"

"No. Not at the moment, dear boy." She grinned. "I hardly ever order officers to fuck me. Only enlisted men, and very seldom them, because it's bad for discipline."

"Are you saying the colonel ordered you to fuck him?"

"Danny dear," she said patiently, "first, he couldn't—I've got the rank. Second, he wouldn't have had to. I'd fuck Guy any time. For any reason. Because he's technically my superior officer and I don't want to rub in the fact that I'm the one who's commanding. Because it'd make things go smoother on the mission. Because it's interesting to get it on with somebody half my size. I'd fuck a Krinpit if it would help the war effort, only I don't know how we'd bring up the kids. But," she said, "a girl's entitled to a certain amount of non-goal-oriented recreation, too, and Danny, I really have the fondest memories of you from last year in Bulgaria."

Fully relaxed, she rummaged under her for her clothes and pulled out another joint.

Dalehouse watched her lighting it. Her body was tanned over every inch—no bikini marks—and looking a lot better than the fishbelly white that came after a while on Jem. She scratched between the crease that hid her navel and her pale pubic hair, exhaled peacefully, and passed him the joint. The thing was, Dalehouse conceded to himself, that he really had the fondest memories of her last year in Bulgaria, too, and it did not seem to matter that he also had some bad memories.

"You know the thing that gets me about you?" he asked. "You make me laugh about a hundred different ways. Lean over this way, will you?"

When they had used each other up, they rested for a moment. Then Margie jumped up and dashed into the water again. Dalehouse followed; they splashed and roared; and as they came out he was astonished to discover that suddenly he didn't feel quite used up anymore. But Margie was calling up the bluff, "Tinka! Time hack!"

"Thirteen twenty hours, ma'am!"

Margie slipped into her fatigues quickly and leaned over to kiss Dalehouse as he was standing with one leg in his pants. "Time to get back. I've got a busy afternoon before the dance, and Danny, I'd appreciate it if you'd do something for me."

"What's that?"

"Teach Tinka how to do that balloon thing this afternoon."

"Why?"

"I want her to run an errand for me. It's important."

He considered. "I can get her started, anyway. But I don't know if she can learn it all in a few hours."

"She learns fast, I promise. Come on—I'll race you back!"

They ran the hundred meters. Marge got off first, but by the time the outpost was in sight Dalehouse had caught up with her. As he passed she reached out and took his hand and pulled him back to a walk. "Thanks for the exercise," she panted.

"Which exercise—swimming, running, or fucking?"

"All of them, dear Danny." She breathed hard, and then, just before they got within earshot of the perimeter guards she halted him. "One thing I ought to mention to you," she said.

"What's that?"

"I just want to set the record straight. With Nguyen Tree I'm fucking. With you I was making love."

Twelve on perimeter guard, two in sick bay, three in the comm shack, and eight more on the other twenty-four-hour details that always had to be manned: that left over a hundred and twenty people in the Food camp, and nearly every one of them was at the dance. Marge congratulated herself as she flung through a hora. It was a big success. When the dance ended and the rhythm changed to something Latin, she shook off the three men who came toward her. "I've got to sit this one out and catch my breath," she said. "After the next number I make my little speech. Then you're all on."

She retreated behind the little stand and sat cross-legged

on the ground, breathing deeply. Marge Menninger's parents had endowed her with good genes, and she had taken care of the equipment; after a long day and a solid hour's dancing she was not tired and her wits were all about her. And the day had been not only long but good. She had got the camp over their scare about the loss of the three people by treating it as if it didn't matter. She had brought them all together in the dance. She had laid the groundwork for Tinka's little mission, organized an effective perimeter guard, broken the back of the job of unloading and stowing cargo, and begun six other tasks equally important. And she had got it on with Dan Dalehouse, on terms of her own making but obviously acceptable to him. That was a personal matter, but not unimportant. Marge was careful to keep an eye on long-range prospects. And as a possible permanent future pair, if permanent pairing turned out to be the way things were going to go on Jem, Dalehouse was the best bet she had yet identified.

It was Marge Menninger's conviction, recent but certain, that this job was what she had been born for. The important thing was to do it the right way, which was her own way, which had to be laid out from day one. No false starts. A happy camp —plenty of work to keep them busy and plenty of time to enjoy themselves. And a productive camp. Jem belonged to her and hers, and now they had it.

While she was waiting for the cha-cha to end she considered the next day. Ship One would be empty, and a team could be started on separating the two halves and moving them into position in the perimeter. Dalehouse or Kappelyushnikov— which? the Russian, she decided—Kappelyushnikov could be briefed on Tinka's mission, or at least enough of it so that he could escort her partway to the Greasy camp. A work team could be organized to start putting up poles for the farm plot. She would meet and learn to know at least six of the advance party; in two weeks, she should know everything she had to know about everyone in the camp. Orders would be cut naming Guy Tree as her G-1 and Santangelo as G-2. The others she would wait on; there might be people she hadn't met yet who should have the jobs. And, if things went well, during the three hours she allowed herself for a midday break, she would go for a walk in the woods. If you could call them woods. They needed to be dealt with too: Knock down some of those skungy ferns, scoop out some farm ponds to drain that soggy swamp. It would work—all they needed was a couple of bull-dozers. Which reminded her that she needed at least to make a first approximation of a requisition list for the next ship-ment from Earth. That couldn't wait. With all the fuss the civilians were kicking up, Marge Menninger wasn't sure how many more shipments there would be. She already knew a number of goodies she wanted, but the old-timers would probably think of more. So she would need to talk to some of the old-timers. Morrissey, Krivitin, Kappelyushnikov—she would fill in the others later.

The smell of pot from beyond the stand pleased her. She thought of lighting up before getting up to make her speech —it was another way of showing her personal style. But it had been less than half an hour since the last one, and Marge knew her tolerances exactly; it might make her fuzzy.

The cha-cha ended, and the girl at the tape machine, look-ing toward Margie, switched it off. Marge nodded and climbed the stand.

The laughter and buzz dwindled as the hundred-odd peo-ple turned to face her. She smiled out at them for a moment, waiting for silence. They looked exactly like the plebes at West Point had looked, exactly like the audience in the Senate hearing room, like every audience she had ever faced. Marge was in touch with her audiences; she could always make them like her, and for that reason she liked them.

"Welcome to the first weekly Food Bloc Expedition Satur-day Night Dance. I'm Colonel Marjorie Menninger, USA, and I'm your camp commander. Some of us already know each other pretty well by now. The rest of us are going to get to know each other very well very soon, because when you come right down to it we don't have much choice, do we? I'm not worried about that, and I hope you're not. We are a pretty select bunch." She allowed her gaze to drift past the audience to the edge of the lighted area, where two of her grunts were holding another while he vomited, and added, "Although you might not know that at first." A small laugh, but genuine. "So let's start getting to know each other. Guy? Saint? Where are you?" She introduced Tree and Santangelo as they stood forth. "Now Vince Cudahy—are you there? Vince is a mathematician, but he's also our chaplain. He used to teach at Fordham, but he's agreed to be nondenominational for the purposes of this mission. So if any of you want to get married, Vince is authorized to do it." Small chuckle. "He's a little old-fashioned, so he'd prefer it if you're of different sexes." Somewhat larger laugh, but a little questioning note in it. "And in case you do," she went on, "or even if you don't, you ought to meet Chiche Arkashvili. Cheech? There she is, our medical officer. Try not to get sick over the next twenty-four hours, because she's still setting up. But then she'll be ready for business, and back home in Ordzhonikidze her specialty was obstetrics." No laugh at all this time. She hadn't expected one. She gave them a moment to draw the logical conclusion and then pressed it home. "As you can see, we're planning a permanent base, and I'm planning to make this the best duty any of you have ever had so that a lot of you will want to re-up and stay here. And if you do—and if any of you take seriously what I've just been talking about and decide to settle down and have a family on Jem, I'm offering a special prize. A thousand petrobucks for the first baby born in our camp—provided you name it Marjorie, after me." She waited a beat and added, "Two thousand if it's a boy." She got the laugh she wanted and closed it out. "Now on with the dance." And as the music started she jumped off the platform, grabbed the first man in reach, and started them all going.

For the next half-hour Marge Menninger played hostess, at which she was very, very good. She danced with the men who didn't much dance, kept the music going, made sure the drinks kept coming. What she wanted was for everybody to have a good time. The next day was time enough for them to start thinking about permanent colonies and how much choice they would be likely to have about extending their stay. When chance permitted she got a word in with the people who had known what she was going to say, asking how they thought it had gone. It had seemed to go well. It made her feel good, and she found she was really enjoying the party. She drank with the drinkers, smoked with the dopers, and danced with everyone. It was safe enough now. When the time came to shut the dance down Tinka would let her know, and meanwhile Tinka would keep an eye on her colonel.

Coming back from the brand-new latrine, Marge paused to enjoy the sight of her people having fun. It was going to be all right! They really were a good bunch, hand-selected, fit, well trained. Whatever she had said to anyone else, in a secret, inside part of her heart Marge had felt a small but unsettling fear that her first really independent command might take qualities she hadn't known she would need. So far, not. So far, everything was going precisely as she had planned, according to the priorities she had laid out in her own mind. Priority 1, safeguard the integrity of the unit. And it was safeguarded; she could see the perimeter guards in regular patrol, a little disgruntled at missing the dance but carrying out their orders meticulously. Priority 2, accomplish the mission assigned. And that was well on the way. Priority 3, subject to accomplishing 1 and 2, make it a busy and happy camp. And that looked good, too.

She walked around the outskirts of the dance, nodding and smiling, not quite ready to get back on the floor. Tinka appeared beside her, one hand on her government-issue pouch, looking questioningly at her. Marge shook her head. She didn't need another joint just then. She was feeling happy and relaxed, but just the littlest bit light-headed. Part of it was the smarmy heat and the peculiar instability that came from weighing only about three-quarters what she had been used to for ten years. But she was feeling a little edgy, too, and checking dates in her mind, she thought she knew why. When she came near the medical officer she said in her ear, "Got your freezers going for the sperm and ovum bank yet, doc? Because I think I'm getting ready to make a donation."

"Noon tomorrow we'll be ready," Chiche Arkashvili promised. "But the way the boys and girls have been disappearing into the bushes, I don't know if we'll need it."

"Better to have it and not need it than need it and not have it. If I could, I'd—"

She stopped. "What would you do, colonel?"

"Forget it. Don't let me keep you from urgent business," said Marge amiably, and watched the doctor go on toward the latrine. If she could, she'd get a whole stock of frozen sperm and ova from Earth, because the bigger the gene pool you started with, the better the chances you'd have a healthy, stable population in another two or three generations. But she was not quite ready to put that request in her next letter to Santa Claus. She would have quite enough trouble with the items she was already determined to requisition, and from Christ's own number of light-years away her powers of argument were limited.

A few meters away the Bulgarian girl was in some sort of altercation with Stud Sweggert, the sergeant Marge had put onto the first of her ships. Normally she wouldn't have interfered, but there was something she wanted from Dimitrova.

"Tinka," she said softly over her shoulder.

"Yes'm."

"Stay with." Marge went up to the arguing couple, who stopped as she came close. "Sorry to break this up," she said.

Dimitrova glared at her. Feisty little prunt; it crossed Marge's mind that her first impulses about Ana Dimitrova might have been best, but it was not a useful thought anymore. She discarded it.

"There is nothing to break up, colonel," the girl said. "The sergeant wished to show me something I did not want to see."

"I bet he did, honey," Marge smiled. "Will you excuse us a second, sergeant?" And, when he was out of earshot, she asked, "How is your Indonesian, Dimitrova?"

"Indonesian? It is not one of my four-oh languages, but I believe I could translate a document satisfactorily."

"I don't want a document translated. I want to know how to say, 'Good morning. Where is the baseball park?'"

"What?"

"Shit, lady! Just tell us how to say it."

Ana hesitated and then, with some disdain, said, *"Selamat pagi, dimana lapangan baseball?"*

"Um." Marge rehearsed it to herself for a moment, glancing at Tinka. The orderly shrugged. "Well, write it down for me. Now, how do you say, 'Have you a map?'"

"Saudara punja peta?"

"Got that?" asked Marge, looking at the orderly. "Not sure? All right, Dimitrova, take Tinka to my office and write it out for her. Make sure she gets it right." For a moment she thought the Bulgarian might object, but then she nodded and the two of them started away.

Sergeant Sweggert was still standing there, three meters away, watching her with calm interest. Margie laughed. "What are you doing, sergeant—waiting to ask me for a dance? Or do you want to show me that little thing you were so anxious to drag out for Dimitrova?"

"Hell, colonel. You've got me all wrong."

"I bet I do. Sweggert," she said good-naturedly, "you're not a bad guy, but it's against my policy to, ah, fraternize with enlisted men. Except in an emergency, of course. And what you've got to show has been widely seen already, I guarantee you."

"Ah, no, colonel! It was educational. They got a tame gas-bag here, and it's real interesting."

"Yeah?" She looked at him more closely, and from the way he stood, the way his head sank into his shoulders, she realized that the man was pretty full of something. But he was also

RA, and whether they chose to call the present time night or day, as a practical matter Kung made it pretty close to broad daylight. "I'll take a look," she decided. She followed him behind the cook-tent, and there was one of the balloonists, clinging to a rope and singing softly and mournfully to itself. It was much bigger than the female she had seen at Camp Detrick, but obviously in some sort of trouble.

"What's it saying?" she demanded.

The sergeant said with a straight face, "I really don't know, ma'am. You want to hold him a minute? Just pull down on the rope."

Margie looked at him thoughtfully for a moment, but he was right—it was interesting. She pulled on the rope. "Damn thing's strong," she complained. "Hey, Sweggert! What are you doing?"

He had leaned down and pulled something out from under a tarpaulin. "Just a strobe light, ma'am."

"And what are you going to do with it?"

"Well," he said cunningly, "I haven't never seen it, but the guys say if you give one of these things a flash it's real interesting."

She looked from him to the sad, wrinkled face of the balloonist, and back. "Sergeant," she said grimly, "it damn well better be or I'll have your ass on toast. Flash your fucking strobe."

"Is that an order, ma'am?"

"Flash it!" she snarled. "Or—"

And then he did.

·FIFTEEN·

AFTER FOUR DAYS of trying, Ana was finally granted permission to use the radio for a call to the People's camp. When the communications clerk signaled *go*, she leaned forward and spoke in Urdu into the microphone. "This is Ana Dimitrova calling from the camp of the Food-Exporting Bloc. I wish to speak to Ahmed Dulla, please."

The comm clerk switched off the microphone and said, "Now you wait. It usually takes about ten minutes for a return message."

"Message? Can I not speak directly to Dr. Dulla?"

"Not with the Peeps, honey. We transmit a message, they transmit an answer. If they feel like it."

"How very queer. Well, thank you, I will wait outside." As she left she added, "Please call me when the answer comes."

"Count on it, sweets."

What a nuisance, she thought crossly, sitting lotus-legged in the warm electric-heater glow from Kung overhead. Still— ten minutes! She had waited much longer than ten minutes to hear Ahmed's voice. And at least his plight could no longer be as serious as she had feared at first. The word was out in the camp that the People's Republics, through what superhuman exertions one could hardly imagine, had succeeded in reestablishing communication with their outpost on Jem. A ship had landed—a small one, to be sure, but at least they were no longer helplessly dependent on the other colonies for the means to survive. How that must have angered Dulla!

Around her the camp was very busy. Nearly a hectare had been cleared and seeded on the slopes above, and the stanchions were in place for the lights that would make the seeds grow. Power would be next, and that was already being attended to. The Food Bloc at last had its own solar-power plant in process of assembly, and meanwhile there was a nuclear-fueled steam plant already in operation—small, expensive, but reliable.

Ana was the best of the three translators in the camp and, since the disappearance of Harriet Santori, the only one who seemed capable of picking up the fine structure of an only partly understood language. Her Krinpit was quite imperfect, and there seemed little chance to practice it. For the burrowers she had spent much time with this James Morrissey, who seemed to have taken them as his personal reason for existence; but none of it had come to much. The microphones he insinuated so gently into the tunnels sometimes picked up a scrap or two of squealing, chittering, half-muffled sounds; but evidently the burrowers detected them at once and avoided them—when they didn't steal them. More than once Morrissey had pulled out a probe and found the working head neatly disconnected.

But with the balloonists she had become almost fluent. She had worked closely with Professor Dalehouse, so far only by radio; the intriguing but frightening prospect of soaring with him under a cluster of bags of hydrogen was for some indeterminate time in the future. Then the Russian pilot, Kappelyushnikov, had taken off with Colonel Menninger's orderly and a cluster of hydrogen tanks on some foolish, secretive errand, and she had been ordered off the radio until further notice. Instead she was assigned to clerical work in the tiny hospital, where there was no clerical work to speak of, since it had as yet no real patients.

But. Regardless. No matter what the small frustrations and annoyances, was she not on Jem, only a matter of a few score kilometers at most from Ahmed? Not to mention the dizzying excitement of being on Jem at all. Another planet! Circling another star! So far from home that not even the sun itself could be found in the ruddy Jemman sky! She had not yet dared to go out into the jungle (though others had, and returned safe and excited at the strangenesses they had seen). She had not even swum in that great lake, or sea, so temptingly near; she had not thought to bring a bathing suit, had not yet found time to make one, and certainly would not follow the custom of those others who frolicked in nothing at all along the beach. Just now she could see a batch of them splashing and shouting. They were supposed to be working on the hydroplanes that were being assembled at the water's edge, but their thoughts, she would warrant, were far less on transportation than on the animal joy of the beach.

Not, she thought justly, that that in itself was wrong; why should they not? It was not Ana's concern if other persons had moral standards different from her own, so long as they did not try to inflict them on her. And splashing would in fact be great fun in this muggy heat—

"Dimitrova!" She jumped up and ran inside the tent for her answer, but it was only:

"Ahmed Dulla is not available at present. The message will be given to him."

In English. And English with a very bad accent, at that; whatever Heir-of-Mao had sent, it was not good translators. She thanked the comm clerk, concealing her disappointment, and strolled toward the perimeter. Off duty, not time to eat, too early to sleep; what should she do since she could not do the thing she wanted most?

Really, it was too disappointing! Where could he be?

She was annoyed to discover that she was beginning another headache. How infuriating! For some reason she had not had very many in her first days on Jem—perhaps because everything was so intensely exciting that she had no time to think of headaches. She did not want one now. Ana was an industrious person by nature, and it occurred to her that idleness was not likely to prevent the headache, but only to make it worse. What to do? If she only had a proper costume, how agreeable it would be to help the boatbuilders on the beach. Or to climb the slope and assist in planting—but no, at the moment they were only plowing, and she did not know how to run the tractor. The power plant? She knew nothing of it, of course, but she had sturdy limbs and a willingness to use her muscles. Why not?

Unfortunately, as she approached she discovered that one of the noncoms working on the project was Sergeant Sweggert.

She changed course and walked briskly away.

She had avoided Sweggert since the night she had come back with the colonel's orderly and found the two of them in rut, out in the open for all to see! Of course, no other had seen. Nan had turned away at once, sweating with embarrassment, and there had been no one else, or all the camp would have been talking of it. Tinka would not speak, Sweggert would perhaps not dare to, and the colonel—well, Ana did not have the delusion that she understood the colonel. But Colonel Marge Menninger she had not been able to avoid, and the woman had said nothing of the incident, had in fact showed no signs that it had ever taken place. That bleached American, copulating with a man whose name she perhaps did not even know! No, that was unfair; they knew each other.

But certainly not socially. Oh, yes, to be sure, she would blame it on the aphrodisiac effect of the—the mist, she put it to herself, that the wounded balloonist emitted. One had heard all about that by now. Still, how appallingly lewd! Not to say—what was the word?—"tacky."

Ana found herself at a guard post in the perimeter fence, and at once it became clear what she wished to do. "I am going for a walk," she told the corporal in charge, who shrugged and watched impassively as Ana squeezed between the strands of the barbed wire.

In a few steps she was out of sight of the camp.

If she could not see Ahmed, at least she could see Jem. She pushed through the violet-oily growth, here all flickering with blue-green lights, and paused to listen: tiny skittering sounds from the underbrush, the rustle of the plants in the wind. There was no wildlife here that would harm her, she had been assured. Because of the presence of the camp, there were not many animals at all. Some had been frightened away, some poisoned away; where the garbage details had brought a day's collection of slops into the woods and buried them, you could see the ferns withered, the crabgrass ground cover dry. Terrestrial biochemistry was as hostile to Jemman as the other way around, but the Jemmans had not had a Camp Detrick to make them salves and injections against the rot.

But what was left—how fascinating and how strange! Forests of plants like ferns, but fruiting and with woody stems; succulents almost like bamboo (the hollow stems would make good structural materials, and Ana's thrifty soul instructed her to tell the colonel not to waste precious iron on tent stakes anymore); vines like grapes, with hard seeds no doubt meant to be spread in the excrement of small animals (if any survived in this part of the forest); and the mangrovelike giants called "many-trees," a dozen or more trunks linking together at the crown, which made a canopy over her.

She stopped and looked around. There was no question of getting lost, she reassured herself, as long as she kept the red-glinting water in sight on her left. At any time she could simply climb down to it and return along the beach.

And there was no question of being tired here, either, when one climbed so lightly over fallen logs and rocks. It was an excellent time for taking a nature stroll, she thought, squirming between the trunks of a many-tree that glittered blue-green in firefly beads—if only her head did not hurt so.

In front of her was a lump of fungus, gray-pink and without lights of its own. It looked quite like a brain, she thought. In fact, rather like her own. Since the brain splitting had been done under local anesthesia she had seen every step, sometimes in the mirror overhead, sometimes in the closed-circuit likris screen. That was how her brain had seemed to her, quite remote and unfeeling. Even when the sharp hooked blade had halved it in one smooth motion, it had been hard to connect that sight with the insistent dragging pressure that was all she felt. . . . Later, when they were reconnecting some of the necessary nerves, she suddenly felt the reality of it. She would have been ill except for the surgeon's motherly scorn. "A great strong girl like you!" she had laughed. "No. Nonsense! You will not vomit." And Nan had not. . . .

What was that noise?

It sounded like distant sticks rattling against hollow logs and someone moaning. It was the sort of sound she had heard before, on tapes at Camp Detrick. The crustaceans, yes! But perhaps not the social race. Perhaps those wild and surely dangerous ones that had been only rumored—

The human voice that came from behind her was severe. "Is it sensible for you to be alone here, Ana?"

In Urdu! With that stern compassion she had heard so often! She knew before she turned that it was Ahmed.

An hour later, a kilometer away, she lay in his arms, unwilling to move lest she wake him. The Krinpit's sound was always audible, sometimes near, sometimes moving farther away; she smiled to herself as she thought that the creature had surely been near while they were making love. No matter. It was not a matter for shame, what she would proclaim anywhere. It was not at all like that American bleached blond, because—well, of course, because it was with Ahmed.

He twitched, snorted, and woke up. "Ah, Ana! Then I did not dream this!"

"No, Ahmed." She hesitated and then said in a softer voice, "But I have had that dream many times. . . . No! Not so quickly again, please, dear Ahmed—or yes, whenever you like; but first let me look at you." She shook her head and scolded, "You are so thin! Have you been ill?"

The black-bead eyes were opaque. "Ill? Yes, sometimes. Also sometimes starving."

"Starving! How terrible! But—but—"

"But why starve? That is simple to answer. Because your people shot down our transports."

"But that is quite impossible!"

"It is not impossible," he contradicted, "because it happened. Food for many days, scientific instruments, two ships —and thirty-four human beings, Ana."

"It must have been an accident."

"You are naive." He got up angrily, pulling his clothes together. "I do not blame you, Ana. But those crimes are a fact, and I must blame someone." He disappeared behind a many-tree, and after a moment she could hear the splashing of his urine against the bole.

And also another sound: the Krinpit's rattle and moan, growing close again. If only she had had more time with the tapes at Detrick! But even so, she could distinguish a pattern that was repeated over and over. *Sssharrn*—, and then two quick notes: *eye-gone*.

She called weakly, "Ahmed?" and heard his laugh.

"Ah, Ana, does my friend frighten you? He will not harm us. We are not good for him to eat."

"I did not know you had such friends."

"Well, perhaps I have not. No. We are not friends. But as I am the enemy of his enemies, we are allies at least. Come along, Sharn-igon," he said, like a householder strolling a puppy, and came back into view.

Scuttling lopsidedly behind him was a great nightmare creature, rattling and moaning. Ana had never been so close to an adult, live Krinpit, had never quite realized their size and the loudness of their sounds. It did not have a crab's claws. It had jointed limbs that waved above it, two that tapered to curved points like a cat's claw, two that ended in fistlike masses of shell.

It paused, seeming to regard Nan, although as far as she could tell it had no eyes. And among the sounds, she recognized words in Urdu! Syllable by syllable, it scratched and grumbled out a sentence.

"Is this one to die?"

"No, no!" said Ahmed quickly. "She is—" He hesitated, then emitted sounds in the Krinpit language. Perhaps it was his accent, but Ana could not understand a word. "I have told him you are my he-wife," he explained.

"He-wife?"

"They have a very rich sexual life," he said.

"Please, Ahmed. I am not ready for a joking little chat. The Krinpit said 'to die,' and what does it mean?"

"Naïve Ana," he said again, looking at her thoughtfully. Then he shrugged. He did not reply, but he unwrapped a ruddy-brown leaf from an object he had been carrying. It was a flat metal blade, broader at the end, the edge razor-sharp. The hilt was sized to fit a man's hand, and the whole thing half a meter long.

"Ahmed! Is that a sword?"

"A machete. But you are right; it is a sword also now."

"Ahmed," she said, her heart pounding harder than the throbbing in her head, "some days ago three persons from the Food camp were killed. I have thought it was an accident, but now I am not sure. Shall I ask you if you know anything of this?"

"Ask what you like, woman."

"Tell me!"

He thrust the machete into the loamy ground. "All right, if you will have it so, I will tell you. No. I did not kill those Fats. But yes, I know of their death. I do not mourn them, I hope many more will die. And if it is necessary for me to kill a few, I shall not shrink from it!"

"But—but— But Ahmed," she babbled, "dear, gentle Ahmed, this is murder! Worse than murder, it is an act of war! Suppose the Food Bloc retaliates? Suppose our homelands do not accept this as a mere struggle far away, but themselves retaliate on each other? Suppose—"

"Have done with your supposing!" he shouted. "What can they do to retaliate? Bomb Pakistan? Let them! Let them destroy Hyderabad and Multan, let them bomb Karachi, let them wipe out all the cities and burn the whole coast. You have been there, Ana. How much of Pakistan can be destroyed? What bombs can blast through mountains? The people will survive. The leeches that flock to the cities to beg, the government parasites—yes, the intellectuals, the proud bloodsuckers like you and me—what do I care if they all die? The people in the valleys will live!"

She was silent, frightened, searching for words that might sway him and finding none. "Ah," he said in disgust, "what is the sense of this? But do not be angry with me."

"Angry? That is not what I feel," she said miserably.

"Then what? Hatred? Fear? Ana, what are we to do? Let them starve us? We have one small ship to save us, and what have the Fats and the Greasies? Navies! And if the fighting spreads—" He hesitated and then burst out, "Let it! Let all the rich ones kill each other. What do we care? Remember, six out of ten human beings on Earth are ours! If there is war on Earth—if only a million survive, then six hundred thousand of them will be citizens of the People's Republics. And here—"

She shook her head, almost weeping. "And here? Sixty percent too?"

"No. More. On Son of Kung—if anyone survives—one hundred percent ours."

·SIXTEEN·

THE RAINS were all around, squall clouds driving toward them, squall clouds already past them, up toward the Heat Pole, where the raindrops fell a kilometer or two and then evaporated, never striking the hot, salt ground. The flock was spread out over a kilometer of sky, and grumbling in dissonant chords.

"Have patience," Charlie scolded them. "We must stay, must stay."

And they echoed, "We must stay," but it was poorly sung.

No matter. Charlie had promised his two-legged friend that they would stay on station, waiting to observe certain strange and incomprehensible events, and the flock would do as he vowed.

Still, it was uncomfortable to him, like an itch or a sunburn to a human being, to have the swarm in such disarray. The place he had promised to watch was upwind of the camp of the Big Sun. It did not do to come too close to that. Many of his flock, and even more of other flocks, had been punctured or burned by the far-striking missiles of that camp, and so he had to try to keep the flock from drifting toward it, seeking every counterflowing gust, and still avoid the squalls as much as possible. Dalehouse had told him that it would be difficult. But he had also said it was important.

Charlie rotated his eye patches over the entire horizon. No sign of the aircraft he had been told to expect. But he did see a vagrant drift of thistledown and spinner silk moving across the hills below. A crosscurrent! He sang his flock together and vented gas.

The swarm followed, dropping into a level where the wind took them away from the rain to a likely-looking area of updraft. They followed well, everything considered. Expertly he guided them under the base of a fair-weather cumulus, and they rose with the drift.

The song of the swarm became contented. It was at the top of these invisible pillars of rising air that the best feeding was found: pollen and butterfly-seed capsules, the small, soft creatures that filled the same ecological niche that insects did on Earth, dried salt particles from the wavelets of landlocked seas, and even tinier things. A flock at feed was queer-looking, with every fin and frill extended to trap whatever touched it. It was also at risk, or once would have been. It was a favorite time for the *ha'aye'i* to knife in, slashing every bag they passed and tearing the life out of the victims before the helpless gaze of their flock-mates. Helpless no more! Charlie sang a boastful song of his great friend Danny Dalehouse, who had given them the far-striking weapons that drove the *ha'aye'i* a hundred clouds away. Or sometimes did. Now each male and some of the females in his own flock had the weapons, and the *ha'aye'i* had come to recognize Charlie's swarm and avoid it.

Although, in truth, it was no longer as tempting to the predators as it had once been. So few were left! Once there had been hundreds, now fewer than a score.

There was still no aircraft on the horizon, nothing happening on the mesa upwind of the camp of the Big Sun. Charlie relaxed and fed with his swarm, and as he ate he became more mellow. He led the flock in gentle songs of childhood and joy.

There had been a time when Charlie was a tiny pip-sized pod, pumping mightily to bulge the creases out of his little gasbag but still tied to the ragged end of his sailing ribbon and to the winds that bore it where they liked. Gusts blew. Air-to-air lightning spat all around him. Because he had no real control over his altitude he was sometimes tossed up through the tops of towering convection clouds, with the dull red sun hot on his tiny balloon and actual stars shining through the murky sky; other times he was so low that he brushed hills and fern trees, and shelled or furred creatures clutched after him as he spun by. Eighty out of a hundred of his brood-mates died then, in one of those ways or in some other. Ten more died almost as soon as their drift-ribbons fell away, when they were tasty hors d'oeuvres for the *ha'aye'i*, or sometimes for the protein-hungry adults of another chance-met flock. Or even of their own. Only a few out of each hundred survived to reproduce. And then there were still the *ha'aye'i*. And the storms. And the clutching beasts from below.

But still—to be a balloonist! To soar and to sing! Above all, to share the chorused flocklore that united them every one, from the tiniest pod to the leaky, old, slow giants that even the *ha'aye'i* scorned. Charlie's song was triumphant, and all the flock around him stopped their greedy gobbling to join in the harmony.

Still his eye patches rotated watchfully toward the mesa; but still there was no sign of the airplane or of the New Friend he had been told would rise from the spot. And they were drifting with the cloud, away from the camp of the Big Sun.

Many of the flock were sated now, softly singing their private courtesy songs of thanksgiving. They were a fine flock, although, Charlie admitted, very few in number.

He sang to them, "Stop feeding, stop feeding! We must go!"

"Go where, go where?" grumbled a chorus of the slower and hungrier ones, and an individual song sounded above the choir.

Faintly: "I must eat more. I die." That was the old female, Blue-Rose Glow. Her bag had been meanly seared when half the flock was set aflame.

"Not now, not now," sang Charlie commandingly. "Follow!" And he sang the new song, the duty song he had learned from his friend Danny Dalehouse. It was no longer enough to float and sing and replenish hydrogen and breed. Not anymore. Station must be kept and the mesa observed. And the camp of the Big Sun must be avoided, and the *ha'aye'i* guarded against, and the swarm kept together; so many imperatives, both the new and the old! And so he led them through their slow, bobbing dance, crisscross with the winds.

For a long time he led them, watching ceaselessly as he had promised. Even so, it was not he who first saw the thing. From far behind, old Blue-Rose Glow sang feebly, "There is a new Sky-Danger."

"Catch up, catch up!" he commanded. "You sing poorly." It was not sung in unkindness but only because it was true.

"I leak," she apologized. "Nevertheless it is there, almost in reach of the Earth-Dangers, far away."

He rotated his eye patches and rose to another air current. There it was. "I see the Sky-Danger," he sang, and the rest of the flock confirmed. It was not a *ha'aye'i*. It was the hard mechanical thing from the camp of the Middle Sun, as he had been told. In it, he knew, was the Other Friend who had sometimes soared with Danny Dalehouse, and also the New Friend he had not yet seen.

It was all as had been said by Danny Dalehouse. The biplane slunk in at treetop level and set itself down on the dry mesa a dozen kilometers upwind of the Greasy camp. While the swarm watched, Kappelyushnikov and a female person emerged and began to fill a net of balloons out of tiny tanks.

When the New Friend's cluster began to swell and she rose gently from the ground, the aircraft took off again, turned quickly, and slipped back down the slope toward the distant ocean-lake. The New Friend rose into the prevailing poleward wind and drifted directly toward the camp of the Big Sun.

Charlie dared come no closer, but he saw her venting gas as she approached the camp. She tumbled into the underbrush somewhere nearby; and it was all as had been foretold.

"The thing is done," Charlie caroled triumphantly.

"And what now?" asked the swarm, milling around him, staring after the New Friend as she fell.

"I will ask the air," he sang. His little insect legs fumbled at the switch of the hard, shiny speaker-to-air Danny Dalehouse had given him. He sang a questioning greeting to his friend.

He tried twice, listening between times as Dalehouse had taught him. There was no answer, only an unpleasant hissing song of static and distant storms.

"We must go near to the camp of the Middle Sun," he announced. "The speaker-to-air cannot sing so far." His skilled eyes read the signs of the clouds and the fern tops far below, seeking the currents he wanted. It was too bad that Dalehouse could so seldom soar with the flock these days because of the hated ha'aye'i of his own kind, but Charlie knew that once they were in line of sight the speaker-to-air would bring his song.

"Follow!" he sang. He swarmed the flock around him. They dropped, all fourteen of them, through a fast-moving layer of stratus cloud into the backflow near the surface.

When they emerged, old Blue-Rose Glow was gone, the leaks in her bag finally too great to allow her to remain airborne. So was the young female called Shrill-Squeal, nowhere in sight, even her song no longer audible.

By the time they approached the camp of the Middle Sun

and Charlie began to sing through the radio to Dalehouse, there were only twelve left in the flock.

Marge Menninger looked up as Kappelyushnikov came in from the orderly room, closing the flap to her private office behind him. "Any word?" she asked.

"Danny has had radio from gasbag, yes. Your friend was seen to descend near Greasies, all in order."

"How long ago?"

"With gasbags, who can say? Perhaps some hours. Not long after I departed spy-drop scene."

"All right. Thanks." After he left, Marge started to call the communications tent, then decided against it. If the Greasies radioed that they had rescued Tinka, blown helplessly off course, the communications clerk would let her know. And he hadn't. So the Greasies were playing it covert and slick, and what was Tinka up against in their camp? Had they figured out that she really wasn't there by accident? Could she . . . ? Were they . . . ? Wasn't it . . . ? Questions multiplied themselves in Margie's mind endlessly, and there was no straightforward way of getting answers. You could get your ass lost in those swamps of contingencies and subjunctives.

That was not the way Marge Menninger ran her life. She made a decision. In one hour exactly she would have the comm clerk radio a query to the Greasies, and until then she would put it out of her mind. Meanwhile, lunch was fifty minutes away, and what to use that time for?

The fifteen notes she had made to herself on this morning's calendar had all been checked off. All current projects were on schedule, or close enough. Everyone had been assigned tasks. The first hectare of wheat was in the ground, sixteen different strains competing to see which would thrive best. The perimeter defenses were in order. Three turrets still sat on the beach, ready to be put where needed when she wanted to expand the perimeter or establish another post. She looked at the 1:1000 map, two meters long and a meter high, that covered almost all of one wall of her office. That was something! It showed every feature within a kilometer of where she sat—seven creeks or rivers, a dozen hills, two capes, several bays. Grid references were not enough, they needed names. What better way to name them than to let individual members of the camp pick them? She would organize a drawing; each winner could name something, and that would give them something to do. She called in her temporary orderly and dictated a short memo for the bulletin board. "Check it with the communications section," she finished. "Make sure we list all the features worth naming."

"Yes'm. Colonel? Sergeant Sweggert wants to see you. Says it's not urgent."

Margie wrote *Sweggert* on her calendar. "I'll let you know." Then she put Sweggert out of her mind, too. She had not yet decided what to do about Sweggert. She had a wide variety of options, from laughing it off to court-martialing him for rape. Which she elected would depend a lot on how Sweggert conducted himself. So far he had had the smarts to keep a low profile around her.

On the other hand, she thought, her authority to court-martial anybody for anything rested on the military chain of command, which extended up from her through the tactran link to higher authority on Earth. And who was to say how long Earth would give a shit about backing her up? Or about whether the colony lived or died? The news from home was bad, so bad that she had not passed all of it on to the camp. The tactran message acknowledging her shopping list had advised that it was touch and go whether she would get everything she had asked for. And requests for further supplies after that shipment were, quote, to be evaluated in terms of conditions at the time of receipt of requisition, unquote.

It was what she had expected. But it was sobering.

On her pad for the afternoon she made two notes: *Medic. —bank okay? Food—6 mos. estimate firm? Stretch 1 yr w rationing?*

It was a damn nuisance that the agronomists all seemed to

be Canadian! Margie needed some smart and private help—smart, because how they managed their crops was quite likely to be life-and-death for the colony; private, because she didn't want the colony to know that just yet. If she got everything on her shopping list she would have plenty of seed stock. But who knew whether she had the ones that would grow best?

Dismiss that thought, too.

Forty minutes left.

She unlocked the private drawer of her desk and lit a joint. Assume the shopping list all gets delivered. There was enough on it for pretty fair margin against most kinds of disasters, she thought, and there was no sense worrying until she had to.

The requisition list included a good chunk of personal things for Margie herself: clothes, cosmetics, microfiche sewing patterns. With the patterns there would be enough variety in styles to suit everyone in the camp, male or female, for a good long time, assuming they found some way of producing fabrics to make the patterns on. It would be nice to have some pretty clothes. She was already beginning to feel the absence of Sakowitz, Marks and Sparks, Sears, and Two Guys. One day, maybe, she thought, drawing a deep hit. Not Sakowitz, no. But maybe a few boutiques. Maybe some of the people in the camp had sewing or tailoring skills, and maybe it was about time she started locating them. She flipped the calendar ahead a few pages and made a note on a virgin page. That Bulgarian prunt was the kind of girly-girl who would like to sew, possibly even as much as Margie did herself; she had been pretty morose after her long walk in the countryside, but she did her work and might need something to occupy her mind. It didn't seem that she wanted a man for that purpose; at least, she had thoroughly discouraged Guy Tree and Cappy and Sweggert . . .

Sweggert.

"Jack, send the sergeant in," she called.

"Yes'm. He's gone back to the perimeter, but I'll get him."

As she leaned back, marshalling her thoughts about Sweggert, the handset buzzed; it was the communications clerk. "Colonel? I was just talking to the Greasies about Sergeant Pellatinka."

"I didn't tell you to ask them."

"No'm. But I kept sending on her frequency like you ordered, and their radioman cut in to ask if we had lost her. So I said she didn't answer. So they said they'd send out a party to look for her."

Margie sat back and took a thoughtful drag on the joint. According to the balloonists, there was no way the Greasies couldn't have seen her come down. So now they were overtly lying.

Sergeant Sweggert shared a number of traits with Marge Menninger. One of them was that he was willing to go to a lot of trouble to get things right, and then if he saw a chance for improvement he was willing to do whatever it took to make them righter. When he perceived that moving the Number Three machine-gun emplacement two meters toward the lake would improve the field of fire, he moved it. Or his squad did. The fact that it took five hours of backbreaking work did not affect his decision. He lent a hand to put the HMG on its tripod and swung it to check the field. "Fucking lousy," he told the crew, "but we'll leave it for now. Get that ammo restowed."

He crouched behind the gun, swiveling it through full traverse. It was an act that gave him pleasure. As far as the shore of the lake on the extreme left and the beginning of the fern forest on the right, there was no way that any sizable creature could approach without being a clear target for the gunner. The claymores and smoke bombs were emplaced and fused, and his command-post detonating radio was keyed to each of them. The floodlights were in position, with quadruple redundancy. At any given moment only a quarter of them were lit, searching the entire area around the perimeter. Every hour that quarter went off and the next quarter came on so that any burned-out bulbs or wiring deficiencies would distribute themselves equally and could be fixed in the downtime. In actual combat, of course, they would all be on. Most would be shot out, but not in time to let anyone cross that perimeter. Not alive.

Although, he admitted to himself as he climbed out of the dome, the chances that anyone would try a straightforward frontal attack were very small. Maybe an attack from the sky. Maybe by long-range rocket fire. Maybe not at all. This whole fucking shoot-up was crazy, if you asked Sergeant Sweggert. What the fuck was there to fight about in this asshole place without a bar or a town or even, for God's sake, a decent tree or field? If you had asked him, that was what he would have said, in total sincerity, but it would not have stopped him from fighting for it.

And inside he was swearing. The colonel wouldn't have kept him waiting like this a week ago. If she was going to shaft him, what was she waiting for? . . . "Sarge." He looked up. "They're calling you from the orderly room." He turned idly and saw the corporal waving.

"Aggie, take over," he ordered. "If I come back and that ammo isn't restowed, it's all your asses."

He strolled back toward the HQ tent and walked in. Marge Menninger was eating out of a mess kit, reading from a small-screen viewer. She didn't look up. "The perimeter's looking good, Sweggert," she said. "Got that machine gun back in place?"

"Yes'm. Colonel? There's a bunch of gasbags around, and that one we been using is about used up. We'll be relieved in a couple of minutes. Can we get a fix from the new ones?"

She put down her spoon and looked at him. After a moment, she said, "Just who do you mean by 'we,' soldier?"

"Oh, no, ma'am!" Jesus, she was touchy! He knew he was close to trouble. "I don't mean nothing, ma'am, just that the detail's been working hard and they need a little break. We'll

—they'll come out of it in an hour, and the relief'll be there anyway."

She studied him for a moment. "That's four-oh, Sweggert, but only half the detail. Keep the rest sober."

"Sure thing, colonel. Thank you, colonel." He got out of there as fast as he could. Shit, he should've been more careful, knowing how she felt and all. Not that she was all wrong. If he hadn't been drunk he wouldn't have done it. But, shit! It was worth it. Remembering the way she had been with a skin full of the balloonist mist, his groin grew heavy.

When he got back to the detail he looked at them with some disapproval. Corporal Kristianides was skinny and had sideburns all down her cheeks, but she was the best he had to pick from. "Aggie, take Peterson and four others; you're on duty till the relief shows up. Kris, you and the rest come along with me. We're gonna take ourselves a jizzum break. Anybody don't want to come, switch with somebody don't want to stay. Let's move it."

The balloonists were out over the ocean-lake now, half a kilometer away and low. Sweggert marched his dozen troops across the camp to the empty tents at the end of the company street; he would do it in the open if he had to, but damned if he wouldn't take a little privacy when he could get it. The tethered balloonist, further than ever from recuperating, had been moved there days since, along with the strobe light.

Sweggert stopped, swearing. Nan Dimitrova and Dalehouse were talking to the balloonist, and only a few meters away the Russian pilot, Kappelyushnikov, was complaining about something to Colonel Tree. Privacy, *shit.* But it didn't matter; he had Colonel Menninger's permission, and she was the one who counted. He retrieved the strobe and pointed it toward the hovering swarm.

Predictably, Dalehouse butted in. "What do you think you're doing, Sweggert?"

Sweggert took time to aim the strobe and flash it to bring

them in before he answered. "Gonna have a little fun. The colonel said it was okay."

"Hell she did! Anyway—"

"Anyway," Sweggert interrupted, "why don't you go check with her if you don't believe me? Would you move a little, sir? You're getting between them and the light."

Ana Dimitrova laid her hand on Dalehouse's arm to keep him from replying. "It is not fun for the balloonists, Sergeant Sweggert. To experience sexual climax is very painful and debilitating. As you can see, this one is seriously affected. It may die."

"What a way to go, hey, Ana?" Sweggert grinned. "Take it up with the colonel—hey, Dalehouse! What are you doing?"

Dalehouse had switched on his radio and was singing softly into it. Colonel Tree, beginning to pay attention, walked toward them, and Sweggert turned to him. "Colonel! We have Colonel Menninger's permission to get the Loonies in for a fix, and this guy's telling them to screw off!"

Tree stopped with his hands clasped behind his back and nodded gravely. "A dilemma," he said in his soft child's voice. "It will be quite interesting to see what they do."

What they were doing was spreading themselves all over the sky, some dropping lower to catch the onshore breeze, others hesitating. They were singing loudly and discordantly, and the sounds came distantly from the sky and tinnily from the radio in Dalehouse's hand. Sweggert stood rock-still, controlling the rage that was building up in him. Fucking Cong! When you had the CO's permission, that was all you were supposed to need! Why wouldn't Tree back him up?

"Gimme that," he growled, reaching out for Dalehouse's radio.

But Dalehouse's expression had changed. "Hold it," he snapped, and sang a quick phrase into the radio. The answer came back as a cascade of musical phrases; Dalehouse looked startled and Ana Dimitrova gasped, her hand to her lips. "Tree," he said, "according to Charlie, there's some Krinpit down the beach, and they're eating a couple of people."

"But Krinpit do not eat human beings," objected Colonel Tree, and Sweggert chimed in:

"There's nobody down there. Nobody's gone through the perimeter all day."

Dalehouse repeated his question into the radio and shrugged. "That's what he says. He could be wrong about the eating part, I guess—he doesn't have a very clear concept of killing, except to eat."

Sweggert put down the strobe. "We better tell the colonel," he said.

Colonel Tree said, "That's correct. You do so, Dalehouse. Sergeant, form your squad on the beach in thirty seconds, full combat gear. We're going to see what's happening."

Half an hour later Marge Menninger herself, with thirty armed grunts behind her, met the first party coming back along the beach. There were no casualties, or at least none from the Food Bloc, but they were carrying two people. One was in a sort of sling made from two jackets knotted together, the other on Sergeant Sweggert's shoulder, fireman-carry. They were both dead. When Sweggert put his burden down it was obvious why he had been easy to carry. Both legs were missing, and so was part of his head.

The other body was less mutilated, so that Marge Menninger recognized her at once.

It was Tinka.

Marge stood numbly while Sweggert made his report. No Krinpit in sight; they had got away, so far that they couldn't even be heard. Both people were dead when they got there, but recently; the bodies were still warm. For that matter, they were still warm now. And the man had had a packet in a waterproof wrapping inside his shirt. Margie accepted it and tore it open. Microfiches—scores of them. The man's ID card, which showed that he was the Indonesian Tinka had gone to contact. A pair of child-sized spectacles—flat glass, not optically ground. Why glasses? For that matter, how had the two got here? Had they been caught as spies and then somehow escaped? And how had they come the long distance from the Greasy camp to the beach where they died?

By the time they got back to the base, she had an answer to at least part of the question, because Dalehouse reported that the balloonists had spotted something farther down the beach that looked like the remains of a deflated rubber boat. She swung the tiny glasses from their elastic band as she listened, nodding, taking in all of it as information to process, not quite ready to take in the information of Tinka's death as a pain to feel.

She looked down at the glasses. They were now almost opaque.

"That's interesting," she said in a voice that was very nearly normal. "They must be photosensitive glass. Like indoor-outdoor sunglasses." She glanced up at the sullen red coal of Kung overhead. "Only what in the world would anybody want with them on Jem?"

·SEVENTEEN·

SIX KILOMETERS down the shoreline from where he had slain the Poison Ghosts, Sharn-igon paused in his flight to scratch out a shallow pit under a bluff. He needed to hide because he needed to rest.

Digging was always dangerous for a Krinpit because of the Ghosts Below. But here it was unlikely they would be near—too close to the water. They did not like to risk their tunnels flooding. And the many-tree on the bluff above him was a good sign. The roots of the many-tree were distasteful to them.

As he settled himself in, Sharn-igon wondered briefly what had become of his cobelligerent, the Poison Ghost Dulla. He did not feel concern, as one might for a fellow being. He did not think of Dulla in that way. Dulla was a weapon, a tool, without "being-ness." After they had slain the Poison Ghosts Dulla called "Greasies," they had both fled, and of course Dulla had fled faster and farther. Sharn-igon did not think of that as a betrayal. If he had been the nimble one and Dulla the slow-moving, he would certainly have done the same. Dulla's utility as a tool lay in his speed and in the way he was able to speak words to other Poison Ghosts that caused them to hesitate, to be uncertain, while Sharn-igon had time to come in upon them and kill. It was so very easy to kill Poison Ghosts! A few slashes, a blow with the club-claw—it took no more than that. Sometimes they had weapons, and Sharn-igon had learned to respect some of those weapons. But the two on the beach had had so little—a bright-sounding pop-gun whose tiny bullets bounced off his shell, a thing that squirted some sort of foul, stinging smell that made him feel queer and unpleasant for a moment but did not slow him in the kill. Such as they he could kill with or without his tool, the Poison Ghost Dulla.

He switched his carapace back and forth to wedge himself deeper in his pit and rested, his hearing receptors watchful toward the water, his feelers drilled deep into the soil to listen for vibrations from any approaching Ghosts Below. It was the burrowers he feared, more than any danger from the water or the beach.

Of course, in normal circumstances an adult Krinpit in shell was a match for a dozen of the Ghosts Below—as long as he could stay on the surface, or at least in sound of it. In the open, Ghosts Below seemed deaf, running almost at random. But these were not normal circumstances. Sharn-igon was not only weary; he felt sick. He felt irritable, tense, bloated—ready, he would have said to his he-wife (but Cheee-pruitt was months dead, his carapace dry), to stridulate and jump out of his shell. But it was not the right time for that. He was not due for many months yet, so it couldn't be normal pre-molt tension.

Abruptly his sphincter loosened. He regurgitated every-thing he had eaten in a great flood—meat of deafworm, scraps of chitin of crabrat, half-digested fruits and fungi and leaves.

Vomiting left him weak but calm. After resting for a mo-ment, he covered the mess over and then methodically began to clean his shell. No doubt the Poison Ghosts were taking revenge for being killed on the beach. It had to be their scraps of flesh still caught in Sharn-igon's chelae that were making him ill. That—and the inner sickness that had claimed him when the Poison Ghosts first came to his city and began the remorseless chain of circumstance that had taken all joy from his life.

Krinpit did not cry. They had no tear ducts; they had no eyes to have tear ducts in. They did have the emotion of sorrow, and no culture-driven taboos against expressing it in their own way. That way was stillness. A quiet Krinpit—or as close to quiet as a Krinpit could get—was a weeping Krinpit.

For most of an hour, once he had polished the last dried particle of alien blood off his tympanum, Sharn-igon was nearly soundless: a rasp of claw against carapace, an occasional respiring moan, little else.

Unbidden, sounds of happier times echoed in his mind. He heard Cheee-pruitt again, and the little female—what was her name?—whom they had impregnated and who bore their young. She had been a dulcet creature. She had had almost a personality of her own, along with the bittersweet appeal of any mated female, her young growing and eating inside her until too much was destroyed and she died, and the brood polished her carapace clean and emerged to the loud, exciting world of their wife-father's back.

But everything was changed now.

It was all the fault of the Poison Ghosts! Ever since the first of them had arrived and Cheee-pruitt—dear, lost Cheee-pruitt—had had the unwisdom to try to eat it, Sharn-igon's world had fallen apart. Not just Cheee-pruitt, all of it. The Krinpit he had mobilized against the Poison Ghosts Dulla called Greasies had been punished severely. His own village-mates had been attacked from the air in reprisal, and so many of them were dead. And how many had he succeeded in killing in return? A few. Hardly any. The two on the beach, the handful that he and Dulla had surprised at the outpost—not

enough! And all of Dulla's plans had come to little: the Krinpit village nearest to the Fats had wavered and wobbled, promised to join in an attack and withdrawn the promise; and
meanwhile all he and Dulla could do was skulk around like
crabrats, looking for strays to attack and finding none. Until
the two came out of their sinking vessel—

There was a sound from the water.

Sharn-igon froze. It was not possible for him to be wholly
silent while he breathed at all, but he did his best.

He listened out of his shallow cave and heard a small, almost inaudible, blurred echo from the water. A coracle. And
in it what seemed to be a Poison Ghost.

Another to kill? It was approaching. Sharn-igon thrust himself out of the cave and reared up to defend himself; and then
he heard his own name shouted across the beach: "Sharn-
igon!" And then those barbarous sounds that were the name
of his mistrusted ally, or his truced foe: "OCK-med doo-
LAH."

He scuttled across the sand, half to greet Dulla, half still
ready to kill, as Dulla yelled and pleaded. "Hurry! The Fats
will be searching this whole coast. We must get out!"

With Sharn-igon aboard, the coracle rode very low in the
water. It could not easily sink. Its cellular shell entrapped too
much air for that. But it could swamp.

Crossing Broad Water it often did, and then both of them
splashed and bailed and kept a watchful eye or ear for Ghosts
Above until they could get under weigh again. The little sail
helped them when the wind blew fair, but there was no keel.
When the wind shifted, the sail had to come down and they
had to paddle. It seemed to take forever; and Sharn-igon felt
increasingly ill; and at every stroke or splash the grim recrimi-
nations continued.

"But for you, my he-wife would still be alive."

"You are foolish, Sharn-igon. He tried to kill us; it is not our
fault he died of it."

"And my village was attacked, and another village destroyed entirely, and I myself am ill."

"Speak of something else, Sharn-igon. Speak of the promises your Krinpit made to join in the attack on the Fats and how they broke them."

"I will speak of my sorrow and my anger, Ahmed Dulla."

"Then speak also of mine! We too have suffered in fighting with you against the common enemy."

"Suffered?"

"Yes, suffered! Before my radio was destroyed—by you, Sharn-igon, by your clumsiness!—I could hear no voice from my camp. They may be dead, all of them!"

"How many, Ahmed Dulla?"

"A dozen or more!"

"A dozen or more of you have then died. Of us, how many? Of persons, two hundred. Of females, forty. Of backlings and infants—"

But it was not until they had crossed Broad Water and Sharn-igon heard the silence from his city that he perceived the immensity of the tragedy. There was no originated sound! There were only echoes—and what echoes!

Always before, when he crossed Broad Water, the city had presented a bustling, beautiful sound. Not this time. He heard nothing. Nothing! No drone of immature males at the waterfront shredding the fish catch. No songs from the mold-eaters on the Great White Way. No hammering of stakes to build new palisades on the made land on the point. He heard the echo of his own sounds faintly returning to him and recognized the shadowy outline of the mooring rocks, a few sheds, one or two boats, some structures half destroyed, a litter of empty carapaces. Nothing else.

The city was dead.

The Poison Ghost Dulla chattered worriedly to him, and Sharn-igon made out the words. "Another attack! The place is empty. The Greasies must have come back to finish the job."

He could not reply. Stillness overcame him, a great, mourning silence so deep that even the Poison Ghost turned toward him in wonder. "Are you ill? What is happening?"

With great effort Sharn-igon scratched the words out on his tympanum. "You have killed my city and all my back-mates."

"We? Certainly not! It could not have been the People's Republics; we have not the strength anymore. It must have been the Greasies."

"Against whom you vowed to protect us!" roared Sharn-igon. He rose on hind legs to tower over Dulla, and the Poison Ghost cringed in fear. But Sharn-igon did not attack. He threw himself forward, out of the coracle, with a broad *splat* that sent the waves dancing. The water was shallow here. Sharn-igon managed to keep some of his hind feet on the oozy bottom, while enough of his breathing pores were above the surface to keep him from drowning. He charged up the shoreline, scattering the littered water in a V of foam.

The tragedy made him still again, at every step and at each fresh echo. Dead! All dead. The streets empty except for abandoned carapaces, already dry. The shops untended. The homes deserted. Not a living male, not a female, not even any scrambling, chittering young.

Dulla waded through the stink of dead and floating marine animals, towing the coracle and staring about. "What a horror!" he exclaimed. "We are brothers now more than ever, Sharn-igon."

"All of my brothers are dead."

"What? Well, yes. But we must be as brothers, to take revenge! We must be allies against the Greasies and the Fats."

Sharn-igon reared up, trapping him against the wall of a ruined shed. "I now need new allies, Ahmed Dulla," he ground out, falling upon him. In the last moment Dulla saw what was to happen and tried to escape. But it was too late; his quickness was not enough when he dodged from the snatching claws only to take the full force of the murderous club of chitin that stove his head in.

When he was quite sure Dulla was dead, Sharn-igon staggered away, blundering through the dried shells that had once been friends, to rest creakily against the wall of a shop he had once known.

He took little satisfaction in the death of one more Poison Ghost. He did not even mourn any longer for the death of his city. A nearer pain touched him. His joints were aching, his body felt bloated, his carapace seemed to be sundering at the seams. It was not his time. But there was no doubt about it. Alone in the open tomb that had once been his home, with no one to care for him while he was helpless, he was beginning to molt.

·EIGHTEEN·

AT 0130 HOURS, Major Santangelo, along with the pilot-engi-
neer who had brought in the third ship, reported in.

"Some good news, Margie. There's a coal outcropping in
the Bad Hills, two kilometers up. Plus we can burn wood and
biomass, and Richy here says we can make a steam boiler with
plates from one of the landing craft. If your turbine arrives,
that means we can drive the generator up to full capacity, fifty
kilowatts, without using up our fuel reserves."

"When?"

Santangelo looked at the engineer. "Ten days? Call it two
weeks."

"Call it one week," Margie snapped. "What about alcohol?"

"Well, Morrissey's got a kind of a yeast—something like a
yeast—anyway, he's getting fermentation. Should be putting
the first batch through the solar still tomorrow. You can probably smell it."

"Saint, I can *taste* it. I need that alcohol to stretch out the
airplane fuel!"

280

"I'll goose him along," Santangelo promised.

"Do it," said Margie. When they were gone she picked up the handset and called the radio shack. "Any ETA yet?"

"No, ma'am. They're still in orbit, figuring a minimum-energy descent." She hung up. At least the resupply ship was in orbit around Jem, not light-years away. But that last little step was a killer. The captain had radioed that his maneuvering reserve was low and he was waiting for the most favorable approach. That might be days! Worse than that. If the Cape had launched them without plenty of reserve, that meant things were seriously wrong at the Cape. Even wronger than the coded tactrans from Earth had indicated, and that was wrong enough.

She looked at her watch: 0145. "Send in Dr. Arkashvili," she called, and the medic came in on cue, bearing a cup of steaming black coffee.

"Medical supplies, Margie. But a little sleep would do you more good."

Marge sniffed the aluminum cup rapturously and took a scalding sip. "I wish they'd land," she said fretfully. Among the goodies on her shopping list were coffee beans, or seeds, or whatever it took to try to grow coffee for themselves. Otherwise the next couple of years, anyway, might be coffee-free. Of course, the Greasies probably had some growing already, to make that vile stuff they handed out in the little brass pots, but they weren't likely to give any away. They weren't giving anything away now, not even information over the radio; and the Peeps simply were not answering at all.

At least the camp was gratifyingly healthy, according to the medic's report. The antiallergens were standing up well, and there was nothing else in the Jemman environment to make a human being sick. A few headaches, probably from the climate and from the switch to a twenty-four-hour day; some dentistry; an appendix that needed watching; a request for a vasectomy—

"No," said Margie sharply. "Don't do any vasectomies. Or laparoscopies, either."

The doctor looked thoughtful. "You're going to have some knocked-up personnel."

"You're supposed to be able to handle that, right? Anyway, give them the pill, diaphragms, condoms—anything reversible or temporary. I get along fine with an IUD, and I can always take it out if I want to have a baby."

"Which you might?"

"Which all of us females may damn well have to, Cheech. That's an order: everybody capable of breeding *stays* capable. How's the baby bank?"

"Coming along fine. I've got twenty-eight ova in cryonic hold, and about a hundred sperm samples."

"Good, Cheech, but not good enough. I want a hundred percent compliance with that. If anything happens to anybody, I don't want his genes lost. Or hers. They don't take up much space, do they? Then I want, let's say, four samples from each, and—what are you grinning about?"

The medic said, "Well, it's just that a couple of the ova turned out to be prefertilized. They're fine. They'll keep in the deep-freeze indefinitely, but whenever you want them reimplanted we won't have to go to the bother of getting them started."

"Hum." Margie scratched thoughtfully. "I'm almost sorry you took the sample; we could start having kids any time now. Who were they? Come on, Cheech, none of this medical confidentiality; I'm your commanding officer."

"Well, one was Ana Dimitrova."

"No shit! Whose kid?"

"You can ask her if you want to. I didn't."

Marge shook her head wonderingly. "I would have guessed her about last," she said. "And the other one? Now, wait a minute! It couldn't be me! The IUD—"

"The IUD doesn't keep an ovum from getting fertilized; it only prevents it taking root and developing."

Margie sat back and stared at the doctor. "I'll be damned," she said.

Nguyen Dao Tree was ten minutes late for his 0200 appointment, and he arrived sleepy-eyed and irritable. "This twenty-four hour day of yours is not comfortable, Margie," he complained.

"You're not the one to bitch, Guy. I took the midnight-to-eight myself. If you'd spend your sleeping time sleeping instead of tomcatting around with every woman in the camp—"

"As to that, Marjorie," he said, "I much preferred when you and I slept on the same schedule."

"Yeah. Well. Maybe we'll have to do something about that, Guy, but right now we're late for inspection." She swallowed the last of her coffee, now cold but still delicious, and led the way.

Complaints aside, the three-shift day was working well. On the plus side, the perimeter was well guarded, the hectarage under cultivation was growing by nearly two thousand square meters every day, the each-one-teach-one training schedule Santangelo had set up so that the skills of the community were shared among several persons (what if Chiche Arkashvili died? or their one and only surviving agronomist?) was on track. On the minus, aerial surveillance showed large numbers of Krinpit roaming around the woods, coffee was not the only food item to be running low, and the resupply ship still could not give a firm landing time.

Margie allowed one hour of each day for her inspection, and she used every minute of it. No white-glove chickenshit. The inspection was rough and dirty; if everybody was doing their job and the jobs were being done, that was it. Her Bastogne grandfather had not cared if the troops were shaved, only if they could fight. And Margie had learned the skills appropriate to a fortress under siege.

That was what they were. No one had attacked the perimeter, not even a wandering Krinpit. But they were isolated in a world of enemies. From spy satellites and balloonists, from the breaking of codes and from what little could be gleaned from their infrequent radio contacts, above all from the contents of the Indonesian's pouch, Margie had formed a pretty good idea of what the Greasies were up to. Or had been up to a few weeks earlier. They had occupied the Peeps' camp; they had requisitioned quantities and varieties of personnel and equipment that made her drool. Even her letter to Santa Claus (who might or might not be hanging in orbit, waiting to come down her chimney) had not been so greedy. They had subdued the local autochthons, apparently by killing off all the nearby Krinpit and shooting down any balloonist who came near. Their burrowers they seemed to have tamed. And they were using them for minerals exploration, because it seemed the Greasies had perched themselves on a Kuwait of oil and a Scranton of other fossil fuels. They had devised an enzyme, or possibly it was a hormone—the information had been unclear—which took Krinpit out of action as effectively as 2, 4-D had dried up the jungles of Vietnam, by causing them to molt. They had acquired something from their Creepies that let them make building materials out of dirt, as the burrowers themselves hardened the interior surfaces of their tunnels. They had—Christ, what had they not done! If only her father had listened to her and given her the support she demanded, how gladly and competently she could have done the same!

Not that she had done badly. But for Marge Menninger there was no such thing as second best, and the Greasies at that moment controlled the entire planet. Barring the dozen hectares her colony sat on, it was all theirs. Their aircraft roamed it at will, so the spy satellites said. They had three separate colonies now, counting the one that had once belonged to the probably no longer surviving Peeps. And apart from the rare occasions when she dared send Kappelyushnikov on a quick survey flight (what would she do if there were some unexplained "accident" to her one and only aircraft?), she was blind except for what the satellites and the few living balloonists could tell. She had even grounded Danny Dalehouse. Not only because of the risk to him—but that was a reason in itself, she admitted privately; she did not want him killed—but because the electricity that made his hydrogen was better used for floodlights to protect the camp and make the crops grow. Also she had apprenticed him to the agronomist, along with Morrissey and the Bulgarian girl—wait a minute, she thought to herself; Dalehouse and Dimitrova? Maybe so. Probably not. They had been friendly, but not *that* friendly. But then who?

For that matter, she thought, looking at Guy Tree as he chattered away about contingency plans in the event of a major Krinpit attack, who was the father of her own sort-of child? Dalehouse? Tree? That son of a bitch Sweggert, with his cute little tricks? They were the most likely candidates, but which?

In other times, one part of Marge Menninger would have contemplated with sardonic amusement that other part of Marge Menninger which really, dammit!, wanted to *know*. At present she had no room for that sort of amusement in her mind. The thought of mentioning to Nguyen Tree that the two of them might be in the process of becoming somewhat delayed parents crossed her mind just long enough for her to dismiss it. It promised some good comedy, but it also promised complications she did not want to handle. First things first.

"Are there any archers in the camp?" she asked.

Tree stopped in the middle of explaining his proposal for arming a couple of canoes. "What?"

"People who know how to shoot a bow and arrow, dammit. We must have some. I'd like to organize a contest, part of the sports program."

"Very likely so, Marjorie. I don't believe there are any bows and arrows, however."

"If they know how to shoot them, they know how to make

them, don't they? Or anyway, it'll be in the microfiches. Get started on that, please, Guy. We'll give prizes. Coffee, cigarettes. I'll donate a bottle of Scotch." The thought that had crossed her mind as he spoke of how he planned to mount a light machine gun in a canoe was that the supplies of ammunition for the guns would not last forever, either, but she wasn't ready to say that even to her second in command.

Tree looked puzzled, but paused to make a note in his book. "It would be a useful skill for hunting, I suppose."

Margie nodded without replying. Hunting what? Every animal they had seen on the surface of the planet was well enough armored to laugh off any homemade bow—a conspicuous blunder on the part of evolution in this place, she was convinced. But she let it go.

As they were inspecting the power plant a messenger from the communications shack trotted up. "Ship's on its way in, colonel," she reported, panting. "They've already retrofired. We ought to see them in a couple of minutes."

"Thank God," said Margie. "Put it on the PA. Guy, get twenty grunts for unloading. Tell Major Arkashvili to stand by in case they land rough."

They didn't land rough. But they didn't land right, either. The drogue chute deployed handsomely, the craft came swinging down on its cluster of three big chutes they jettisoned on schedule, and it came in on its rockets. But it never made it to the beach where the others had landed. It came in almost a kilometer short and dropped into the jungle and out of sight.

The good part was that no one was hurt. The fifteen persons on board all came into the camp on their own power; and twelve of them were both young and female. God had answered Margie's prayer that far, at least. The bad part was that everything on the ship had to be manhandled over eight hundred meters of bad terrain, through jungle and over half a dozen ravines. No matter. They were there. And as Margie scanned the bill of lading she began to relax. It was all there, every last thing she had asked for, and more besides. Seeds and hand tools, weapons and training manuals. It was not enough—there was no such thing as enough—but it was all she had hoped.

First priority was to get everything movable inside the perimeter of the camp. That meant organizing working parties and armed guards to go with them. No Krinpit had been spotted near the landing site, but the woods were full of them. It wasn't until the first detachments began straggling back with cases of food and boxes of microfiches, folded bicycles and crates of electronic parts, that Margie relaxed long enough to greet the new arrivals. She shook each hand, spoke each name, and turned them over to Santangelo for assignment to quarters. A short black major hung behind. "I've got something for you, colonel," he said, patting a dispatch case. "In private, if you please, ma'am."

"Come ahead. Vandemeer, is it?" He nodded politely and followed her into her office, where he placed his dispatch case on her desk.

"This is it, ma'am," he said, unsnapping the case.

It was not a dispatch case. When he had undone the snaps the side peeled back and revealed a microprocessor with a liquid-crystal panel. He touched one of the buttons and it sprang into light, displaying a row of close-typed symbols.

"There's your guidance, ma'am. There are twelve satellite busters in orbit, and these are the controls."

Margie touched it. A warm feeling grew in the pit of her stomach and spread, an almost sexual excitement. "You're checked out on this, Vandemeer? Can you locate the Greasies' satellites?"

"Yes, ma'am. We've got acquisition and lock on four of theirs, including their main tactran receiver. Also the Peeps; they have two, but they don't seem to be active." He expertly punched a combination into the processor, and the colors of the symbols changed. "Green lights are ours. Red are Peeps. Yellow are Oilies. The lines that are still white are standby. If anything else comes within two million klicks the guidance system will track and identify it, and one of the spare birds will lock on."

The warmth was spreading. That had been the biggest and most important item on Margie's Christmas list, and the one she had been least sure of getting. Now the sons of bitches survived at her pleasure!

"Thanks, major," she said. "I want you to show me how to work this thing, and from then on I want it in your possession or mine, twelve hours a day each, until further notice."

"Yes, ma'am," he said unemotionally. "And I have something your father asked me to hand to you personally."

It was a letter, not a microfiche. A paper letter, in an envelope with her name on it in Godfrey Menninger's own handwriting. "Thanks, major," she said again. "Go get settled in, and take the controller with you." As he turned, she added, "Major? Are things pretty bad at home?"

He paused, looking at her. "Pretty bad," he said. "Yes, I would say that, colonel. They're pretty bad."

Margie stood holding the letter for a moment. Then she jammed it in her pocket and went out to see how the unloading was coming along, because she wasn't quite ready to get the uncensored word on how bad "pretty bad" was.

Putting it away did not let her forget it was there. While she was chewing Sergeant Sweggert out for talking up two of the new girls when he should have been shifting cargo, she was fingering it. When she was breaking up an argument over what had become of a case of flashlights—"Jesus, colonel, I just put them down for a second; I thought one of the other guys took them!"—her hand returned to it. When the mess tent called a halt for breakfast, she could resist no longer, and she took her tray and her letter back into her office and ate while she read.

Marge, honey,

You've got it all, everything on the list. But there's no more where that came from. The Greasies have ordered our rigs off the Mid-Atlantic Ridge. It's a bluff. We're calling it. But every drop of booster fuel is now sequestered for missiles until they back down—and then there's Peru. The Peeps have flanged up a phoney "election," and we're not going to sit still for it. So we'll be at full military alert for months to come, maybe longer than that.

You're on your own, honey. Figure at least a year. And it may be more than that, because the president's being threatened with impeachment, maybe worse—there was an assassination attempt with two National Guard tanks last week. I told him what to do. Declare martial law. Send Congress home. Crack down all around. But he's a politician. He thinks he can ride it out. If he does, that means the rest of his term he'll be trying to score brownie points with the voters, and that means cutting back a lot of important programs.

And one of them might be you, honey.

I wouldn't be telling you this if I didn't think you could handle it. But it looks as if you'll have to.

That was all, not even a signature. Margie sat with the letter in her hands and minutes later noticed that she had forgotten to finish her breakfast.

She no longer wanted it, but neither would she waste food —especially not now. She forced herself to eat it all, and it wasn't until she had swallowed every scrap that she realized the sound of the camp had changed. Something was wrong.

While Sergeant Sweggert was eating he heard two sounds, not very near and not very loud. They sounded like shots. No one else in the mess tent seemed to have heard anything. He scraped the plate of its canned ham and dehydrated eggs, picked up the big chunk of bread, and strolled toward the entrance, still chewing.

There was a third shot.

This time there was no mistake. Some dumb son of a bitch was playing with his piece. You couldn't blame him—if Sweggert got a Krinpit in his sights he would have been tempted to blow it away, too. But three shots was wasting ammunition. He speeded up and headed toward the perimeter. As he rounded the cook tent he saw a dozen people standing around the uphill emplacement peering up the trail toward the spot where the resupply ship had landed. Others were converging on the post, and by the time he reached it there were twenty, all talking at once.

The shots had come from the trail. "Who's out there?" he demanded, grabbing Corporal Kristianides by the shoulder.

"Aggie and two grunts. They decided to get another load in before they bucked the chow line. Lieutenant Macklin just took a patrol up after them."

"So sit down and shut up till they get back," Sweggert ordered; but it was an order he didn't want to follow himself. It wasn't like Aggie to shoot up the jungle. The crowd was getting bigger; Colonel Tree came trotting up, looking like a little China doll, then half a dozen from the mess tent, then the colonel herself. Ten people were talking at once, until the colonel snarled, "All of you, at ease! Here comes Macklin. Let's see what he has to say."

But Macklin didn't have to say a word. He came stepping along the worn place that had become their path, carbine at port arms, looking both ways into the jungle. As he got closer they could see that the two men behind him were carrying someone, and the last soldier was backing toward them, carrying her weapon as Macklin carried his.

What they were bringing in was a body. It was female, and that was all you could say. The face was unrecognizable. When they dropped her down, it was plain that not only the face had been attacked. One arm was shredded up to the shoulder, and there was a bullet hole between her breasts.

"Krinpit," snapped Major Santangelo.

"Krinpit don't have guns," said Colonel Menninger, tight-lipped. "Maybe Krinpit, but they had company. Tree! Check the perimeter. I want every weapon manned and a reserve at every point. Santangelo, fall the off-duty troops in. Give Sweggert and me two hundred meters, then follow us. Sweggert, take three people, and you and I are going to take the point."

"Yes'm." He spun around, took Corporal Kristianides's gas-operated recoilless away from her, and picked three from his squad at random while Colonel Menninger was listening to Lieutenant Macklin's report. He had got only about halfway up the trail, where he found the casualty and a couple of spilled and ransacked cases of supplies. Where the other two were he didn't know. He had come back for reinforcements. Marge Menninger listened to no more. She turned him over to Major Santangelo and signaled Sweggert to move in.

At twenty-second intervals they dogged it across the open space that was the field of fire, reforming under the arch of a many-tree. As Sweggert waited for the others, he could hear the rattle and moan of some shelled creatures, but not very near. The next man in heard it too and turned a questioning face to Sweggert, mouthing the word *Krinpit*. Sweggert nodded savagely and motioned silence. When Colonel Menninger crossed the field of fire, she trotted ten meters past them, then dropped to a knee and looked around warily before raising a hand and ordering them in.

Fucking hairy, thought Sweggert. It was like that bitch to pick him for something like this! She'd had it in for him ever since he had it in her. He hand-signaled the rest of the patrol to move up one at a time, two on one side of the trail and the other with him and the colonel on the other, and when they had made their run he waited ten seconds and then sprinted to drop down beside the colonel. "That's where they got her," he breathed, pointing ahead on the trail, where half a case of fluorescent tubes lay crunched and scattered on the ground.

"I see that, sergeant! Keep moving, I don't want Santangelo running up my ass."

"Yes'm." He stooped low, dodging through the underbrush, and flopped down. The distant Krinpit rattle was still audible, but not closer. The patrol leapfrogged through the jungle until the bulk of the resupply ship loomed ahead, with its tramped-down clearing before it. He waved to catch Colonel Menninger's eye, then pointed to the top of a many-tree. She nodded, and when his turn came again he raced for the nearest of its trunks, slung his GORR over his shoulder, and started up the clump of growth. It was not much like climbing a real tree; it was easier. The flat, arched branches were like a series of steps, and the stalactitic growths that hung down between them made good handholds. The problem was that it was hard to see. Sweggert had to change position twice before he could get a clear view of the rocket.

What he saw was the base of the ship, and right in front of it the bodies of the other two grunts. They had been savagely mutilated. There was no sign of Krinpit, and the sounds he had heard seemed to have gone farther away.

Sergeant Sweggert began to feel a little better. Why the fuck should he worry about Krinpit? They were noisy bastards; there was no way one of them could get within twenty meters with him hearing it. And then the GORR would take care of it. Of course, he speculated, maybe they weren't alone. Maybe there were a couple of Greasies with them. But what did that matter? Greasies were Greasies—they were spics, Ay-rabs, or limeys—and the day hadn't come when he worried about meeting one of them in the woods. He pushed his cap back and settled down. If anything showed up in that clearing he would blow its ass off, and meanwhile he had the entertaining spectacle of Margie Menninger silently worming her way forward on the ground, almost right under him. Off to the other side of the trail somebody else was moving, equally silently; he swiveled the GORR to sight in on it, but as the figure slid between bushes he saw that it was one of his own patrol. He returned the gun and slowly centered it on Marge Menninger, moving the cross hairs in the reticle down from the base of her skull to her hips. Wouldn't it be nice, he speculated, if he could give her one she'd never forget, right up the old—

The faintest of sounds behind him made him freeze.

A little too late, he comprehended a mistake in his thinking. Krinpit and human beings were not the only creatures on Jem. As he started to turn he saw a skinny, stretched-out creature, longer than he was tall, climbing toward him with at least half a dozen legs, while others held what looked like some kind of a gun. The damn thing was wearing sunglasses, he thought with surprise, trying to bring the GORR around. He was too slow. He never heard the shot that went through his head.

Marge Menninger was the first one back into the camp. She didn't wait for the cleanup; once they knew what they were looking for, the forty armed troops scoured the area. All they got was three of the burrowers, but one of them was the one who had killed Sergeant Sweggert. You were always a lucky son of a bitch, she thought; now you don't have to worry about a court-martial for rape anymore. She collared a passing man and sent him running toward the communications tent, and before she was in her office she heard the announcement coming over the PA: "Major Vandemeer! Report to the colonel on the double!"

She met him at the door. Good man, he was trotting over half-dressed, but he had the case with him. "Open it up," she snarled. "They're arming the Creepies against us, guns and glasses. That's what Tinka was trying to get back to tell me. Move it, man!"

"Yes'm." But even the stolid Major Vandemeer fumbled as he undid the snaps. "Ready, ma'am," he reported, fingers poised.

The red fury in her mind was balanced by the warmth

spreading at the base of her belly. She scratched vigorously and snapped, "Take 'em out!"

"Who, ma'am?"

"The Greasies! Bust their birds, all of them!" She watched the complicated ritual and then frowned. "While you're at it, take the Peeps' out too."

·NINETEEN·

GODFREY MENNINGER woke up wondering who was shaking the foot of his bed.

No one was. He was alone in his room, exactly like a hundred thousand Holiday Inn or Howard Johnson's Motor Lodge rooms all over the world. There was the phone on a nightstand beside the bed, the TV set staring grayly across at him from the long desk-plus-chest-plus-luggage-rack that stood against the wall. The phone was almost the only visible element that made it different, for it was a push-button jobber with colored lights flickering across its face. The other element of strangeness was harder to see. The drapes over one wall covered an immense likris display panel, not a window. There was no point in having a window. He was two hundred meters under the earth.

It was 6:22 on the clock.

Menninger had left orders to be awakened at seven. Therefore it was not a call that had awakened him. Therefore there were only a couple of other possibilities, and none of them were attractive. God Menninger considered picking up the phone or switching on the TV or pulling back the drapes over the likris situation screen, any of which would have told him at once what was happening. He decided against doing so. If it had posed an immediate threat he would have been notified at once. Margie's disciplined and hierarchical approach to problem solving had not been taught at West Point; it had come to her on her father's knee. If she was good at putting unwanted thoughts out of her mind, he was superb. He dismissed the question, slipped into his brocaded robe, went into the bathroom, and made himself a cup of instant coffee with tap water.

God Menninger's waking-up minutes were precious to him. He was of the opinion that both his marriages had failed because he had been unable to make either wife understand that he was never, not ever, to be spoken to for at least half an hour after waking. That was coffee time and summoning-up-strength time and remembering-what-he-had-to-do time. Conversation destroyed it. A weakness of Godfrey Menninger's character was that he was apt to destroy anyone who infringed on it.

The coffee was at just the right temperature, and he drank it like medicine, swallow by swallow, until it was down. Then he threw off the robe, sat cross-legged on the bed in the half-lotus position, let his body go calm, and began to say his mantra.

Godfrey Menninger had never really understood what happened among his neurons and synapses when he practiced transcendental meditation, nor had he ever really tried. It did not seem to do any harm of any kind, except to cost him some twenty-four hundred seconds out of every twenty-four hours. He seldom discussed it with anyone else and therefore did not have to defend it. And it seemed to work. Work how? Do what? He could not exactly have said. When he did it he felt more confident and more relaxed about his confidence. That was not a bad return on the investment of less than three percent of his time. As he sat, his body withdrawing from him, the reiterated *ta-lenn, ta-lenn* of the mantra becoming a sort of drapery of sound that surrounded him without being present, his whole brain became a receptor. It contributed nothing. It only perceived. On the inside of his eyelids he saw faces and shapes that melted into each other. Some were beautiful and some gargoyles. Some were etched in the sharpest of drypoint lines. Some seemed to be beaten out of gold. They held no emotional content for him. The demon snarls did not frighten. The loveliness did not attract. They were only there. Wispy chains of words floated past his consciousness like snatches of conversation from the next table at a restaurant. They spoke of ultimata and megatonnages and a remembered caress and the need for a haircut, but there were no imperatives in them anywhere. The circulating memory that pumped them past his mind sucked them away again without residue.

More than two thousand kilometers away and half a kilometer down, inside a submarine belonging to the Fuel Bloc, a vice admiral in the Libyan navy was programming The One That Had His Name on It. Menninger did not know it. His thoughts floated free into infinity in all directions, but all directions lay within that inner space of his mind. He could not have done anything useful about it if he had known.

The bed moved again.

It was not an earthquake. There were no earthquakes in West Virginia, he thought, bringing himself up out of reverie, getting ready to open his eyes. It was sharper than an earthquake would have been, more quick and trivial than the slow battering of a crustal slip. It was not particularly strong, and if he had still been asleep it might not even have awakened him. But it was something. And then the lights flickered.

Two hundred meters down in the side of a West Virginia mountain, the lights were not meant to flicker. A ^{239}Pu megawatt generating plant, vented through a kilometer of piping to emerge on the other side of the hill, was immune to most external events. Lightning bolts did not strike transformers underground. Winds could not tear loose a line, since there were no lines in the open air. And then, tardily, the flickering colors on the base of the telephone all went out. A single red light flared, and the buzzer sounded. He picked up the phone and said, "Menninger."

"Three missiles came in, sir—near misses. There's no structural damage. Point of origin backtracks probably to near Sinkiang province. The city of Wheeling is out."

"I'll be there in a minute," he said. He was still coming up from his meditation, and so he did not look at his own situation panel, but he also did not stop to shower or shave. He rubbed deodorant on his armpits—French whore's bath, but good enough—ran a brush over his hair, pulled on his coveralls and shoes, and walked briskly down the placid, beige-carpeted corridor to his command room.

The situation map was alight from end to end.

"Here's your coffee," said General Weinenstat. That was all she said. She knew his ways. He took the cup without looking at her, because his eyes were on the board. It displayed a Mercator projection of the earth in outline. Within it, bright red stars were targets taken out. Bright blue stars were also targets taken out, but on the wrong side: that was Washington and Leningrad and Buenos Aires and Hanoi and Chicago and San Francisco. Broken red profiles in the ocean areas of the map were enemy missile-launching vessels destroyed. There were more than a hundred of them. But there were also nearly sixty broken blue ones. Pulsating targets, red and blue, were major concentrations not yet destroyed. There were relatively few of them. The number decreased as he watched. Kansas City, Tientsin, Cairo, and the whole urban complex around Frankfurt ceased to exist.

The second cup of coffee was not medicine but comfort. He took a sip of it and then asked, "What's their remaining second-strike capability?"

"Marginal, Godfrey. Maybe one hundred missiles operational within the next twenty-four hours, but we're cutting that down all the time. We have almost eighty. And only two of our hardened installations are scratched."

"Local damage?"

"Well—there are a lot of casualties. Otherwise, not bad. Surface contamination is within acceptable limits—inside shielded vehicles, anyway." She signaled an orderly for a coffee refill and added, "Too early to tell about long-lived isotope capture, but most of the Corn Belt looks okay. So's Mexico and the Pacific Northwest. We did lose the Imperial Valley."

"So we're not bad for now."

"I would say so, yes, God."

"For the next twenty-four hours. Then they can start to redeploy." She nodded. It was a known fact that every major country had squirreled away missiles and components. They were not at ten-minute command like the ones in the silos or on the subs. They could not be launched by pushing a button. But they could not be taken out at long range, either, since you didn't know where they were hidden. He added, "And we can't look for them, because the satellite busters have half-blinded us."

"We've all-blinded them, Godfrey. They don't have an eye in orbit."

"Yes, yes, I understand," he said testily. "We've won the exchange. The damn fools. Well, let's get to work."

Menninger's "work" was not directly related to the exchange of missiles that was remodeling the surface of the earth to a facsimile of hell. That was not his responsibility. It was only a precursor, like a friend's retiring to the bathroom to fit in her diaphragm while he slouched, waiting, on the edge of the bed. She would not need his advice or his help at that stage, and neither would the Chiefs of Staff while the actual fire fight was going on. His involvement would be central immediately thereafter.

Meanwhile, one of the damn fools had finished the programming and was trying to round up enough of a crew for the launch. It wasn't easy. The neutron bomb had done just what ERW weapons were supposed to do—penetrated the carelessly scant meters of water and the steel tube of his submarine and knocked out most of the crew. The Libyan vice admiral himself had taken nearly five thousand rads. He knew he had only hours to live, but with any luck his target would have less than that.

Three hours' sleep was not enough. Menninger knew that he was quick-tempered and a little fuzzy, but he had trained his people to know that too, and they made allowances.

At five-minute intervals the map disappeared and the likris screen sequenced itself through a round of ten-second displays: profiles of industrial capacity destroyed and remaining, curves of casualties, histograms of combat-effectiveness estimates. In the Ops Room next to God Menninger's command post, more than fifty persons were working on overdrive to correct and update those figures. Menninger hardly glanced at them. His concerns were political and organizational. Rose Weinenstat was on the scrambler to the Combined Chiefs every few minutes, not so much to give information or to get it as to keep them aware, every minute, that the most powerful unofficial figure in government had his eye on them all the time. His three chief civilian liaisons were in touch with state governments and government agencies, and Menninger himself spoke, one after another, with cabinet officers, key senators, and a few governors—when they could be found. It was all US, not Fats; the rest of the Food Bloc was in touch through the filter of the Alliance Room, and when one of them demanded his personal attention it was an intrusion.

"He isn't satisfied with me," General Weinenstat reported. "Maybe you should give him a minute, Godfrey."

"Shit." Menninger put down his pen at the exact place on a remobilization order where he stopped reading and nodded for her to switch over.

The face on his phone screen was that of Marshal Bressarion of the Red Army, but the voice was his translator's. "The marshal," she said, sounding tinny through the scrambler, "does not question that you and the Combined Chiefs are acting under the President's orders, but he wishes to know just who the President is. We are aware that Washington is no more, and that Strongboxes One and Two have been penetrated."

"The present President," said Menninger, patiently restraining his irritation, "is Henry Moncas, who was Speaker of the House of Representatives. The succession is as provided in our basic law, the Constitution of the United States."

"Yes, of course," said the translator after Bressarion had listened and then barked something in Russian, "but the marshal has been unable to reach him for confirmation."

"There have been communications problems," Menninger agreed. He looked past the phone, where Rose Weinenstat was shaping the words "in transit" with her lips. "Also," he added, "I am informed the President is in the process of moving to a fully secure location. As the marshal will realize, that requires a communications lid."

The marshal listened impatiently and then spoke for some seconds in rapid-fire Russian. The translator sounded a good deal more uptight as she said, "We quite understand, but there is some question of lines of authority, and the marshal would appreciate hearing from him directly as soon—hello? Hello?"

His image faded. General Weinenstat said apologetically, "I thought it was a good time to develop transmission difficulties."

"Good thinking. Where is the son of a bitch, by the way?"

"Henry? Oh, he's safe and sound, Godfrey. He's been ordering you to report to him for the last hour or so."

"Um." Menninger thought for a moment. "Tell you what. Send out a radiation-safe team to escort him here so I can report. Don't take no for an answer. Tell him he'll be safer here than in his own hole." He picked up the pencil, scratching the pit of his stomach. Which was complaining. He wanted orange juice to build up his blood sugar, a stack of flapjacks to give a foundation for the next cup of coffee, and that cup of coffee. He wanted his breakfast, and he was aware that he was cranky because he was hungry. "Then we'll see who's President," he added, to the air.

On the edge of the Bahía de Campeche the Libyan vice admiral had got his crew together and his submarine up to two hundred meters, running straight and level. None of them were functioning well, with prodromal diarrhea and vomiting often enough so that the whole ship smelled like a latrine, but they could serve. For awhile, at least. They did. Libya's naval doctrine called for one big missile instead of a few dozen little ones. As this one big one broke the surface of the gulf it was immediately captured by a dozen radars. The scared but as yet untouched tourists on their lanais in Mérida saw bright, bad flashes out west, over the water, as a Cuban cruiser locked in and fired ABMs. None of them caught it. It was a cruise missile, not ballistic, easy to identify but hard to predict as it drove itself north-northwest toward the Florida panhandle. A dozen times defensive weapons clawed at it as it crossed the coast, and then it was lost to view. There were plenty of installations along the way charged with the duty of detecting and destroying just such a weapon, but none that were functioning anymore.

The latest picture from Margie showed her with one foot on the shell of a dead Krinpit, looking tired and flushed and happy. It was as good a picture of his daughter as God had had since her bearskin-rug days, and he had it blown into a hard print for his wallet. General Weinenstat looked at it carefully and passed it back to him. "She's a credit to you, God," she said.

He looked at it for a moment and put it away. "Yeah. I hope she got her stuff. Can you imagine her mother? I told her

Margie wanted some dress patterns, and she wanted me to put in about a thousand meters of fabric."

"Well, if you'd left her raising to her mother she wouldn't be getting the kind of efficiency ratings you've been showing me."

"I suppose not." The latest one had been nothing but praise, or at least up to the psychologist's report:

Latent hostility toward men due to early marital trauma and mild inverse-Oedipal effect. Well compensated. Does not affect performance of duties.

I really hope that's so, thought Godfrey Menninger. Rose Weinenstat looked at him carefully. "You're not worrying about her, are you? Because there's no need—wait a minute." General Weinenstat touched the thing in her ear that looked like, but wasn't, a hearing aid. Her expression turned somber.

"What is it?"

She turned off the communicator. "Henry Moncas. His shelter took a direct hit. They're trying to find out who's President now."

"Shit!" Godfrey Menninger stared at the remains of his breakfast for a moment and saw none of it. "Oh, shit," he said again. "It looks bad, Rosie. The worst part is we never had a choice!"

General Weinenstat started to speak, then changed her mind.

"What? What were you going to say, Rosie?"

She shrugged. "No good second-guessing, is it?"

He pounced on her words. "About what? Come on, Rosie!"

"Well—maybe moving into Canada—"

"Yeah. That was a mistake, all right. I'll give you that. But not ours! The Greasies knew we couldn't let them move troops into Manitoba. That was Tam Gulsmit's mistake! Same with the Peeps. Once we were engaged we had to take Lop Nor out—quick, clean, minimum casualties. They should've accepted it instead of retaliating—"

But he could hear voices within him denying it, speaking in the tones of Tam Gulsmit and Heir-of-Mao. "We were safe moving troops in to protect the tar sands, because we knew you couldn't afford to invade." "You shouldn't have bombed Lop Nor. You should have known we would have to retaliate." The voices within God Menninger's mind were the only voices they would ever have again. Heir-of-Mao lay with eyes bulging and tongue protruding from his lips, dead in the deep shelter under Peking, and the atoms that had once been Gulsmit's body were falling out from the column of fire over Clydeside.

The Libyan missile had bypassed Atlanta and Asheville and Johnson City, matching their terrains against the profiles imprinted in its memory. The safety interlocks on its thermonuclear charge were falling away one by one as its tiny, paranoid brain began to recognize its nearness to the thing it was unleashed to destroy.

"It's bad, Rosie," said Godfrey Menninger at last, rising to return to his desk. Maybe he should have let Margie's mother have the raising of her. Then Margie would probably have had a husband and a couple of kids by now. And perhaps—perhaps the world would have been a different place. He wondered if he would ever hear from her again. "Rosie," he said, "check Houston. See if the communication links with Jem are holding up. With the other colonies, too, of course."

"Right now, Godfrey? Give me ten minutes; I've got a call coming in from the DoD."

"Ten minutes is fine," he said; but before the ten minutes was up he was dead.

·TWENTY·

THE CORACLE first appeared between showers, far out over the water. In the pit beside Ana Dimitrova, Corporal Kristianides—no, Lieutenant Kristianides now, she corrected herself—stood up and turned the field glasses on it.

"Krinpit," she said. "Son of a bitch. Lay your gun on it, Nan, but don't fire unless I tell you to."

Unnecessary order! Not for worlds would she have fired. Not until she saw for herself that there were only Krinpit in the boat, and not Ahmed Dulla. Perhaps not even then, for this insanity of guns and shooting was awful even to play at. She had not yet had to fire at a living being, was far from sure that she could, and had said as much; but no one wanted to hear. But the good thing about her machine gun was that it had a telescopic sight, and she was glad enough to aim it.

The coracle disappeared into a squall, but not before she had seen that there was no human being in it, though it was large enough for several.

305

When it appeared again it was larger and nearer, and she could see that the single Krinpit was working furiously to keep it bailed and the trapezoidal sail intact, and paddling to bring it straight into the camp. By then everyone had seen, and at least a dozen weapons were pointed at it. Over the PA system Guy Tree's voice shrilled an order to hold fire. Down on the beach Marge Menninger stood, a GORR under her arm, oblivious of the rain that soaked her. Ana wiped the wet off her sight as carefully as she had been taught and looked again. She had no skill at recognizing individual Krinpit by sight, but this one did not look familiar.

Disappointment of a hope. But what a foolish hope, she scolded herself. How improbable that Ahmed would once again miraculously appear. And even if he had, who was this Ahmed who had taken her and used her and left her again? He was not the person of Sofia, she thought gloomily, and roused herself and tried to think more constructively.

It was a failure. There was so little to think constructively about! The world she had left was blowing itself up, and the world she had come to seemed determined to do the same. What went on in the secret conferences among Marge Menninger and her warrior knights in the headquarters shed she did not know, nor wish to. But it might well be the death of all of them.

The Krinpit was in the shallows now. It raised itself and splashed over the side, and the coracle bobbed away as it lurched ashore. It seemed to be in bad shape. It staggered in a half-circle on the shore and then fell to the ground with a painful crash as Colonel Menninger and half a dozen of her warriors formed a wary perimeter around it.

Perhaps they would kill it, she thought. Well, let them. Everyone else was standing and staring, but Ana's attention wandered—until one of the riflemen came running toward her.

"Dimitrova, front and center!" he was calling. "It's the one that speaks Pak! Colonel wants you to come translate!"

When Ana Dimitrova was nineteen years old, precocious senior at the University of Sofia, candidate for the callosectomy that would forever sunder the two halves of her brain and lead to a distinguished career in translation, she had watched a film on the subject. It was not her choice. They would not accept her application without it. The first part was quite tedious, though instructive, as it described the anatomy of that senseless and defenseless kilogram of pinky-gray jelly that mediated and transformed and commanded all the senses and defenses of the body. Before her very eyes a surgeon took a human brain in his hands and peeled away tissue to expose that great suety bridge that connected the two halves and that, in her, she would ask someone to sever. There was a long explanation, quite hard to follow, of how nerves crossed, so that the right half of the brain seemed to take responsibility for the left half of the body, and vice versa: strange quirk of anatomy! She saw how the nerves carrying visual impressions intersected at the optic chiasma, but not completely—as though prankish evolution had tired of the joke and decided not to finish it. All that part of the film was difficult to absorb, as well as unsettling to look at. But then there were some comic parts. Each half of the brain commanded its own network of afferent and efferent nerves. The efferent nerves, the ones that directed action, were spared in the resection or reconnected afterwards, which was why the split-brain people were able to walk without stumbling. Most of the time. The afferent nerves, the ones that accepted sensory impressions from the world, were kept apart. So each half of the brain could receive and process and store its own information, not shared with the other. That was why translation became easy.

But.

But some kinds of afferent input were not value-free. They produced glandular responses. They caused emotions. This was where the comic part came in. The film showed a woman, one of the earliest volunteers for the surgery. She had an earplug in one ear and was reading from a prepared text. The voice-over narration explained what she was doing: delivering a translated talk to a mathematical congress. But while one half of her brain was reading and translating and speaking, the other half was listening to the words coming in over the earplug; and those words were the filthiest of scatological jokes. The woman began to stammer and falter, and over her face spread the rosiest of blushes, though the operating half of her brain had not an idea in the world why. Blushes. Stammers. Headaches. Depression. They were the symptoms of leakage from one half to the other. The scar tissue that blocked the flow of impulses through the corpus callosum let each half of the brain work efficiently on its own. But feelings seeped through. All the time Ana Dimitrova was translating for Colonel Menninger she could feel them pounding at her—

"He says that as the People's Republics are no longer a force, he wishes to help us against the Fuel Bloc."

"Fucking great. What's he going to do, scratch them to death with his sharp little feet?"

—and the headache was the worst she had ever had: sickening, sandbag blows at the base of her skull. She felt nauseated and was not helped by the Krinpit.

Sharn-igon was repulsively ill. Even the dull, recurrent rasp of his name—Sharn-igon, Sharn-igon—was badly played, like a defective radio. His carapace was a sickly yellow instead of the rich mahogany it had been. It was cracked and seamed. At the edges of it, where undershell joined the massive armor of the top, seams did not quite join, and a thin, foul liquid oozed out.

"He has molted," she explained to the colonel, "and feels he is about to molt again. Perhaps it is because of the chemicals the Fuel people used against them."

"You don't look so fucking great yourself, Dimitrova."

"I am quite capable of continuing, Colonel Menninger." All the same, she moved away from the Krinpit. The exudations of his shell had darkened the sand around him, and the smell was like rancid fat. Moving did not help. The headache, and the pain behind it, grew with every moment.

Marge Menninger ran her hands through her wet hair, pulling it back so that her ears were exposed. She looked almost like a little girl as she said, "What do you think, Guy? Have we got ourselves a real blood-hungry tiger?"

Colonel Tree said, "One does not refuse an ally, Marge. But the Greasies would eat these jokers up."

"So what is he saying exactly, Dimitrova? That he'll tell all his Crawly friends to attack the Greasy camp if we want them to?"

"Something like that, yes. What he says," she added, "is not always easy to understand, Colonel Menninger. He speaks a little Urdu, but not much, and he speaks it *very* badly. Besides, his mind wanders. It is a personal matter with him, to kill. He does not care who. Sometimes he says he wants to kill *me.*"

Menninger looked appraisingly at the Krinpit. "I don't think he's in shape to do much killing."

"Must one be well for that?" Ana flared. "I am sick in my heart from talk of killing, and from killing itself! It is a wicked insanity to kill when so few persons are still alive."

"As to that," said Margie mildly, raising her hand to stop Guy Tree from exploding, "we'll talk another time. You look like shit, Dimitrova. Go get some sleep."

"Thank you, Colonel Menninger," Ana said stiffly, hating her, perhaps hating even more the look of compassion in Margie's eyes. How dare the bloody trollop feel pity!

Ana stalked off to her tent. It was raining hard again, and lightning lashed over the water. She hardly felt it. At every step the throbbing in her head punished her, and she knew that behind the headache a greater pain was scratching to come out. Pity was the solvent that would melt the dam and let it through, and she wanted to be by herself when that happened. She stooped into the tent without a word to the woman who shared it with her, removed only her shoes and slacks, and buried herself under the covers.

Almost at once she began to weep.

Ana made no sound, did not shake, did not thrash about. It was only the ragged unevenness of her breathing that made the black girl in the other cot rise up on one elbow to look toward her; but Ana did not speak, and after a moment her roommate went back to sleep. Ana did not. Not for an hour and more. She wept silently for a long time, helpless to contain the pain any longer. Hopes gone, pleasures denied, dreams melted away. She had held off accepting the thing that the Krinpit had said almost in his first sentence, but now it could not be denied. There was no longer a reason for her to be on Jem. There was hardly even a reason to live. Ahmed was dead.

She woke to the loud, incongrous sound of dance music.

The storm of silent weeping had cleared her mind, and the deep and dreamless sleep that followed had begun the healing. Ana was quite composed as she bathed sparingly in the shower at the end of the tent line, brushed her hair dry, and dressed. The music was, of course, that other of Marge Menninger's eccentricities, the Saturday night dance. How very strange she was! But her strangeness was not all unwelcome. One of the fruits of it had been the patterns and fabric that had come in the last ship. Ana chose to put on a simple blouse and skirt, not elaborate, but not purely utilitarian either. She was a very long way from dancing. But she would not spoil the pleasure of those who enjoyed it.

She cut past the generator, where the Krinpit was rumbling hollowly as it scratched through the clumps of burnable vegetation for something to eat, a guard with a GORR trailing its every step, and visited the fringe of the dance area long enough to get something to eat from the buffet. (Of course, she had slept through two meals.) When men asked her to dance she smiled and thanked them as she shook her head. The rain had stopped, and sullen Kung glowed redly overhead. She took a plate of cheese and biscuits and slipped

away. Not that there was far to go. No one walked in the
woods anymore these days. They lived and ate and slept in a
space one could run across in three minutes. But all who
could be there were at the dance, and down by the beach were
only the perimeter guards. She sat down with her back against
one of the machine-gun turrets and finished her meal. Then
she put her plate down beside her, pulled her knees up to her
chin, and sat staring at the purple-red waves.

Ahmed was dead.

It was not much comfort to tell herself that her dreams had
been foolish to begin with, that Ahmed had never taken her
as seriously as she had taken him. Nevertheless, it was true,
and Ana Dimitrova was a practical person. She had learned
the trick of dissecting pain into its parts. That she would never
see him again, touch his strong and supple body, lie beside
him while he slept—that was purest pain, and there was no
help for it. But that she would never marry him and bear his
children and grow old by his side—that was only a spoiled
fantasy. It had never been real. That loss could not hurt her
now, because it was of something she had never owned; and
so her pain was diminished by half.

(But, oh, how that half still ached!)

She wept gently and openly for a moment, then sighed and
rubbed the tears away. What she had lost, she told herself, she
had lost long ago. From the moment Ahmed came to Jem, he
had become a different person. In any event, it was over. She
had a life to make for herself, and the materials to make it
from were all in this camp; there was nothing else anywhere.
You should dance, she scolded herself. You should go up
where they are laughing and singing and drinking.

Plainly and simply, she did not want to. It was not merely
that she didn't want to dance, not yet. It was more deep and
damaging than that. Ana, translating for the Krinpit, had
heard enough of what was going on in the minds of Marge
Menninger and Nguyen Tree and the other hawks who directed the fate of the camp. So much madness in so few

minds! They were determined to carry on a war, even here, even after Earth had blown itself into misery! And yet there they all were, smiling and bobbing around the floor. Her own brain had been divided by a surgeon's knife. What had divided theirs, so that they could plot genocide in an afternoon and drink and cavort and play their sexual games at night? How Ahmed would scowl at them!

But Ahmed was dead.

She took a deep breath and decided not to cry again.

She stood up and stretched her cramped limbs. The Krinpit was lurching slowly down toward the water for a drink after his unappetizing meal, the soldier wandering after. She did not particularly want to be near him, but she needed to rinse her plate—either that or carry it back to the cook tent, which was too near the dance floor. She kept her distance, paralleling his scuttling path, and then she heard someone call her name.

It was the Russian pilot, Kappelyushnikov, sitting cross-legged at a gun pit and talking to Danny Dalehouse, on duty inside it. Why not? Ana changed course to approach them and wished them a good evening.

"Is truly good, Anyushka? But Danny Dalehouse has told me of death of Ahmed Dulla. I am deeply sympathetic for you."

There it was, the first time someone had spoken of it to her. She discovered that it was not impossible for her to respond.

"Thank you, Visha," she said steadily. "What, have you become a monk that you do not dance tonight?"

"Is no one I care to dance with," he said gloomily. "Also have been having most interesting discussion with Danny on subject of slavery."

"And what have you concluded, then, Danny?" she asked brightly. "Are we all slaves to your mistress, the beautiful blond colonel?"

He did not answer directly, but chose to be placating. "I know you're upset, Ana. I'm sorry, too."

"Upset?" She nodded judiciously, looking down into the pit at him. "Yes, perhaps. I must assume that my home has been destroyed—yours, too, I suppose. But you are braver than I. I am not brave; I become upset. It upsets me that what has happened on Earth is now to happen again, here. It upsets me that my—that my friend is dead. It upsets me that the colonel intends to kill a great many more persons. Can you imagine? She proposes to tunnel under the Fuel camp and explode a nuclear bomb, and that upsets me."

Why are you doing this? she asked herself; but she knew that she could not accept more sympathy without crying, and she was not ready to cry before these men. At least she had diverted them. Dalehouse was frowning.

"We don't have any nuclear weapons," he objected.

"Softheaded person!" she scoffed. "Your mistress has what she wants to have. I should not be astonished if she had a fleet of submarines or a division of tanks. She wears weapons as she wears that cheap perfume. The smell of them is always around her."

"No," he said doggedly, peering up at her, "you're wrong about the nuclear weapons. She couldn't conceal that from us. And she's not my mistress."

"Do not flatter yourself that I care. She may have her sexual excesses with whomever she likes, and so may you."

Kappelyushnikov coughed. "I think," he said, "dance has suddenly become more attractive."

As he stood up, Ana put her hand on his arm. "I am driving you away. Please forgive me."

"No, no, Anyushka. Are difficult times for all, nothing to forgive." He patted her hand, then grinned and kissed it. "As to myself," he said, "I see beautiful blond colonel roaming about alone, and perhaps she wishes to dance or otherwise relate to some new person, such as I. Also do not care for cheap perfume worn by big cockroach. You do not yourself desire to dance? Or otherwise relate? No. Then stay with friend Danny."

They watched him walk steadily toward Marge Menninger, strolling past her checkpoints. They heard her laugh as Cappy spoke to her; then he shrugged and moved on toward the dance floor.

The Krinpit, in his random stagger around the beach, was coming closer. It was true that the stench of his exudations was strong. So was the sighing, droning sound of his presence. Ana listened, then said gloomily, "This one is muttering about his love now," she said. "It was killed somehow, I cannot tell how. I think Ahmed had something to do with it, and it is for that that it is determined to kill human beings. But it had become Ahmed's ally! Dan, is not that lunacy? It is as though killing has become an end in itself. It no longer matters who is killed or for what possible gain the killing is done. Only the killing itself matters."

Dalehouse stood up in his shallow rifle pit, looking up the hill toward the dancers. "She's coming this way," he said. "Listen, before she gets here. About her being my mistress—"

"Please, Danny. I spoke without thinking and because I am, yes, upset. It is not a time to worry about personal matters."

Clearly he was not satisfied and would have pursued the subject, but Margie was now too close. She paused to light a cigarette, studying the Krinpit and its guard, now a model of military deportment, his recoilless at port arms as the colonel approached. Then she came smiling over to Danny and Nan. "Getting it on, are you?" she said amiably. "When was the last time you checked your earphones, Danny?"

Guiltily Dalehouse clapped the phone to one ear. He had been neglecting the buried microphone probes, which were supposed to warn of burrowers digging toward him under the ground. There was no sound. "Sorry, Margie," he said.

She shook her head. "When you're on duty, that's *colonel*. And when I say frog, you hop. Now that that's understood," she said, smiling sunnily, "would either of you folks like a hit before we talk some business?"

"I am not in the habit of using narcotics," Ana said.

"Pity. Danny?" She watched while Dalehouse filled his lungs, and as she took the stick back from him, she said, "I want you to draft your gasbag friend. One hundred and—" She glanced at her wristwatch. "One hundred and eight hours from now, give or take a little, we're going to hit the Greasy camp, and he's going to be our air arm."

Dalehouse coughed and spluttered. "He—he can't—"

"Take your time, Danny," she encouraged. "While you're getting your breath, just listen for a moment. Storm's over. Looks like we've got maybe five or six good days. I'm taking fifteen front-line effectives, plus you, Danny. We'll mop up that camp without breathing hard. Only I don't want to take a plane, and I don't want you or Cappy floating around up there where they can see you, and that leaves Charlie."

"Charlie can't fight!"

"Well," she said reasonably, "come to that, I don't figure you for your real Geronimo trained killer, either. But I don't expect it of you. You communicate. Charlie observes. The Greasies won't pay any attention to one more fartbag hanging around—"

"Bullshit they won't! They've been shooting balloonists down all along."

"Danny," she said, "I'm not asking your advice. I'm giving you an order." She dragged on the joint, down to the last centimeter, and then carefully rubbed it out and pocketed it before exhaling. "You see," she said, "the Greasies are going to come to the same conclusions I did, only it'll take them a little longer. One of us has to run things. The only way to do that is to knock the other out. All Charlie has to do is hang in there with his radio and keep us posted if they send up a plane or put some people out in the woods. I'll bring the company up overland. But we're naked without air cover. We need to know when to get out of sight. That's easy enough for him, right?"

"Well, sure. But—shit, Margie. He's almost the last survivor. It's a lot to ask—"

"But I'm not asking, Danny. You keep making that same mistake. I'm ordering. If he doesn't, he'll make a nice flame." She scratched under her belt, regarding him amiably. "So after the dance I break the news to the camp, and tomorrow this time we're on our way."

"To atom-bomb the Fuel Bloc," said Ana bitterly.

Marge Menninger's face froze. After a moment she said, "I guess I'll let that pass, Dimitrova. I didn't specifically order you to keep your mouth shut. But I won't let it pass again. What you hear when you're translating is *classified.*"

"Holy Christ," Dalehouse said. "You really have a nuclear bomb?"

"Bet your ass, Danny. You've got a piece of it right there in your ground mikes."

"Where? You mean the plutonium power-packs? That's no good, Margie—colonel, I mean. There's not enough of them. Even if there were, you couldn't flange them together to make a bomb."

"Wrong and wrong, Danny. Takes eighteen hundred grams and a bit to fission. I have a little over six thousand grams, all tidied away in the stores marked 'fuel replacements.' All this was planned a long time ago, and they'll fit together because some pretty high-powered weapons people designed them to do that before the first ship took off. Oh, it's not one of your hundred-megaton jobs. Maybe not even a kiloton, because I don't have containment to keep the parts together very long. But I don't want a big one. I don't want to wipe out the Greasy camps, I want to own them. I want to take out their ammunition and their food stores, and I know just the place to put baby for that. Then they can beg."

She looked serene and innocent as she said it, and Dalehouse responded with shocked disbelief. "That's—that's unprovoked aggression! A stab in the back!"

"Wrong, Dalehouse. That's preemption. The Greasies don't have a choice, either. They just haven't figured it out yet."

"Bullshit! It's what the Japanese did at Pearl Harbor all over again!"

She opened her eyes wide. "Sure, why not? There was nothing wrong with Pearl Harbor, except they fucked it up. If they'd gone on to take out the carrier fleet and follow up with a landing, history would be a lot different. You'd be saying 'Pearl Harbor' the way you say 'Normandy' now, only you'd be saying it in Japanese."

She seemed quite pleased with herself, but then she hesitated. She sought a dry place on the ground and sat down before adding, "But I will admit to you two dear old friends from Bulgaria that right now I'm scared and tired and not what you'd call real happy with the way things are going. I— what's the matter with that thing?"

The Krinpit was staggering closer to them, moaning and stridulating. Ana listened. "He is quite hard to follow. He is speaking of Poison Ghosts and Ghosts Above—that is, of ourselves and of balloonists. He seems to have us confused in his mind."

"All enemies look alike after awhile, I guess. Tell him to back away. I don't like the way he smells."

"Yes, Colonel Menninger." But before Ana could summon up the commands in Krinpit-Urdu, Margie stopped her again.

"Wait a minute. What was that?" There had been a voice on the PA system along with the blare of dance music.

"I couldn't make it out," said Dalehouse, "but I do hear something. Out in the woods. Or in the air—"

Then the dance music abruptly died, and a scared voice replaced it. "Colonel Menninger! All personnel! Aircraft approaching!"

The sounds were clear now, two sets of them: the whickering putt-putt of a helicopter, and a quicker, higher sound. The dancers scattered.

Over the trees two shapes appeared. Neither was moving very fast, but they came without warning: the Fuel helicopter and a stub-winged STOL plane, one they had not seen in the

air before. They did not come in peace. Soldiers strapped to
the pods of the helicopter were firing incendiary rockets while
wing-mounted machine guns on the STOL strafed the camp.
The fixed-wing plane made a roaring run that took it out over
the water; then it rose, turned, and dived in again. On its
second pass the guns did not fire, but four tiny rockets leaped
out from under the wing, streaked into the store shed, and set
fire to a row of tents.

The Greasies had not been so slow after all.

Here and there, around the camp and inside it, perimeter
guards and the more quick-witted of the dancers were beginning to return the fire. Margie jumped to her feet and began
to run toward the nearest rocket launcher, and then, on its
third pass, the stub-winged plane swerved toward her. It was
using both machine guns and a flamethrower now. As the
bullets stitched toward her, Margie dodged and fell, almost
beside the Krinpit; and the creature rose up high above her.
It launched itself, two hundred kilograms of half-molted
body, on top of Marge Menninger.

Sharn-igon knew that this would be his last molt, terribly
premature, agonizing, fruitless. He would never experience
the satisfying itch of his new carapace as it hardened and
stretched over the soft inner pulp, never feel the sexual stirring of the newly shelled and embark on the quick conquest
of a female with a he-mate. As the Poison Ghosts Above
zoomed in toward the camp, he tried to warn these new allies.
But they were deaf to the brilliant sounds from over the trees,
deaf to his warnings.

The pain was too much.

It had been his intention to assist them in killing each other
to the maximum extent possible, and then to kill the survivors
himself. But perhaps he had done all the assisting he would
ever do. The agony of his new shell, already beginning to
crack again, tormented his thoughts. The blinding sounds of
the aircraft and the explosions dazed him.

There was only one Poison Ghost left that he could kill. It would have to be enough. He raised himself on his pitifully soft-shelled limbs, leaned forward, and crashed down on top of her just as the soft, deadly tongue of the flamethrower licked at them both.

By then the whole camp was firing at the aircraft—or that much of it that was still able to fire. But the planes were out of reach. They hung out over the water, a kilometer and more away, the helicopter dancing lightly, the STOL turning in small circles, and did not return to the attack.

The next assault came from another place.

A scream from one of the machine-gun pits, and the two soldiers in it were down, ripped to shreds. Out of the pit came a long, limber, black shape wearing tiny goggles and racing on its dozen limbs to the nearest knot of humans; and another behind him, and another.

The burrowers managed to kill more than ten of the survivors. But that was all. Even with the sunglasses they were no match for trained human soldiers on the surface of the planet. If the planes had continued their attack—but they didn't. The human defenders quickly rallied, and at the end there were fifty burrowers stretched out on the ground, soiling the sand with their watery black blood. No more came because there were no more in the nest to come. That burrow had been wiped out.

Dan Dalehouse stood peering out over the sea while one of Cheech Arkashvili's assistants bandaged a deep gash on his arm. The planes were gone. In the middle of everything, they had quietly flown down the coastline and away.

"And why didn't they finish us off?" he asked.

There was no answer.

·TWENTY-ONE·

By THE TIME they found Margie Menninger, still alive, the fight was long over and the camp was almost functioning again.

She had lain under the dead and stinking Krinpit for more than two hours, stunned, half-suffocated, unable to shift the gross dead weight on top of her, her limbs twisted painfully but unhurt. Like the djinn in the bottle, at first she would have given a king's ransom to her rescuer. When they finally heard her sand-gagged attempts at a bellow and dug her out, what she wanted to give was death.

They helped her a few steps away, with their heads averted from the stink. She gagged and swore at them, and when they tried to help her stand she collapsed and vomited into the sand again. The doctor came running, but a doctor wasn't what Marge needed. What she needed was to get the cesspool stench of the Krinpit off her and out of her nostrils. She let Cheech strip off her coveralls and assist her to the edge of the water, and then she splashed around until the smell was gone and she could walk again. Limpingly, yes. But under her own power. Wearing a bra and bikini panties, with her gun belt over her shoulder, she walked up the shore past the dead Krinpit, seared into a sort of omelette of meat and shell, until someone came up with a terrycloth robe. She was giving orders as she walked.

Why had they stopped?

The camp had been at their mercy. With great precision they had knocked out the heavy weapons on the first pass. There was not a rocket launcher or a machine gun untouched —nothing but hand weapons. Of the hundred eight persons in the Food camp, twenty-two were dead, nearly fifty were wounded or burned. The planes had been unscathed. The burrowers had been wiped out entirely, but if the planes had finished their work first, the burrowers would have had an easy time with the survivors. Why? The timing had been exact. As soon as the planes had stopped shooting, the burrowers came out. That could not have been a coincidence, and the goggles the burrowers wore were proof that the Greasies had prepared them for the job. But then they hadn't followed through.

Why not?

But thank God for poppa and his parting gift! A metric ton of ammunition had been blown up, but there were metric tons left untouched by virtue of the spare supplies in the final ship. Tents burned and food was destroyed. But there was more. If Cappy's airplane had been stitched across by machine-gun fire, there were spare parts to fix it. And that greatest of gifts, the six kilograms of ^{239}Pu in its carefully crafted sheaths—that was still intact. The dead were irreplaceable, of course. Worse still were the casualties, because some of them were not merely a loss but a debit. Nguyen Dao Tree, who had lost a leg and a lot of blood to go with it; six persons badly burned, two others with serious abdominal wounds—a whole cluster of damages for Cheech Arkashvili to try to repair. For each one of the worst off, there was the cost of an able-bodied person to tend him. There was no tent still standing big enough to hold them all, and so Cheech had put them onto cots dragged out of the damaged tents, out in the open. Some of the bedding was scorched, and if it began to rain again they would be in trouble. But for now they were as well off as they were likely to be, Margie thought as she moved among them.

One of them got up as Margie approached: Lieutenant Kristianides, one whole side of her body in gauze and antiburn dressing. But functioning. "Colonel," she said. "I had to leave the radio—"

Marge glanced at the doctor, who shook her head. "Get back in bed, Kris. Tell me about it later."

"No, I'm all right. When they shot the tent up I ran out. But I left the tape going. I was getting their chatter, only it was in all different languages."

"Thanks. Now get back in bed," Marge ordered, and looked around. "Dalehouse, front and center!" she called. "Check the radio shack. If the tape's still working, give me a yell."

He didn't look too good himself, she thought as he put down the tray of dressings and headed up the hill without a word—but then, none of them did. Especially herself. Margie's own tent had been totaled, and she was wearing fatigues belonging to a woman who would never again need them— not unfair, but she had been a taller and fatter woman than Marge Menninger.

When Dalehouse called her, she had forgotten about the tapes. But she went up to the shack, which was unburned and not really harmed except for bullet holes, commandeering Ana Dimitrova on the way. The tape was voice-actuated, and Dalehouse had already found the right place to begin. Ana put on the earphones and began to translate.

"First one of the pilots says, 'On target,' and the base acknowledges. Then there are some carrier noises, as though they were going to transmit and changed their minds, and then the base says, 'Suspend operations at once. Do not attack.' And one of the pilots, I think it is the Egyptian, says in a different Arab dialect, 'Strike already in progress. We have taken out their weapons dump. Body count around twenty-five.' Then there is some mumbling that I cannot make out, as though they are talking at the base with the transmitter on but not close enough to pick it up. And then the base says, 'Urgent. Suspend operations immediately.' And then the other pilot, the Irishman, says they are observing from over the water, waiting for instructions, and then the base orders them to return without further attack. That is all there is on the tape until they get landing instructions later on."

"That's it?" Margie asked.

"As I have said, colonel, yes. There is nothing else."

"Now, why would they change their minds in the middle?" Margie asked. Neither Dalehouse nor Dimitrova offered an answer. She hadn't expected one. It didn't matter. The Greasies had declared war, and if they backed out in the middle of it that was their problem, not hers. She would not back out. To Marge Menninger, the attack on her base—*her* base!—answered all questions right there. *Why* didn't really matter. The only question was *how*—how to carry the fight to them, and win it.

"Can you dig with that shoulder?" she asked Dalehouse.

"I guess so. It's not bleeding."

"Then go help Kappelyushnikov dig graves. Dimitrova, you're a radio operator now. No transmissions. Just listen. If the Greasies say anything, I want to hear about it right away."

She left them and headed for the surviving latrine. She didn't particularly need to go to the bathroom; she just wanted to be alone for a moment to clarify her thoughts. She ranked her way to the head of the line, closed the door, and sat there smoking a cigarette and staring into space.

There was no question in her mind that she could win this war, because she had some powerful cards to play. The plutonium store was one of them. The other was Major Vandemeer's little dispatch case. There were still four birds in orbit; one could hit the Greasy main camp, and another their Farside base, anytime she gave the order—and that would be that.

The trouble was, she didn't want to destroy the Greasy facilities. She wanted to acquire them. The birds and the bomb were overkill, like trying to take care of a mosquito with a mortar.

No. It would have to be a straight overland operation. Maybe the plutonium, if it could be placed exactly right. Not the missiles. It was a pity the Greasies had launched their preemptive strike before she was quite ready to launch hers. But not a disaster. The worst thing about the raid was that her cadre of effectives had been seriously reduced. How was she going to mount her retaliatory strike without grunts?

Marge Menninger had just taken the only decision that gave the human race a future on Jem, even though she didn't know it.

"The only good thing about all this," Dalehouse said to Kappelyushnikov, "is that most of the casualties were military. At least now we can get on with the real business of the expedition."

Kappelyushnikov grunted and threw a few more spadefuls of dirt before he answered. "Of course, is so," he said, pausing and wiping sweat off his face. "Only one question. What is real business of expedition?"

"To survive! And to preserve. God knows what's happening on Earth. We may be all that's left of the human race, and if anything's going to be left of, what, maybe five thousand years of science and literature and music and art, it's here."

"Very discouraging amount of responsibility for two gravediggers," Kappelyushnikov commented. "You are of course right, Danny. We have saying in Soviet Union: longest journey begins with single step. What step do we take now?"

"Well—"

"No, wait, was rhetorical question. First step is apparent.

Have finished covering up graves of now absent friends, so you, Danny, please step up to colonel's headquarters and report burial services can begin."

He jammed his spade into the dirt and sat down, looking more despondent than Dalehouse had ever seen him.

Dalehouse said, "All right. We're all pretty tired and shook up, I guess."

The pilot shook his head, then looked up and grinned. "Am not only tired, dear Danny, am also very Russian. Heavy load to carry. We have other saying in Soviet Union: in thousand years, what difference will it make? But now I tell you the truth, Danny. All sayings are bullshit. I know what we do, you and I and all of us. We do the best we can. Is not much, but is all there is."

Dalehouse laid down his spade and trudged up the hill to the headquarters shack, thinking hard. A heavy responsibility! When you looked at it carefully, there was no way to preserve everything; so much that was irreplaceable would inevitably be lost—probably already was lost. There was not much chance that the Arc de Triomphe and the British Museum and the Parthenon had all survived, not to mention some billions of fairly irreplaceable human beings. It was hard for Danny to accept that he would never again see a ballet or listen to a concert. Or fly in a clamjet or drink in a revolving restaurant on top of a skyscraper. So much was gone forever! And so much more would inevitably vanish as they tried to rebuild....

Yet there was one great asset not yet destroyed: hope. They could survive. They could rebuild. They could even rebuild in a better way, learning from the mistakes of the past, on this virgin planet—

There was a knot of people gathering around the headquarters shack, and Marge Menninger, with a couple of her aides, was trotting up to join them. Dalehouse hurried his pace and arrived in time to hear Ana saying, "This message just came in, Colonel Menninger. I will play the tape for you."

"Do it," snapped Marge, out of breath and exhausted

Dalehouse moved closer to her. She seemed near to collapse. But as the tape player hummed and scratched, she pulled herself together and stood listening intently.

Danny recognized the voice. It was the black air vice-marshal, Pontrefact; and what he said did not take very long.

"This is an official message on behalf of the Fuel Exporting Powers to the Food camp. We offer an immediate and permanent armistice. We propose that you remain within twenty kilometers of your camp, in the direction toward ours, and we will observe the same limits from ours. We request an answer within one hour."

There was a pause, as though he was shuffling papers in his hand, and then the rich Jamaican tones began again.

"As you are aware, our air strike against your camp was provoked by your destruction of our satellites. It was ordered only after full exploration of all alternatives. Our intention was to wipe your base out completely. However, as you are also aware, we terminated the strike after inflicting relatively minor damage on your base. The reason for this decision is the reason for this offer of armistice now.

"Our star, Kung, is unstable. It is about to flare.

"We have been aware for some time that its radiation level has been fluctuating. Within the past twenty-four hours it has become more extreme. While the air strike was in progress we received information from our astrophysicists that a major flare will occur in the near future. We do not have an exact time. Our understanding is that it may occur as early as forty-eight hours from now, and almost surely within the next two weeks. If you accept our offer of armistice, we will transmit all technical data at once, and your people can make their own judgments."

The voice hesitated, then resumed in a less formal way. "We have no knowledge of conditions on Earth at present and suppose you have none as well. But it is clear that for all practical purposes we on Jem are alone in the universe at this time. We think we will need all the resources we have to prepare our camp for this flare. If we continue to fight, we suppose we will all die. I do not propose that we work together. But I propose that we stop fighting, at least until this crisis is past." Another pause. Then: "Please respond within an hour. God help us all."

Margie closed her eyes for a moment while everyone waited. Then she opened them again and said, "Call them back, Dimitrova. Tell them we accept their offer, ask for their technical data at once, and say we will be in contact again when we have something to say. Folks, the war is over."

Ten minutes later, the whole camp knew it. Margie had gone on the public-address system, played the tape from Marshal Pontrefact, and broken the news of the disaster and the truce. She had called a general meeting for 0300 hours, about ninety minutes from then, and ordered Alexis Harcourt, the nearest thing they had left to an astronomer, to go over the data from the Greasies and report before that time. Then she turned to Danny Dalehouse and said, "I don't have a bed anymore, but I need about an hour's sleep real bad."

"There's a spare in my tent."

"I was hoping you'd ask." She peered up toward the sullen glow in the clouds where Kung was hiding and shook her head. "It's been a son of a bitch of a day," she said as they picked their way toward the tent row. "And it's not over yet. Know what I'm going to do at the meeting?"

"Am I supposed to guess?"

"No way, Danny. You'd never make it. I'm going to announce the impending retirement of Colonel Marjorie Menninger from active service."

"*What?*"

"Pick your teeth up, Danny, and don't just stand there," she advised, tugging him along. "We're going to convert this place to civilian government, effective as soon as the emergency is over. Or maybe before. I don't care. Maybe all you guys who're bitching about the army way of doing things are right. I have to say that my way hasn't been working out too well, everything considered. So I think we're going to need elections for a new government, and if you want my advice you'll run."

"For what? Why me? Margie, you get me all mixed up!"

"Why you? Because you're practically the only original settler left, you know that? Just you and Cappy. Because nobody hates your guts. Because you're the only person in the camp who has the age and experience to handle the job of running things and who isn't a soldier. Don't let me pressure you. It's your decision. But you've got my vote. If," she added in a different tone, "anything we decide makes any difference at all now."

They were at his tent, and Marge paused at the flap, staring up at the sky. "Oh, shit," she said, "it's beginning to rain." It was—big drops, with promise of more behind them.

"The casualties!" he said.

"Yeah. We're going to have to get them under cover. And that's a pity, Danny, because I was kind of hoping we could catch us a little R and R before the meeting."

In spite of everything, Danny could not help himself. He laughed out loud. "Marjorie Menninger, you are some kind of strange. Get in there and get some sleep." But before she turned, he put his arms around her for a moment. "I never would have thought it of you," he said. "What converted you to civilian values?"

"Who's converted?" Then she said, "Well, maybe it was that fucking Krinpit. If it hadn't been for him, you'd've been burying me a little while ago, too. I didn't trust him, either, but he gave his silly life to save me."

With so few of them left, they didn't really need the PA system to cope with the fifty-five or sixty persons listening, but they hooked in one speaker for the benefit of the casualties who were well enough to hear, in their tents down the hill. The rest sat or stood on the wet planks of the dance floor in the sullen, steady rain while Marge Menninger spoke to them from the little dais. She turned the stage over to Harcourt.

He said, "A lot of the data from the Greasies isn't astronomy, it's geology. They've done a lot of digging. They say there seem to be flare episodes every twenty or thirty years. There's no set pattern, but by the amount of ash and char, they think your average flare involves about a seventy-five percent increase in radiation spread out over a period of a week or more. That's enough to kill us. Partly heat. Mostly ionizing radiation.

"Now, when does it happen? Their best guess is ten days, —give or take ten days." There was a murmur from the audience, and he nodded. "Sorry about that, but I don't have the training to make it any closer than they do; in fact, I'm only taking their word. The picture I get is of slowly increasing heat over a period of a couple of weeks. I think we've been having that, and maybe it's why the weather has been so lousy. Then the flare. Surface temperature goes up to maybe three-fifty degrees. That's Kelvin—say, somewhere between where we are now and the boiling point of water. I don't *think* it goes over that, not for very long, anyway. But there are peak flares, and they're like striking a match. If anything can burn, it will. Apparently the forests burn, but maybe not right away—they'd probably have to dry out first. Then the flare recedes, the temperature comes down, the air drops out moisture, and you get rain to put out the fires. Probably a hell of a lot of rain, over a period of weeks or months. Then you're back to normal."

"Only dead," somebody called out from the audience. Harcourt spread his hands defensively.

"Maybe not. If you're in shelter, you might survive." He started to continue, then stopped himself. Margie came up beside him.

"You don't sound too confident."

"I'm not. The—ah, the geological record doesn't inspire much confidence. The Greasies took cores from more than a hundred different sites, and they all showed the same pattern —recurring char and soil, back thousands of years."

Dalehouse stood up. "Alex," he called, "why hasn't it killed off everything on the surface of Jem long ago?"

"You're asking for a guess? I guess it has. At least all the vegetation. It burns off, then regrows from roots, most likely. Seeds probably would survive, though. And those drenching rains after each flare would give the new growth a good start in fertile soil—the char's great fertilizer; primitive man used to slash and burn to get his farms started, back on Earth. I don't know about the animals. I'd guess the Creepies would be all right in their tunnels if they didn't starve to death waiting for new growth to live on. Probably a lot of them do. Maybe the same for the Krinpit, because it would take a lot to kill them off. They don't have to worry about being blinded by the radiation, because they don't have any eyes to begin with. And those shells are pretty good armor for their vital organs. Probably get a lot of mutations, but in the long run that's as much good as it is bad for the race."

"What about Charlie?"

"I don't know. That's harder. I guess a really good flare might wipe out damn near all the adults. But that's when they spawn, and the spawn might survive—also, no doubt, with a lot of mutations. I'd say evolution moves pretty fast here."

"Well, look," Margie cut in, "if all these things can survive, why can't we?"

Harcourt shrugged. "They're adapted, we're not. Besides, I'm talking about *races* surviving, not individuals. Maybe as few as one percent live through it. Maybe less." He looked around the audience. "One percent of us leaves how many?" he asked.

"Yeah," Margie said slowly. "Well, I think we get the picture. We need to get under something big enough to stop both heat and radiation, and we need to do it in a hurry. Got any ideas on what we can make a roof out of?"

Harcourt hesitated. "Not a clue," he confessed. "Certainly

the tents won't do it. Oh, and I should mention the winds. They probably get pretty fierce, with all that insolation. So anything we did build would have to stand up to maybe two-hundred-kilometer-an-hour hurricanes. Maybe more. I, uh, I thought for a minute of using the Creepies' tunnels, and that might work—for some of us, anyway. But I doubt more than ten percent of us would live through maybe two or three weeks underground without very good ventilation and certainly without air conditioning—and that air down there is going to get *hot.*"

There was a silence while everyone considered possibilities. Then Kappelyushnikov came forward. "Is one thing we can do," he announced. "Not many of us. Maybe fifteen, twenty. Can get in return capsule and go into orbit."

"It's just as hot there," Marge Menninger protested.

Cappy shook his head. "Is only radiation. Steel hull reflects ninety-nine percent, maybe. Anyway, plenty. Only problem— who decides which twenty lucky people go up?"

Marge Menninger thought for a moment, then said, "No, that's a last ditch, Cappy. There's another problem with it: what do those lucky fellows do when they come down again? There aren't enough of us left now. I don't think twenty would be enough to survive. If we went up—strike that; I'm not saying I would be one of the 'we.' If anyone went up, it'd be just as smart to keep on going. Try to get back to Earth. Maybe go to one of the other colonies. The chances would be as good as coming back here when the whole planet's fried."

Harcourt nodded but corrected her automatically. "Not the whole planet."

"What?"

"Well, only half the planet. Our half. The part that faces Kung. The far side probably wouldn't even notice there was a flare going on. That's no good for us," he went on quickly, "because can't live there; we don't have time to build an airtight heated dome and move everything— What's the matter?"

Margie had burst out laughing. "Son of a bitch," she said. "Shows how wrong you can be when you start trying to trust people. Those bastard Greasies aren't giving us a square count! They didn't stop fighting because they wanted to make peace. They stopped because we were as good as dead anyway!"

"But—but so are they—"

"Wrong! Because they *have* a Farside base!" She shook her head ruefully. "Folks," she said, "I was going to make a real magnolious announcement about turning the reins over to civilian government, only now I think that's going to have to wait. We've got a military job to do first. When this side of the planet goes, they've got that snug little nest on the side that never gets radiation from Kung anyway, and they couldn't care less if the son of a bitch blows up. That's going to be a nice place to be. And we're going to take it away from them."

·TWENTY-TWO·

THESE WERE THE mesas and canyons of the high desert. Danny Dalehouse had flown over them in less than an hour and seen them only as quaint patterns in an unimportant carpet beneath. Marching over them was something else. Kappelyushnikov ferried them in as close as he dared, three at a time, once four, with the little biplane desperately slow to wallow off the ground. He made more than a dozen round trips and saved them a hundred kilometers of cutting through jungle. Even so, it was a three-day march, and every step hard work.

Nevertheless, Dalehouse had not felt as well in weeks. In spite of bone-bruising fatigue. In spite of the star that might explode at any moment. In spite of the fact that Marge Menninger's shopping list had overlooked a supply of spare hiking boots, and so he limped on a right foot that was a mass of blisters. He was not the unluckiest. Three of the effectives had been unable to go on at all. "We'll come back for you,"

Margie had promised; but Dalehouse thought she lied, and he could see in the eyes of the casualties that they were certain of it.

And still he would have sung as he marched, if he'd had breath enough for it.

It had been raining on and off for nearly forty hours—mean, wind-driven rain that kept them sodden in the steamy heat even when it let up, and chilled when it drenched them. That didn't matter, either. It was regrettable, because it meant that Charlie and the two remaining members of his flock could not keep in touch with them visually. (He had had to take the radio away from the balloonist before they left—far too easy for the Greasies to intercept.) Whenever the clouds lightened, Dalehouse searched the sky for his friend. He never saw him, never heard his song, but he knew he was up there somewhere. It wasn't serious. The weather that kept Charlie from scouting danger for them kept the Greasies from providing it.

There were twelve of them still toiling toward the Greasy camp. They had left the rest of the survivors—the highly impermanent survivors, if this expedition didn't do what it was supposed to—back at the base with orders to look as though they were twice as numerous as they were. Margie herself had transmitted the last message to the Greasies: "We are beginning construction of underground shelters. When the flare is over we can discuss a permanent peace. Meanwhile, if you approach we will shoot on sight." Then she pulled the plug on the radio and crawled into Cappy's plane for the last ferry trip.

They had less than ten kilometers to go—a three hour stroll under good conditions, but it would take them all of a day. It was scramble down one side of a ravine and crawl up the other, peer over the top of a crest and scuttle down its other face. And it was not just the terrain. They were all heavily loaded. Food, water, weapons, equipment. Everything they would need they had to carry on their backs.

The red cylinders marked "Fuel Elements—Replacement" were the worst. Each cylinder contained hundreds of the tiny clad needles and weighed more than a kilogram. Twelve of them made a heavy load.

At first they took turns carrying the puzzle pieces that would unite to form a nuclear bomb. One of the tricks was to make sure they didn't unite prematurely, and at every stop Lieutenant Kristianides supervised the stacking of knapsacks so that no two bomb loads were within a meter of each other. The chance was very small that they could in fact be dropped, kicked, or jostled into a configuration of critical mass. Making that happen on purpose when desired had been a serious challenge for some of the best munitions experts on Earth; for that purpose they carried another twenty kilos of highly sophisticated casing and trigger. Without that there was no real danger—or so Marge assured them all. But they were careful anyway, because in their guts none of them believed the assurance. Perhaps not even Marge.

At the end of the first march Margie had gone through the party, checking loads. When she came to Ana Dimitrova, sitting hugging her knees next to Danny Dalehouse, she said softly, "Are you sterile?"

"What? Really! What a question!" But then Margie shook her head.

"Sorry, I'm just tired. I should have remembered you aren't." And she grinned and winked at both Dalehouse and Ana; but when they picked up packs again Nan's load was changed to water flasks, and limping old Marguerite Moseler was carrying the fuel rods.

Margie looked terrible, and at every stop she seemed to look worse. Her plumpness was long gone. The bone structure of her face showed for the first time in years, and her voice was a rasp. More than that, her complexion was awful. When the Krinpit had buried her for two hours, its molting juices overrode her defenses. A day later she had broken out in great purplish blotches and a skin discoloration like sunburn. She said it did not hurt; there, too, Dalehouse thought she lied.

But he thought she was telling the truth about one very important thing, and perhaps that was the reason he could not repress a feeling of cheer. The bomb they were carrying would not be used.

He had been the one to propose it, and she had accepted the idea at once. "Of course," she said. "I don't want to destroy their camp. I want it, all of it—not only for us, but for the future of the human race on Jem. The bomb's best use is as a threat, and that's what we'll use it for."

He said as much to Ana at their last halt before coming in sight of the Greasy base. "She's planning for future generations. At least she thinks it's worth keeping your chromosomes intact."

"Of course," said Ana, surprised. "I have that confidence too." And so, Danny Dalehouse was discovering, did he. Bad as things were, he had hope. It carried him through that last belly-crawl, three hundred meters in the drenching rain, into the muddy cave that was their point of entrance for the burrower tunnels under the Greasy base. It sustained him while Major Vandemeer and Kris Kristianides painfully and gingerly assembled the parts of the detonator and fitted the fuel rods into it. It survived after Margie and Vandemeer and two others wriggled their way into the abandoned courses and disappeared from sight. The part of his life, of all their lives, that they were living through at that moment was misery and fear. Maybe worse than that, it was self-reproach; they were doing something that Dalehouse could not think of as noble or even tolerable. It was a holdup. Armed robbery. No better than a mugging. But it would be *over*. And a better time would come! And that hope kept him going for two full hours after Margie and the others had crawled away. Until Kris Kristianides, looking scared and harried, checked her watch and said, "That's it. From now on, everybody stay inside. Face the wall. Hands over your eyes. When the fireball comes, *don't look up*.

Wait ten minutes at least. I've got goggles. I'll tell you when you—"

Then they drowned her out, Dalehouse first and loudest. "She's going to do it! But she promised—"

"Shit, Dalehouse, she couldn't keep that promise! The Greasies would think it was a bluff. She's going to take out their arms and food just like we planned, and then we'll move in and wipe them up."

"What insanity!" cried Ana. "There'll be nothing there! The fallout will kill us if we go into the camp."

"Maybe. I've got a counter; we'll check everything out. The important thing's the planes. If we get them we can get to their base on Farside." She hesitated. She had been carefully rehearsed in all this and had carried the secret with her for more than a day. But she had dreaded this moment. If it had not been for her burns, she would have been in the warrens with the colonel and the major, and a lot happier there than she was here. "Anyway," she finished, "there's nothing we can do about it now. She'll blow the bomb in the next ten minutes. Get your faces down!"

And then, at last, hope was dead.

For the Brood Mother, too, all hope was gone. Blind and alone she moved slowly down through the tunnels to the only place left for her to be.

The thirty-meter level was for pups and outcasts. It was a place to play growing-up games or, at the end of all games, a place to die. Mother dr'Shee had never been there before. She had been a biddable pup, trained early to responsibility. As a tiny thing she had found it tingly-thrilling to listen to the stories of the half-growns, shivering in delight as she groped for the teat in her nurse's sheltering silk. But she had never explored the adventurous levels for herself. Not once. She had known that the time would come soon enough when, at the end of her life, she would drag herself down to see those old, unvisited levels and die.

In that she had been partly wrong. It was time to die, and she was there. But she could not see.

With dignity the Brood Mother raised her forebody to its fullest stretch and called, "Is anyone near?"

There was no reply. No sound. No scent except the stale, spoiled smell of elders long dead. She tried again, not because she had any hope of being answered, but for the sake of being methodical. "Person or pup, can anyone hear my voice?"

Nothing. If there had been an answer, it could only have been one of the wild young males who roamed the upper corridors, seeking only to kill. But there was not even that.

So another of her senses had become useless to her. Hearing meant nothing when there was nothing to hear.

It was a pity she was blind, but she bore no malice toward the Two-Legs who had burned out her eyes with their stroboscopic lights. She had in any case revenged herself upon a number of them in advance—for poisoning her tunnels, for abducting her young, for perverting the brood into new and vile practices. Most of all for coming to disturb her life in the first place. She had fought against it all, against the Two-Legs and sometimes against members of her own brood turned against her by the new ways of the Two-Legs. And now the tunnels were empty, and she was blind. *Tssheee!* It would have been less—less *final* to be here and alone if she could have seen at least an occasional phosphorescent glimmer of fungus or decay. What was left of her senses? Taste no longer mattered. There was little to eat. Smell was unrewarding, with neither males nor pups to nuzzle. She could still feel the powdery dust floor beneath her, the curving wall at her side. Dr'Shee took comfort from being tightly enclosed, as she had been through all the happiest parts of her life . . .

Which was now over.

She stretched and sighed a feline, purring sound of despair. She was beginning to be very hungry. The Two-Legs had ruined most of the food stores when they poisoned the tunnels to get at her and her few surviving allies. But the tunnels stretched ten kilometers in all directions. Somewhere there would be something, in this immense engineered warren that had been her world. She did not seriously think of seeking it. A Brood Mother did not debase herself to prolong a life that was over.

Woomp—

The tunnel around her moved. It was not a shake or a tremor, but a deliberate and almost peristaltic movement. Mother dr'Shee had never before experienced such a thing. Burrows sometimes crumbled, Krinpit invaded them, the rains might wash through a roof. But for all the earth to move? Such a thing could not happen! For the Brood Mother such an event was exactly as disquieting as it would have been for a fish to scull its tail and yet not move, or for a human being to feel the air about him turn glassy and shatter.

And then, from thirty meters above and more than a kilometer away, she heard the sound that followed. It was more than a sound; it was a pressure in the air that stung her ears and left them filled with a distant, discordant chatter, like the peeping of a hungry litter. But there were no pups to cry for her, ever again.

For some reason Margie's right knee was only scraped and sore, while the left one was bloodily gouged, the leg of the coverall worn through, the skin itself long since rubbed away. It was harder and harder for her to keep up with the two ahead of her. God had not intended her to crawl through tunnels ninety centimeters high for hours on end. . . . Which God she meant was not quite clear. To spare her knee she tried for awhile a three-legged gait, putting a little weight on her left toes, the rest on right leg and hands. That was a bummer. She wound up with the worst cramp she had ever had in the calf of her leg. She had to stop and press it out while Vandemeer behind her almost caught up and the two ahead kept on going. So then she speeded her pace and ripped the knee still more.

She paused and glanced at her watch. Still more than a quarter of an hour before the device would go off. Before that the two grenades they had left at bends in the tunnels would bring down enough dirt to tamp the explosion; and they were a good kilometer away by now. Probably far enough for survival, if not comfort. "Take ten," she shouted. She rolled over and rested her limbs, breathing hard of the stale and tainted air. Funnily, it was not really dark in the tunnels. That she had not expected. Once her eyes had adjusted, she could see little will-o'-the-wisp lights, so faint and pale that they hardly had color at all. Swamp gas, foxfire, Wilis—whatever they were, they were welcome.

She heard a quick, quiet scuffle down the tunnel behind her, then a *thwuck.*

Then silence again.

"Van?" she called. "Major Vandemeer?"

The dirt walls swallowed her words, and there was no reply. Painfully she rolled herself over, turned herself around, and crawled back.

The mouse-droppings odor was very strong. She touched the switch of her little helmet light and saw that the major was dead. One of the burrowers had been here, and the dart that protruded from Vandemeer's face proved it.

"Shit," whispered Margie, and then belatedly lifted her head and drew her pistol. The light showed nothing for sure down the crooked, uneven tunnel—was that a glint of something? a reflection from an eye? She fired twice.

When she looked again there was nothing there. But every few meters there were little side passages and bays, and a dozen Creepies could be waiting there for her to turn her head.

She almost raised her voice to call the others back but stopped herself as she was opening her mouth. For what?

They could not bring the major's body back. Doubled over as it was—he seemed to have been turning when he was shot—he almost blocked the tunnel. Maybe that was the last service he could render his cause—to slow down pursuit.

There was a better way. She had two grenades left. She pulled one off her belt, set it to ten clicks, turned around, and scuttled as rapidly as she could after the others. When she had counted a hundred seconds, she dropped, locked her hands over the back of her neck, and waited for the distant, muffled thud that told her she had dropped a part of the tunnel roof down to bury the major.

When the grenade went off, it occurred to her that it was strange she had not caught up with the others. "Sam! Chotnik! Sound off   !" she cried. They didn't answer; they hadn't heard her order to stop. She left the helmet light on and hurried after them, the pain in her knee no longer signifying. When the red numerals on her watch told her it was time for the nuclear blast, she still had not caught up.

She rolled over on her back again. For this blast it did not matter whether she protected her neck. She would be killed or she would not, and the only factor that mattered was whether there was enough earth between her and the explosion. There should be. When the impellers drove the sets of plutonium needles in to mesh with each other, there would be a nuclear blast. But not a big one. They would not stay in contact more than a few microseconds. If she had placed them right, they would expend their force up through the roof of the tunnel, carrying the Greasies' arms stores with them, and not much else. If she had placed them right. She was far less sure of that than she had pretended to Vandemeer and the others. The maps that Tinka and the Indonesian had given their lives to get to her were extremely complete and clear. But reading them in the open air was one thing; trying to follow them as you crawled from level to level underground was something quite different. She was not even sure that they had followed the same route on the way out as going in. They should have drawn a silken cord after them or broken off bits of gingerbread cookies for a trace—

At that moment the explosion occurred. Right on time. And she was still alive.

It was not even frightening. It was, she thought, as it would have been in her mother's womb if her mother had fallen. Some external event had taken place. But here in the tunnel she moved with the ground, and even the sound of the explosion was too huge and slow to be frightening.

So that part of the plan, at least, had worked. Now, if Kris could rally the patrol to the attack— If they remembered their radiation ponchos and the wind was not too unfavorable— If the Greasies did not pull themselves together fast enough to resist— If the bomb had been in the right place after all— There were too many ifs. Her place was with her troops, not here.

A sighing, slithering sound a few meters behind her caught her attention. She turned the headlamp toward it and saw that a section of the roof had collapsed into the tunnel.

Shaken loose by the nuclear blast? Maybe. More likely not. Creepies had been known to try to trap a foe by plugging tunnels before. She was terribly easy to find and follow, with the trail of blood from her knee.

It was time to get out of there. Doggedly detaching herself from the pain and from the fear that one of them was silently creeping up behind her, she resumed her crawl.

In ten meters her head struck dirt.

She turned on the light again. It was fresh dirt. The burrowers had closed both ends of the tunnel. She whirled quickly. Nothing moved behind her. She was alone.

Margie Menninger said to the wall, "The most basic human fear is of being buried alive." She waited for a moment, as though hoping someone would answer. Then she pulled out her pistol with one hand and reached for her entrenching tool with the other. It wasn't there. Then she remembered she had left it where they assembled the bomb.

Fingers then.

She dropped the pistol and tore at the dirt plug with her bare hands. Furiously. Then in terror. At last because there was nothing else for her to do.

From horizon to horizon, as far as Charlie could see, there was a solid undercast of clouds, and taller ones poked up all around. The storm was weakening off toward the ocean, but here, somewhere above the Greasy camp, it had been hours since he had seen the ground at all, days since he had last seen the little party of his friend 'Anny. And it was impossible to stay on station! At all levels up to ten thousand meters and more the wind was strong and solidly toward the Heat Pole, and it dragged him remorselessly away. Charlie could read the fraying of the anvil-shaped tops of the cumulonimbus; it showed that at fifteen thousand meters there was a return flow. But he and the two females of his flock who survived were worn and tired. They had lost much lift. It took them forever to reach those lofty levels.

As they labored upward a new flock came sailing down from the Pole, and Charlie led his tiny fragment to join it, eager for a new audience for his songs about the new friends from Earth, hungry to hear songs he had not heard before. It had been long and long since he had joined in a proper eisteddfod, and his soul ached for it. The new flock was small, fewer than sixty adults, but there were voices in it he had never heard, and he sang greeting toward them with joy.

White light lashed across them.

The flare caught them all by surprise. Charlie was one of the fortunate ones. He was facing away from the blast, and so he was not blinded at once. He saw the high cirrus starkly outlined, blue-white against the sullen, crimson Jemman sky, saw the shapes of the new flock picked out in brighter, sharper colors than he had ever seen. Minutes later he heard the sound, and behind him and below a new thundercloud boiled up out of the undercast.

Chorus of welcome became a dirge of pain and fear. Charlie could only reply with a lifting song. The seniors of the new flock took it up, and the swarm dropped ballast, belched swallowed hydrogen into their sacs, and rose. A few did not. They were not merely blind; they were in too great pain to respond.

Although they were far from the blast, when the winds struck, the swarm was thrown helter-skelter across the sky. Charlie had never felt such gusts before. Always in other storms there had been warning—gathering clouds and the deadly play of lightning to tell them it was time to swallow hydrogen and ride out the storm, or soar to escape above it. This time there was no warning and no escape. His feeding flaps and winglets felt as though they were being torn out at the roots. Captive of the huge sail of his surface, he was thrown through the new flock, caroming off their seniors, cannoning balloonets out of the way.

And then, without warning, he felt the familiar creeping tension of the surface of his gas sac and recognized the sweet, stinging odor of the females. Estrus, swarming time, time to breed!

The spinnerets of the females were working furiously now, spraying threadlike ova and pheronomes into the air. All around the swarm, the air was fragrant with the demand to breed. For Charlie, and for all the males, there was no question about what to do next: hive up, spray milt, soar back and forth through the stinging mist while their teats elongated, convulsed, spread their seed. The skins of their air sacs tightened, drawing the features of their tiny faces into caricatures. Behind the expressions that looked like pain was pain. The overtures to sex were no joy to Charlie. They were like being locked in an Iron Maiden with acid-tipped spikes. Only the relief that came when the semen squirted out made the pain end.

But it was wrong, wrong!

Charlie sang out his question and his fear, and the new flock sang with him. What breeding was this, with the flare coming from the enemy ground and not the sky? What was this heat that smote them like a fist, following on the thunder and the wild gales? Charlie could see that in the turbulence most of the silklings had been missed by the milt. They were all over the sky. Within his own body he could feel it was wrong. Where was the bubbling of hydrogen to replenish his sac, radiation-stung out of his body fluids? And what—what was this monstrous, bubbling cloud that was growing so fast it was drawing them all toward it?

And that was the question that answered all the others and put an end to questions forever for Charlie as the searing heat of the nuclear cloud burned out his eye patches, cracked his gas sac, touched off the hydrogen that spilled out, and ended his songs for always.

·TWENTY-THREE·

As NUCLEAR EXPLOSIONS went, it was inconsiderable. Less than a kiloton, it would hardly have been noticed in the multi-megaton blasts that had scoured the surface of Earth. When the imploding grenades forced the bright plutonium needles out of their sheaths to mate, they were in contact for only a few microseconds before their own immense reaction drove them apart.

But by then the explosion had occurred. The needles, the shell, the walls of the tunnel around them had been vaporized to a hot gas, billions of atmospheres of pressure, irresistibly determined to escape. It escaped. Within a few thousandths of a second it had formed its pipsqueak fireball, fifty meters across, racing upward at five hundred kilometers an hour, brighter than Kung, brighter than Earth's sun, brighter than hundreds of them put together. The fireball grew and soared, first bright red with its burden of nitric acid, then whitening and losing its brightness as it began to cool.

Even through closed eyes that stark flare was visible to the people huddled in the cave, and the shock front that swept over them shook the cave and their bodies. The noise was immense. After it, over the echoes, Kris Kristianides was shouting, "Stay down! Don't open your eyes! Wait!" For nearly ten minutes she kept them there, and then, slowly, she peered through half-closed lids and the dark goggles and announced they could get up.

Tentatively they poked their heads over the ridge. Squinting, they saw what Marge Menninger had done.

The nuclear cloud boiled tall through the layers of stratus. It had punched its own hole in the rain clouds, but its mushroom top was out of sight. Nearer, the Greasy camp seemed hardly touched: a shed blown over, a couple of tents burning, people moving dazedly around.

"She—she missed the base!" cried Kris, and Danny Dalehouse could not tell whether her tone was angry or glad. But what she said was true. The bottom of the blast was half a kilometer away from the camp toward the Heat Pole. Marge had got herself lost. The half of the blast that went into explosive pressure had wasted itself on the sand and succulents of the steppe.

But the third that went into heat had done better. The nearest persons in the Greasy camp were staggering around, blind and in agony. No one had given them goggles. No one had warned them not to look toward the blast.

"Check your pieces," Kristianides ordered. She had taken the goggles off, and under them her eyes were red. But her voice was determined. "Put on your cloaks. Let's go. We're moving in."

Dalehouse stood up and pulled the plastic poncho over his head like an automaton. (Would that really protect against any fallout at all?) He picked up his recoilless and slapped a cartridge into the breech. (Why am I doing this?) He started off with the others in a ragged line of skirmish, all nine of them walking slowly toward the Fuel base.

At every step he was telling himself that it was wrong. Wrong tactically: the nuclear blast had knocked out no more than a few unfortunates, and they were likely to get their heads blown off by the survivors. Wrong strategically: they should never have allowed themselves to get into this position. And wrong, most wrong of all, morally. What kind of world were they fighting for when they killed people without warning?

Dalehouse looked uneasily back and forth at the others in the line. All were staring straight ahead at the Fuel camp. Didn't any of them feel the way he did?

He stopped in his tracks. "Kris," he said, "I don't want to do this."

She turned slowly so that the muzzle of her gun covered him. "Move your ass, Dalehouse."

"No, wait, Kris. Let's—"

She said tightly, "I was expecting that from you. We're going in there. All of us. Colonel Menninger set this up, and I'm not going to let it go to waste. Now move it."

The others had stopped to look at them. None of them spoke; they only waited while Dalehouse watched the barrel of the GORR come into line with the bridge of his nose. He sighed deeply and said, "No, Kris." And then he stood there as her expression changed and hardened and he realized that, yes, she was going to pull the trigger—

"Put down your rifle, lieutenant," Ana called.

She was behind Kris and a little to one side, and she had her own gun pointed firmly at the lieutenant's back. "I do not wish to kill," she said, "but I, too, do not want to attack this camp."

Dalehouse didn't wait to see what would happen. He stepped forward and took the GORR from Kristianides's hands. He threw it back over the crest of the hill they had just crossed and then followed it with his own. After a second Ana did the same, and so, one by one, did the others.

"You fucking fools!" Kris raged. "They'll shoot you down like rats!"

Dalehouse did not answer. He stared toward the Greasy camp, where a few persons who were not blind or incapacitated had begun to appear. They had weapons, and they were gazing at the drama on the hill.

Dalehouse raised his hands over his head and began to walk steadily toward them. Out of the corner of his eye he saw Ana doing the same thing. Maybe Kris was right. Maybe one of those armed people kneeling in the shelter of a smoldering tent would begin to shoot. But it was out of his hands. Whatever guilt there was, it would not anymore belong to him; and for the first time in months he felt at peace.

·TWENTY-FOUR·

AND SO, AT THE LAST, what can one say of them? What is to be said of Marjorie Menninger and Danny Dalehouse and Ana Dimitrova—and of Charlie and Ahmed Dulla, or of Sharnigon and Mother dr'Shee? They did what they could. More often than not, they did what they thought they should. And what can be said of them is what can be said of all persons, human and otherwise, at the end: they died. Some survived the fighting. Some survived the flare. But in the long run there are no survivors.

There are only replacements. And time passes, and generations come and go.

And then, what can one say of that beautiful and powerful woman named Muskrat Greencloud An-Guyen?

One can say that she bears the traces of Margie and Nan and some of the others. Some through the passage of chains of DNA, some only because of what they did or who they were.

any of them, of course, because they are all
dead; she is a replacement.

she is not a single person. She wears three
, or a hundred if you count the subjective
tereotypes other persons carry around that
uskie An-Guyen." To a former lover, she is
ty companion of a weekend at Lake Hell. To
n, she is the docent who leads them through
the zoo. To your average registered Repub-
f the Boyne-Feng Metropolitan Area, she is
e who supervises the machineries of govern-
, of nongovernment. Muskie is one hundred
behind the Six Precepts of the Jemman
No strong central government is the last and
ortant of them. "Government" is a dead
uskie, burned out in the Blast and starved in
It has been gone from Jem this century and
ts to see that pawkish horror back, least of
obsolete as armies and indolence and waste.
it so, if it demands her last drop of blood as
t sacrifices by her militia volunteers and gift

Muskie is, let us look at the three principal
show the sultry and satisfied world of Jem.

se is Muskie the nurturer. She provides more
e food for Boyne-Feng, and nearly all of it
underground. She does not do it by herself,
er as she stands in the gallery gate. The
coming on duty. The bad old days of "own-
overnment did. Muskie is not an owner. She
g equals. But she is a special one.
k she looks like a Virginia planter overseeing
s like a Shensi landlord accepting squeeze
armers in her paddies. This would be deceiv-
ing. There is no ownership. There is not even any compul-

sion. The tokens the Krinpit laborers give her one by one as they scuttle past to the underground farms are not extorted. They are gifts. They are freely given. If Muskie is not pleased with the gift of one of them, she does not reproach him or order him to give more. She simply refuses it. Then the Krinpit chooses to go back to his village, where he may freely starve. A meter or two past Muskie's station the Creepie overseers spray the Krinpit with anti-allergen lacquer. No force is employed here, either. If the Krinpit do not choose to make gifts to the overseers, they need not turn back. The overseers will then choose not to spray them. The Krinpit will then itch or molt or die as a consequence of exposure to the terraborn crops they handle. It is the Krinpits' right to choose this if they wish. There is absolutely no compulsion, by anyone, of anyone, at any time. That is part of the Six Precepts.

The Krinpit know this and rejoice in their freedom—not to mention rejoicing in the radios, the gaily raucous drums and zithers, the chemical intoxicants, beads and metal tools that they prize. These are freely given to them when they freely give up the tokens that Muskie has freely given to them at the end of each voluntary work shift. The Creepies also know that this is true. They are also grateful, especially for the Two-Legs' improvements on their savage old burrows, and they freely assist the stronger, bigger Krinpit laborers by instructing them in where to plant the floor crops of mushrooms and the roof crops of potato and yam. They too now rejoice in the possession of beads, devices, and intoxicants their rude progenitors never knew. The balloonists know it—what fun they have with their taped music and their repeated orgasms! And, of course, Muskrat Greencloud An-Guyen knows it really well. She has everything she wants. Perhaps the best part of what she has is the certain knowledge that the Six Precepts are always followed, and so justice is always served, and everybody else on Jem—and that means everybody, Krip or balloonist, stranger or son—has everything, too. Though not usually as much of everything as she.

Then there is Muskie the civil volunteer. Not merely a discussant or a participator, like everyone else. She is a selection judge who gives freely of her time to serve the whole community, even at holidays.

She leaves the agricultural galleries and goes aboveground into the warm, bright dome of Fat City. Muskie is still a sturdily beautiful woman. She is tanned by the ultraviolet lights of the pool-grotto, tall, solid rather than plump; she weighs sixty standard kilos, but she has a fifty-centimeter waist, and her lovers prefer her to partners half her age. Eyes follow her as she comes smiling into Remembrance Hall, removes her slacks and slicks for comfort, gives Ring-Greeting to all, and reclines on a foam couch. "I would like to begin," she says sunnily. The other six volunteer selection judges agree that they, too, would like to discuss the issues of the day.

Most of the issues are routine, and consensus appears at once. (They are all saving themselves for the big one.) From his place under the bust of Mother Kristianides, wide-browed and serene as she looks down on them, Roanoke t'Schreiber describes the progress in cleaning up Lake Hell. All the city's sewage is being pumped there. The native aquatic life is being satisfactorily killed off, since *Escherichia coli* is antibiotic against most forms of Jemman life. "Another two million bowel movements and we'll have it sparkly clean," he comments. Sod House Flareborn looks up from inspecting her ten-centimeter fingernails to wonder if the militia should be freely given extra tokens, since so many of them have unfortunately (though voluntarily) given up their lives in the exploration of additional Creepy burrows and the liberation of distant camps of Krinpit. All agree that this seems desirable. The woman in militia fatigues who has been hovering by the door leaves with a smile of satisfaction.

Then Muskie's face clouds and she observes, "I have heard that there has been another tactran from Alphabase."

There is silence in the chamber. This is the issue that holds the seeds of dissent, and even change. No one really wants to get into it. All the judges stir uncomfortably on the couches under the busts of the ancestors, each waiting for the others to speak.

At last t'Schreiber offers an opinion. "I, for one, think it was unwise of our predecessors to attempt to resume space exploration. They freely gave much value to put new tactran satellites in orbit. What have we gained? Sorrow and confusion." He lists the contacts made: a garble that *might* have been from the Martian colony; pitiful pleas for help from old Earth itself; a dozen cocky messages from the base at Alpha Centauri suggesting an attempt at an actual flight to and from Jem. From the rest of the universe, nothing.

Muskie waits uncomfortably, shifting position and scratching just above the plaque of her string bikini. Then she says, "I wonder if we should answer messages from Alphabase anymore."

No one responds.

Therefore it is agreed; and the judges turn to speaking of the gratifying growth in human population—from one hundred eighty survivors to eighteen hundred in the third generation, and now nearly a quarter of a million in the sixth. There is no longer a fear that humanity might not survive. On Jem Man flourishes.

This reminds Muskie that her newest baby is about ready to be born. She speaks softly into her telephone to the hospital. The mare is in the delivery room even at that moment. But the news is bad. The baby was born dead.

"I blame myself," says Muskie to the doctor remorsefully. "Sarah Glowbag—was that her name?"

"Mary Glowbag," the doctor corrects her.

"Yes, Mary. She was nearly sixty years old. I should have invited a younger mare to brood my baby."

"Don't let it spoil your day," consoles the doctor. "One must expect a failure now and then. Nearly all of your children have lived, and remember, you have three others in the oven right now."

"You're very kind." Muskie hangs up with a smile. But the news has upset her—and just at Christmas, too. "I would like to leave now," she tells the other judges, and of course they also wish to close the discussion and return to their homes.

And then there is Muskrat the mother, the honored one at the head of her family.

This is no small part of her. Her family is huge. Forty-four living children, the dozen oldest long since having made her a multiple grandmother, the three youngest still unborn in the borrowed wombs of other women. (She reminds herself to make a voluntary gift to Sarah, or Mary, Glowbag for her kindness in carrying her most recent implanted ovum to term. Not as large as usual, of course; after all, the child had been born dead.) At Christmas all of them will come to give her Ring-Greeting, and she looks forward to the day with pleasure.

But not all of a family's concerns are pleasurable. As she walks across the pleasant gardens toward the place where she sleeps and keeps her belongings, a short, pale youth pushes toward her through the shrubs. He is d'Dalehouse Dolphin An-Guyen, and he is one of her sons. He has been running. He is breathing hard. Muskie sighs and says, "How nice of you to hurry to give me Ring-Greeting, Dolph."

He stops and blinks at the pretty Christmas many-tree in the center of the garden, with its ring-shaped lights and yellow Star of Earth at the top. Obviously he has forgotten about the holiday. Muskie sighs again. "Merry Christmas anyway, Dolph. I know you're going to reproach me some more. Sit down and catch your breath first."

They sit on a pressed creepystone bench under a grape arbor. (A few raisins had survived the flare-storm under a bunk in that Outpost of the People. From the six germinable seeds that were found in them had come all the wine on Jem, and this arbor.)

Muskie does not look at her son. She knows that in spite of

his faults, he is too well brought up to begin before she has given him encouragement, and she wants him to feel the peace of this place. All around the garden are the statues of the First Generation, the eighteen Mothers in gold, the fifty-two Mares in crystal, the eighty-nine Fathers in granite quarried from the cliffs under the Heat Pole. (The twenty-one survivors who contributed no genes to the pool, even by cloning, have statues too, but they are ranged outside the park. None of them were even mares.) There are further distinctions in the statues. The eighty-one survivors who returned from Farside have their names picked out in frost-etched silver. The thirty-two who survived in the burrows under the Outpost of Food when the flare caught them before the ferrying to Farside was complete are marked in ruby. And the sixty-seven others—few of them viable—who survived the flare in caves, under machines, inside space capsules, or wherever they could hide from the rage of the star are marked in orange chrysolite, the color of flame. That was six generations back. Muskie could have been descended from 2^6 of them, more than a third, but actually only eleven are truly her ancestors, with considerable overlap. (For instance, she is quintuply each descended from Marjorie Menninger, Ana Dimitrova, Nguyen Tree, and Firstborn McKenzie, the tiny phocomelic child born to the one woman who survived both the nuclear bombing of the Outpost of Fuel and the flare. She lived only long enough to bear her damaged child, but the child was marvelously fertile.)

When Muskie feels that this holy place has done all it can for her son, she scratches below the waistband of her slacks and says, "All right, Dolph, you may as well say it."

He cannot wait to get the words out, he is so impatient. "All right, I'll say it! You've made a mistake, Mother Muskie. We can't say no to Alphabase!"

" 'Can't'?"

He is doggedly stubborn. Even ferocious. "Yes, that's what

I said, *can't*. It's a crime against the human race! Jem's rotting away before your eyes, Mother Muskie. This is the best chance we've ever had to get things going again. They've got high-energy technology on Alphabase! Do you know what it means, what they're suggesting? They're able to put ten tons standard into the tachyon charge state—we couldn't do that to save our lives."

"Dear Dolph," she begins, sweetly reasonable, "we have more pressing problems right here on Jem. Do you know how many wild flocks of Loons there are? Krips who still wallow in savagery? Creepies unreached and unbenefited. We have a duty—"

"We have a duty to humanity!" he cries.

"Yes. Certainly! And we are carrying it out. Our ancestors gave their lives to save us, and we are true to the Six Precepts. There is no tyrannical government, no coercion, no contending nationalities here. We haven't raped Jem, we've wooed it. We live off renewable resources, while the Alphs are back to industry and all the evils of technology."

"Dear God," he shouts, *"resources?* The quarter-million of us don't begin to scratch the surface of them! Do you know that fossil fuel is *forming* faster than we use it?"

"Good! Proper! That makes it renewable. But be reasonable, Dolph dear. Why spoil everyone's happiness by striving for something foolish? Suppose everyone wanted to do what you say. Who would mine these fossil fuels?"

"Krips. Creeps. People. Machines! I don't care. If they don't want to, they should be ordered to!"

Muskrat is shaken. "You have spoiled my Christmas," she says sorrowfully, and walks away. What a shame! A foolishly stubborn boy and an incompetent mare, and her whole holiday was ruined before it had rightly begun. Dolph is her favorite son, or often is. She admires his tiny, quick body and his bright mind. But what rot, really! What a bore! Why can't he accept paradise like everyone else and be happy in it?

Dolph's holiday is spoiled, too, and he sits on the creepy-stone bench so angry and frustrated that he does not even hear the carols beginning.

A'es'e fi'eles,
lae'i 'riumphan'es.

If only she could be made to understand! The winning of Jem had cost so much in blood and pain. Not just in that first terrible year. Over and over again, every time Kung had flared in those first decades. There had been eight flares since the days of the ancestors, and only the last two or three had been fairly painless. Plenty of warning. A frenzied rush to ionproof the domes and hustle essential perishables inside. A week of confinement while the star raged, a year or so of one or another kind of scarcity until the planet replenished itself. But that left half a dozen sieges of misery, the first worst, but all of them catastrophic. Was all that to go for nothing?

Veni'e a'oremus,
'Ominum.

A Creepie overseer darts whickering past him toward the many-tree, followed by four noisy Krinpit gardeners in their bright red and green Ring-Greeting coats of lacquer. He becomes aware of the choir belatedly.

—save us all from Sa'an's power
When we were gone as'ray—

Hell of a season of joy this is, he thinks to himself. Season of suicide! Time of deciding to die on the vine while all the rest of the galaxy goes on to who knows what triumphs of technology and adventure! Glumness battles Christmas inside him. Gradually glumness loses. He remembers what the Creepie had been carrying—palely glowing ultraviolet strobes—and decides to stroll over to the Christmas many-tree.

The Krinpit are pushing away benches and picnic tables to

make room, moaning and clattering to themselves; they finish and scuttle away. The Creepie positions his strobes and waits for orders. On the tree itself, the tethered ballonists are singing their little hearts out.

> Schlaf im heilige ruhe,
> Schlaf im heilige ruh'.

All around the tree young people like him are removing their clothes and slipping in between the gaily decorated trunks. "Time to start!" they cry; and the Loons begin the jolly, lively "Good King Wenceslas." Obediently the Creepie touches off the strobes. The Loons gasp and continue to sing and begin to emit their milt, and all under the lovely tree the couples link in the traditional Rings.

And Dolph can stand it no longer. Gloom loses. Christmas wins. He flings off his clothing and plunges into the trunks of the many-tree. Why fight Utopia? he thinks to himself. And so in that moment he completes the process of growing up. And begins the process of dying. Which is much the same thing.

PRAISE FOR
LOIS MCMASTER BUJOLD

What the critics say:

The Warrior's Apprentice: "Now here's a fun romp through the spaceways—not so much a space opera as space ballet.... it has all the 'right stuff.' A lot of thought and thoughtfulness stand behind the all-too-human characters. Enjoy this one, and look forward to the next." —Dean Lambe, *SF Reviews*

"The pace is breathless, the characterization thoughtful and emotionally powerful, and the author's narrative technique and command of language compelling. Highly recommended." —*Booklist*

Brothers in Arms: "... she gives it a geniune depth of character, while reveling in the wild turnings of her tale. ... Bujold is as audacious as her favorite hero, and as brilliantly (if sneakily) successful." —*Locus*

"Miles Vorkosigan is such a great character that I'll read anything Lois wants to write about him. ... a book to re-read on cold rainy days." —Robert Coulson, *Comics Buyer's Guide*

Borders of Infinity: "Bujold's series hero Miles Vorkosigan may be a lord by birth and an admiral by rank, but a bone disease that has left him hobbled and in frequent pain has sensitized him to the suffering of outcasts in his very hierarchical era.... Playing off Miles's reserve and cleverness, Bujold draws outrageous and outlandish foils to color her high-minded adventures." —*Publishers Weekly*

Falling Free: "In *Falling Free* Lois McMaster Bujold has written her fourth straight superb novel. ... How to break down a talent like Bujold's into analyzable components? Best not to try. Best to say 'Read, or you will be missing something extraordinary.'" —Roland Green, *Chicago Sun-Times*

The Vor Game: "The chronicles of Miles Vorkosigan are far too witty to be literary junk food, but they rouse the kind of craving that makes popcorn magically vanish during a double feature." —Faren Miller, *Locus*

MORE PRAISE FOR
LOIS MCMASTER BUJOLD

What the readers say:

"My copy of *Shards of Honor* is falling apart I've reread it
so often. . . . I'll read whatever you write. You've certainly proved yourself a grand storyteller."
— Liesl Kolbe, Colorado Springs, CO

"I experience the stories of Miles Vorkosigan as almost
viscerally uplifting. . . . But certainly, even the weightiest
theme would have less impact than a cinder on snow
were it not for a rousing good story, and good story-
telling with it. This is the second thing I want to
thank you for. . . . I suppose if you boiled down all I've
said to its simplest expression, it would be that I immensely enjoy and admire your work. I submit that, as
literature, your work raises the overall level of the
science fiction genre, and spiritually, your work cannot
avoid positively influencing all who read it."
— Glen Stonebraker, Gaithersburg, MD

" 'The Mountains of Mourning' [in *Borders of Infinity*]
was one of the best-crafted, and simply best, works I'd
ever read. When I finished it, I immediately turned back
to the beginning and read it again, and I can't remember
the last time I did that."   — Betsy Bizot, Lisle, IL

"I can only hope that you will continue to write, so
that I can continue to read (and of course buy) your
books, for they make me laugh and cry and think . . .
rare indeed."   — Steven Knott, Major, USAF

What do you say?

Send me these books!

Shards of Honor 72087-2 $4.99 _____
The Warrior's Apprentice 72066-X $4.50 _____
Ethan of Athos 65604-X $5.99 _____
Falling Free 65398-9 $4.99 _____
Brothers in Arms 69799-4 $5.99 _____
Borders of Infinity 69841-9 $4.99 _____
The Vor Game 72014-7 $4.99 _____
Barrayar 72083-X $4.99 _____
The Spirit Ring (hardcover) 72142-9 $17.00 _____
The Spirit Ring (paperback) 72188-7 $5.99 _____
Mirror Dance (hardcover) 72210-7 $21.00 _____

Lois McMaster Bujold:
Only from Baen Books

If these books are not available at your local bookstore, just check your choices above, fill out this coupon and send a check or money order for the cover price to Baen Books, Dept. BA, P.O. Box 1403, Riverdale, NY 10471.

NAME: _____

ADDRESS: _____

I have enclosed a check or money order in the amount of $ _____.

POUL ANDERSON

Poul Anderson is one of the most honored authors of our time. He has won seven Hugo Awards, three Nebula Awards, and the Gandalf Award for Achievement in Fantasy, among others. His most popular series include the Polesotechnic League/Terran Empire tales and the Time Patrol series. Here are fine books by Poul Anderson available through Baen Books:

FLANDRY • 72149-6 • $4.99 _____

THE HIGH CRUSADE • 72074-0 • $3.95 _____

OPERATION CHAOS • 72102-X • $3.99 _____

ORION SHALL RISE • 72090-2 • $4.99 _____

THREE HEARTS AND THREE LIONS • 72186-0 • $4.99 _____

THE PEOPLE OF THE WIND • 72164-X • $4.99 _____

THE BYWORLDER • 72178-X • $3.99 _____

THE GAME OF EMPIRE • 55959-1 • $3.50 _____

FIRE TIME • 65415-2 • $3.50 _____

AFTER DOOMSDAY • 65591-4 • $2.95 _____

THE BROKEN SWORD • 65382-2 • $2.95 _____

THE DEVIL'S GAME • 55995-8 • $4.99 _____

THE ENEMY STARS • 65339-3 • $2.95 _____

SEVEN CONQUESTS • 55914-1 • $2.95 _____

STRANGERS FROM EARTH • 65627-9 • $2.95 _____

If not available at your local bookstore, you can order all of Poul Anderson's books listed above with this order form. Check your choices and send the combined cover price/s to: Baen Books, Dept. BA, P.O. Box 1403, Riverdale, NY 10471.

Name _____

Address _____

City _____ State _____ Zip _____

THE BEST OF THE BEST

For *anyone* who reads science fiction, this is an absolutely indispensable book. Since 1953, the annual Hugo Awards presented at the World Science Fiction Convention have been as coveted by SF writers as is the Oscar in the motion picture field—and SF fans recognize it as a certain indicator of quality in science fiction. Now the members of the World Science Fiction Convention— the people who *award* the Hugos—select the best of the best: *The Super Hugos*! Included in this volume are stories by such SF legends as Arthur C. Clarke, Isaac Asimov, Larry Niven, Clifford D. Simak, Harlan Ellison, Daniel Keyes, Anne McCaffrey and more. Presented and with an introduction by Charles Sheffield. This essential volume also includes a complete listing of all the Hugo winners to date in all categories and breakdowns and analyses of the voting in all categories, including the novel category.

And don't miss *The New Hugo Winners Volume I* (all the Hugo winning stories for the years 1983–1985) and *The New Hugo Winners Volume II* (all the Hugo winning stories for the years 1986–1988), both presented by Isaac Asimov.

"World Science Fiction Convention" and "Hugo Award" are service marks of the World Science Fiction Society, an unicorporated literary society.
